STILL MURDER

Finola Moorhead was born in 1947 and brought up in Mornington, Victoria. Her second novel, *Still Murder*, won the Vance Palmer Prize for fiction in the Victorian Premier's Literary Award when Joan Kirner was Premier. Finola became a full-time writer in 1973 and has been actively and theoretically involved in the development of the women's liberation movement in the 1970s, and as a radical feminist since the 1980s. She has received major grants from the Literature Board of the Australia Council and now lives on the mid-north coast of New South Wales. Her latest novel, *Darkness More Visible*, continues the story of Margot Gorman.

Other books by Finola Moorhead

Quilt, a collection of prose (Sybylla, 1985)
A Handwritten Modern Classic (Post-Neo Press, 1985)
Remember The Tarantella (The Women's Press, 1994)
Darkness More Visible (Spinifex Press, 2000)

STILL MURDER

a novel

FINOLA MOORHEAD

Introduction by Marion J. Campbell

Spinifex Press Pty Ltd
504 Queensberry Street
North Melbourne, Vic. 3051
Australia

women@spinifexpresss.com.au
http://www.spinifexpress.com.au

First published 1991 by Penguin Books Australia Ltd
Published in the UK 1994 by The Women's Press
This feminist class edition published 2002 by Spinifex Press Pty Ltd

Cover design by Deb Snibson
Original edition-typesettng by AdverType Vic.
Second edition typeset by Palmer Higgs Pty Ltd
Printed and bound by McPherson's Printing Group
Editor: Jackie Yowell

National Library of Australia
Cataloging-in-Publication data:

        Moorhead, Finola.
        Still murder.

        ISBN 1 87656 33 0.

        1. Police - Australia - Fiction. 2. Policewomen -
        Australia - Fiction. I. Title.

        A823.3

This publication is asssted by the Australia Council, the
Australian Government's arts funding and advisory body.

to the memory of my mother,
Leslie Mary Moorhead, née White, 1906–1983.

Acknowledgements

I wish to thank for their direct help during the composition of *Still Murder:* Virgina Fraser, Jenny Maiden, Kaye Moseley, Jennie Curtin, Lisa Pearman, Denise Thompson, Margaret Roberts, Geoff at my local video shop, Mary Lou Moorhead, Jan McKemmish, Helen Potter, Janne Ellen Swift and Jackie Yowell.

Aphorisms used in Part Four IV selected from *The Oxford Book of Aphorisms* (John Gross, OUP, 1983).

This novel was written while I was in receipt of a fellowship from the Literature Board of the Australia Council. Their financial assistance is gratefully acknowledged.

This work is entirely fiction. Any similarity to any living or dead person is purely accidental.

F.M.

CONTENTS

INTRODUCTION

Marion J. Campbell

Still Murder was marketed by its original publishers in 1991 as 'a
mischievous but deadly serious murder mystery'. When it won the
Victorian Premier's Literary Award for Fiction later the same
year, however, it was more likely its claim to be 'serious
literature' rather than its generic status as 'popular fiction' that
attracted the judges' attention. Although this prize no doubt
boosted sales of *Still Murder* in the literary market, it was not
clear whether a book as experimental in form and as difficult in
style as this one could win over a substantial portion of the crime-
fiction readership. The dichotomy between 'serious' and
'popular' fiction continued to underwrite the controversial
reception of *Still Murder* in feminist circles, where it was asked
whether a text could engage seriously with the crucial issues of
lesbian politics while at the same time observing the protocols of a
murder mystery. Revisiting a decade later a novel I'd read with
enthusiasm when it first came out and taught with conviction over
many years — and finding my enjoyment and admiration for it
reassuringly still intact — I'm inclined to call *Still Murder* a
cross-over novel. By this I mean that it not only combines politics
with entertainment, and radical experimentation with 'reliable
pleasures',[1] but also that it centres a male-dominated world on

---

[1] Jan McKemmish, 'Reliable Pleasures', in *Killing Women: Rewriting Detective
Fiction*, ed. Delys Bird (Sydney: Angus and Robertson, 1993), pp. 73–86.

female experience. These features make *Still Murder* a surprising and significant novel, in both political and literary terms.

As a cultural category, 'serious literature' has often been opposed to the popular on account of its self presentation as intellectual, elitist and masculine. In a similar way, the idea of the aesthetic has frequently been formed against the political by people who value objectivity and universality more highly than partiality and commitment. Critics have always been more interested than writers in these ideological exclusions and distinctions, which turn literature into an escape from everyday realities rather than an engagement with them. As soon as feminist literature identifies itself as a separate and specific kind of writing, it intervenes to change not only what gets written about, but also the ways in which it is both written and classified. Feminist writing is fuelled by a political obligation to 'represent' women in both the imitative and political senses of that word. It therefore understands that to depict new kinds of reality requires new forms of writing, which must also engage new audiences. At all three levels — content, form and readership — feminist writing is both political and popular.

Writing about her book a couple of years after it first came out, Finola Moorhead categorically stated that '*Still Murder* is not a genre novel.'[2] Her reason for refusing this designation is not that her novel is experimental rather than popular, or aesthetic rather than political. It is because it is feminine rather than masculine: 'it has a women-identified central reality'. By contrast, the world of conventional crime fiction is male-dominated: typically, it enables heroic, individualistic and masculine detections of crimes which are often embodied in the passive figure of a murdered woman. In *Still Murder*, however, the victim is a man, and the murderer and detective are both women. But these obvious displacements are merely outward signs

---

[2] Finola Moorhead, 'Equal Writes', in *Killing Women: Rewriting Detective Fiction*, ed. Delys Bird (Sydney: Angus and Robertson, 1993), p. 99.

that alert us to Moorhead's more thoroughgoing reassessment of the sexual politics of both crime as a social disorder and of crime fiction as a cultural form. Moorhead writes a crime novel because she wants to investigate and reevaluate what counts as crime and criminality in a male-dominated society. She also wants to think about the ways in which cultural forms like novels can perpetuate or change the way people experience the world they live in.

The title of Moorhead's novel also evokes another framing device remote from the literary genre of crime fiction. This is the pictorial genre of 'still life', that realistic mode of depicting objects which is designed to trick the eye into mistaking the represented for the real. 'Still murder' first switches our attention from the conventions for representing life to those which represent death. Furthermore, it implies a conflation of genres. For in Moorhead's skilful handling of these effects, the statically pictorial form of still life (in which art is taken for life) is overlaid by the chaotically temporal processes of detection in crime fiction (which turn life — and death — into art). This aesthetically framed and authenticated depiction of 'murder' in the title of Moorhead's novel is the first sign we are given of its ironic critique of the rules of the genre it deploys.

Understandably, the question of whether feminist politics can be advanced within the confines of an ideologically conservative form – and if so, to what extent — has stimulated productive discussions and debates. Finola Moorhead is among those who believe that because lesbian feminist writing is committed to changing the existing social order, genre fiction — which inevitably reproduces it — is politically not an option for women-centred texts. Moorhead's analogy with 'still life' indicates that her concern with genre is largely technical. In this context *Still Murder* is more like an analysis of a crime novel than an example of one. Nevertheless, it is impossible to discuss this novel without providing some standard definitions of the genre it subverts.

Classic crime fiction is conventionally understood as a masculine genre that mediates the ways in which individuals relate to the larger social structure. Society is often represented by the nuclear family, which is seen on the one hand as what must be protected from crime, but on the other hand as the place where the guilty secret of criminality originates. The processes of detection are like the processes of law. Both are concerned to identify and convict an individual whose essentially evil nature (in theological terms) or emotionally damaged personality (in psychological terms) is responsible for the crime. In these structures, guilt is always individual, and never collective or social. The detective is figured as someone whose knowledge of criminality makes him a mirror image of the criminal. He accordingly pays the price of heroic isolation for his ability to discover a person equally isolated by his perverted nature. In this classic formulation, both hero and villain are featured as masculine, and are further connected through their dual roles as protectors and violators of feminine virtue. In structural terms, crime fiction is typically dominated by plot, which ensures that a complex but logically determined sequence of events is always resolved clearly at the end of the novel. The 'clues' which enable this resolution to occur are not material traces in the real world. Instead they are rhetorical figures in the text. In other words, the process of detection in which the hero is involved is reflected in the process of reading the novel that narrates his activities. And so when the status quo is finally and comfortingly restored — which is one of the main pleasures offered by genre fiction — it is guaranteed by fiction rather than by fact.

Such characteristics justify the description of classic crime fiction as a masculine genre. But there is of course another well-known and lengthy history of the form, which focuses on women's engagement with it as both writers and readers. Although popular female practitioners tend to increase the 'feminine content' of the form by introducing such things as women detectives and domestic settings, they nevertheless preserve the generic structure of classic crime fiction and consequently its masculinist assumptions. More recently, however, programmatically feminist writers have attempted to demystify the male power of the detective by such devices as rewriting it as female professionalism.

More significantly, in redefining what counts as crime they treat it as systemic rather than individual. Their stories accordingly establish a different relation to knowledge and power, and entail a different reading of sexual politics.

In this context *Still Murder* offers an anatomy of both sexual politics and social corruption, as well as the connections between them. It provides us with all the ingredients of a classic crime thriller. But instead of marshalling them sequentially and conclusively, it reveals them randomly and teasingly – rather like the pieces of the jigsaw puzzle which its central characters construct and deconstruct throughout the novel. The point of this puzzle is not to painstakingly put together the pieces until they reveal the hidden picture — but instead to play with clues and patterns, to establish connections, to pass the time, to conceal as much as reveal. But the novel is like a jigsaw not only in being cut into pieces but also in being framed. It is an aesthetic object obliged to respect the boundaries placed around it, which limit what it can know and tell. Technically, the novel is a series of fragmented texts in different modes: newspaper clippings, diary entries, notebook jottings, computer printouts, letters. It does not offer any unifying point of view because each character knows only a part of the truth. No coherent narrative emerges from its disordered chronology and sequence. Most importantly, the parodic nature of the resolution prevents readers from wrapping up the story in a single meaning or truth. *Still Murder* fosters doubts rather than producing clarification.

By radically dislocating the highly codified form of the novel of detection, *Still Murder* draws attention to what I see as its central concern with the nature of crime itself. Although 'an unidentified body ... wrapped in leaves and buried beneath a crop of marijuana plants' is discovered at the beginning of the novel, and although both that body and its murderer are eventually identified, the process of detection is continually obstructed, and so much so as to seem irrelevant by the time it is concluded. The mystery that *Still Murder* presents to its readers is the mystery of *what* crime has been committed: is it murder, rape, war, treason, betrayal, drug dealing, police corruption? Perpetrators of the crimes themselves are even harder to identify. For this novel refuses either to singularise crime or to individualise those responsible for it. Certainly the novel reveals its female murderer, though in passing rather than at the end. But her identity — no secret anyway for most of the text — is much less important than questions of motive and responsibility. Patricia is never formally called to account for her actions because those who know what has happened (including the readers) recognise a network of involvement and a collective guilt. In any case, the worst crimes are those which are never called by their true names and are punished only in the guilty consciences of their perpetrators: Patricia, for example, is much more preoccupied with her moral responsibility for her sister's death than she is with her physical murder of her husband.

Still Murder deals with the problem of male violence. Framed by two male texts, it opens with a 'confession' from one of its 'criminals' (the war hero and Vietnam veteran, Peter Larsen) and closes with the tying-up-the-loose-ends explanations of its master detective, Samuel Lake, who is a fellow soldier and blood brother to Larsen. Although these two men are involved in covering-up rather than committing the murder of Steven Phillips, both are deeply implicated in the wider field of male violence as epitomised by war. Larsen's guilt centres on his rape of a ten-year-old Vietnamese girl, sold by her father and brutalised by the soldiers who were supposed to be protecting her. For Moorhead, women and children are the emblematic victims of war. But she also understands the physical, sexual and psychological devastation suffered by young men like Peter, who are randomly conscripted to fight in a foreign war. Even more important than the bodily and mental scars inflicted on them in war was the alienation of returning Vietnam soldiers from their own community and their own generation. Patricia, who was Peter's girlfriend before he was sent to Vietnam, can no longer be his lover, his companion and the mother of his unborn child. Instead she becomes an increasingly objectified sexual fantasy — worshipped, spied upon and eventually protected without her own knowledge. Patricia's husband, Steven, is the man who avoided the draft, by chance rather than conviction. He finds that his possession of a desirable woman is not enough to assuage his sense of being both alienated and emasculated, conditions represented through his nefarious activities as philanderer, spy and informer. The Vietnam war not only divided men from men, men from women, and soldiers from civilians. It also separated those able to indulge in the luxury of a voluntary political protest from those who were forced to surrender their own will to military discipline. The major crime encompassed by Moorhead's novel is Australia's involvement in the Vietnam war, and the terrible dislocations, divided loyalties and inescapable guilt that it effected in Australian society. Crimes committed against the Vietnamese people are also acknowledged, although they are depicted less vividly.

The Vietnam war provides Moorhead with more than an occasion to reexamine masculinity. For it was also the moment of a new understanding of femininity. Here in Australia as in the United States, the galvanisation of the peace movement and the moratorium protests in the late 1960s coincided with the development of feminism as a political program. The origins of second-wave feminism in the divisive conflicts of the Vietnam war are a source of guilt as well as strength in women who struggle to understand their collusion with male violence as well as their victimisation by it.

The story of the novel's central character, Patricia Phillips, illustrates this dilemma. Patricia's innocence is destroyed by the loss of her lover, Peter, to the war, and her decision to abort their unborn child. These betrayals are sealed by her marriage to Steven. As feminist politics and theory come to engage her intelligence and take up her energy, Patricia increasingly finds her emotional and sexual satisfactions among women. But when her husband attempts to rape her female lover, the pressures of her life become unbearable. She murders Steven in one of those fits of unknowing which, in patriarchal society, evince the 'madness' of femininity. She uses the military 'skills' she has acquired through watching Vietnam war films in an effort of identification with Peter and their lost son. Voyeuristically watching her through the window of her home, Peter covers up the crime and saves Patricia from its legal consequences. In doing so he is exercising the male prerogative to protect women, even from themselves. Patricia's subsequent madness illustrates the self-division of the woman who is not allowed to claim full knowledge of herself. Instead, she is 'known' only through the structures of male society, watched, spoken for and framed. When she attempts to disrupt the frame and speak for herself, her speech is elliptical and fragmented. Patricia's story thus emblematises both the difficulties of representing women and the contradictions of feminism.

The formal investigator in this novel, Senior Detective Constable Margot Gorman, is the uncomprehending inheritor of 1960s feminism. A young, educated professional on her way up, Margot is intelligent, strong and independent. These qualities, however, she sees as emanating from her own individual character, without understanding that they are part of her political legacy from an earlier generation of feminists. Sexually straight and professionally committed to being one of the boys, Margot must be inducted into the community of women by learning to trust her female instincts and to interpret her feminine experience. As the detective figure, Margot is ironically the most mystified character in the novel. Deliberately kept in the dark by her boss, patronised and threatened by her colleagues, and exploited by her former husband, she is treated as a pawn in that great game of corruption which has made the New South Wales police force infamous. In the course of her investigation, Margot learns more about herself and the vulnerability and violation of women than she does about the murder of Steven Phillips. And what she learns comes mainly from personal contact with the murderer, Patricia, who is supposedly under Margot's surveillance. Treated as mentally disturbed and subject to hallucinations and fantasy, Patricia is the true site — albeit an oblique and even duplicitous one — of knowledge in this novel.

She has achieved wisdom from her reading of feminist theory as well as from her long experience of the loves and betrayals of women and men. Beyond her education at the hands of Patricia, Margot's understanding is pieced together from contacts with a string of other women who practise amateur detection. These include Patricia's sister, Julie, who is her rival and accomplice in the family drama of their youngest sister's death; Jane, the Catholic nun who believes in liberation theology and 'justice at home'; Hattie, the Aboriginal investigative journalist; and Angela, the bored and busybody socialite.

While Moorhead treats her female detective with an ironic sympathy, she offers a more wary account of another professional woman who is also engaged in surveillance and detection. Anne Levin is a psychiatrist, a practising doctor and academic, who treats Patricia while she is in hospital. Although Patricia's diary reveals the games she plays with Anne, the doctor has the last word in summing up her patient's mental state, and specifying her possible motivations and actions. Anne represents the professional and theoretical codification of knowledge-about-women. Her therapeutic practices enable her to 'detect' the putative causes of Patricia's behaviour and to confine her even more securely than the processes of law and justice. Patricia avoids legal conviction through the agency of her lover's loyal and powerful friends. But she escapes incarceration in a mental hospital only through the help of her own real and imagined family. As is so often the case in crime fiction, in *Still Murder* the nuclear family is revealed by the processes of psychoanalysis to be the site of both violence and guilt. But it is also a place for reimagining human relations — beyond the barriers of age, class and gender — and for attempting to make a future that is not merely an image of the past.

Gillian Whitlock has claimed that 'the price of radical experimentation with form is audience and commercial appeal'.[3]

---

[3] Gillian Whitlock, '"Cop it sweet": Lesbian Crime Fiction', in *The Good, the Bad and the Gorgeous: Popular Culture's Romance with Lesbianism*, ed. Diana Hamer and Belinda Budge (London: Pandora, 1994), p. 105.

That opposition is no longer inevitable, I think, and especially not now when Finola Moorhead's successful feminist classic is being republished. As a crossover novel, *Still Murder* has introduced both feminist readers to crime fiction and genre readers to feminism. It is a novel that continues to demand discussion, commentary and debate. Unlike a 'still life', it is not textually self-sufficient, since it continually breaks out of its frame to engage with contemporary realities. As a political novel, *Still Murder* acknowledges the social conditions its readers live in; it is engaged in refashioning both readers and society as it imagines a different world. I am very pleased that this timely reprint of *Still Murder* will stimulate a new generation of readers to engage in the continuously relevant debate about the nature of social violence and sexual conflict.

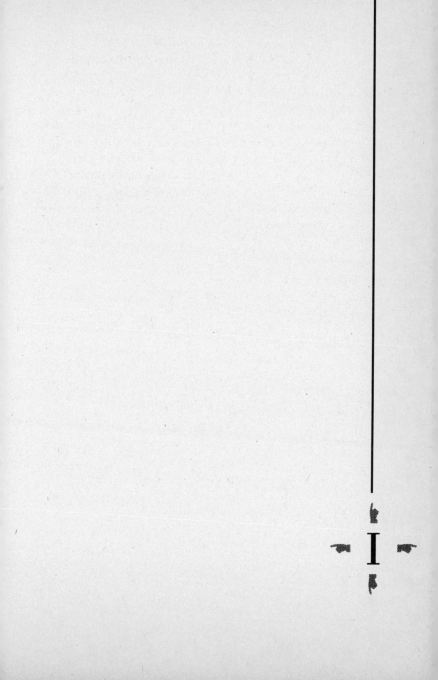

I

PETER LARSEN
The Confession

My name is Peter Larsen and I'm as pissed as a parrot. I have
been watching you Patricia, Pat, Trish, whatever they call you.
Not my name for you.

I belong to the roughest RSL Club in Newcastle—you know
the type—the sort with the young mothers and kids in the lobby
around tea-time, waiting and swearing and worrying
with their shopping and plastic bags of dirty nappies, crawling
kids crawling and lap-kids bawling, shouting to each other,
being tolerated by a doorman in dress-shirt and bow-tie. I can
find my kind of club anywhere. I'm a stupid shit but I'm writing
this down for you now. I bought my bloody old ute from the
biggest bastard of a used-car salesman in the smallest yard,
because he had this deaf Alsatian bitch who'd lie on her back for
a piece of pizza behind a rickety wire fence. Work it out, I can't.

The dream of the fathers, the dream of the grandfathers—the
dream of my forebears—was of ships, doorways to the new
world. Vikings. Fierce Arctic blood raged in their brains under
long blond hair and pulsed in the veins of their mighty arms and
shoulders—bulls of men. The heroes of Norway were men of
heart and fury.

My grandfather left the land of skiers and sailors and came to
the new world here—Australia. He broke away from the north

3

Norwegian small town, which was tight and cold, yet wild and proud and tough as boots cracking on rock and ice. He broke away, turned away from the tears of the women with contempt. And with equal contempt looked down on his father for betraying the little Peer Gynt who sails inside every Scandinavian male, from artery to artery, vein to vein, and through the heart and back again. My grandfather broke the rules, left the girl pregnant and worked a ship to Sydney rather than suffer the shame of staying a beaten man, a cowed and hunched, bewildered, disappointed shotgun-husband in constant struggle with father-in-law, prisoner of conscience; nothing but a bored, boring provider, beating the kids when the epidermis got too tight to hold the amount of fire-water he had to consume to live behind the bars of tradition and righteous living.

I remember his eyes, those fierce, rheumy, blue eyes glittering like flick-knives as he lay crippled on the lounge in our living-room, consumptive and shrunken. Vikings, he growled, were the toughest when other nations were beaten into effete little bishoprics.

Did my father have a sister, a brother, in Norway, somewhere near the Swedish border? My father wanted to know. In contrast to his own father, he was a family man right down to his workman's steel-capped toes; a family man for whom blood resided in chalices of love and respect; a dignified man with the soft eyes of the Christian, who, when he needed to lull himself to sleep or rest on a journey by train, would take up sentimental tales of invalids with an almighty faith managing to move mountains and having miracles happen at their pathetic bedsides, tracts on cheap paper with silly drawings. Dissolving in gratitude to God at the end, my father would sigh and close his eyes and dream not of furious masculine obsessions but of peace and goodwill; a nice man who for all his saintly troubling got buckets of contempt hurled at him from beneath the woven coverlets of granddad's couch.

I vowed to write to you in the middle of the Welcome Home Parade, October 3rd, 1987. It came to me like a bolt of inspiration amidst our ridiculous relief and gratitude. A rocket of dignity, powered by anger, shot up my spine. Lovers alone are interested in life stories, and I've never told a soul.

The old man died when I was thirteen. I must have told you this. That was the right age for him to do it, for already I knew all his obsessions, both fable and truth, off by heart, with all their changes and embroideries. I knew them so well that when he was gasping his last rattling breaths into lungs like storm-torn sails, having nothing else to say, I repeated them to him. I gave voice—a teenage, breaking boy's voice with a broad Australian accent—to the sagas, lived or imaginary, that were going round his head, and had since he was a boy. I didn't want him to live a moment more, not because I was sick of his coughing and the smell of his rude ready-rubbed tobacco, like the rest of the household was, not because after so many years he was out of his misery, but because I had a girl to see, a girl who had promised to lift her skirts and show me sex, and I couldn't go until the death had happened.

When it did I was released and half an hour later I was in a concrete pipe up at the development site, clumsily groping and blushing like hell. We never even got our clothes off, and now, as a memory, it is overshadowed by the immense importance of my grandfather's death and the fact that I was there breathlessly giving account of the Count on his mission of revenge. I was saying, 'The Count of Monte Cristo would only fight a duel for a trifle and given his skill he would most certainly kill his man, but that is too quick an end for his real enemies. He believes in an eye for an eye and tooth for tooth.' Sweet journey, my forebear, you gave me … Excuse me it's time for … I snuck out of the house, omitting to inform my mother of the momentous occurrence, for the simple reason I didn't want her to stop me. A date is a date and no other time had been planned. I have forgotten the girl's name.

I confess to you that I have become a peeping tom and a drunkard. And that I'm a mean bastard of a practical joker. So? There's meaner than me. According to my friend, Swan, your husband is a traitor. He betrayed his country. On some espionage errand for the CIA he bellowed when a group of our fighting men were in hiding, hardly breathing. Called attention to their presence, responsible for their death. But Swan says we have no proof.

Why does a man do this? I don't know, maybe taste for betrayal is the answer. Perverse power-mongering. He probably betrayed the demonstrators and the draft-dodgers as well, but that doesn't surprise me. Betrayal is power, if you look at it from a weasel's viewpoint.

It is strange that allies should envy each other so much, but the Yanks, according to my theory, wanted to pull the Aussies down a peg or two, because we were better jungle fighters and that got up their noses. They were losing whole camps because they would have prostitutes, house-maids, lackeys, inside barracks. And who could tell one Vietnamese from another? Who was South, friend, and who was South, Cong? Beyond being big, they hadn't got a clue. Whereas we have been great jungle fighters ever since the fall of Singapore, and New Guinea is almost a border.

Swan's been watching your husband for years because he suspects a Chinese drugs connection. My theory: it was all an American dirty trick using drugs and a certain hippie's taste for betrayal. But I'm just a drunk with a big mouth and a wilderness of sagas tucked away in the mountains and fjords of my brain.

Bodies mean nothing when you've seen the napalm fall on human skin and kids running around like chooks with their feathers alight.

I've watched your spouse and he's a real shit of a bloke. No mates for whom he would stick out that narrow neck which has felt only the steel of a razor. By the way, who put all those mirrors in your house? Him?

The Count could hate, and my grandfather taught me that hate makes a man strong. Hate is stronger than love, he said. He loved the woman he left pregnant. He never said so, but I know, because as a lad I listened, and now I've lived, I know that love and desertion are compatible. He hated the small-town narrowness and predictability more. He was a bitter man to the end, both envious and contemptuous of my father, who chose to live and serve the woman he loved for the length of his life.

Our son would be like that, and such a handsome lad. How old would he be now, love? Eighteen, nineteen. He'll be married at the age of twenty-two to his childhood sweetheart, a natural businessman maybe in electricals or real estate. I imagine him. He is virile and has children straightaway and lots. There is no conscription, no dirty, stupid war to muck up his brain, his good looks, his healthy sexuality or his children. He lives, I reckon, in a small city, small enough for him to make his mark and big enough for there to be cash and opportunity. Maybe it's Queensland where the beaches are long and lapped by the crystal waters of the Coral Sea. Been there, been everywhere.

I'm writing again, after seventeen years. Hello Felicity. Last wrote from Saigon—sweet, romantic, erotic shit. Did I say, 'dear Patricia' or 'dear Felicity'? I can't remember.

The coral sands are white as bone and patterned as fossils. The beach is death. The wrecks of the yachts on the reef, dragged by huge seas of the past up onto dry land, provide shelter for the castaway. I gaze past the broken hull over the still water to the fringe of surf. It doesn't matter. Nothing matters in the lotus-eating climes except the constant slapping of thoughts, like the ocean lapping the shore. Get stoned, forget it. Drumming repetitious humiliation for you too—I saw it, day after day. For a while I thought you were deaf not to rage against that puny tide. All too exasperating for a man to bear. How could you bear him? I went away and came back again, went away, married, and came back again, took the wife up to

Newcastle, away from Sydney. But I couldn't settle down, couldn't handle myself in polite company. After a few arrests and many disappearances I finally left her with our blonde-haired little girl. I sang my forebears' songs of courage and despair, knowing, like granddad, the girl and the woman are better off without me.

My obsession grows like the mighty baobab tree, just getting bigger, every day.

Between the old man's death and the war, I had five, maybe six, years of good clean life in my good clean family. Played Rugby League and thought that was courage — ploughing through the big men's legs, wrong-footing them and out-running them with great spurts of superhuman strength; coming into the clubhouse and feeling the team, the masculine mateship of sport, where if you hurt all over you feel a hundred times better, you drink faster and laugh louder and the slaps on the back are as tender as kisses and you get gruff and surly because you've got to hide the tears of sheer joy. And cricket in the summer. Mum, Dad and the other kids would sometimes come and lend support, and Dad would take on duties like the good Christian father he was and Mum would make sandwiches.

Those games and all those summers sit on the blank wall like one single slide. Then I am a boy out of school with a driving licence and a wish for a car and dreams of going bush or sailing to Scandinavia and seeing everywhere in between, nothing worrying me — only petty realities, like having to earn money or study.

Alley cats sit on the fence and watch. You stick out food and they take it carefully. They watch the tame pussy being cuddled and bossed, played with and combed, and they groan in disgust. Death, they say, before that happens to me. The feral feline knows the mark, the exact point up to which fear is needed. The caution lights flash on and every nerve in your system quivers with attention.

This wild cat loves the clubs of New South Wales and the pubs of western Queensland and north-western Australia, where there is always an old digger, always some bloke, who knows something about who you are before you speak and likes it. There's a wisdom in the eyes of these outback cockies: something to do with their readiness to stay silent and watch a mug like me perform, shout the bar, spill my guts or just expound on the state of the world. I haven't met a man from the sticks who didn't love the land as he raped it. The land is like a terrible woman to them. She breaks their hearts when she sees their vulnerability and she dries the clay into deeper ruts month after month with the determination of nature's revenge. Then she laughs, she laughs buckets of silver rain and the reflection of her laughter is carpets of delicate wildflowers as far as the eye can see. This is their very own land, no matter what the acreage. They pretend to own it, they'll die saying they own it, but really they're panting after a perverse mistress who has the strength and fury of hell and the loving embrace of the gorgeous earth. Human women will leave them. The wives can't take the competition of the mistress, nature herself.

There are lonely men everywhere and I love them and I am welcome. They understand me when I'm drunk and babbling, when I cry soldier's tears of guilt into the foam of fresh beers. They agree with me when I abuse the Yanks for their perfidy or women for their incomprehensible indifference, or else they mildly disagree so a good old meaty discussion can get going and the whole bar's having fun. The drunk lady, who is always there, always says something loud and different. If the disagreement were aired in the sober light of lecture rooms it would be so deep everybody would be left shaking their heads. But alcohol makes the brain cells wobble and no one really gets to the point. They waddle round the tracks of their own concerns and in the middle is something that hurts. I reckon it's the betrayal of dreams. Each self has betrayed itself, and probably others, so there's self-sorrow and guilt mixed like two fruits in a jelly, inseparable.

This country is large enough to take in all the wanderings I figured I needed. After Vietnam, the world did not attract me. Some stranger, some foreigner in his foreign place mistaking me for an American would get no answer but a fist in the jaw, because my anger is a millimetre from the surface, and it surfaces so quick no word is that fast. There's a great big, sad warmth in outback Australia that I'm part of.

I have no head for business, Felicity. I like to dream and run risks for the hell of it. I've got dope growing all over the countryside. Sometimes I harvest it, sometimes I don't. Never give my seeds away. Always got young plants in the car, carrying them here and there. They'll grow in the bush on their own pretty well after they're about a foot high if you mulch deeply. My clientele are all mates, nearly all Viet vets.

Among the native pines of the Pilaga scrub, I light my campfire, roll a smoke of grass and tobacco, watch the flames, dream of you, love. I have to measure reality against the glow in the coals. The moving pictures in the fire are witches dancing in a golden cave. Or the hot hell my dad feared. I have him in me in wanting a miracle to turn up beside my bedroll. Leave that house. Turn up beside me like a vision.

I sit in the bush a while and I can't stand not seeing you. I up and arrive in Sydney to skulk and sneak with my secrets.

I'm remembering those short days between school and war. I remember the feeling of love in my hot blood, which turned my tan scarlet on my cheeks, and your look at me that first day. In a grimy coffee shop at university, your long hair hid your face and the pages of the book you were reading. Hey, I said, with my wide Norwegian grin, can you show me ...? And you looked up. The world changed. I didn't even know where I wanted to go any more. As I stood shaking and raking all the bits of my frame back together, you looked me up and down, with that peace, love and fucking honesty we had in those days. You appraised me. Fit footballer, with long limbs and muscles anybody could have confidence in, I loved myself in your look, and laughed.

The entire time I was with you I laughed and when I wasn't with you I went around singing 'Patricia' to the tune of 'Maria' from *West Side Story* in strong voice, trained from years of hymn-singing, and my mates started calling me a hairy goat. Neither of us studied at all and then I was called up and you got pregnant. So it was a hill of passion and a valley of despair as only heroic lovers can have, as only young lovers can have, as only passionate people like Cathy and Heathcliffe can have, nothing mellow about it, nothing permanent as in plans and house mortgages, just something eternal. Like Adam and Eve we were cast from the Garden of Eden for the flaw of being human. I had my fair curls cut off and joined the troops, who were next best — mates. In the army I renamed you 'Felicity'.

Patricia. I had to get away, piss off and kill myself or something. It's almost a year since I started this. It won't get lost. I've been torn between hating you and wanting to punish you and needing more than ever to talk, to be yours in some small, humble measure.

I was spooked by seeing your house change into the witches' cave I saw in my campfire. Wimp-features wrapped his rifle in canvas and put it in the car about four o'clock and drove off, saying 'cheerio' for the weekend. I was watching you through the window. You were, suddenly, crazed, frenzied, throwing bits of material over electric light globes. You stripped naked, put on all your jewels and a raincoat and went out shopping. I snuck through that terrace house in Lilyfield that you had made into something Egyptian, a den of decadence with incense burning, to check that no chiffon would burst into flame. I was out by the time you got back. Then your girlfriends came. Late at night, when I came back from the pub, the others were naked too.

There seemed to be more than there were; you hadn't covered the mirrors. I was privy to a porn show.

Like the weak old bugger that I am I took myself to the Barrier Reef. The old jalopy the shyster sold me turned out all right. Tried everything to keep myself away, even bought secondhand books to read. I discovered a dog-eared paperback in a dusty book exchange among the Mills & Boon romances and Western comics, and opened it to find the author, Agnar Mykle, quoting Alexandre Dumas: *'But,' said Franz to the Count, 'with this theory, which renders you at once judge and executioner of your own cause, it would be difficult to adopt a course that would forever prevent your falling under the power of the law. Hatred is blind; rage carries you away; and he who pours out vengeance runs the risk of tasting a bitter draught.'*

'Yes, if he be poor and inexperienced, not if he be rich and skilful…'.

Then Mykle goes on: *'The deepest of all wounds are those that touch one's self esteem and masculinity; and that is why a man never hates so hugely as when someone has stolen or disfigured or ravished or killed or spied on the woman he loves.'*

I want to hate someone I can kill—not you, Felicity, no, no, no, not my goddess. A man.

'Arrogant' is a word of praise when assessing a fine sportsman's performance. In that case the bloke is so confident in himself, he can't lie about his qualities. They're there for all the world to see, he can see them himself. But 'arrogant' has a flipside meaning. It is the assumption that you're better because you are privileged. Like the copper outback who says ' You're a drunk black bum', delivering an insult designed to hurt. But who sells them liquor, who denies them houses? The victim can't help himself, can't change, because he hasn't got the power. Your husband thinks he knows women, but he's *arrogant*. Mostly you waft through it like an ethereal being, too beautiful to be bothered.

Through the windows I have seen him degrade you. I'm not saying I haven't said similar things to women. Not to you, though, never.

You were already married to him when I finally decided to try to find you. I had deserted you; yet at the same time I had carved your statue and put it on a pedestal. I couldn't face the human being and preserve the perfect memories of my passion and delirious happiness. To say the war ruined my life would not be the truth. The war freed me from the chains of banality; ordinary I can never be.

Swan it was who told me where you lived. He went from army sergeant to police sergeant in one afternoon. I used to show your picture round at mess when I was merry from beer-drinking and bleary-eyed soldier shouting. Swan reckoned he recognised you when he attended a traffic accident. That was a full ten years after the picture was taken. You were still striking. I never believed him when he said he found a picture of me in your purse, because that's just the sort of thing an old soldier would say to one he thought wasn't keeping things together too well. He knew I was besotted and he knew I was one of his best men and that there is a link between the two, something akin to a death wish. It makes a man not care for his own skin much.

The one leave I had with you, when I couldn't help being violent and impatient, shook me up. Your look then was like the swapcard pair of that first look, and it was pity. The self I saw reflected in that look I loathe. It has haunted me ever since. You've got to give me another look up and down—give me a me I can live with.

Even when I knew where I could find you I didn't try until after several years of wandering around the outback and the cities of Australia. But you were always there, my Felicity.

October 3, 1987. Remember that date, it's a big one.

Four of us in The Team were the best of mates: Swan—the sarge, regular army, Training Team—and Frank, Paul and me, conscripts in the elite unit. The AIF were barracked, we worked out in the villages and saw a lot of action. The Welcome Home

Parade was our own little reunion. Even though we'd been in contact often, this was the four of us together. The public recognition and respect somehow made us closer for a day.

Vets have a habit of blaming themselves. It's a part of the manhood of soldiery to take the consequences of war. We talked like we never talked. Even Paul Murphy was his old self. Soldiers have to believe they're fighting for right. Every uniformed fighter is a crusader, a knight, at heart; he believes in the principles of freedom and fraternity. The whole machine relies on his courage and idealism. When the machine breaks or his body and mind breaks, his courage and idealism or some version of them has to live on. After Vietnam it tends to be a pathetic and constant ability to blame ourselves for any damn thing. It's crazy because the other thing essential to the running of the machine is obedience. The good soldier follows orders without question or hesitancy, and that's a part of his pride and that's a part of his courage. To blame us for the stupidity of Canberra and Washington is so patently unfair it's no bloody wonder we feel bitter; and in many cases the direct insults from the protesters and their supporters undid us completely.

My mate, Paul, is a case in point. Now he's a weed and crippled in more ways than one. He always was a shrewd little bugger but he was trying to readjust to having half the body he used to—his mobility was intrinsic to his cheek, his charm, his cunning, the way he'd dart about.

I got a message about eighteen months after we demobbed that Paul wanted to see me. So I went there, to the green steep hills of inland Gippsland. He was trying to believe the debriefers and psychologists when they sent him back to the farming village he came from. I suppose they thought he could become a fixture in the local pub in his wheelchair or something. I just wished he could have had my dad and mum when I saw what his parents were like. His mother was one of those women set on automatic whine and his father was an unemployed yes-man, a pretty lowdown member of the species, if you ask me. That was all right, he could handle the shortcomings of his own flesh and blood.

But he had loved his teacher in high school. I say love; he said it was a stupid crush. This teacher humiliated him on the street as he clumsily tried to manoeuvre his chair where there was no footpath. He'd called out to her in his cheeky way for a bit of assistance and she turned on him and gave him scorn and peace-love polemic.

If there had been more of us there would have been a civil war in this country in those days, passions ran so high. When I arrived he was a broken bloke; her lack of compassion was the straw that snapped that little camel's back. He's a mean kind of guy now, irreparably buggered.

Some of the others have become wheelchair champions: sprinters, basketballers; or one-limbed swimmers; or simply great blokes, who because they have to take so much, give twice as much back and their women love them. Just as there's a knight-crusader hidden in every man, there's a nurse at the heart of every woman. If two people can find that bit in each other, then it doesn't matter about disability, somehow. I'm sounding like my dad.

I terrified that bitch of a teacher before I took Murf away from Victoria forever. If she hadn't had nightmares before about masked rapists turning up in her precious home to slide a cool blade along her throat, she will now. She saw the muscle that could snap the ulna and radius of her thin forearms with a flick. 'Men are everywhere,' I growled, whispering delicious threats into her shell-shaped ears, 'and some have a sex as long as a hose, as wilful as a snake, that can strangle their common decency and go after any woman any time, especially you.' I was avenging her robbery of Paul's last hope in the human race, that's all. Like the Count of Monte Cristo I was skilful and honourable in my vengeance. Instead of raping her or physically hurting her at all, I made her feel that she was beneath contempt. To scare her more I capped it with a beautiful lie. 'I'm a cop,' I said as I left her unbruised at the spot in her house where I caught her. You see, Patricia, I can be a mean bastard when it comes to revenge. I am guilty of giving a woman who betrayed the Florence Nightingale in her soul nightmares. Full stop. I take that stain on my battle-scarred armour all the way to the pearly gates.

Went to a meeting for our war memorial fund-raising and afterwards there was a bit of crying into our beers. Another crazy like me lives in a shack on some commune's land outside Canberra. A bunch of us ended up there, getting further into the fierier liquids. Freezing shit of a place, though the snow gums were nice in the dawn. Built a fire fit to burn Moscow or Rome. The remnants of an old team of losers staggering around on the sharp grasses and twigs of the Australian bush. We laughed at everything, and a moment later we're sinking into a pit of despair, drowning in grog and feelings. All the anger was swirling around like licks of flame, yet none of us felt obliged to fight. Perhaps we were too drunk to punch. No, each one of those blokes is precious. Damned precious to the others, and of next to no value to himself.

I'm still drunk and I haven't been able to sleep. We have to invent our own heroism from here, and just setting foot in Saigon in uniform is enough for a cove to join the parade. The real heroes of that time probably hide because living the peace has not been so heroic and they know it. Writing to clear the record. You've got to know a bit about me. In my words.

National service to fight in Vietnam ... national service to fight in Vietnam! Imagine that happening now? National service to fight ... conscription exclusively to fight *there*! Imagine them taking these little twenty-year-old-shit-yuppies now and putting them in uniform and making them fight? The wrong generation was sent! We were fucking called up, called up through the mail ...Wham bam!...a fucking mob of sheep! Live export.

We went first to Marrickville Army Barracks then to the bush then to the jungle then Saigon. The government made us fight our poor little twenty-year-old bums off. Gave us Asian prostitutes. We were taken from harmless dope-smoking uni parties to the madness where the cheapest way out of your own fucking head was dope. Or booze. The government sent us a bloody note, then boy it's off with your hair. It's off with your paisley body-hugging pointy-collar favourite shirt and it's into the dormitory with a bunch of other callow handsome youths. A few laughs. I remember that shirt. I remember a moment really early. We didn't know each other but this bunch of strangers with new and identical hair-cuts suddenly starts singing 'I love my shirt I love my shirt'.

Half your friends stayed home and got into trouble and the other half, your new mates, were stuffed one way or another. Imagine them sending these right-wing materialist selfish kids now! Now, I reckon, the young girls would put white feathers on cowards who wouldn't go to battle for king and country, like the first-world-war women, rather than protest on the streets yelling 'Save our sons!'

I couldn't get the same kind of fuck afterwards.

We had been made into men with headaches and nightmares and hearts wrecked by seeing and touching bodies in pieces. Then we were supposed to cool off, relax, by fucking strange frightened Asian girls, who were so brutalised by what was going on around them enjoyment was out of the question. Especially with a huge white barbarian who couldn't control his prick in a fit, who wanted to come so quick to get it over with because pleasure had become pain.

The pain was in your head, sometimes, and you wanted the body's pleasure to drown it, kill it. In Saigon I'd have a quiet meal by myself. Vietnamese food. And I'd remember my mother and sitting at the kitchen table on a Saturday about eleven o'clock, eating chops, potatoes, peas and grilled tomato, ready to rush off to cricket where I could bowl and bat and throw down the stumps, and my girl-friend would be watching thinking I was the ant's pants. Very occasionally and only for the smallest moment when the hunger was being covered did I feel that eager innocence in Saigon.

'Remember Fosters was ten cents a can,' one bloke kept shouting the other night.

'Dysentery! I nearly died when I first arrived.'

There is nothing like that half-tragic laughter, the fellas together. All of us bemoaning our jaundiced appetites and knowing we wouldn't have that special thing with each other without them. At times like that I'm glad I never came back to you. Proud of being a rogue elephant.

Vietnamese food is not bad, a bit bland. Now, in Vietnamese restaurants, I don't get the peace. Perhaps they recognise me, perhaps this one, that one, recognises my face. This girl serving me I might have fucked when she was ten...that woman over there, she looks like that prostitute I hurt. I couldn't help it. I want to say that, but then again she probably isn't the one. How could there be so many of them here and not one of them be one of the ones that I hurt? I mean, I wanted to hurt and be hurt.

Maybe some of these Vietnamese here are the same brutalised people who mobbed in Saigon, ratted on each other, scuttled around trying to make a quick American or Australian buck, offered you their sister or their daughter, wanted little favours even an ordinary old nasho private could provide. If they've forgotten, how come I can't? How dare they forget if I can't? I mean, they were there too, weren't they? It was worse for them. It was a fucking civil war for them. Maybe their cousins were blowing them up.

We're all affected psychologically. Came back short-tempered, jumpy.

'But time heals, mate. It gets better.' It has to. Just imagine putting these kids through that! Imagine getting their minds off the Stock Exchange! They don't want their minds off the Stock Exchange.

'They wanted our minds off something and the only thing I can remember is not giving a shit about anything except giving a girl a good time, feeling her fresh body sweat and shudder with pleasure and doing a bit of talking about changing the world and listening to the Beatles and Dylan and the Stones and the

Grateful Dead and LSD-tripping and skinny-dipping in the
Lane Cove River. I mean 'National Service' would be all right if
it were for everybody everywhere for a short time and not just
because they needed bodies in a war.'

'Hear hear.'

All the fellas talking and sharing the same things and yelling
over one another, whispering and being honest in a way I don't
think many soldiers after the other wars were capable of...
because anger, jealousy, resentment, mix with pride and a
brand of mateship that says I wouldn't have missed it for quids.

I turned mean at one point when an image of the women at
your party wouldn't leave me alone; it teased me in the coals of
our bonfire. Frank was there. Frank, that mountain of a man,
listened to my story. I hadn't seen him for ages because he'd
settled down with another bloke by the name of Morrie, a real
queen. He was really angry with you, Patricia.

I never told my mates your real name, I said you were called
Felicity, for happiness. With your name being Felicity I could
make you anything I liked, and I ended up putting you on a
pedestal. When I finally came home, a hero-warrior, I wanted to
drop down on my knees in front of you and beg you to marry me.
I cried big round tears into your imaginary skirt, sniffing your
fine perfume, wanting you and vulnerable to you in a way I
wouldn't, couldn't be to anyone else. Well that's the way it should
be. A man goes off to war, he fights like a demon because he has
a woman and she's safe, he comes home and he climbs into her
womb and there he weeps.

They are selfish women who want to take women away from
men, who don't respect what men do and can do, what men know
of the dovetail between life and death. Perhaps they know the
other end of the plank, birth and life, maybe. They took over
while the soldiers were away, between '65 and '75. Even when
we came home, it took us a while to settle down, a long while to
regain any power in the civilian region. They were in positions
of power; in the universities, their books were being published;
they were responsible for a lot of the Women's Movement. You

see I find out about these things, Patricia.

If they were women who needed a man in bed, that's all they gave him. In their minds they were shitting on men, and people were listening. It was all different when we came back, the world had changed. We'd been off fighting an Asian 'enemy' who wasn't even the real enemy because they had made no claim on our home town. The enemies within had taken over, not really just in the head, in the policies, the ideas, writing graffiti saying they were everywhere: 'War is menstruation envy'.

If we hadn't gone, it might have worked out more even, but our position was weakened. The draft-dodgers and the dykes had taken over. Men wanted to wheel baby-prams through the supermarkets. They wanted something of the mothering role; men who didn't were accused. I've been in hippie communities up in northern New South Wales and I can tell you there is no less wife-bashing and child-rape there, no more and no less.

We were accused, and we only followed orders. Again it's classic: the cowards take over while the warriors are at war. During the two world wars the women took over and that was right and proper because when the soldiers came home, their wives and lovers shifted aside saying, 'I've kept the hearth warm. I've been speaking to your boss and he reckons he'll find you a place.' They had looked after everything for the return, just as the soldiers had kept a photo near their heart on the battlefields, war mattering for both in a kind of equal and opposite way. With us it was different. We fought the wrong enemy. Well, I saw that when I returned. And I vowed that if ever any one of them took my woman away from me, I'd act like a tribal warrior and I'd go out and avenge my honour.

I confess to having drunk now forty-eight hours or more.

One thing I know—perhaps the only positive thing—is that my mates, especially Frank and Swan, would do anything for me, even if it was insane. And I'd do likewise.

Is the soft flesh in the light of lamps draped with silk scarves the enemy? Are these soft images sent to haunt me in the coals of fires because I saw it all through your windows? Am I getting messages?

Let's not forget that there was a war in our times, girls. Those healing hands are needed over here. The boys are damaged, girls. But you have forsaken us. I curse myself for my morbid spying; if I could stay ignorant...would that make me less dangerous? There are loose grenades rolling around out there. The slightest bit of rough road is likely to set them off. At cars, shoppers in the shopping mall, at rival bikie gangs, at anything. The legacy of war is rigid control. If it cracks, splits, breaks open, it's the fury of jealousy you have to contend with.

I might have walked through mine-fields under bombardment, and done all manner of dangerous things, but gathering up the courage to give you this, Felicity, is going to be the hardest task of my life.

As truthfully as I can put it, your warrior,

Peter L. Larsen
New Year's Day, 1989

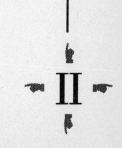

II

JOURNALISTS
Press Cuttings

The *Sun-Herald*, Sunday 5 March 1989

Marijuana Discovered in Wiley Park

Yesterday. Half a dozen Indian Hemp plants were found in Wiley Park, Wiley Park. The park is undergoing reconstruction as a continuation of a Bicentennial beautification project started last year. The marijuana seedlings, still with the evidence of jiffy pots around the roots, could not be expected to grow in the wet clay. Police are treating the discovery as a practical joke, a spokesperson said.

The *Sunday Telegraph*, Sunday 5 March 1989

Strange Dope Find

Police were called to Wiley Park yesterday afternoon following discovery by a nun of an immature plantation of Indian Hemp. The small number of marijuana seedlings seem to have been dumped late Friday night or early Saturday morning.

Sister Mary said she noticed the plants, which had not been there the previous day, when she was walking home across the park after calling the numbers at a regular Bingo afternoon run by her church.

The reason the dope was planted carefully and mulched with surrounding gum leaves baffles police. Sr Mary said it was an attention-seeking gesture, the type of action characteristic of a lonely person in need of love. She is assisting police with their enquiries.

The *Age*, Monday 6 March 1989

Religious Sister Helps Police

SYDNEY, Sunday. Sister Mary Ignatia reported her discovery of a marijuana plantation to police yesterday afternoon in Wiley Park, Wiley Park, a south-western suburb of Sydney.

The nun, a well-known and popular identity in the Roman Catholic community, has been calling the Bingo numbers at the local church hall since she retired from teaching senior science at St Benedict's, Punchbowl. She said she noticed the illegal plants as she walked home across the park. Sister Ignatia told the *Age* that she alerted police to the possibility of something suspicious being concealed under or near the plantation.

Members of the Homicide, Narcotics and Ballistics squads were called to the park late Saturday afternoon. No official information has been released.

The *Glebe*, Wednesday 8 March 1989

School Show Stopped

The South Annandale Primary School concert, scheduled to take place at the new Bicentennial amphitheatre in Wiley Park last Sunday, was postponed after the discovery of a marijuana crop in the area. Choirmaster, Mr Rex Johns, said the school was hoping to hold the concert next Sunday.

The *St George Voice*, Wednesday 8 March 1989

Missing Legs Eleven

Miss Elsie MacNamara and Mrs Ahme Pahuda, long-time Punchbowl residents and regular Bingo players, pictured here with fellow player, Mrs B. A. Bently, of Wiley Park, will be without the services of their regular caller this week. Sr Mary Ignatia, affectionately known as Legs Eleven, has been calling the numbers at St Benedict's Church for the past six years. Miss MacNamara expressed concern for her health, but the *Voice* believes the nun to be fighting fit. So, take cheer, ladies. All will be back to normal Saturday week.

The *Western Courier*, Wednesday 8 March 1989

Exclusive Interview with Nun Discoverer

Local identity and much-loved philanthrope, Sister Mary Ignatia of the Little Sisters at St Benedict's, Punchbowl, after her discovery of marijuana in Wiley Park on Saturday, made calls not only to the local police but also to the Chief of Homicide and the Drug Squad of NSW.

Police are reluctant to reveal any details or to take Sister Mary Ignatia's suggestions seriously.

Sr Ignatia said that she surmised we could be dealing with a very clever murderer with a confused and evil turn of mind who decided quite cold-bloodedly and with dedicated intention to conceal his or her foul deed by covering the greater crime with the lesser. Or there may have been heavier narcotics hidden in the recently graded clay.

When asked why she assumed there was more to her weekend discovery than meets the eye, Sr Ignatia replied, 'Why not? It's obvious. The question is why would the murderer, or whoever, want to bring attention to his or her crime?' Sr Ignatia is determined to keep police digging until they find what she *knows* is there.

As an ex-pupil of Sr Ignatia's, I assure you the police will end up listening to her.

H.P.

The *Sydney Morning Herald*, Thursday 9 March 1989

Body in Banana Leaves

Dramatic developments in the marijuana plot mystery

The area around the site discovered by a social-working nun last Saturday afternoon in the south-western suburb of Wiley Park has been cordoned off by the police.

An unidentified body is believed to have been wrapped in leaves and buried beneath a crop of marijuana plants. The gruesome discovery was made after a local nun, Sr Mary Ignatia of the Little Sisters of Jesus, Punchbowl, stumbled upon a young transplanted marijuana crop in the park on Saturday afternoon when she was returning from calling the numbers at the local Bingo hall.

While police are refusing to release any details, a source close to the investigation last night confirmed that the body had been wrapped in banana palm fronds and carefully bound with string, 'not unlike an Egyptian mummy'.

The value of the crop is estimated at no more than $3,000 and it is understood that police believe the drugs were planted to disguise the freshly-dug earth.

However, if the marijuana was planted to be noticed and removed, no explanation has been given as to why police continued to dig on the site, apparently to a depth of almost two metres. A bystander who wished to remain anonymous saw the removal of a body in a body-bag late Wednesday afternoon.

Homicide Detective Inspector Harold Clarke is expected to take over enquiries. Detective Inspector Clarke told the *Herald* from his home last night that although he is a devout Catholic he does not consider anybody above the law.

Speaking hypothetically, he said, a nun could be a murderer and suddenly, struck by guilt, want her crime discovered.

The *City Lights Review*, Friday 10 March 1989

E.T. in AIDS Scare

Grant Lout, the super-snout, has been nose to the ground on the Wiley Park body mystery. He discovered that the grave-concealing dope was odd. Something akin to Egyptian embalming fluid was found on the few heads he managed to steal from the drug store in stir. The remarkable plants are said to contain the secret of eternal youth.

Some Johnny Appleseed, a good guy according to Grant Lout, decided to blow somebody's secret nest-egg skyhigh by planting it in a common garden frequented by nosey nuns. These virgin, dynamo dollies of the cloth never let anything pass them by without a thorough investigation as to how God's work is progressing in the vale of tears.

After sampling some of the remarkably enhanced grass, Grant Lout put forward a theory, of which he himself has no doubt, that the body in the grave was the alien personage who brought back to Earth this mind-shattering substance.

They are covering up the horrible truth because of its awful implications. He may have died of AIDS, or worse, Chicken Pox. Not only our own solar system but other solar systems could be infected. Therefore all varieties of intelligent life-forms are likely to produce deformed kiddies. The consequences are too terrible to imagine.

But as only such great brains as super-snouts and nosey nuns can in fact imagine them, there's nothing to worry about.

Super-snouts and nosey

nuns have not yet turned their big crania to speculations as to how an alien might have contracted a sexually transmitted disease here. We people of Paddington wish to know which public toilet is so ill-lit that dalliancers may be unaware of the species type emerging from the next-door cubicle.

As ridiculous as that sounds, *City Lights Review* wishes to point out that insane behaviour should be taken into account as the world is largely run by madmen and that Stanley Kubrick's *Dr Strangelove* was a documentary and we should not forget it.

III

STEVEN PHILLIPS
Hardcopy 'Personal'

Add files to desktop:

CATHERINE	3/3/89
JULIE	3/2/89
LETTER Ci	14/12/88
LETTER Cii	19/12/88
LETTER Ciii	13/1/89
LETTER Civ	20/2/89
PATRICIA	4/3/89
PHONE Ci	20/1/89
PHONE Cii	5/2/89
SSP	4/8/88
ROO	12/9/88
VICKERY	31/1/89

File: JULIE REVIEW/ADD/CHANGE Escape: Main Menu

My wife's sister. I confess to a short affair with her years ago, not successful. She's uptight, anal retentive. I love the daughter, Samantha. (Love kids generally. Especially my own nephews and nieces.) Suspicious type anyway: wouldn't trust her bank manager. Makes money: tourist industry. Married an Italian who couldn't keep up. He was as thick as two bricks. Tiles, Melbourne. Julie is all talk and opinions but with half the substance of her sister. Overheard her telling Trish that she thought I must be a closet gambler. Patricia responded in her wonderfully vague way with, 'Do you think so?' Julie would try to drive a wedge between us. I must have hurt her severely. She has something against me. Glad she lives interstate, otherwise she'd have me up for molesting Samantha or something. Hates me.

Trish needs a protector in this world of wolves. Overheard Julie after the funeral trying to make Trish leave me, even offering to support her until she got on her feet. That's a laugh. I laughed, interrupted, she went as red as a beetroot and, to my knowledge, hasn't brought it up again. Basically Julie's scared of me. She is not quite sure what I might do, or might have done. I like keeping the prying little gossip guessing.

File: PATRICIA   REVIEW/ADD/CHANGE   Escape: Main Menu

Patricia Gaye Vickery married me, Steven Sligo Phillips, in the summer of 1974. She wore a white dress speckled with violets and I hired for myself and my brothers lavender tuxedos and all the photos were taken in the Botanical Gardens with Sydney Harbour Bridge rearing in the background. Of all the wedding photos my mother has, of all her sons, on the lounge-room wall, mine are the kookiest, happiest and most colourful and Patricia is certainly the most beautiful wife. They are also the most dated photos she has. It is as if I died. For the later ones are all of grandchildren and we're childless.

We've been in and out of love a thousand times. She buries her head in books. She can't get enough reading. She would be happy on a desert island with a library. She works only in the arts and crafts and sells her creations at Balmain Market. She dreams and daydreams. She wouldn't have a clue about the wheeling and dealing in the greater world. She has her secrets and I have mine. At times I've broken into what she's thinking about and found myself disappointed and bored.

So it is better to have it surrounded by mysterious silence. That keeps my interest up more than actually knowing. She is too generous and altogether too precious for this world. I'd kill anyone who touched her roughly or hurt her at all. She is my china doll, as David Bowie would say. You don't ask china dolls to bear your children, that's how I handle it.

I don't go to my mother's house anymore because I don't want a tour of the latest photos. I don't want to have my own mother glance down surreptitiously so that I think my fly must be open. She catches me every time. I would have made a great dad, but when it comes up between us, Patricia's inscrutability becomes a wall. Thick invisible bricks separate us and she pretends she hasn't heard, sometimes. Sometimes she throws a tantrum. Sometimes I get angry. Sometimes she says she will think about it. What makes me grind my teeth is that she has all the say, and doesn't say anything. Years ago when neither of us wanted children, she would talk about it in the vein of: 'Brats about the house is the last thing I need, Steve. I think I'd go mad. I'm just too selfish.' I can't explain to my mother: my wife is so selfish she won't have children, Mum, sorry. No, I think I'll have to put my creativity into writing.

I must ask her where my new socks have gone.

File: CATHERINE   REVIEW/ADD/CHANGE   Escape: Main Menu

The little bitch. See letters and record of phone calls.

File: ROO   REVIEW/ADD/CHANGE   Escape: Main Menu

Met about March '88. Roo, real name Rosemary, is the first 'radical' lesbian I have got to know. Not the first lesbian by any means, but the first of the ugly feminist type. Hairs under the arms, great huge shoulders with a brickie's tan from wearing singlets in the summer with no bra, big swinging tits, big belly, big thighs, big rude laugh. Her hands always seem oily from the massaging she does. She bites her fingernails. No man would want her, but from the way she talks you would think she had been through the wringer of constant harassment. A wolf-whistle is rape to that type. Mix Ma Kettle with Gertrude Stein and put her birthdate around the early 1950s in somewhere like Perth or Launceston, have her coming to one or all of the big cities for the Vietnam demonstrations, and you have Roo. I find her immensely amusing.

File: VICKERY   REVIEW/ADD/CHANGE   Escape: Main Menu

The old witch is dead, finally. Anyone who has had a drunk for a mother-in-law will sympathise with me. She was impossible. The house always smelt of spilt white wine. Even urine. I couldn't bear it. Pathetic. Brown furniture and a dark old upright piano crowded into a small room she called her parlour, cluttered with the knick-knacks and gim-cracks of a bygone and depressing era. She would get her schooner of moselle and teeter it on the edge of somewhere and start tickling the ivories. Oh my god. She would smile sweetly to me, saying, 'Steve, you could afford to get my pyanny tuned, you know.' Yes, but I'd be too embarrassed to get anyone to enter this establishment, I'd mumble under my breath. Three minutes was too long for me in that place. Eventually Patricia had to go there alone. Even Julie avoided it if she possibly could. But the little money-grubber was around often enough as the end drew near, you bet. A house in Lane Cove, even falling to bits, would be worth a nice amount. I wouldn't be surprised if she got the lot, actually, seeing the old girl got to hate me so much. She'd cut Patricia out of the will to spite me. I wouldn't put it past her. Patricia herself is so other-worldly she'd hardly notice. There's nothing more disgusting than an old drunk flirt.

Me. Bought a little computer, so I've got to use it. Write files on people. Might as well include me. Other people use their PCs for games, in which, for all the technology involved, the main aim is to kill, to knock off aliens. Don't want to do it. Don't want to get RSI again.

For me the great days of our times were the sixties. For me the great god of the Greek pantheon is Dionysus. For me the sixties were Dionysian, when peace, love, flowers in the hair, romping naked near the streams, getting ecstatic in the hills, proclaimed days of sexual liberation. They were days when men bonded with women and became caring and nurturing. We decided to hate war and dress in soft clothes and wear our hair long. We took on the warriors and won. Dionysus was Zeus just as Jesus was God the Father. Both of them did miracles with wine. Dionysus's mother was struck by lightning and he was sewn into his father's thigh where he incubated until nine months were up and he was born. And he was born to dance and lead the ecstatic women out into the wild and make them happy and free with his satyrs and sileni and phallic symbols. He sent women mad.

What I like about this god are his tricks and his games and his masks. I love to mask myself and be the one who knows what's really going on. Which is why—it doesn't matter now if I write it—I did one single job for the CIA during the Vietnam war when I was prominent on the campus as a peace-campaigner. Surreptitious adventure was alluring. I dressed as a cameraman and went to Vietnam, picked up a package, heroin, and came home on a troop ship.

Now I go into the bush with a gun—into the wild with a phallic symbol—and dream of remembered pasts. But I hated the troopers. If I knew which one had fucked Trish and he was on that ship I would have overdosed him or knifed him in the back quietly late at night and slipped him overboard. Only dreams, I never hurt anyone. Anyway I didn't need to, she was mine.

My biggest ambition is to perpetrate a hoax like the bloke who sold the Hitler diaries to the *Sunday Times*.

It wasn't hard to let Trish have other lovers even though she was mine. They were different from the soldier; she didn't love them and she was stoned most of the time. That was the freedom of the great days. I wanted Trish to believe she was as free as me.

We all knew those days would get out of hand. I voted for Fraser knowing he'd bring in a razor gang and slash back all the reforms of the Whitlam government. Another thing no one knows. I voted Labor next election of course.

Anyway, the frenzies of Dionysus were tamed by Apollo, who admitted him to sit at his side at Delphi.

IV

MARGOT GORMAN
Police Notebooks

10 MARCH

The wicked are always surprised to find the good can be clever.
Vauvenargues, 1746

'Detective Senior Constable Margot Gorman,' my boss emphasised my recent promotion. He waited for me to grin, then said, 'I've got to take you off that case. You may have been seen more than once.'

'Not likely,' I responded, automatically. I'm quick on the uptake and offence takes me a split second. Anybody on the Dogs would think twice about suggesting that I'd been seen. But he was National Crime Authority.

His great craggy face rearranged itself into a hearty laugh. 'We can't be too careful.' School prefect, Army Captain, leader of men, Detective Inspector Samuel Lake inspires confidence, expects and gets loyalty. From the boys. I've yet to prove I'm one of them.

'Sorry, sir.' Half the time I pretend I'm offended anyway.

'How would you like to work on your own?'

Just when I was figuring, planning, to be the best member of a team he'd seen. I shrugged. In the New South Wales Department, being put on a job on your own has secondary messages to do with the faction-fighting between the Cleanskins and the Black Knights, as they're dubbed. The

corrupt have a lot of power and I'm not exactly a favourite
with them. In fact, one of the reasons I applied for this job, and
maybe even why I got it, was to get out of the way for a while.
The layers of secrecy within the Authority make it in some ways
safer and in other ways more dangerous for me.

I gritted my teeth. Who are we after, Detective Inspector?
What's the game plan? I've got the kind of head that needs to
see the overall objective first, then work at details,
conscientiously.

He asked, 'How would you like to cycle to the job each day?'
They do their homework. I've become very serious about two
wheels since Barry and I broke up. It's a way of letting off
aggression. It takes me about forty kilometres to work off a
temper. Come back exhausted but rippling fit.

'Mixing work with pleasure hadn't occurred to me, sir.'
He could tell by my tone that I wasn't happy. On the other
hand I was curious and I would be saying yes. Enthusiasm
on hold, looking at him through the straight strands of fair
hair I let fall across my brow (a technique well practised in
front of the mirror when I was thirteen), I tried to question him
as to how I was on my first job with the National Crime
Authority. Explained that even though I am abrupt, I like
working with a team. I like having a partner. And I'm not
ashamed of being clean.

He listened to me and ignored what I said. 'Congratulations,
Detective Senior Constable Gorman.'

He'd die if he realised I cherished the ambition to be
Commissioner one day. The first woman Commissioner of Police
in the state of New South Wales will be a working-class girl from
Wollongong—me.

Work is about all I've got at the moment. I live in a unit in
Dulwich Hill which I managed to buy with my half of the
proceeds from the other place and a mortgage I can handle. I'm
not sneezing at my present wage, especially with the overtime

I get. I'm comfortable. Work. Bikes. Touch football. Throw myself in barefoot. Mud and slush. I was born with more vitality than most, it seems. Maybe they want to see what I'm capable of, maybe it's because of the promotion. The bait's on the hook and I'm biting. I eased off. I'll put the best part of myself into it.

'It's tricky, Margot. I can't tell you much. Absolutely no gossip, okay?'

I nodded. 'What is it, sir?'

'Call me Swan, woman,' he laughed. 'Everybody does.' Anyone with the surname Lake is likely to get Swan as a nickname, and it's not because he's graceful. Definitely not. He sat behind his desk just oozing power and humour like a poker-player who is bluffing but really does have three aces and two kings in his hand. No choice but to trust him.

'Find out why this handsome woman has suddenly gone mad,' he said, showing me a photograph. Long black hair, high cheek-bones and the eyes of a movie star, long lashes made longer by mascara. I frowned. The snap was a few years old. 'And protect her,' he growled.

Detective Inspector Lake briefed me alone for this assignment. There are four chairs in his office, apart from his. Usually we sit together and hear where each will be and what his or her job is. Margot, you watch the mad-lady. Bob, you cruise with the taps. Wong, get gambling: we know they're laundering the money through the Mah Jong Palace in Dixon Street. Jessie, you walk the streets. They're not obliged to tell you everything, they never do. But sitting there alone, holding a glamour snap, being asked to protect a mad woman, felt decidedly odd to me. Incidentally, find out why she's gone bonkers.

'Why ...' I started, stopped. 'What ... do I look for?'

'Visitors, contacts, the usual.' Reputedly, one of the best is Swan. I'll be there to cover his back in any situation, and he better know it. He's obviously got others on it and doesn't want even a shiver of recognition to pass between us. Secrecy, Margot: remember, you're with the Authority now. Reputation is a fortune, as Nanna would say.

He changed the subject. Apparently my going off the booze has upset one or two of my colleagues. They don't feel so comfortable with me anymore. 'I've never seen Swan drunk and I've never seen him knock back a drink,' one of my new colleagues said. I got the feeling that my sobriety was one of the reasons I was there. Not one for the ladies, Swan. He was turning an insult into a compliment, saying don't break ranks. This particular case required someone who wasn't into releasing her pent-up tension in the beer halls and bars, talking shop. He seemed to know a lot about me. I wondered if he knew the real reason I gave up the grog.

He laughed in his godfather way. I respect him. While all the subtle messages came through loud and clear, basic instructions were vague. I started to probe. Swan's got a neck like a front-rower in rugby league. He stuck his finger under his collar and pulled. Warning: you're getting a bit close.

'Simple guard duty at a mental hospital?'

He nodded. 'I hear you're a great one for the notebooks, Margot?' Police are issued with both diaries and notebooks. The latter are simply to assist your own memory. Some coppers don't bother, others jot down bare minimum, but I like getting into it. It's good to know what really went on, especially when you're working a lot with surveillance, in case you get tripped up on point of fact. There are rooms in the back of cop shops all over New South Wales full of unread notebooks. Diaries and running sheets show the job you've done. I keep my notebooks. Nobody minds, but somebody noticed. And it was significant enough to pass on. Perhaps because I chose the deluxe model, with aphorisms in it.

'So?' I was suspicious.

'Ah,' he gave out a big sigh. I was afraid he was going to caution me about corrupt officers of the law and the nasty habits of their criminal friends whose hearty fear of written words takes them to extreme lengths, but no.

'Tend to keep an accurate record myself, Margot,' he confided.

'Just in case …' he hesitated. 'Truth matters in the long run.'

Drove home feeling that Swan had given me a special handshake.

11 MARCH

War is the father of all.
Heraclitus, c. 500 BC

Hilarious article in *City Lights Review* about the marijuana body mystery. But what I can't understand is why they pulled suspicion on themselves by planting the dope. Why not just bury the body where it can never be found?

How come they wanted to draw attention to it?

Not looking forward to new job, starting Monday. Terrified of boredom.

13 MARCH

It is more dangerous to be a great prophet and poet than to promote twenty companies for swindling simple folk out of their savings.
Bernard Shaw, 1914

There I was undercover, edgy and ready, in a green uniform.

She was standing with the droopy spinelessness that loonies get after a while. Several centimetres taller than I and a good bit older than the picture I had. Uncertain what to do, what foot to put her weight on, where to look. She frowned and stared at the grass between her ankles. Shaking her head wildly now and then.

Perhaps she thought being institutionalised would protect her from the rude realities of the everyday world. Complete absence of security in the grounds surprised me when I rode around getting my bearings. Anybody can come and go. The place seems to be sleeping in some bygone time, generous space in the midst of tight-packed, overpriced terrace-houses. Shabby and quiet, all the city sounds at a distance.

Nursing and keeping this woman under surveillance would require some tricky manoeuvring as I don't know who around here knows my real profession, the nursing sisters or the aides. I got the job in the regular way on Friday afternoon. Interview, issued with uniform, told the rules. They must have a big turnover. My references provided by Swan were excellent. I'd have to pull my weight. I actually don't mind that. Never been short on energy.

Standing against the grey sky, the steel structure of the Iron Cove Bridge behind crawling with vehicles, my lady was distressed, squeezing her hands as if they were wet nappies, a woollen cardigan hanging loosely from bony shoulders. She was pointing down into the car-park between the soccer ground and the bay. I went over.

A character in shorts was yanking his car-door handle. A girl was running out of my sight. I had to stop myself being a cop for a moment. That lad needed a talking-to.

'Fuck you. Fuck you dry,' he was shouting at the girl, over and over.

Patricia Phillips, my mark, turned on me, 'Isn't that a terrible curse? "Fuck you. Fuck you *dry*!" Where did he think it up? Such misogynism. Yet he must love her, in his way, I suppose, or why would he be so upset? They have come, you see, to a romantic setting, a lovers' lane, a place to park and neck, I expect.' She acted so upset about a couple of strangers. 'He calls out such terrible things. Now I won't be able to stop thinking about it.'

'What?' I spoke like a clumsy nursing-aide. 'Thinking about what?'

Now, sitting with her, I realised I'd have to talk to her, a lot, if my presence was going to be accepted.

'Rape,' she said.

Vice and domestics are not my cup of tea.

I started to take her by the arm when she screeched like a

spoilt baby, protesting. I was dragging her away from an exercise book and some pens. She wouldn't let me touch them but was perfectly happy to come with me, hugging them to herself.

I don't want this gig for too long. Got to think of a way to make my report, move on and up. Get among the power-brokers. Out of the dead-end wasteland of womenstuff.

14 MARCH

In all private quarrels the duller nature is triumphant by reason of dullness.
George Eliot, 1866

Getting the hang of the job, i.e. nursing. She goes to her shrink and wanders about reading and talking to herself. No visitors. Drugs: Largactil, major tranquilliser; Benztripine, to counteract side-effects; and prescriptive Codeine. They tell me she's schizophrenic.

15 MARCH

Free love is sometimes love but never freedom.
Elizabeth Bibesco, 1951

I think I'd fancy a sweet boy, some gentle bloke. Just for sex. Barry, apart from his size, was a weak chap, I suppose. Liked games. Kids' games. I've got it. A jigsaw!

16 MARCH

Life is a great bundle of little things.
Oliver Wendell Homes Sen., 1859

Today I went to the hospital with a good old-fashioned jigsaw puzzle. Two thousand pieces.

'Let us sit down and do a jigsaw puzzle, just you and I.'

'I'd prefer to read or write a book,' she responded, raising her already arched eyebrow higher.

Mad ladies generally are not my forte. I'd prefer a violent man because inbuilt in them somewhere is a sense of the limits; they know when to give in. Not women. When they fly off the handle, they're off. Surrender to simple authority doesn't occur to them.

'A jigsaw puzzle is a pleasure we don't go in for much any more.' I was proud of thinking of it.

'Haven't you got any work to do?'

She liked the idea of a jigsaw puzzle. Good.

'First there are colours, areas of colours, slowly collected in loose piles, bits, pieces, this, that, here, there ...'

I wondered if she saw my condescension as professional or personal. I sounded like someone at a cocktail party trying to hide the fact that daddy was a miner at Wollongong, which mine was. She has a sort of middle-class height and social presence. Me, I'm just a no-frills hard worker.

We had carefully put out the pieces when suddenly she kicked the card-table up in the air. I had found that card-table in one of the empty wards halfway up the road—no small feat.

'Now they're all over the place, like a madwoman's breakfast.' I was annoyed. Well anyone would be.

The pieces were on the floor. She swore at me.

'How can I find two thousand things this size?' Her eyes were frantic. 'And with all these fruitcakes wandering around ...' Then she turned vicious. 'You're an insensitive frigging bitch. Why didn't you say "dog's dinner" or "ploughman's lunch"?'

'Because "dog's dinner" is something revolting and "ploughman's lunch" is the common fare of the working man.'

I couldn't back off at that point, not that I ever back off. She wasn't going to take to me if I wasn't interesting in the verbal department, I could see that.

'I am revolting ... or mad. And, I suppose a common man's lunch.'

'Good,' I remarked drily. I slid down to my knees and began putting pieces into the box. 'We become familiar with the pieces and the subject matter, slowly.'

'We?' She sounded confused.

'The point is, one can't sit around and cry all day, every day.'

Then she started gabbling vulgarities and abusing me, kicking into my ribs as I crawled around after the pieces on the floor. But her confidence was slipping away. The kicks I was getting now were feeble compared to the mighty punt that sent the card-table flying. You wouldn't think both came from the same person.

Later.

Got home, slipped into shorts and rode and rode in the wet dark to get the exhilarated feeling.

Swan said just keep a report in my diary. When anything unusual happens, ring him. The NCA sure is secretive. He gave me his private number—direct line, bypassing the switchboard.

17 MARCH

Poetry heals the wounds inflicted by reason.
Novalis, late 18th century

A week at it and time seems both long and flown. My unknown colleague can take over for the weekend. I'm going down to Wollongong—see the olds before their trip. Surf and sleep in. In my single bed.

23 MARCH

*Alas! it is not the child, but the boy
that generally survives in the man.*
Sir Arthur Helps, 1835

It's been raining, day after day. I'm used to getting wet going to work, towelling off and changing there. I am considered an oddball but that's a good thing. Normal around here.

There was a bit of a struggle when we started the jigsaw. I wanted to separate out all the pieces with straight sides, first, and she kept mixing those up with others of similar colour. She seemed to enjoy undoing my logical step-by-step approach every time I turned my back. I explained that we'd never get going on it unless we had the borders.

'The god of wine and mirrors,' she shook her finger at me, 'violated women's boundaries.' She then worked conscientiously sorting out the edges of the picture for a few minutes.

'That is madness, nurse. Self-loss.' She laughed without mirth, and said, 'Then they try to heal it with further ecstasy.'

'Largactil is not supposed to make you high. It's to stop your hallucinations.' I guessed I'd got it right, and tried to sound pharmaceutically informed. Meanwhile, together we had managed to piece together a corner.

'She has lost herself in his house of mirrors and she does not know whose face she sees in her beatific visions, his or hers. He drives her mad with his femininity.'

'His femininity? Is he a transsexual? A transvestite, maybe?' I got up and brushed my hands down my uniform, hoping that she would get interested in the jigsaw.

'Femininity is a male construct. It belongs to him.'

I wondered if it was my job simply to watch her and keep her safe or to watch her to ascertain whether or not she was insane. The latter would be more interesting in that she may be playing an active role in some criminal activity.

She is the type of woman I have had precious little to do with. Artsy, middle class, rarely seen down at the station, suspicious of cops from demo days.

Jigsaw puzzles keep going while you talk, and take ages, and everybody gets intrigued by them if they have time on their hands.

Time on their hands these people certainly have.

So have I, surprisingly.

This place is getting to me. It must be one of the biggest empty spaces in Sydney, with vacant buildings, open parkland and gardens. Today it was so still, so calm, so peaceful. Crickets in the unslashed fresh-bladed grass are choirboy-voiced, the flat-bottomed clouds that hang overhead are reflected on the ripples of Iron Cove, along with an almost-white sun and eggshell-blue bits of sky. The bay laps soundlessly like some milky oil. The silence and warm sunshine, after so much rain and gloom, makes you lift up your nose and notice, listen. The constant hum of traffic along Victoria Road: the cars going around the Drive across the water from here seem pulled like an endless toy. An old codger from El Alamein Cottage keeps up a constant yell-moan. If we didn't hear it every day I guess he'd sound as if he really were in pain, poor old bugger. It's like going to another planet, to work here.

Seagulls suddenly take off from somewhere in hectic argument—that oak?—in too much disagreement to make a flock. My mates reckon I'm turning green; well, there are times I wouldn't mind being on the other side of the lines. For instance, I'd like to save the south-east forests.

A plane comes over so low that if the paint were peeling on its undercarriage we would see it, almost. A shag dives, a small pleasure cruiser glides by, going in the direction of the Apia Club.

Sometimes I see her looking at the water, making movements as if she's trying to gain someone's attention or pretending that she is drowning. I have grown used to her madness in a way. It fits the scene.

They've made a drain where there was a creek at the end of

the bay, a moorage for fishing boats, a little pier, and opposite that, Rodd Point, surrounded by brightly rigged yachts and sailboards like butterflies around a shrub. Rodd Island is an enviable piece of real estate, owned by Sydney Harbour National Park. No one seems to go there except the ranger who lives there. It's like the homestead and the home paddocks of some squatter's station plopped into an arm of the harbour. On the hill an elegant sandstone clock-tower watches without telling the time, or rather tells of a time that's gone. Then there's the old section of the hospital, where I believe there are nurses training, their union headquarters and other facilities, but my business at this place doesn't take me up there.

A brick-burning chimney is the only other man-made thing to protrude from the skyline of trees. There's a wonderful variety of trees — stands of poplars, birch and weeping willows, firs, cypresses, oaks and so on from England, plenty of gums. The creek that runs down from the tennis courts to the chapel must have been someone's folly. He has made an artificial waterfall, a mossy pond, stone bridges and sort of conversation-pit semi-circles, all of heavy stone, planted with exotics and palms. But now it is dark and damp and littered with used Southern Comfort bottles.

She and I take walks. Along the other side of Wharf Road, which slices through the grounds from Balmain Road to Iron Cove, there is a line of vacant residences, which remind me of a street in a country town in the fifties in some arty movie. Why can't they put some of the homeless — preferably single women with kids — in these places? It is not as though this lunatic asylum is locked or off-limits to the public: there's always traffic going down there, dog-walkers, joggers. On Saturdays there are soccer matches. Anyway it's so quiet; it has a deserted feel, an air of neglect. You wouldn't know there were loonies being fed in the loud rattle of the wards, if you were outside. Unless you happen to see the tractor delivering trolleys of bain-maries containing steamed cabbage, limp beans in litres of salted water and pre-heated casseroles to the ward-kitchens.

Today they had chicken à la king lacquered by a clear sauce, with cubed carrots, grey capsicum, boiled potatoes; apple-crumble and custard.

Nearly two weeks and it feels like an eternity.

24 MARCH

Experience is a good teacher, but she sends in terrific bills.
Minna Atrim, 1902

'It is a serious existence trying to understand civilised behaviour.' She met me with this when I came into work.

'You could write my Thought for the Day,' I joked as I got behind the trolley and started wheeling, but she didn't laugh. They don't when you expect them to, these people.

I waited for her to come out of the psychiatrist's office and we walked down the road. She stopped under a tree and smiled.

'Do you think it is a kingfisher?' She pointed up at a plastic bag caught in the branches.

I discovered that in her scrapbook there are letters, newspaper cuttings, her thoughts scribbled around the page. A madwoman's diary. I didn't let her see me slip out a newspaper cutting. I didn't want to upset her. She is easily disturbed. Yet she left it there. She must know that I, or anyone, could read it.

The cutting was about the body in Wiley Park.

27 MARCH

Makes of men date, like makes of cars.
Elizabeth Bowen, 1938

Initially I was pleased because I could ride my bike to work. I have a machine I built myself for just under a thousand dollars, twenty-five gears, single-notch subtlety. I have clocked times through the suburbs of Sydney that make some traffic boys spew with envy. Drummoyne to Paddington—nineteen minutes. But now after a frustrating weekend, the highlight of which was going to the movies with Angela, I'm not pleased at all. Not only was the movie boring beyond belief, it was black and white. *Wings of Desire*. Angela, of course, raved about it. I'll give her a miss for a few months if she's going to throw her superiority in my face. And the ride is too short and the weather too bad.

Better than sitting in an unmarked car watching a door? I watched that door fifteen hours a day for three weeks when I first changed from a suburban station to the NCA. Now I work exclusively on secret operations. Vast webs of intrigue designed to snare the wealthy barons of crime, but which catch the gnats and flies who do their bidding. Watching doors, trying not to drink take-away coffee, trying not to snap at Nicky, who was with me a lot of the time, for smoking in such a confined space—it was, as it happened, terribly exciting. They might be the little guys, the tail, but if we yanked we didn't know what we'd pull out—a dinosaur-sized Chinese dragon of organised crime operated by skilled racketeers with truly mean and single-minded intent. If they suspected for half a second that I was glancing at their doorway—assuming it was the right doorway—they would not have had a qualm about despatching this particular bronzed Aussie. The high heels and tight skirt would have cramped my style of self-defence, had it come to that. It didn't. They didn't suspect that this girl was a good cop, and mission was accomplished. Door watched, heads counted, suspicions affirmed. The characters were as nasty as we thought, working for the kind of money that makes all human life, including their own, worthless. Cowards value life more than these chaps do, and cowards are the pits.

The madwoman's scrapbook was the first indication I had that murder might be involved here. When I was talking to the boss

I didn't get that particular odour, actually. Cases have about them a particular scent. A great detective always has an instinct, a hunch, about what's going on. Swan didn't give me the impression that I was working at the blood-spilling end of the operation, rather that I was guarding a contact, a go-between. That, I think, is what leads me to wonder if the insanity is real and if the hospital is not some clumsy hide-out. Swan's attitude lacked the spike, as if he had two options going: I succeed, I fail. Both were covered.

These cuttings might mean nothing, and I don't want to go flying off at the mouth on the grounds of some sneak reading. This is one job the boys can't do without me. Well, they're not going to take the info without my understanding it first.

Maybe her life is in danger. Follow orders, Margot. Resist the crazy lazy routine of the hospital, Margot.

After lunch today, she had a copy of Shakespeare tucked under her arm, like a clutch-bag. She stared at the jigsaw picture for a few minutes. And said, 'The picture is a skeleton which is fleshed muscled veined organed nerved sensed out with preoccupations, philosophies, pasts, sensibilities, guesses and experiments. Don't you think, nurse?' She tapped the box casually.

She walked past me. Her shadow fell in front of her. I found a few pieces that fitted together and smiled up at her.

She wasn't watching me. 'At present, a group portrait. The clouds. The clouds. The clouds. The clouds are intriguing in themselves, but it seems there is a strange traveller there ... both a trick of the eye and a quirk, this character.'

She turned and stared through me. She whispered, 'Leni di Torres is Frida Kahlo in me.' She hugged her Shakespeare and jiggled it like a baby. 'Perhaps in the material world there is only shape, light, shadow, form in the sky at evening. Frida haunts me.'

She sat beside me. 'But ghosts ride up there and you can see them if you try.' She put the book in front of me. I opened it with the satin ribbon attached to the binding.

'*Enter Polonius,*' I read aloud, while she played with the jigsaw.

' *— My lord, the queen would speak with you and presently.*

'*— Do you see yonder cloud that's almost in shape of a camel?*'

'*— By the mass, and 'tis like a camel indeed.*'

'*— Methinks it is like a weasel.*'

'*— It is backed like a weasel.*'

'*— Or like a whale.*'

We laughed. She must know it off by heart. I stared at her, trying to get an idea of why I am being paid to watch her, a normal loony. Clever. Brilliant, probably. Certainly not *feeble*-minded.

'Starting with ignorance and the intention to not remain so, nurse, with time, patience and enjoyment, you'll get snatches of character as real as riders in the clouds. Stick around.' She pulled her scrapbook out from under my elbow.

Swan rang.

'No visitors, boss. Nothing has happened since I got there. Except I turn a mean hospital corner.'

'I'm sure you do, Margot. Just stick with it for a while, okay?'

'Have I got a choice?'

'Yes.'

Sure, what choice do I have?

'How's it going?' He coughed kind of politely.

'Well today we went to the clouds with Shakespeare and other angels.' I heard him take a drag of his cigarette and a drink of something.

'Come in Thursday: six, six-thirty?'

'Right.'

Maybe I'll mention the murder then.

*The more serious the face, the
more beautiful the smile.*
Chateaubriand, 1849

Strife for Margot. I won't have to wait until Thursday, for I've
already been frightened off.

Watch your mouth, Margot, watch your step, Margot. And
don't come to the office. I wanted some kind of reassurance. I
asked a couple of colleagues what they knew about the Wiley
Park stuff. All they said was it had grown very hush-hush very
smartly. And smart girls know what that means. This smart
sheila knows it means big boys are involved. In the State force
you might get away with blue murder, but it's not easy because
other police know. Talking with each other serves the purpose of
keeping things in check. The NCA is so clandestine in its
investigative methods it wouldn't be hard to get away with it. For
a law enforcement body, it's almost outside the law. Gossip's got
to be contained within the boundaries of your own mob. The left
hand of justice is not to know what the right is doing. These were
old mates I was chatting with, but Swan was livid. He was in no
mood to answer any of my questions. The point of my job was to
be kept from me too. I fumed. Silently. In the end just asked
whether she was in danger. If there was one murder in the
pattern, perhaps another could occur. My sarcasm was
scintillating.

Swan's reaction makes the newspaper cutting in her
scrapbook worrying. He said very quietly that he was more
concerned about me. I feel no threat to my person except the
slow malaise of tedium, I responded. I am after all an
ambitious, energetic woman.

Then his tone changed. 'Under no circumstances, Margot, is
Harry the Heat to get wind of where you are and what you're up
to. Good night.' Click.

The more secret I'm expected to be, the more I want to write
down everything. It helps me think.

Detective Inspector Harold S. Clarke is, I think, in Criminal Investigation, but there was some rumour that he had gone or is going to the Internal Security Unit. Or was it Homicide? It is in their best interests to keep pretty shady about the ISU, as cops checking up on cops is not a happy lot. Especially in New South Wales at the moment, morale being as low as a dam in a drought.

Harry 'the Heat' Clarke is a Cleanskin, so the story goes. A whistle. He was a member of some Catholic organisation, the Knights of the Southern Cross. He is a tall, lean, deceptively kind-looking chap with a stoop. His son is also in the force, family within a family. As tough and righteous as they come, Harry. I found him quite pleasant, if a bit condescending because I'm a woman and he believes women should sit behind the counter, type up complaints and make the tea.

And how clean is Detective Inspector Samuel 'Swan' Lake? As clean as a bloke who keeps a record of the truth, should it matter 'in the long run'. His phone call left me with an uneasy feeling though.

She seemed sane today. But she was getting upset. A nurse would offer a pill, advice, something practical. A cop is curious. I pry all the time, making judgements. She was caught in a dilemma involving the nature of time. My assessment of her fitness to plead would be 'No way'. Someone who cannot take a game seriously is certainly mental.

'Doing the jigsaw puzzle,' she said, picking up pieces that were in some sort of order and throwing them in the air and trying to catch them on the back of her hand, 'is a meditation on stillness. I like that.'

With the rain outside, the world is in constant motion.

'The buyer is given a box with the picture on it, a bag of pieces, a clue on the side of the box as to how large it is and how many pieces make it up.' She looked quickly around at her fellow patients. Most were sleeping, or lolling in a drugged state, or repeating the same actions over and over.

'Time out, as it were. Time ticking by while one constructs an instant.' She framed her eye and clicked at the jigsaw pieces lying on the card-table.

'As the crippled traveller was walking the other day, the burden got heavier and heavier. You know how I am sometimes in quite another reality?'

Mmm, I nodded.

'The crippled traveller is a favourite of my shrink's.'

It sounded simple the way she said it. Easy to agree to agree with.

'There is this instant here, still. In that reality movement never stops. It is a river. The river of humanity, flooding like vermin over everything. And nothing can stop it. I am caught up in it, screaming, "Why am I carrying shit I don't need?" '

In doing a jigsaw, you do have the picture on the box. This is necessary and does not detract from the mystery of where the bits fit together or the pleasurable anticipation of the picture emerging.

'When you go to an art exhibition and see a group portrait, without a programme, you don't know who the people are or why they are looking this way,' she mused.

I could not see in this gentle woman any inkling of crime or association with it. 'In painting,' she continued, 'there is always a form and perspective: sky, foreground, ground.'

There are still many blank spaces that I will have to fill in to find out why she is of particular interest to the NCA.

'Group portrait, body in the distance.'

What has 'the Heat' Clarke to do with it? A sense of foreboding is making me paranoid.

'There must be subtle changes of shade and tone in a single colour. And much similarity of colour.' She still picked up bits that were stuck together and tossed them. I didn't like it. I wish I knew who was working with me. Was it another nursing-aide? An orderly? A doctor? A gardener? An inmate?

'Some stark contrasts. If there isn't either of these, then the shapes of exact colour must be completely distinct. Careful examination reveals that each piece is unique.'

'Yes, but leave the ones we've done where they are,' I pleaded.

She glanced at me with such a shrewd expression that I realised she was sending me up. My care about finishing our jigsaw puzzle had me in her power, for she was prepared to break the rules. She could get up and walk away, leaving me frowning down at hooks and eyes, concentrating, having to concentrate. Sharp-sighted as she is, she couldn't know what I was really thinking about.

Which of us was in danger?

And why?

29 MARCH

In our ideals we unwittingly reveal our vices.
Jean Rostand, 1928

Loonies are so self-absorbed. They have ingrown minds, no wonder they're in so much pain.

I found her today, drifting. She was swaying with her arms out trying to be a tree.

When she saw me, she said, 'The body is in the distance. The body is in the distance.'

'Body?' My god, she is uncanny. She caught me thinking like a homicide detective, which I am not, never have been, nor has any other woman in the NSW Department that I know of. Murderers, I was thinking, want to be discovered.

'The body of woman is a space,' she continued, 'or a place for man. It is a background, a location, a context against which he can pit his enormous, fragile ego, so that he can take on an autonomous identity.'

'Too abstract for me, I'm afraid,' I mumbled. Swan is a fool putting me on this case.

She screeched. 'If that is not the soul of insanity, what is, nurse?'

'Lucky this is a mental asylum: no one will notice your screaming here. Everybody's doing it,' I commented, and walked back to the card-table.

'And you're doing my jigsaw!'

Oh no, she was going to kick it all over the ship again.

'Touchy.'

But the bodies that litter the international drug scene are not strictly murdered, just disposed of, removed, terminated, to be found or not found according to the professionalism of the gun. 'Killings' they're called, not murders.

'Don't you see, while a woman is a place, a space, like an horizon, in someone else's movie, in someone else's collage, or bloody jigsaw, she can't have a place of her own. Does this make sense to you?'

She appealed to my mind and I looked away. I looked across at the other nurses ushering the shufflers this way and that, making them do things, like eat, sleep, walk and sit in a particular chair. Thought I should get back to work.

'For instance, if you take maternal and feminine out of woman … are you listening to me?' She could see I was trying not to. Her stuff was getting too uncomfortable. I live in a man's world and, my god, I'm going to make it there, madwomen pecking or not.

'Get back to your frigging work then. Workers of the world unite! Surrender your brains to the god Mammon, let him regurgitate them and throw his vomit like crumbs on the ground for you dumb bitches to eat. Get back to work and leave my frigging jigsaw puzzle alone.'

'Yes, I better do my bit.' I got up and smoothed down my uniform. She stopped me.

'Wait a minute. I know you have been sneaking looks into my book. I've seen you.'

My first reaction was to deny, or apologise and explain if I had to, but she was curling her lip up under her nose.

'Well you leave it around. I'm curious.'

'But don't you see? You're not! You're a second-rate snivelling shit, you're not listening to me.' With that she swept away like Lady Muck. She called back over her shoulder, 'Shit for brains.'

I laughed. Rolled up my sleeves and got into it, giving cheek to the other noodles, getting them to giggle and eat up.

30 MARCH

Faith makes many of the mountains which it has to remove.
W. R. Inge, 1931

Thursday — when I should be having a meeting with my boss. It's downright dangerous leaving someone like me hanging, suspended. Beyond the philosophising and the psychology of the woman, there must be some ordinary facts about her life I could find out.

'Where is your husband?' I asked. She was lying down. It was afternoon.

'He prided himself on knowing my mind, though he didn't, couldn't,' she grinned up at me from her bed, grasping the blanket like a child. 'I had a little teddy bear that I cuddled and called cute. I wiped its bum and giggled. My sister, Julie, had one too. We thought up dirty girlish games. I fed it with a spoon and put it to bed and kissed its snout. And when I grew up I got a hubby bear. I had another sister, Kerry Anne, but she never had a hubby bear. She was pushed under a train.'

Just before I left, she handed me a poem. I had seen her working at the table copying it down from her exercise book.

Standing by her bed, I skimmed it, a spiel of agony and passion which seemed to rationalise why a woman should kill.

'Do you think a woman could kill another woman?' I asked.

'Certainly.' Her answer was prompt. 'In the case of euthanasia.'

'But that's not what this is about, is it?'

'Not exactly. It's the monologue of a victim.'

I folded the page and put it on the bedside cupboard, and said apologetically, 'It's too long for me, I'm afraid. I like one-liners.'

She yawned. 'We live in a swamp, nurse. It takes all types to maintain the ecosystem.'

At least, boss, you've given me an interesting person to guard, and I've been doing that. She has hardly been out of sight when I'm on duty.

31 MARCH

Neurosis seems to be a human privilege.
Freud, 1939

This morning she ran through the corridors yelling, 'Snip off their dicks, clip off their pricks, let us have eunuchs and all will be well!'

She grabbed the male nurse in the crotch quite violently. He, poor poof, had to go off for an hour to calm down. He will never like her again. They used to be fairly friendly. She is unpredictable. She was waving one of her newspaper clippings. They are not news any more. Time for this woman is her own commodity.

I manhandle her out of the ward. 'Have they found another body or something?' I ask her, gesturing at her news cutting.

She swung around and focussed intensely for a second. 'So. It is not I who am dead then?' She threw the cutting in the air and shrugged.

I picked it up—a feature article with a couple of lines marked with pink pen. *Rap fans in baseball caps punch the air to the beat rally-style. Rap has the style of a political rally with the domination of women as its most salient platform.* I screwed it up and tennis-served it into the bin.

'No, you're not dead.' We walked to the wire railing of the yard. 'Do you feel you are?'

'Only a mad woman goes haring around shouting what all women think, isn't that so, nurse?' She plucked leaves from the oleander bush and watched them float to the ground.

'I suppose I have to find that out,' I said wearily. I took the oleander leaf she was crushing, remembering it was poisonous.

'You'd think the youth would want to make it better, rather than worse.'

'Rap, as far as I can see, is just a way of dancing.'

I wanted to get on my bike and ride around Iron Cove at breakneck speed. I wanted to talk to her about that, about things I'm interested in as if she were sane, a real friend. I could lend her my stop-watch and have her cover for me. Then daily I could break my own record, perhaps. This desire hits me during work hours. I could do it on my days off, but I don't. I watched the rowing eight on the water with envy. She followed my eyes in the manner of a caring aunt.

'I'd like to see how fast I can ride around Henley Marine Drive.'

She smiled the beautiful smile of serious faces, and said, 'Why don't you?' Just like a friend, a mate.

'I'll be no more than twenty minutes. Let's walk up here. You can cover for me.'

She shrugged, okay. I unlocked my bike. We walked up to the other end of the hospital. Her voice lost all pretence of insanity. 'You asked me about Steve yesterday. Still interested?'

I pulled on my shorts and whipped off the uniform while she spoke.

'Gone are the days of lying together in bed, reading the latest *Forum*, of him pretending to know Clyde Packer and Bettina Arndt. Well, perhaps he did know her at Sydney Uni. Or perhaps he always lied to me. All history. All down the tube. Always reading about sex in bed, what could I expect? He read about depravity the night he did it.'

As I yanked the tee-shirt over my singlet, I asked, 'Did what?'

'Raped her.'

'Who?'

'My lover, Cath. Off you go.' She pushed the bike with that expression non-sporting people have that makes them all seem like sissies. I wondered where the strength of that first kick of the card-table had gone.

'Now she has disappeared,' she called after me.

When I rode I was not concentrating on speed although my thighs didn't stop pumping. The rotten carbon monoxide air caught painfully in my throat and probably made my lungs filthy. Still, cycling helped me think. So, she had a girlfriend, a lesbian lover? And the lover's disappeared, raped by the husband? Now it's getting clearer. I immediately thought of the body in Wiley Park: no one had even said whether it was a man or a woman.

I had an appointment with my boss tomorrow—Saturday—a nice whack of overtime, a day of training and instruction. I had to find out more.

When I came puffing back to the tree I had left her under, she was nowhere to be seen. On the ground, anchored by the stop-watch, which hadn't been started, was a poem. I looked around and saw her in the middle of the rugby ground in King George Park, waltzing.

On the left of the page the poem was typed; on the right, it was in Pat's handwriting:

A chook with no head,
a recently beheaded chook.

Waiting for the meal.	*They shall*
The last supper.	*grow not old*
Eucharist.	*as we who are*
Blackguard, blaggard.	*left grow old.*

(The recent suicides,
boys in love with death.)
Drink my blood.
Eat my flesh.
Live eternal life.
Boys men war religion.
Christ.

Age shall not
weary them nor
the years contemn.
We will not
remember them.

The earth had cooled overnight and with the humidity in the air of late, with all the rain and clouds, a mist had formed over the water. In the whitish stillness there were few about, someone walking a dog, and she dancing and skipping towards Iron Cove Bridge. I mounted the bike and caught up. It was a worry now, how long we'd been, me lured away from duty. I turned her around.

'When he came home, a hero ...' She gestured towards the change-shed and toilets. Was that someone going in there, or am *I* seeing things now?

'The young warrior home from the wars, that sort of thing?' I asked vaguely.

(My reports were reading very cryptically: 'Watched subject, mad? sane? Normal day. Man taking an interest? Not sure.')

'When he came home, a hero ... if she loved him and took his suffering into her own heart, he was healed. He had her love, and that magical quantity or quality could absorb all the pains and woes of the world for him. That's what he wanted.'

I handed back the poem.

'Love is grief, grief is love. Men are afraid of death and yet they're jealous of the boys who died even in our war.'

'Vietnam?'

She nodded.

'Felicity was beautiful with a big heart. He was handsome and adored her. He was slightly damaged by the war but that was swamped by the fact that she loved him. In his dream.'

'Happily ever-aftering! Did you have children?'

'Oh yes, a boy. But the tower was struck by lightning!' She was being loopy deliberately, in a sane and moderate voice.

'Small cracks would appear now and then. There is my son.' She slapped her fist into her palm.

'Where is he? Perhaps I could get him to visit you?' I took her hand, in the manner nurses have with patients.

'Oh yes, I'd like that. I glided like a Chinese princess or a kept courtesan through those years, enjoying life, making things, and after I told him that women don't want love they want sex, I was allowed lovers. It was a bit rocky, a bit of violence and punishment, red-blooded argument—usually when he hadn't scored and I had. It was rather sordid really, now I look at it. Like foot-binding.'

I hooked the bike bar over my shoulder and we walked around the rocks.

As I was changing back into uniform on the little beach, there she was, standing in the water up to her ankles, almost shouting: 'Napalm's dripping all over the place, booby traps are exploding in their faces, American helicopters are strafing the area and one of them has a blown-off knee-cap and the other risks life and limb screaming "Medivac! Medivac!" while whispering encouraging stay-alive words through sweat-and-tear-streaked grime on his grim face.'

'What's bringing this up?' I asked as she came out of the water.

'I've just been speaking to him.'

'Who?' One slacking-off and she's made contact without my supervision.

'Just my teenage sweetheart.'

I relaxed. She must have been talking to herself, while she waltzed around the oval.

We went up the path. 'What about friends?'

'We watched it all on television—Vietnam ... My friends? Oh, I treated almost everybody the same. To opinionated, boorish types, I'd say something sarcastic and turn away; sometimes I'd turn away from sweet types too. There was nothing I had to risk for friendship's sake—until recently, of course—not like the fellows. They risked their lives for each other. Their bonds went beyond the wall of death.'

Smelt bullshit; she was romancing. I wanted to be brutally curious. I wanted facts.

'What about your husband? When will he come to visit you?'

With a flourish of her wrist, she said, 'It is an evil world out there of which I want no part.'

I got roundly told off by the charge sister when we got back, and threw myself into the preparation for lunch. She was drugged in the afternoon.

1 APRIL

It is difficult to overcome one's passions, and impossible to satisfy them.
Marguerite de la Sablière, late 17th century

Fools' day. Even though I will no more believe that men are angels and women are circus performers than fly on the back of a pig, I rang Angela. I had the information now that my mark had a lesbian lover as well as a husband and other lovers, and if anyone could help me understand without knowing too much or too little, Angela was my man (as my uncle would say).

She responded fulsomely, her style. 'Luce Irigaray considers female homosexuality to be a form of radical rupture in heterosexism and male domination and, at the same time, believes that all sexual practices represented in our culture are effects of an underlying phallocentrism that renders women socially, discursively and representationally subordinate.'

'Thanks, Angela. I understand perfectly.'

'No, Margot, French feminism is really interesting. Freud ...'

'I suppose they don't eat frogs,' I interrupted, 'or elect governments that don't want to blow up Pacific islands and turn New Zealand cheese green.'

'What it's saying, dear, is dykes imagine cocks like the rest of us.'

'Oh, do they?' Not exactly the type of information I was after, but then I wasn't sure what I wanted to know.

'I don't know.'

'Do they get violent with each other?' it occurred to me to ask.

'Don't know, but I'll find out.' The upper-class voice sounded eager.

Words like 'phallocentrism' — even if I could be bothered understanding their meaning — are considered dirty in the police force. Especially if you wanted to criticise it. You're, then, called either a poofter or a dyke, full stop. Even if you're not.

Anyway I had already decided that Swan was interested not in the woman so much as the husband. Just a hunch: his indifference to her welfare on the phone, his care for mine, and the general secrecy. In our business, usually men rather than women are the threatened or a threat, unless a woman who knows too much is prepared to spill beans, jeopardising some man's well-being.

Swan was cold and official. He saw me on his day off. The husband? He'll get me a file, ring me. Lesbian lover? 'You're not that way inclined are you, Margot?' I seethed — the way men get you off the point by saying something personal, just to throw you, just as a joke. Suddenly you're defending yourself against accusations you don't even understand, that are point-blank irrelevant. Then I was thrown: she *had* had contact with the outside. 'While I was on duty, sir?' He knew and I didn't. Who was it? Keep your eyes peeled, Margot. Great job, great job so far. What do you mean? You're looking after her. Thanks for nothing.

Who's an April fool?

I used to take so many pills on the job, to stay awake, to sleep, to stop the headache. Now there's only me and my metabolism. I'm finding it hard to sleep nights. Haven't touched a drop of alcohol for over three months now.

4 APRIL

Life is one long process of getting tired.
Samuel Butler, 1913

The days drip by one after the other.

What did I have? Newspaper cuttings of mysterious body, probably murder. Husband gone. (Note to self: *See his family.*) Lesbian lover, also gone. No visitors. Letter from sister, too busy to come to her aid. Dream fantasies of handsome soldier lover. Then there is a boy.

Frankly, boss, I don't know whether she is stringing me along or what. Has accepted my game of completing jigsaw together. Idea I thought up to give time to chat. Are there clues in her chatter? What the hell am I watching her for? Suspicious comings and goings of others? Guilt? Guard duty, protection— from what? From herself?

I discovered her banging her head against a wall this morning. But maddies tend to act out clichés as if they weren't metaphorical. Why this close cover? Usually, the Authority is concerned with illegal trafficking, and the protected are witnesses, turncoats. Who's watching me? Have I a back-up? Can't confirm that she has seen anybody, or passed anything out. Whom did she see? When? Been through her locker and there's nothing much. Her exercise book is loony tunes, from the glance I've had.

Only uses psychiatric drugs. Went to toilet inside ward. Went to shrink. Seems to think plastic bags caught in branches of trees are birds: bad eyesight? delusions? Everything routine, boss. Except that I'm tossing and turning. Gave me poem about Catholicism. Neither she nor I is Catholic ...

The lump in my throat came when I was thinking about this and Catholicism: eat my flesh, drink my blood, violence, sentimentalism. I've read all of Morris West.

Asked her about the boy. Got more than I bargained for.

'The dry stinging tears on his eyeballs rendered each blink as painful as a stick thrust full-strength into the soft globes. *If thine eye offends thee* ... Those breakable windows into his being needing a scourer—Ajax, elbow grease. The hard, crystallised salt and grime tormented him. He couldn't remove it unless he cried. To make himself shed water from his tear-ducts he would need something like a blade.' After raving like this, she backed away from me, nodding her head and shaking her forefinger.

I worked as a nurse all morning, frowning, while she wrote in her exercise book. The violence of the images in her description of her son seemed uncharacteristic, like the muscular strength she displayed once.

'The boy was born in 1970,' she said at afternoon tea. 'In the video shop he searches for Vietnam videos. The jacket of *Jud* says: *You thought Vietnam was hell. Just wait till you get home ... killing was only a beginning*. The boy hates women, he hated his mother.'

'You?'

She shrugged.

'*One too many mornings and a thousand miles behind*. This sort of Bob Dylan song has the same flavour of past that the American Civil War has for him. The boy wants to go back in time ... Nightmares with tunnels in them, suffocating with dirt in the mouth, or maybe the walls become alive and start breathing, billowing, suffocating.

'He hates women because of his mother. It doesn't matter what anybody says, he is right. He doesn't trust anyone. No friends for the hero. He believes he is so right he is prepared to die fighting for it. The boy practises. No. He looks the enemy in the eye as he passes girls in George Street. He shouted on Australia Day in the crowds at the Rocks, 'What am I gunna do with my hard-on?' All the world hates him but he is secretly powerful, like Jud. Nobody is walking, everyone's riding, riding the monorail like Blade Runner or the boy. Jud refuses favours. The boy learns.'

'A bit of an armchair psychopath, your lad!'

'Yes.'

It wasn't hard to believe he'd leave home. I'd had enough to do with displaced kids to know a lot left quite comfortable houses to live on the street, usually leaving homes with malevolent step-fathers.

So I have information on the boy. What use it is, I don't know. 'Doesn't it bother you that he hates his mother?'

She responded, 'Am I Leni di Torres or not?' She scratched the air with her fingers like a tigress. 'I am becoming Eleanora di Torres, or Leni, who arrives in Australia in a boat made of skins stretched around a frame of whale-bone, her face soft-leathery like a loved old coat from single-handed journeys across the Pacific.'

Leni di Torres was the one of her characters, her selves, who could kill.

5 APRIL

A man is robbed on the Stock Exchange, just as he is killed in war, by people he never sees.
Alfred Capus, 1901

Her hand appears in front of my eyes, a long-fingered brown hand. She holds a square of newsprint, advertising a book.

'*Headhunters*,' I read, '*edited by Matthew Brennan.*'

'I used to be in love with warriors, even though I married a protestor, a campus politician, who quietened down into an ordinary school-teacher.'

'Where is he? Why doesn't he come to see you?'

She ignored me and read: *'To this day, I treasure the memory of the heart-pounding rush of a helicopter insertion, the coppery taste of fear on my tongue, the closeness of my comrades ... Do you find that fear tastes like copper, nurse?'* She glanced at me sharply.

'Copper? I suppose ...' I stopped short.

'Jim Borsos speaking, a member of the 1st Squadron, 9th Cavalry, in Vietnam — the first reconnaissance squadron — 27 oral accounts ... the 9th were called "headhunters" ...'Nam the way it was. Without the apologies.'

This early afternoon was fairly quiet. It was cool and nice outside. Several of the other nurses were attending to their favourite patients. Most were dozing in the mild sunshine. After so much rain, it was a treat for all. Patricia and I went for a walk up the hill to where there are a couple of desolate picnic tables and plastic seats.

'Why so fascinated by Vietnam? And what about the man you married?' She will not give me a straight answer. She can't. Or she won't? I feel stupid.

'In war, someone is shooting, the victim seeks cover. He is intense, he is enduring an intimate moment. At the heart of the experience is the tension between the soldier's body and the surface of the earth he presses himself against.'

'I have to confess I'm a bit addicted to men. Addicted, yes. But I'm sick of the wham-bam-thank-you-ma'ams you always get, especially from the hunks.' She didn't hear me, thankfully. I don't know why I said it.

'Earth with thy folds and hollows and holes, into which a man may fling himself and crouch down ...'

'So?' A kookaburra begins laughing in a nearby gum-tree. Some inmate believes the bird is his friend because I can see, on another table, pieces of fresh meat carefully laid out. An inmate in the kitchen. I smile.

'Don't be thick. It's the rush — that first overwhelming

streaming of the stuff through the arteries and the body, the inundation of consciousness with pleasurable sensations—that every addict says is the experience to which he must return ... like shooting up the heroin that washes away fears of the enemy wave for the duration of the assault ... an addiction.'

'My boss—I mean my ex-boss—was in Vietnam. He loved it.' She is so beguiling I nearly betrayed myself, my job, again.

'Nurse, tell me, do men need war? And if there's no war, violence?'

'They can control themselves.' I turn away from her and wonder where all the workers are. The grass is high and it's too wet for mowers.

'Can they? Always? Or are they smitten with self-hatred?'

'More like self-love, in my experience.'

She read from her scrapbook: 'Self-hatred is too difficult; let's say I love the sense of battle, the rightful war, the wheels of civilisation.'

I can't solve the problem of men and civilisation. I gave up long ago. If you can't beat 'em, join 'em, I say. But I ask her, 'Why does it all matter so much?' History was boring at school. I was more interested in practical subjects, in my image, being popular and getting on. It was important to me and my friends to look good.

'I don't understand, that's all.'

At that moment I thought she was the sanest person I had met. The way she said it.

We sat for a few moments. As far as she was concerned, I wasn't there. She reached in her overall pocket and brought out a handful of pens. She stared through me, looking for inspiration, got some and started writing. I could have been thin air. I moved. Stood, placed one heel then the other on the table. Stretching exercises.

Without looking up, she said, 'Nurse, remember that I am afraid of the sea. I'm sure I will drown.'

'Better get back,' I mumbled. It had been a brilliant idea really, having me nurse as well, because at times she just got too much. I liked mucking in with the other nurses, mostly women. It's the sort of companionship I haven't had since high school.

History was a thick, hard-covered book with tight printing and the dullest teacher on earth.

6 APRIL

It's as easy for the strong man to be strong, as it is for the weak to be weak.
Emerson, 1841

New shift. Weekends. Late start.

When I got to talk to her, she was sitting with all her books spread out over the jigsaw, writing.

'The desire for sex flows, if it flows at all, flows in a certain sense through women, not for women,' I read, over her shoulder.

'A river without end
enormous and wide
rumbles through the world's literatures:
woman as water,
as a stormy, cavorting cooling ocean,
a raging stream, a waterfall;
as a limitless body of water ...
woman as the enticing (or perilous) deep.'

She asked me, did I like it. I didn't want to tell her I didn't want to read it; I'd rather be cavorting in a waterfall. 'Don't understand it.'

'Long-distance swimming is the only competitive sport where women remain superior to men in speed and stamina,' she said.

I nodded.

'A man must have honour,' she was looking particularly serious, 'or the biological brake fails, and his troika hurtles out of control into violence. The woman must swim away at that point. Not an awfully practical solution for most of us.'

I guessed not. She was twirling me around her little finger

and she knew it.

I contemplated this strangely deserted parkland. Saturday. Cooled by the breeze off the water of Iron Cove, kids played soccer and rugby on the ovals. Dog-owners were walking their dogs and the secretaries were doing their three-kilometre jogs. But nearer the wards, it is deathly. Even though the grass is nearly up to your knees, we walked through it. No one plays on the tennis courts. No one swims in the perfectly all-right pool. No one about, only a couple of storemen and packers at the store-house. Hang on, that guy in the overalls didn't look right. Besides, why weren't those blokes working the normal week?

I let the suspicions sink in the torpor I was feeling. For the rest of the day I dreamed of going on holiday somewhere, to mountain-climb, do white-water rafting. Having to deal with the weight of women and madness (for something about her had hooked into my brain) was making me weary. Again my night's sleep was fitful. The sense of foreboding has become a vague nausea. I could do with a drink.

8 APRIL

There are infinitely more ideas impressed on our minds than we can possibly attend to or perceive.
John Norris, c.1691

Coincidence: happened to pick up a brochure on mountain climbing and white-water rafting in Tasmania, on the way to work!

On our walk today, across the soccer field, I turned my back on her and began to stroll away. She snuck up behind me, tripped me up in front of the dressing-shed, put her foot on top of me.

Shocked me again with her strength and agility. Then whispered, 'The boy sent me a poem. He's into rap, you know.'

She began performing, making the stand into a stage, in a jerky singsong beat, strutting with disjointed shoulder movements:

> 'The killing machine the/ultimate instrument
> of revenge next one/on my list video rap
> beat beat beat and rap
> and that's no drum/getting done ultimate
> revenge i'm a factory
> soccer hoodlum mad man jack
> Iceman T Gizmo P Chuck D/initial me the
> ultimate instrument/of revenge off the hinge
> who deals dare/killing machine hey mean
> getting beat and that's no drum
> getting done crack's a tart
> smack's not smart it's tart
> i'll crack box smack/shitman jack is back
> jack is back to take/no flack flak jacket jack.'

I know the son didn't send it. Been checking her mail.

'You wrote it,' I said. 'You know how I know? Because Iceman T and Gizmo P are on the graffiti painting up the road. As well as something about *who dares deals*.'

I laughed at her disappointed expression. Habits of observation die hard. 'However,' I placated, 'it's not bad. A bit young for you, but ...' I pulled down the corners of my lips in considered appreciation.

The old fellows who always sit there with their dogs clapped. Her complete change of face staggered me, for when I had arrived at lunchtime, I caught her sticking a sewing-needle into the skin of her wrists. And refusing to eat.

She bowed. Then she grabbed my arm, began walking me back to the ward and proceeded to lecture me further.

'I am denied both sainthood and martyrdom because there is no god for me. The goddess is dead.' She squeezed my arm and let me go. 'I could be an addict of war movies, you know, they make sure of a good big weep.'

Inside, at the card-table, she said, 'When that lie I am living gets too much, I turn to the feminist books. The heavier, the harder, the more I like them, and this is what they say. They say I have no place. They look back and they say you're not the only one, it's been going on for centuries. Or they look deep and they see that man was the only one who existed in Freud's mind, Marx's mind, Darwin's mind, Saints Paul, Augustine, Aquinas, Cardinal Newman, you name it. For culture, you see, I might as well watch war movies and forget that I don't in fact suffer penis envy, and just absorb the love between the men and feel — more than they, probably — the loss of their mates from enemy fire ... or accident, though few, very few even admit that truth. But, the goddess is dead. We are confronted with mortality. Men failed to invent immortality, though they've killed the Earth trying to. Why so many people find the idea of the emancipation of women so frightening is because it represents the final secularisation of mankind.'

Boss, why did you say 'Find out why she has gone mad'? What has that got to do with police work? Her head's in the clouds. She can't be an underworld stooge; she's not the type. I'm not sure I can say feminism turned the lady's mind.

Report again as formal and brief as can be. Differs from my notebook as much as chalk differs from cheese. As they say. All I can come up with tonight is she is a possible suicide. Remote, but possible. I keep a check on the drugs they give her, as another nurse today was saying that some of the major tranquillisers can have pretty nasty side-effects, including disturbed sleep, constant drowsiness, and severe depression.

Four days off the job of nursing. Two off police work. A lot of good hard exercise, new diet, new resolutions about the old demon drink.

Carrying my diary of events since beginning the job, I entered the boss's office, a bit worried about the vagueness of my findings. At times he can be as hard a man as you'll get. He wasn't in, so I waited. A month into the job and I felt I had nothing. Except a lethargy I seem to have caught from the place itself. Asylum in the middle of Sydney. A beautiful spot, really, if you don't go beneath the surface of the Cove and see how dead the marine life is.

The woman is beginning to affect my brain, my equilibrium. A fact I've got to hide from Swan, a situation I have to fight in myself. For all my ambition, it's only a job. Remembered that at touch-football, sloshing around in the mud.

When Swan came in, he said she escaped.

'What?'

'Don't worry, Margot. The fellas from Mission Beat took her back. Apparently she was stoned out of her tiny mind.'

Another bubble of air formed in my bowels. Too many lentils.

Swan handed me a despatch case. 'Take your time with it.' He left.

This was proof that I was not alone on the job after all. Inside the case were photographs in an album, files on Steven Phillips, odd bits and pieces obviously pilfered from Pat's home. Plainly, we, the NCA, were interested in the bloke. The web of criminal activity is woven finely through all strata of society, from politicians and respectable businessmen to known hoods in the back alleys of Surry Hills. And joining these threads were little knots of police on the take, bag-men, go-betweens and cover-uppers. Liars. Thinking this, skimming through the contents of the despatch case, I felt the first edge of gratification that I had for weeks. I am one of the team, guarding the woman of the piece, albeit doing a girl's job, nursing. Another girl's job is a street-walking gig, fish-net stockings up your arse, wobbling around William Street in stilettos, a strapped shoulder-bag carrying a firearm, hiding a bleeper, making eyes and watching behind a mask. At least in nursing I could feel a little more together, more at one with myself.

While doctors and lawyers feature quite frequently in the chain of corruption, teaching is a profession that usually doesn't. Unless the teacher gets himself elected to a municipal council. Phillips' correspondence with the Education Department showed him to be a contentious bastard, peppering them with letters of complaint. No evidence that he stood for the union though.

My boss was back.

'Coffee, Detective?' he asked, 'or can I get you something healthier?'

I reached blindly into my pack and brought out a peppermint tea-bag and gave it to him.

The manila file was full of protest press cuttings and university newspaper articles, circa '68, '70. A face was ringed with marker pen. His name was highlighted as the author of several articles and, for a year or so, on the editorial crew and standing for election in the students' union. Steve Phillips. Life on campus looked completely different then. For the few months I was at Sydney Uni, there was a rush to get out the gates around five. Here they were sitting in the vice-chancellor's office, locking themselves in all night ... Long-haired freaks with their tight shirts and flared jeans.

'The husband. A real Abbie Hoffman, isn't he?' Swan had come back in with my herb tea and his instant coffee. 'I wonder if Phillips has committed the final act against himself.'

'You mean that American who committed suicide a while back? What was that fuss about? Who was he?' The look I got from my godfatherly boss was one of complete contempt for my youth. I flexed my leg muscles and glared back aggressively.

'Okay,' he smiled at me indulgently. I'm not sure that's what I asked for. 'He finished his degree and went teaching like a good little radical. Married her '73, '74. They've been together ever since. No children, probably by design rather than infertility, though one can never be sure with the likes of him. All puff and no balls.'

Most Vietnam veterans hated peace-protestors. But Swan was a cut above the norm, not usually prone to mob emotions. The fact that he can make up his own mind, and quickly and impartially, makes him a good leader.

'See that one, burning registration papers? He's right in the camera shot, isn't he? He's not burning his own. He wasn't drafted. All the time' — he gestured across this impressive record of student radicalism—'the creep is working for a foreign government.'

'These are ASIO files.'

'Too right. ASIO think he was probably spying on our spies. Our spooks stood out like umpires on a footy field. The Americans were far more subtle. Those were the halcyon days of dirty-tricks campaigns. If it worked in Chicago, it'll work in Sydney.' His brows were still down. 'Askin wouldn't have minded—not that he would have been told.'

I nodded. I was about eight or nine at the time.

'Students were the enemy of the secret service in the days of J. Edgar Hoover. All commies. But the CIA didn't send their own men undercover all the time, just dangled some money and seconded from the students themselves.'

'Why would a student do it?' I asked. Were we working with ASIO on this case?

He shrugged. 'Steve Phillips and his ilk? Some people just love to betray those that trust them. It gives them power, the feeling that they're in the Big Boys' team.'

He talked about the games played in espionage circles and the psychology of those who carried the drinks. So maybe Patricia's husband was both student radical and some sort of agent then—but I really wasn't interested as Swan went on about Vietnam, Indonesia, the Whitlam government. My job was specific.

'Patricia?' I interrupted. 'I think I've found out she does have a son. Not his, apparently.'

Swan ignored me. 'What have the CIA been up to in the past twenty years, bringing down governments, starting wars, laundering money, arms trading with both sides in the wars they start, bankrupting banks, companies, through extreme and at times inept corruption. Putting their pretty penny into international drug syndicates. Soldier-of-fortune jockeys. Above and beyond the law.' Detective Inspector Lake leaned back in his desk chair, put his hands behind his head, rested a foot on his waste-paper basket and made a face.

'Not fond of Yanks, sir?' Behind my mask of dogged obedience, I was shrewd.

'Nope, they're stupid. Found that out in Saigon, ma'am.' He laughed his infectious laugh. And I felt I had a good captain.

I contemplated the pictures of Steven Phillips. There was something really attractive about him, engaging. 'How did we get this charmer's file. Did we steal it or are we helping them?'

No answer. 'Where's your report?'

I handed over my police-issue diary.

Swan's face has three expressions. Anger, when his eyebrows, nose and jaw seem set in rough stone. Laughter—whether or not that's happiness I don't know, but he has got one of those ugly faces that joy transforms, all the world laughs with him. And inscrutability, a wise blandness, and you've Buckley's chance of figuring what he's thinking, or feeling. The diary evidently moved him to neither anger nor laughter.

'Generally routine. If you call nursing in a mental hospital, listening to fantasies, routine for a cop.' I wanted to make him smile.

'Listen, Margot,' he said, suddenly getting up. 'I've got a million things to do. Take that stuff home, and come and see me in a couple of days.' Quick dismissal.

'Did you hear my question, Swan?' Bum stuck to seat,
determined.

He cleared his throat. 'I've a wide acquaintanceship, my dear.'
Placed his hand under my elbow. I stood up quickly and left.

13 APRIL

> Men are miserable by necessity,
> and determined to believe
> themselves miserable by
> accident.
> Leopardi, c. 1834

Rejuvenated at the hospital today, half cop, half nurse. Saw
more than I had been seeing. For instance, she did have
contact outside. I was making a bed. Saw it through the
window. It was deliberately casual. With a dykey broad
walking a dog. Went through her locker. A book has arrived,
a biography of this Frida Kahlo that she mentioned. Weird
paintings. Absolutely horrible.

She spoke to me only once. 'Went and saw Brendan,' she
said.

'Brendan?'

'My son, the street kid.'

'Oh. I heard you'd escaped.'

'I'm a voluntary patient, nurse. I can come and go as I please.'
She read all day at the table where the jigsaw is half done.

14 APRIL

> Admissions are mostly made by
> those who do not know their
> importance.
> Mr Justice Darling, 1889

Looking through the photograph album. A biggish one of her in
a sixties ball dress and a sash and a crown. Even with false-
looking blackened eyelashes, lacquered beehive helmet and full

lips whitened to non-existence, she has star quality. Something the camera can catch through all her changes of fashion. A littler one shows her with long hair, parted in the middle, with a tiny mini-skirt and calf-clinging boots. Then another with her hair teased out in tight curls and her whole body covered by flowing batik except for bare feet.

Why am I looking at this stuff? The NCA is concerned exclusively with organised crime. I work for the NCA, and I can see no connection between organised crime and what I'm doing, unless there's some Asian triad dating back to the Vietnam days that has something to do with hubby. In a photograph I see a skinny bloke with a long neck, lots of hair those days, small eyes. Has he aged by thickening? By balding? I'll keep a look out for types hanging around her at the hospital in case he turns up. I think I'd recognise him. Obviously, he's who we're interested in, and I'm watching her. She's the bait, he's the fish. The fellow I think I've seen a couple of times is thick-set, shortish, sandy-haired.

In the album I noticed some snaps had been removed, by the clean tear of the cardboard, I'd say quite recently. No pictures of the boy, Brendan. Not even as a baby.

16 APRIL

I love to pray at sunrise—before the world becomes polluted with vanity and hatred.
The Koretser Rabbi, 18th century

'Margot Gorman, in from the cold in her cyclist's shorts! What's this?' Swan took the pages from my lap, leaving me to be embarrassed about the muscle above my knees and the skin-tight black lycra.

'I can change. I have a change of clothes in my pack if it disturbs you, sir.'

'No, don't bother.' He was fiddling with the despatch case I had returned. 'Any help?'

I nodded.

He started talking about treason again, and told me the code name for Phillips was 'the Phantom'.

It was somehow getting out of my league. I was having to listen to feminism and fantasies and here he was talking about espionage, complete with cute code names. I leaned over and gave him the cutting from her scrapbook: 'Exclusive Interview with Nun Discoverer', from the *Western Courier* of March 8. 'Any bearing on the matter in hand?'

He sighed. 'This, Margot, is the first connection I have between his disappearance and the body in the park. Probably nothing. She's mad, isn't she?' His eyes flickered in a fourth, shifty, expression I hadn't seen on his face before.

'Do *we* know anything about this mystery body?' I insisted.

'Aha. Later.' His mild wise-monkey look returned.

'She seems obsessed with Vietnam.'

'Maybe she knows more than we think she does, Margot. As a woman, do you think you could live for fifteen or so years with a man and not know him?'

I felt him humouring me, the way fatherly types can with me and get away with it. 'Perhaps that's why she's cracked, Swan.' I didn't want to have to go into my sleepless nights and the irritating theories and poems. 'Well, she is more concerned with a warrior chap, but I don't know whether he's a figment of her imagination. She reckons she ducks in and out of reality. One aspect of her is pretty vicious and violent, another so … um … so, soft skirt.'

'You may be dealing with a killer in a victim's clothing. Be careful, Margot.' He pulled the collar away from his thick neck and then perversely tightened his tie.

'Well, I'm not a psychologist, but there is a certain amount of guilt, you know, in how she sees things.' I felt I was grasping for attention.

'Not necessarily her.' He impressed his point by leaning forward, hands on desk, an action which changed into a dismissing one, taking his weight as he rose.

The fantasies of the woman must have got under my skin, because I found myself thinking of the word 'trust' in my relations with Swan, for the first time ever. In the Gothic world of her schizophrenia, where a battle of the sexes rages for centuries, where did I stand? On the fence, collaborating, or with my own sex? A flash of loyalty made me want to defend her. Of course a woman can kill if she has a cause.

'We didn't suspect her of anything like that: we want her watched because we want him. She might reveal what happened in the recent past to occasion (a) his disappearance, (b) her own collapse if it helps in looking into him, and (c) certain unsettling developments on an international level.' He lifted his suit-coat off the hook on the back of the door.

'Sir, what sort of developments?' Come on, Swan, I murmured under my breath, I'm your mate.

'Big crime. Don't you worry about it.' He put his arm around my shoulder.

'We found that she had a frequent line of lovers beating a path to her door. And he, weasel, didn't seem to mind. He seemed to bank it, have it there if he needed to throw it at her. But she's a spider, Margot.'

I shook my head. I didn't think so. 'What about her son?' I asked.

'She hasn't got one. I imagine he's impotent. You could find that out, I suppose.' I got the feeling that he didn't care.

He opened the door and we began walking down the corridor, and as I passed fellow-NCA operatives I wondered who else was working on my case.

'Are you sure there's no son? And of all of this about her husband? Is it waterproof or still a bit conjecture—I mean about the CIA and so on?' I was almost running to keep up with the Detective Inspector's long strides.

'I'm sure. There's no reason why she should know though. In fact, I reckon it is unlikely that she would have the faintest idea. She probably thinks he's a good guy, understanding, libertarian, free-loving. Weasels fool women more easily than the soldiers and heroes.' Raised his eyebrows.

He stopped at the door of the stairwell, pushed his shoulder into it and continued talking to me there. He lit a cigarette, leaned against the wall and relaxed.

'What people can't understand is how much fun Vietnam was. I loved it.'

I coughed politely.

'You haven't become an anti-smoking fascist have you, Gorman?' He handed over my diary. 'Facts about mystery body being kept close to the chest I'm afraid.'

'Tell me something so ...' I begged, letting my fair hair fall over my eyes in that habit I've got.

'I suppose I could tell you the method of murder and burial. Throat was cut from behind, and the blade of the knife was screwed up into the cranial cavity and the brains mushed. Particularly brutal. This method reminds the press boys of Vietnam and the vets, who are enjoying good public relations these days, so we're not saying anything at all. Understand?'

I understood, I had a job to do, and it wasn't a homicide investigation. The hair tickles the bridge of my nose until I can hardly bear it, then I flick it back.

'Get out to the range for some pistol practice or into the gym, work out, punch the bag, let off steam. Don't worry for a while.' By taking schooners of soda water, I was still managing to get around the coppers' code: you can't trust a mate who won't drink with you. That includes women. I give the excuse that I'm training and on a strict diet, and have to double the effort of chumminess. It's not hard, I like them.

My Smith and Wesson .38 is a heavy little gun. It's always in my handbag or pack and I never use it. I stood at the range steadying my right hand with my left, pressing the trigger, feeling the recoil, bored with the game. I can't imagine a woman killing a stranger like this, like the troopers who see the enemy in their sights, aim carefully, and pow. If there was a second to think Why?, would an ordinary woman shoot? No, says one half of me and the other says, yes, of course, if she was trained to and was following orders. Kicking and punching the bag I was beating shit out of someone, myself, my frustration, my confusion. Some days are just bad days. I made myself sore.

24 APRIL

Good taste is better than bad taste, but bad taste is better than no taste at all.
Arnold Bennett, c. 1908

The weather was dreary for days on end. Rain, rain, rain—as grey and boring as that black and white movie. The only excitement was when Pat started kicking and scratching another patient after a session with the psychiatrist.

I gave up on the bike and drove to work, my shift starting in the afternoon. Playing Dolly Parton on the car stereo: *Single bars and single women with a single thought in mind ... toothbrush in your purse ... couldn't get much worse ...* Bought a box of condoms at the 7/11 store when I stopped for milk and a chocolate bar on the way home. Just because they were there, displayed near the cash register. What I do in my own time is my business.

25 APRIL

Take away leisure and Cupid's bow is broken.
Ovid, 1st century

Time to read the newspapers in the morning. Students at China's three major universities go on hunger strike. Pro-democracy. Detective Inspector Harold S. Clarke answering questions about the murder. Giving nothing away. Time to do the crossword.

As I came down the road into the hospital I passed a motorbike going out being ridden by a big woman. There was a dog on the petrol tank. A lot of people walk their dogs along the jogging path. She could have been taking him for a walk or she could have been visiting. Force of habit, professional curiosity, I memorised the rego and detailed the dog as a little black Border Collie cross. Needle nose.

Our jigsaw was sky and frame with some of the scene appearing. Part of the trees and the same trees reflected in water. After the patients' tea at four-thirty, around five, there is time for me to sit. The other nurses don't mind. I do my bit. The women on the ward don't ask questions. Brian is not a poof after all, says one of the girls. I notice him now.

I sat beside Patricia on the verandah overlooking the water. She is at the card-table, arranging pieces that look as if they belong to the costumes of people in the picture. Now, alongside Shakespeare, she carries the biography of Frida Kahlo. The pictures in it are nearly all self-portraits. I couldn't see why with that talent she didn't paint something sellable.

And returned to the jigsaw. A lot of grey: could be clouds, or clothes.

Patricia answered my queries about her sister, Julie. 'She's a business woman, mucho fond of money. Her loneliness frightens me. The loneliness of judging others, of being judged correct by herself, a loneliness that creates itself and multiplies itself … my horrible sister.' Why did she want to impress on me how awful her sister was? Sisters are sisters.

She handed over her scrapbook and flipped it open at the page with the photographs, pointing out who was who.

A small, slightly brown snap with deckle edges shows three fair girls playing on swings in a park. There are several others of the two together. They must be sisters: the same colouring, similar features, foreheads, eyebrows, chins. Yet you would not remark on Julie's looks. She hasn't the high cheekbones or the deep-set eyes. In fact, their eyes are quite different: Julie's have dominant lids. In all the photos, Pat retains a fundamental beauty, and sort of camera serenity, whereas in Julie you can see all her moods, from grumpiness to cheer, while her clothes are classic good taste and don't change all that much.

There is one picture of the other sister, Kerry Anne, by herself. She stands on a city street in her school uniform staring uncompromisingly back at the professional photographer. My aunt Jo has a couple of similar childhood photos, taken when wandering photographers roamed the city. This sister's face is thinner. Her nose is long. She looks serious for a kid.

'Jealousy,' Pat said, 'is like Frankenstein, stitched together out of many little, insignificant things.' She made the monster and she had to sleep with it. Some days, she said, there was nothing else for her emotionally but this sister-loathing.

My contact with one of my sisters is similar—the voice on the other end riles you, the indrawn breath, the boredom—it's always like the first time you've tried to have it out. But of course, it isn't. My sister's thin patience implies here we go again, and I'll listen so long then make an excuse and get off the phone. She hears only the quibbles, to which she responds without any effort to resolve them. Perhaps an insincere promise or an irritable apology, but never anything which gets down, down, down to the truth. Then, stubbornly, never again will I ring her, never. She can fry. I think it probably swings both ways. I have a few problems with my sister, but I'm not perfect, either.

'Did you happen to read this letter Julie sent a few months ago?'

I shook my head, and she handed it to me. I *had* read it before.

'You said she couldn't do a thing when your mother died; you had to do everything.' A kind of mild torture, competition, et cetera, happens in all families. But they're there for each other in the end, I find. Real sisters. When you need them.

'She grieved, there and then, at the funeral. I didn't have a moment to grieve. I was so tired. Like an empty biscuit tin. Dreams had been hollowed out of my sleep, or my head as I had no sleep, no sleep to dream. Jangled nerves ... rattle. Of course, they played the wrong music as well.'

I was watching Brian and he was watching me, just getting an understanding going, and I wasn't concentrating until she mentioned her husband.

'Beg yours?'

'Steve turned on me,' she repeated. 'Kept me awake arguing the night before he left. He told me about how he raped her. He didn't say "rape". He wanted me to punish him in the usual way by booting and scratching and screaming. But I was too tired. I explained quietly, it was the wrong woman.'

'Should he have raped some other woman?' I started to feel angry.

'He didn't say "rape" and I didn't think "rape", then. He tried to force himself on her. She is too sensitive for men. Women like her are out of bounds. He went out of bounds. He cheated. He wanted too much. And too little.'

'Nearly all rapes are of daughters, wives, girl-friends or prostitutes.' I'd seen enough for a lifetime, from eighty-year-olds to eight months. 'Lesbians are not an exclusive group, not to men anyway.'

'They are. They are choosing their own sexuality. He went too far. Too far.' She punched the card-table.

Quietly crying, she mumbled, 'I was a shell looking at a shell; the insides of both of us had changed. Only very vaguely was he the same—the clothes I recognised, the shoulders, the voice, but the man inside ...' She put her head in her arms on the jigsaw. 'I just wanted some sleep. A rest. I thought he'd be back and I couldn't stand it. But I don't know.'

I didn't know what she was talking about. 'Do you know where he is?' I wanted the information to keep coming.

'I imagine,' she said, 'I'm sitting in the cafe where she was sitting, beneath posters and flyers of what's on in Sydney. Handwritten ads: guitar lessons, Swedish massage, assertiveness training, Tai Chi, poetry readings, theatre, bands, martial arts, demonstrations against global violence, someone to share a non-smoking house with two music-loving cats.' She started shaking her head savagely. 'But I can never ever ever go in there again. Even the image in my mind is shattered.'

'Dramatic,' I commented. Putting eyes into hooks, hooks into eyes—making up some of the scene.

Then she was acting, reciting:

'There she weaves by night and day
A magic web of colours gay
A curse is on her if she stay
    To look down to Camelot.'

I interrupted. 'I had to learn that off by heart at school, too.'

'She look'd down to Camelot.
Out flew the web and floated wide;
The mirror crack'd from side to side;
"The curse is on me," cried
    The Lady of Shalott.'

'But you didn't know what you were reading, did you, nurse?'

She waved and I heard a whistle and saw the black needle-nose sniffing at the grass along the edge of the bay.

'Who was that on the motorbike? One of your "sensitive" friends?'

'Friends? Why is love such a tragedy for women?'

She got up. Her face changed. Her voice lost its soft modulation and friendliness. 'You're too young,' she spat at me. 'The personal is political.'

My hands fiddling with the puzzle were grabbed suddenly at the wrists and she pulled me around to face her. Roughly. She is remarkably strong. She threw me back into the chair which nearly fell over.

'Of a type, my friends. Like Roo on the motorbike. She is encroaching on his area, that's why. When she is with her mates, she swears, drinks, talks about sex and conquests, laughs at jokes as sexist as the boys' but different. She is different only in a single way, like the enemy. Dresses similar, acts similar, feels she has the same rights—of territory, of freedom. She is a woman, so she's softer, more devious in love matters. He can't bear it that she gets other women into bed.

He feels his woman is seduced, taken out of his tribe. There's not only anger, and violence in that anger, but honour involved.'

Was she telling me her husband was jealous enough to kill her girl-friend?

29 APRIL

Only a born artist can endure the labour of becoming one.
Comtesse Diane, Maximes de la Vie, n.d.

He is a sweet boy, a gentle lad. The anticipation was heaps better fun than the performance, which in turn was a lot better than the aftermath. Why do I do it? Habit. The old idea that you have to have a man in bed to feel attractive, a full-blooded member of the human race with a healthy appetite for what comes naturally. Getting into bed was easy for both of us, finding anything to say to each other apart from hospital gossip, impossible. He'd shrivel if he knew I was a cop. He did tell me Patricia Phillips had been seeing a bloke, thick-set sandy-haired, when I wasn't around.

My bullshit detector starting ticking like a geiger counter and I concentrated on the jigsaw and put pieces together at a great rate. All the same, why should Brian tell the truth? Other things he gossiped about I knew to be lies.

The lovely grey gown of one of the ladies in the group portrait emerged. Patricia was talking to herself. 'He's learnt and loved the rites of war, the means to kill, he knows how to handle the feelings of killing. The exhilaration of taking life, for a few moments, gives life, gives intensity to feeling alive. He always felt that he took some essential being from those he wasted, took it unto and into himself. He remembered something about each, something he could have if he stole it: an ironic expression, a spark of courage, a look of wonder. There was something they would have that he didn't: sanctuary in the wasteland beyond death. He searched each dying face for that vision in the dovetail of life and death, and each time he killed he knew a little more. And it is okay to kill the enemy. This is why a man is given an enemy, so that he might search through death for his own soul.' She saw me listening to her intently, and got up and walked away. I stayed where I was, remembering what she had said, more than ever convinced that the soldier was dead, and that was why she talked about him so much.

She came back and sat down on the edge of the verandah, hugged her knees, began rocking to and fro. 'Women should be pacificist. But the hippie male was betraying something of his birthright, his masculinity. For a while Peter thought the hippies had an hormonal imbalance, but it was strange so many with the same hormonal imbalance in one generation. Maybe the surfeit of war in the fathers had got through to the genes, the chromosomes ...' Her voice fell away.

I got up and sat near her on the step. 'Who?'

'The long-haired, flower-loving, dope-smoking draft-dodgers missed so much, made themselves as ignorant as women of the unsayable, the horrific, and the blinding intensity of each moment mattering like hell yet nothing mattering. You could go hungry for days; you could walk through the soaking jungle, step over snakes, come within an inch of your life by stepping beside a booby trap; you could run without getting puffed carrying fifty kilos; you could bloody amaze yourself with this feeling that nothing mattered, only now and life at this level. Shopping lists, your mother being diagnosed as having cancer, mortgages, wages, quality of life, speedboats—all these you didn't have to think about. The one thing that mattered like hell was your woman. It was primal. She was always who you were fighting for. Or if you were fighting for freedom, say, well you saw freedom as a woman, your country as your mother. When you flipped, it was when your sense that this woman, your woman, left you, and that's when the freaky things happened. The sense of owning a woman somewhere, the photo of her in your billfold, joking about her, boasting about her, fighting for her, made war bloody beautiful. You were the classic warrior, with muscles that would withstand any attack as you held her close, kept the fragile thing, your other half, in your palm like a captured butterfly. You get awfully mystical in the theatre of war.'

'So you have been talking to your soldier?'

'Oh yes, we've been exchanging secrets across the fence. Those thoughts are his. For me the jungle is a rain forest, a huge living organism, and the fighting men in their tunnels and helicopters and crawling through the trees are maggots, wasps and ants swarming in a destructive frenzy.'

I started working on the jigsaw.

'But your husband—he was a student rebel, wasn't he? A campus personality in those famous years?'

'Oh him. I married him on the rebound. I loved the soldier. I am classic too, you see.' She lifted her head and looked at me. Put myself back to work on the puzzle as I felt her eyes boring into me. I was getting so much of the picture.

'How did you know about my husband?'

Whoops, too relaxed.

30 APRIL

Sometimes in life situations develop that only the half-crazy can get out of.
La Rochefoucauld, 1665

Had a drink with Swan and told him that Patricia Phillips had been seen talking to a man when I wasn't around.

'You can't be expected to watch her twenty-four hours a day, Margot.' He had his wise-monkey expression. I had to be totally honest with this man. A real good copper. I told him how I got the male nurse to talk, I suppose to display my heterosexual health. I mentioned the dyke on the bike with the dog.

He didn't think it important. 'Margot, you're doing a job of work,' he said as he got up and went to talk to a bunch of men by the bar.

So I keep listening. Changing sheets, making beds and serving food. Having our routine walk.

'This foreign shore' — she reached down and picked up a clod of mud—'that we called home was never owned, none of it.' She found my hand with her filthy one and walked me around.

'You run to stand and gaze vaguely. You busily make your way somewhere then you curl up and go to sleep. Like a cat. Are you acting all this?' I gestured to include the grounds, the drugs, the other patients.

'It's mad if you call a cat mad.'

We were walking along the man-made wall of Iron Cove. The sky was heavy with moisture, but not actually raining.

'I dreamed of hills and plains, even the river country and the desert, but lived in the city on the harbour which wore more cloaks than Imelda Marcos had shoes. Always dressed to suit the day, from battleship grey through green to silver, slapping the pylons of the pier, the rocks and sand, with thunder or gentle laps. The drowning element, siren-singing names like Kerry Anne, gone fishing, sailing, waterskiing. All the time testing me.'

'Kerry Anne? Your sister—the one who died?' There was a crash on the bridge. She ignored it.

'My sister could frighten me to death.' She stopped and stared into the water.

'Before she was pushed under a train?' I pressed for a confession of something which would explain her great load of guilt.

'She jumped, I always thought. Kerry was a fish. She tried to drown me. I remember the choking panic of dunking. Fear itself is the sea for me.'

Later. Heavy, narcotic sleep around us, beings barely breathing. We were like two little girls telling each other spooky stories in the dark with muted voices so the parents couldn't hear.

'You're not going to drown. You're not going to kill yourself. You're going to pull yourself together. You're brilliant, you know.'

She shook her head. 'Now I have nothing and all I need, even the weather I choose, and shoes for it. The almighty sea lacks sweetness like a love which is also hate: it merely has a passion as murderous and consuming as any in any family.'

'Dotty, simply dotty.'

'If my great-grandmother and I exchanged places, would I have braved the journey as she did in the scurvy sea of sailing ships filled to the bilges with fortune-seekers?'

'What about Shakespeare's tragedies? You were going to tell me about…'

She circled my wrist with her forefinger and thumb. 'It is horrifying that it is so because it betrays all our comforting myths, our sentiments and hearth-fire warmths, but the family is the bed of destruction, the husbandry of inner corruption in too many cases for it not to be the norm. We rot from inside.' It was almost as if she were preparing to die, clinging onto me, like the Ancient Mariner having to tell her tale, have her say.

'What of love?' she asked melodramatically.

'There are two, says R. D. Laing: when one comes in the window the other walks out the door.' I felt clever, and smiled.

'There are many, I say, and each is barbed with wine-dark thorns. Margot, who's Shakespeare's great tragic heroine?'

'Give me a clue, just a line you remember and I will try and guess.' I had said the right thing. She grinned in the gloom. The night lights were on at ankle level, and the only other light was the shaft angling through the glass door at the end of the ward.

'Okay: *Sister, prove such a wife as my thoughts make thee.* Think about it.'

I had to take all the laundry out before I went home. While I was away, she went to sleep. There had been a quality in our conversation tonight, as if I had turned some corner in the knowing of her.

Even so, I had the eerie sensation that I had been speaking to half-ghost, half-person. The present was lacking somehow. I felt bewitched.

Lamb's *Tales* is the closest I've got to a copy of Shakespeare's plays. I'll read myself to sleep. *Lear, King of Britain, had three daughters ...*

4 MAY

In politics nothing is contemptible.
Benjamin Disraeli, c.1826

Apparently I was doing my job to everybody's satisfaction, most noticeably Swan. I rang in, saying the obvious, trying to find out who was watching when I wasn't there.

Believed him when he said, 'I've got it covered, Margot, don't you worry', and that was it. For the rest, just settle into the torpor of the loony bin, Margot. Fine. Long rides were keeping me sane and fit. I got the feeling my being there was protecting her. Scan the horizon, look both ways before entering and after passing through a doorway. The thick-set man I'd reported to Swan. If I wasn't to worry about that poor skulking bugger, who should I be guarding her against? The slimy charming husband is the prime suspect. They'd had a spat and he might turn up with some nasty retribution in mind, as scorned partners do too often.

This was the trap. He'd return to do her some damage and we'd pounce and nab him for his other, less domestic, activities, saving her further aggravation into the bargain. Neat as two pins, Margot. I can live with that. The 'Phantom' was our man.

5 MAY

One keeps saying the same thing, but the fact that one has to say it is eerie.
Elias Canetti, 1978

Today it was raining, and she was sitting near the window on a straight-back chair, her spine erect, the light on her cheeks catching glistening tears. I stopped making the bed and stared. What a great photograph in black and white it would make. Anyway I yanked the sheets and blankets into tight corners and went over to her.

'Why are you crying?'

'I am thinking about the times Steve was kind to me, of when he was generous and giving. I remember giving in to him. He would beg with his eyes like a puppy or something, and I would give in. I mothered him.'

I noticed she had stopped writing in her special exercise book. It had gone. So had her psychiatrist.

'Was he impotent?' I asked.

'I don't know. What do you mean?' A despair seemed to have settled over her. It didn't matter what I asked her.

'Did you have abortions, take the pill? Why didn't you have children in your marriage?'

'When he was generous, it makes me cry to remember, but I never loved him. I thought I did. I'm grateful for crumbs.'

'You are not going to tell me, are you?'

Hearty, healthy nursey questions. 'I slept with a lot of people. I took the pill, sometimes, not always. He wanted me to, he was adamant about it, because, he said, he couldn't handle it if I was pregnant with another man's child, or not knowing whether it was his or not.' I could take that on board, but it felt like she was making it up.

'Didn't it bother you? Did you ever tell him about your other child? The boy with the rap-poems?' If I wanted a child, I'd have it. A man couldn't stop me.

'Nurse, I want to cry about sentimental things, not myself, not life. Love, what is love? Is it bi-sexual, or are there two

different things? Both essential to women. To men, also, I
suppose. Will it ever stop raining?'

'I've tried to figure out the riddle.' Still jolly.

'What riddle?'

'*Sister* um ... you know, Shakespeare's tragic heroine?'

'Yes, Charmian loves Cleopatra much more than Antony does.
It is not considered a great tragedy because the woman is the
tragic heroine.'

Talking literature and reading seemed to give her more vigour
than anything else, so I sat down opposite her, put my elbows on
the table and my chin in my hands in the eager listening
position.

'For men, too, Enobarbus loves Antony so that he too suffers a
tragedy, a minor one his being a minor character, but it is a
great conflict for a soldier: *When valour preys on reason/It eats
the sword it fights with: I will seek some way to leave him*. That
is so sad, that moment, don't you think? But of course, he can't
stay. Antony is doomed to lose. Antony is not a tragic hero, he
hasn't got the tragic dimensions Cleo has. Cleopatra is a tragic
heroine. Did you get it right, nurse?'

'I didn't, no. That one isn't in Lamb's *Tales*, but I read nearly
all of them. I enjoyed them.' I wanted to make her feel better.

'You could have guessed. She makes the decision that turns
the tide of the war. Her fine moral purpose brings her down. She
is misunderstood, as all women are. Men have no idea of
feminine courage, not even Willy the Bard, though he knew
more than most. The horror is that women betray women. We
betray ourselves, or take the blame anyway. Cleo takes Antony
into the delicious delights of the free-loving East. The harem of
straight spines and articulated muscles of Amazons with
amazing humour. I was blown out by them, and loving him I
thought I had to share it with him. I was committing a sacrilege.
I was asleep, lazy, blind, smug.'

I looked over at the other beds I had to make and back at her.
It was my job to nurse, and she was near-suicidal in my opinion.
When I said this to the charge last night, she said, Nonsense,

that I didn't know what I was talking about. Bugger her, I'd stay and listen.

'He fooled me. He was delighted, chortling like a cock in the henhouse, crowing at dawn. Pranced like a bull along the fence-line of the paddock of milk-full Jersey cows.'

'It's natural ...' What did I know about nature? I read somewhere that snow geese are one of very few species of wild creatures that mate for life. Apes, monkeys, et cetera, at the zoo anyway, mate with whoever is around. I've seen it, all my class at High saw it. We had a crazy biology teacher. He was always arranging excursions and telling us the dirty bits.

7 MAY

Each one of an affectionate couple may be willing, as we say, to die for the other, yet unwilling to utter the agreeable word at the right moment.
George Meredith, 1877

I brought up the conversation again today. I wanted to catch that man. I wanted to earn the pips, take part in the stake-out, see what he looked like, snare the coward.

'You see I justified myself in domestic animal terms, urk yuk. One male among thirty females was no threat at all, in fact quite a pleasure to me, being top cow, first wife of the harem. It is natural for me to trust.'

'Was he jealous?' Of course he was jealous. She nodded.

'Or did he see that my eyes were opening? Maybe I just became too happy and free? He had to "divide and conquer". No matter how much Cleo explains herself, if ever she is given a chance, they wouldn't understand. She lies to be honourable. She is ratted on.'

'Doesn't Cleopatra love Antony?' What threat is a woman who loves her man?

'Of course. And he doesn't love her. Her. He loves his own pleasure. *Though I make this marriage for my peace/ In the*

East my pleasure lies. He doesn't care a fig for her. No matter what she does. She humiliates herself for him and he can't see. He gets boozed when things get too difficult for him. He makes Cleopatra's and her friends' home like a brothel for his soldierly release. He misunderstands her use of feasting and the fruit of the grape. He misunderstands the East, Arabia.'

'When did you start all this study of Antony and Cleopatra?' I sighed because I really wished she'd talk about Steven Sligo Phillips.

'I took a course a few years ago. It got me into the habit of reading Shakespeare, Dostoyevsky, Tolstoy, Dickens. After my mother died I read the feminists.'

Rain patterned the still bay with little stars and made the world grey, the ground underfoot as soggy as a cow yard.

'Cath wrote. Do you want me to read what she said?'

Yes, I said, I did.

' "For my love I have to take full responsibility." What did she mean? Then she was gone. As she stayed away licking the wounds of my husband's rape, she wrote, and I longed for her, grieved for her. She ...'

'Grieved? Is she dead?' Could the spurned husband have killed the girl? Having done that, could he be lurking around now, waiting to deliver the final punishment to his wife?

'The father of the boy went to Vietnam. I looked up all the names of those killed in action, peace marcher that I was. I cried when I read those names. His wasn't there. Now, I suppose, he and I are both mad. Victims in a generation that had everything.'

'You could die for each other, but not say the affectionate word at the right moment?'

She smiled. 'Something like that. In fact, yes. Cleo dies for Antony, but has the affection with Charmian. Charmian and she live together as lovers.'

'Where is the exercise book?'

'I sent it to Cath. But I don't know if I remembered her mother's address exactly.'

Food for thought. The jigsaw puzzle whiled away the time. We were getting the picture.

'Where is he?'

'Who?'

'Hubby bear. He is like the main figure in our jigsaw. The one with the blue sash the colour of the patch of sky?'

'There are men's lies and there are women's lies. He is exactly like that, a hole. A codpiece. An emptiness. Good riddance, my husband, rest in peace if you can.' She laughed, bitterly. Sliced her throat with her thumb and a grimace.

'You wouldn't kill a fly,' I stated. She raised her eyebrows.

'Did they burn my brain when I came here? Erase something. Look, read this. Here I am trying to work out why he killed her, but it's not him.' She flicked over the pages of her scrapbook with practised dexterity, and started reading.

'You were trying to work out why he killed her,' I reminded her. 'Though who the he is and who the she is, I don't know.' Total confusion in the nurse face of my role, while the detective side frowned and figured behind it.

She turned away full of drama, a femme fatale. 'I'm being besieged by personalities: I imagined him for twenty years. Kept a photograph of his laughing face. Do you know, a policeman stole that? It could have been no one else. It disappeared after a car accident I had. I was pretty hurt. My handbag was returned but not that snap.'

'I'm frightened.' She wanted to be hugged, but I couldn't do it. I felt for her though, left high and dry, lonely, sensual, loving, a woman who had not had to see the world if a man was around to hold her at these moments of vulnerability. She would crumble into his arms, or sobbing into the arms of her ladies-in-waiting. Cleopatra, a beautiful woman. I went over to the charge sister to suggest that she be watched tonight as she seemed decidedly suicidal to me.

She began to babble as I put her to bed. 'Leni is not alone on the high seas. She is a dog maiden. She has with her a chihuahua bitch of great age, from her native barrio, and a black-and-white bull-terrier cross who joined her at the docks. The chihuahua finds the rips and tears in the hull for me to fix. Her beady yet big-for-her-body eyes say "a stitch in time saves nine" … fishing line, corks with big needles, leather thongs. I have been dead and since I have constructed my own life it is mine to hobble around in. Death's piss hangs around like the stink of tom-cats. Leni di Torres' arms are tremendously strong. She strangles stray cats when she comes to harbour, for the catgut. Patches on the prow are quite tabby … consumed with doubt … secrets and hiding places pierce the surface … she is making me … jutting through normal parlance, rocks. Trouble.'

I tucked her in gruffly, and asked, 'One last thing. Do you think Leni di Torres is capable of premeditated murder?'

She looked at me quite steadily and nodded. 'Of course.'

Then she was asleep.

8 MAY

How can there be laughter, how can there be pleasure, when the whole world is burning?
The Dhammapada, c. 3rd century BC

Protecting her I am doing my job. From herself, from outside threat. The only threats I can *see* are the bloody drugs. I gather schizies get violent without medication, but these chemicals seem to make her swoon into her imaginary world and accept it. They dull her but they don't dull her despair. Who, on the other hand, is protecting me from her?

11 MAY

Life is an offensive, directed against the repetitious mechanism of the Universe.
A. N. Whitehead, 1933

Day shift again.

During the last few days of sunshine she's been heavily sedated. I pursue the dreary grind of nursing. Occasionally I sit by her, reading or writing, waiting. The sun is the unreal thing, soporific, still, resting lightly over the soggy land, brushing softly the silky surface of the bay. I gaze, she gazes. My job is nothing but watching this woman. I watch her and get my pay. Two pays. I wouldn't say anything about that. Meanwhile, Margot, carry on.

There's something worrying me though: why has she been put under such heavy sedation? There is a new charge sister. Things have changed. The psychiatrist she liked has gone onto bigger and better things at a university somewhere. My ward is someone else's patient now. Maybe the new psychiatrist prescribed stronger drugs? I must look.

There was something curious about this charge sister. I felt it in my water, as Nanna would say, but I couldn't finger it. She was plainly hostile to Patricia. Did she or did she not know what I was about? If so, why should she try and frustrate it? Maybe she was just a malevolent type who liked to make her patients' lives as uncomfortable as possible. Was she a plant? Whose plant? My usually good sense of smell must be affected by the narcotic regime of the mental hospital. In this environment everyone, nurses, aides, doctors, visitors, blue-collar workers, march to a slower beat.

Smokos out in the sun, reading the news. Troops and hunger-strikers shaping up to each other in China, in the wake of Mr Gorbachev's visit there. None of the real divisions in the New South Wales police force breaking through, yet some ripples hitting the media. The journos are no fools. The corrupt networks upset by the restructuring of divisions seem to be holding out. It all seems so distant from me, in this job, as if by listening to the madwoman's conversations and recording them I have stepped up on a rickety bridge, high above the dangerous waters. I am trying to decide whether to go to a function organised by the Surveillance Squad, in lieu of a golf day they were going to have. The course is too wet for a complete round.

The jigsaw puzzle was nearly complete, a big old oil-painting, with trees and sky reflected in a lake, a little cottage with a single line of red fence in the background, a group portrait in period costume.

Up finally, she walked through the ward saying she is dead or a carrier of the dead. I ignored the eagle eyes of the charge and followed her. I don't have to obey a petty tyrant, not even to maintain my cover. Patricia was my main concern and I was worried about her deterioration. Slow poisoning occurred to me as a way of getting rid of her, even though that seemed outlandish. There was a reason I had spent so many weeks caring for her safety. I had an eerie feeling that her death was possible.

Rang Swan. Said, 'Call it feminine intuition, but she's going to die.'

'Don't be stupid, Margot. She's as safe as a church. You're just getting sucked in.'

He squashed me. Remember which side your bread is buttered on, Detective Senior Constable Gorman.

It is not the clear-sighted who rule the world. Great achievements are accomplished in a blessed, warm mental fog.
Joseph Conrad, 1915

She is on Haloperidol now, instead of Largactil. And something called Thorazine.

'I began as a crippled wanderer,' she said, 'and then I learnt that if one is to travel one must carry a burden.' She reached for my hand like an old woman.

'The burden of guilt?' I wondered as I steered her to our card-table. I had never known a jigsaw puzzle to take so long, but then we hadn't really spent continuous hours on it.

'Will I be famous because I'm the murdered, the murderer, the teller of the tale or not famous at all? The truly holy take on others' burdens, sometimes by force, and begin to crawl on bare hands and knees, incomprehensibly ...'

She frowned in a stagey sort of way and stared into the distance. Her breathing became agitated.

'Are you all right?' I asked.

She ignored my question. 'There were characters along the side of the road. Old women, witches from Shakespeare, apparitions from Milton, real or as real as the rest of us, and all they could do was mix up undrinkable brew and speak in untranslatable language. I hardly looked their way. When I was alive. Or when I was dead. Whichever way you look at it. Perhaps I am there now, on the side of the road, being heard but not understood ... Help me.' An ambiguous plea, as she was looking intensely at one piece of the puzzle.

'I think we can fit that here: it's not a piece of cloud, it belongs to his trousers,' I suggested helpfully.

'A camel, a weasel.'

'Yes, well ... It can't be cloud. We've finished the clouds.' I laughed at my own joke and gestured at the clear sky, one of the few this autumn.

'The western suburbs of Sydney stretch out to the foothills of the Blue Mountains. In a jigsaw puzzle of this moment, the immense sprawl of buildings, streets, factories, clubs, supermarkets, brothels and the great variety of humanity there in cars, homes, groups and alone and walking would only be a few pieces. It is a reddish stain of straight edges and broken bricks, spotted by a few early electric lamps.'

I played along. I wanted to contact her, to have her look at me and see me. Only once or twice had she called me by my name. My anonymous nurse status suited her individual construction of her world. Yet she had said 'help me' as if she meant it.

'To make a jigsaw I guess you have your print and you stick it to cardboard, then you get a jigsaw and you saw it into pieces and then you put the pieces into a bag and you mix them all around, and seal 'em, don't lose any, package it and sell it.'

So she played along with me, too. 'Am I afraid of getting help? Am I afraid of the collapse of my inner wall?'

'You're here, aren't you? Here to be healed.' Though there wasn't much sign of her getting better.

'In the distance a body is being exhumed. It is naked, a glance of white in the dark background. Shadowy figures stand erect around it in the bush. As if drawn by red biro, a plastic ribbon marks the site. Almost lost in the darkness of trees and standing police is the young civilian, a stick figure resting on his bike. The foreground obscures the media. But they are there with their OB vans and they will write as briefly as possible the facts as they see them: what, where, when, how, who, how old. All this, deep in the upper left. An instant. Yet no photography, no photographer. The strokes are lines of print, the pigment words, the display between covers and through pages, from mind to mind, in the gallery of the imagination. At first glance it is simple. At first glance everything is simple, this is a matter for the glancer, to see and notice, to analyse and deduce, to enter! Am I the painter or the painted?' Her finger traced the imaginary scene over the old-fashioned one of the jigsaw.

Poetry, a kind of imp, had her entranced. She went on. 'The picture is the sight, the glance, the surface, the appearance of things which is necessarily nothing to do with the real matters, and yet a lot of the culture we're given today is in the still picture. For instance, the advertising hoarding, the image. Three men and three girls, laughing, drinking milk, smoking Players, caressing sheets, the lone rider, his horse, the landscape and Drum or Marlboro. This is advertising but it is also an analogy of how a lot of minds work and actions are taken—like buying a motor boat or an Akubra hat, buying a house, mowing its front lawn. A lot of time is taken *seeming*. And a lot of money. And thought. It must be robbing the reservoirs of desire and passion and belief and identity in the individuals.'

'Yeah, it makes you sad,' I agreed. She made me sad.

She shrugged. 'Picking up scraps of knowledge and placing them on the rocking, sea-like table of my emotional awareness, my life is its own jigsaw puzzle. It ends, I end it. She' —jabbing her forefinger to her own breastbone—'has lost the box. There is no picture of herself. No clues to the length and breadth of her real person. The size of it all. Hints—a straight edge, the frame, and this colour is like this, only it differs slightly in shade, and anyway, they don't fit. There's not enough?' She counted four, five bits.

'Yes there are.' I started concentrating, sorting.

The desperation absent from her voice, she mumbled. 'This is as important as anything, isn't it? I mean, playing. Isn't that what everybody does all the time? They are playing when they destroy the planet, when they replace the gold standard with interest rates, when they pay revolutionaries to maim innocent women and children. But of course these are serious games.' She started wringing the sleeves of her cardigan. Her tone changed. I'm trying to find the frame, the frame of suspense—a series of unanswered questions—or maybe just suspicions that turn out to have a simple explanation, like the man forgot. The letter was not under the door, it was under the carpet and he didn't see it. If he had seen it and saw that I had gone off with my sister to my mother's, then he may not have ... I've had other lovers before—

but what I am getting at is she is not only female but lesbian—he is excluded, this may have been the problem.'

It really was as if she were seeing something in that moment too hard to look at. Insight, reality? Fact. My guts constricted in worry for her. She stared at our jigsaw, the big old oil painting now almost completely revealed through its fretted patterning.

'It is the moment you come to, now, just before the completion, that is the most enjoyable,' I said softly.

'If it were a painting, not a collage—my head, I mean—thick red paint could stand in its glistening oil.'

13 MAY

It is not in human nature to deceive others, for any long time, without in a measure, deceiving ourselves.
I. H. Newman, c.1837

She would not dismantle the jigsaw on the card-table, or let me do it. I could see a coffee ring on it from a cup, and an ashtray was still there. The charge kept on my back all morning, but when I had my tea-break I sat beside the table with Patricia. She is drowsy all the time now. Tired frown-lines and bags under her eyes indicate disturbed sleep.

She mumbled, 'The solid moment, the still life, the picture, is completed. Life is bloody murder. Still murder, just murder.' Absolute gibberish. I emptied the ashtray and got back to work.

When the afternoon drug tray came around I stopped her taking hers because the narcosis was helping neither her nor me. She conspired quite happily.

'*The Brothers Karamazov* is like a good big old painting in a heavy frame. An oil painting, not collage or photo-realism. The old man is basically a puny personality. He is despicable.' She raved on about this story as we sat outside in a weak yellow sunshine. She no longer had the energy to walk. 'There are three legitimate sons and a bastard son, and the old man is murdered by one of them.' She gestured with her forefinger and thumb to show me how thick the book was.

'Who is the murderer?' I asked.

'There are long conversations in it,' she pressed on, describing one—a meeting with a holy man, which takes a hundred pages. 'The old man and his son love the same woman of the town, who has "loved much". The saintly elder bows his head to the ground in front of the son, who seems ruled by his passions. So Dostoyevsky has set up why everyone's going to gossip. Do you read literary novels, nurse?'

She said 'nurse', not 'Margot' — 'nurse', like some nineteenth-century caretaker of children. Sometimes she assumes the grandness of a countess.

'No, popular fiction is more my style. Buy all my books from newsagents. I don't mind the odd historical romance, I suppose.'

My lady smiled at me with a look that also caught her own image of herself, like I was doing her hair and her smile reflected through the mirror.

'The holy elder has no odour of sanctity when his dead body lies in state and pilgrims come to see it. In fact he stinks.'

'Why?' I asked as she got to her feet.

She glided away without answering, straight to the sister who, I saw, nodded and went to the drug cabinet, rattling her keys. For a moment I suspected collusion between them. Odd, hostility was usual. She had the extra pills in the pocket of her cardigan, I knew. The ones I stopped her taking. How often had she done this? Was she collecting enough drugs to damage herself? If she did, what could I do when I went off duty? I still felt this vague suspicion she might be acting: the way she would glance in my direction to see if I was watching her.

The jigsaw was done. I broke it up and put it in its box. She was so out of it when I left. I nicked her scrapbook and took it home. I read it that night.

'"I fell in love. I plunged into a bottomless chasm of savage longing for death, and at the same moment I was hurled toward the burning sun of an intense affirmation of life." My soldier boy's words were poetry of violence. Franco Beraldi wrote: *In a way that has no precedent in human history, militarisation becomes the model, the only available model for every form of social interaction as well as the imagery. From overlay, mutation and from mutation, war.* War makes murder beautiful. Like an ultimate sport.'

On the opposite page, with doodles of arrows and exploding stars and jagged borders, was pasted in a piece of yellow paper: 'We are apologising to soldiers whose crimes we know, now even better than the mothers who marched to "save their sons". We're sorry, boys. We should have been behind you all the way with your rapes, your massacres, your shooting off your rapid fire like wasted sperm into children's mouths in foreign cities in an alien inhospitable landscape.'

Pat has written in pencil in the margin: I can seen no escape except violence.'

14 MAY

A sigh can break a man in two
The Talmud

Today I told her that I had read her scrapbook. I did not want her to die, she was my responsibility. She laughed. She didn't care. I told the charge that I feared she would commit suicide.

As we walked she continued her murmuring. 'They knew what they were doing to good crops and blameless trees in Vietnam when they blew them sky-high and loved the look of flames and smoke and bilious defoliants. They blamed the leaders, the politicians. But the ordinary bloke who was only following orders has a conscience, hasn't he?'

We are walking, weaving our way through the other patients.

'She thinks I am sane like her,' she says to me of one of them, pointing her out. 'She likes the ambience of crazies in pain.'

I thought she was going to attack the patient again.

'Porn is a way not a what,' she suddenly shouts across the ward. 'Graffiti I read somewhere,' she explains. 'I'm getting ludicrous, Margot, rats are climbing up my walls. I'm afraid the evil genius is going to wire me up and singe the thoughts off my brain. I have not signed any paper giving permission.'

I take her by the arm and lead her outside. The rain has started again. 'Tell me about your son.'

'The only animal the boy ever knew was the cat. Cats walking along the top of the fence, one after another, like coolies. On a mission to find gold. That is, to sleep in the sun somewhere.'

'I'm going to have children,' I respond. 'When I'm properly married to a good man. Before my middle thirties I think. Hope.' I grin. I'm determined.

'The first animal he touched was a horse in harness standing at the kerb waiting to jog through the streets taking tourists for a ride. He brushed his hand along its neck, but he was being watched by the girl in the Driza-bone and Akubra hat with a whip so he stopped.'

We sat on the banana lounges on the verandah and watched the rain.

'In the Timezone parlour of games, he learned to drive fast cars, could handle a space-craft as well as Luke Skywalker. My boy. He could smithereen herds, flocks, floods of enemy craft in his own movie. He had power, he won. An enemy was always in his thoughts. The aliens' attack.'

I could imagine her with her son and I said so. It made her savage. She bought into my conversation with a vengeance.

'The boy is a psychopath. As you pointed out, nurse. In every known society, homicidal violence, whether spontaneous and outlawed or organised and sanctioned for military purposes, is committed overwhelmingly by men. The conclusion would seem to be that women should run the world. If we can agree that the greatest threat to human survival over the long haul is posed by posed by human violence itself, then the facts of human violence—the sex difference, and its biological basis—can lead nowhere else.'

She was so articulate I thought she was saving her pills again.

'But I am violent.'

'What do you mean?' I grasped her wrist. I wanted to know. 'Did you take your medication today? Do you feel violent now?' I wished that I had some nurses' training and understood the difference between Lithium and Largactil. All I know is that they mustn't be mixed up.

'He locked himself in his boarding-house room,' she continued, 'playing with a flick-knife, slicing himself— murderer-victim—letting the blood flow. Until the decision to live took him down to the emergency clinic where he had it bandaged up. Then the aliens struck. He received an almighty electric shock among the old televisions and power points in the back of the shop.'

I know it's not strictly NCA business, but I was concerned, not only about her own violence but also her son's. I rang Swan and said, 'We've got to find her son. He's going to kill his mother.'

'That's interesting, Margot,' was his reply.

I screamed at him. 'It's important. I know it.'

'No, he's not, Margot. She's spinning you a line.'

'You don't know her like I do.' I was sobbing.

'Don't side with the tarts, Detective,' he said, delivering what he considers healthy advice. 'Don't go too far.'

About five minutes after I put the phone down, I got an anonymous phone call from someone who had a sock over the mouthpiece. Just a threatening call: I've had them before.

15 MAY

One must be poor to know the luxury of giving.
George Eliot, 1872

I was a wreck from a bad night. Patricia was raving all day. I dived into her chatter like into a soothing pond.

'*Apatico, mediano*, words with more spit than a Mallee landscape. My brain is flat as a dry plain. It is self-critical, and dull in the extreme. What a place to escape! Where I go to, a tatted web knots mystery to mystery in technicolor.' She seemed to have saved it up for me, standing over me as I made beds and mopped floors under the eagle eye of the charge sister.

'Beyond the four walls of the institution may be any manner of thing, and still I say, lie down in the sun whiffing of coconut oil, make of punishment pleasure and vice versa. Sink into the drama of heroic types, with Will m'dear bard boy. Is it now? The moment of intensity, to go ... off? Isolation insulated by figments and schitzy fragments taking with sticky fingers obsession of reality, stolen, holus bolus possession becomes medieval demons with powers, is it now the moment ... to go well and truly mad?'

When I tried to answer what sounded to me like questions, she didn't hear me. I wondered whether this creepy charge sister had put her on another type of psychiatric drug. She suddenly turned and walked away. When I'd finished I found her wandering near the edge of the bay. She stood staring paralysed at the wind-surfers on the bay, chewing her tongue.

We were close to the water then and, if I had been listening only, I may have been fooled again to think she was totally around the twist, but I happened to glance at her eyes and they were searching. Clear, cunning, they were inspecting all the vessels on the water. But she continued spinning her yarn.

'The bruja of the waves, Leni di Torres, drifts on sympatico currents, the leather hull of my craft mistaken for a small whale sunning itself on the surface by the creatures of the deep. My long hands webbed like a macramé net reach down and lift food from the lapping-licking sea, lulling me with lotus dreams. I have rigged up a simple catchment system for fresh water. I gaze at the horizon, crisply drawn, and from here to there, full of oceanic, exotic life like an illustration in a kid's book. As a child she suffered from polio and faced Death, old baldie, with hollowed-out eyes no more than a gleam, in the children's hospital. With weakened legs and a mighty spirit and forearms and shoulders as strong as a cripple's, I went out into the world with the expressed intention of copping no shit.'

Sometimes I think she is on mind-bending stupifiers; at others I think she is making the worst possible effort at convincing me she is mad. She calmly took herself off to the bathroom and returned with theatrical gusto.

'The release is making my insides loose. I race to the toilet, it's beautiful. She doesn't exist because she is me. How can she exist? She is as real as the portrait inside the third eye of a self-portrait by Frida Kahlo. She is to me, in me, in ratio to me, like the infinitesimal doll at the centre of a Russian doll puzzle. And I am an overgrown Alice, wondering.' She was dancing around me. A dervish.

The sister ran down and took her by both arms and held her elbows at the back. She, Patricia, was my charge. Before I could stop myself I reacted like a cop, like someone obviously trained for crisis situations where physical confrontation was a probable outcome. I saw my lady as a hostage shielding a wrong-doer in a siege. I dropped on one knee, gritted my teeth, and felt for my gun. It was only for a second; then I recovered my composure.

Patricia was led away, laughing. Hysterical. I awkwardly arose from my crouch and pulled back my outstretched arms. The sister looked me up and down and sneered. I'd seen plenty of cops use that belittling expression when dealing with suspects. I'd done it myself a few times. I recalled Swan's warning to watch out for myself.

16 MAY

The path of duty lies in what is near, and man seeks for it in what is remote.
Mencius, 4th century BC

After inadvisedly acting like a cop, performing automatically instead of keeping my wits about me, I followed Pat and the charge back to the ward, trudging like the terminally bored and hard-working ethnic women who wear the same uniform as I. Everything was clear because of a fear I felt. Like putting on glasses. I saw how deadened I had become in this gig. The rhythms of work at the mental hospital had etched a pattern of scratches over my grooves, and this slow walk enhanced by an anxiety was like playing an old record on a new hi-fi.' In front of me, the spineless loony was being manhandled by the strong arms of the charge sister as if she were no more than a rag doll. But I felt less than she, so small, because her conversations had acted on my person like the gradual effects of a regular drug. I was addicted to them. But jumping into action had felt good — for a second. Then I was confused.

I was further confused when I entered the ward and everything was back to normal.

Pat immediately began talking to me. 'Spose you thought I'd gone back to the swamps from whence I came and whereto, like Persephone, I descend every now and then, to emerge each time scraping off a different sort of slime ...'

I sat down and listened to her as I usually do.

'I look into my heart and I find no love. I squeeze my fibre and get no drip of loving kindness. The blinds of consciousness won't open, or are they shut? The man I loved could not have done what he did. So um er reality is only as my brain perceives it to be. I am a monster who, being betrayed, growls like a frightened German Shepherd.'

I smiled weakly and noticed the charge was busy not glancing in my direction.

'Steven can never know how much he has done. Never. He justifies himself, or seduces the criminal lawyer. He has tongue, talent, pride, money, looks. Cath would have Buckley's in a court of law.'

Out of the blue I am back on the case, the spectre of the husband throwing its shadow over her features.

'Criminal lawyer? Why would he need one?'

'If life were a series of different subjects for which one was marked individually, he would score very well on some ethically difficult ones, no doubt. The law being a deputy headmaster, he would get off. He is a rapist.'

Was this the same hysterical rag doll of half an hour before? She sat on the metal chair with one knee thrown over the other, her elbow resting on the table supporting her chin a little, staring into the distance, conversing.

'The law being an ass, he would get off.' She looked at me and nodded a question mark. I guess I nodded back. All my weight seemed to be in my ankles.

'He abused me,' she mused. 'I could be violent, as Leni. She is the complete anarchist. The free cripple, as alone as lone can be on the high high sea.'

She suddenly grabbed my arm and pulled me closer. 'In case the police come and commandeer all my stuff, there should be no names. There are no names in pictures anyway.'

Out of nowhere the charge sister appeared. This woman wanted to prove her authority in every action, every mannerism. Simply having it was evidently not enough. She heaved Patricia to her feet. Both looked at me over their shoulders as they went towards the beds. I, left stupidly at the table, checked the time on my watch and decided I could go.

She was laughing, hysterically, I reminded myself. I was tired, riding home. So tired.

It's been raining too much too often. They say it's the greenhouse effect. My mind is foggy.

I am too young to be into feminism. Too practical to contemplate the origin of the species. I reckon I exist on an equal basis with men. But she says we haven't got very far at all. Didn't Persephone go to hell? It's all a matter of individual interpretation … choice … choice is freedom. Who's free? Not a lot of the men I know … I dozed on my bed when I got home with her scrapbook open across my tummy.

Daytime sleep is always racked with dreams. Mine had sex in it. I look up at the clock. Its arms, which are cyclist's legs, point to the nine and the five. I think of my niece who gave it to me. The Police Golf Day will be under way; by now they will be drinking in the club house. I can't settle, reading this stuff. I have no hook on it. I need to see my colleagues, feel the friendship of my own kind.

Fed the cat, found the car keys and went out along Canterbury Road to Bankstown.

The scene in the Club was as I expected. Men jovially enjoying each other's company, many of them wearing bleepers on their belts. Detective Constable Sally Miller was the only woman, apart from two wives who had done the catering. I came in during the speeches. Gerard Clarke was thanking his wife and the lady who sat beside her for the delicious food. They giggled and were loudly applauded. His father, Harry, won a prize with three other old chaps — the old guard. Sergeant Gerard Clarke is considerably bigger and broader than his father, a confident cop and speech-maker. Sally Miller leaned against a poker machine with her partner, both apparently on duty. She smiled and raised an eyebrow, mouthing 'where've you been?'.

Gerard hailed me with an equivalently querying expression. 'We thought you were away, Margot. Townsville or somewhere?' I sat down with Micky Stravros and his crowd. They were talking about phobias: fear of flying, fear of traffic jams — making jokes and telling anecdotes. I glanced up at Sally. She was checking a number on her bleeper and saying goodbye to the clan. Women in the police force could not talk like this about fear. We had to be fearless. I got up and left, feeling very edgy. I should be elsewhere. I wasn't allowed to talk of my job, and Harry S. Clarke was not to get the slightest wind of it. Oh shit. Easy Hills Golf Club carpark was muddy, slippery and by now it was getting dark. Someone moved behind my car and I tripped, slipped, fell. When I got into my car I saw a note on the windscreen under the wipers. All it said was: 'Only a pawn in the game'.

Since I gave up drinking I haven't felt as comfortable with the coppers as I should. But I didn't give up because I'm a prude. I gave up after a gathering such as that. It was down at Goulburn, a great night. Everyone was drunk. The men and boys were drunk. I was drunk. And I was randy. Barry was already sleeping with Susan and everybody knew it. Fair's fair among mates. Myself and another constable—his name was Jim—went to a private hotel and took a double room. The trucks outside moaned with airbrakes all night and the neons lit up the wall in venetian slits. The one overhead light was a fluorescent strip. The place had the grandeur of yesteryear and the smelly dowdiness of now—digs for single men, basically. We paid for a night half of what they paid for a week. Jim was too drunk to get it up. He tried for a while, then he flaked. I was wide awake, wanting. I went down the other end of the passage for a leak. A young Maori was in the bog. Instead of saying 'Sorry, where's the ladies?', I stood at the door watching him. He took my meaning loud and clear and we had each other there and then. In the men's toilet. His legs were as strong as tree trunks and he came standing up, me with my legs around his loins, my arms around his neck, holding on with all my muscles.

In the morning, waking up beside Jim, who was grumpy, embarrassed and hung-over, I vowed to cut out alcohol. We made a pact with each other. I'd say he was great in bed to anybody who asked and he would keep me honest about my pledge.

When I got home there seemed nowhere else for me to go except back to her scrapbook. The television looked boring. There were no friends I wanted to see. My little mind was jumping around my brain like a Spanish flea. I tried to concentrate:

'Once upon a time there was another planet in our galaxy which exploded. Because its inhabitants were driven to experimenting with matter. This planet—Lucifer by name—was then left as a spirit without body, and it entered Gaia, unbidden, and this constitutes cosmic rape. Have been looking again at rape in mythology—Persephone and Hades, Tiamat and Marduk, all the sky-gods of the ancient world (Lucifer was a sky-god). Also the Virgin Mary and God.

'When Lucifer entered Gaia, a world-wide mutation followed, the division of the sexes—the male of the species is the manifestation of this mutation. And I have come to believe that men are the agents of this alien spirit in Gaia, because our planet now houses two incompatible spirits. Lucifer is the interloper; there is something of the cuckoo about him—he is parasitic and lives on the energy of Gaia. As a host planet to such an unholy parasite, we are in danger of losing our very being to succour him.'

I am not exactly the type to understand the radical lesbian viewpoint. But what a story! Could be taken both ways though: men are angels, women animals. All a bit weird. Reminds me of Sunday School where they expected you to accept stories of Joseph in his coat of many colours and baby Jesus doing miracles and God making Adam lie down and go to sleep while he removed a rib and made Eve out of it. Couldn't make sense of it when I was five. Can't now.

Then, a poem:

'i hung a crystal over my words
on the page, it tugged out
wide anti-clockwise circles,
—gullible without faith—
then i moved the rainbow prism to
feint-lined vacancy where it
stayed stone dead in the air'.

Oh, Pat, you must be mad. They've got you in an institution for the insane, so all should be right with the world. At least I'm all right.

After reading for a while I shave in the bath. My bath is the size of a tub. My brown, smooth muscles are what's called 'nuggety'. I love shaving my legs and greasing them before a race. I love the feel of the tight cyclist's clothes, and I love the pain in my thighs and calves as you give that bit extra going up a hill, or into the wind. Wind is the worst thing. I can change my back wheel almost as quick as I can the front. When I shave my legs I'm daydreaming, preparing. I love having an obsession, something to look forward to after work—to be on a bike as sleek and fast as a racehorse. It's why, I say, I gave up the grog and the shit-food. The thing I miss about them is the trust of mates in the force. They miss out on my loose moments when they might take control. Now I don't give them the chance.

Swan is a big drinker, after hours, with lots of mates. He operates with honour within all the unwritten limits. He's a wild gander. Wild geese mate for life, and his wife died a few years ago. She was an army nurse who also served in Vietnam. Swan's honour is charting rocky shallows with my abstemiousness. He's got to run a tight ship, a well-oiled team, and I am a bit dry for him. So he put me to work on my own. Fair enough. I have a fat notebook, now, filled with material I'm sure he's not the slightest bit interested in, and a thin diary. I've been a bishop on his chess board, put into position on the side-lines, guarding a whole diagonal, to be moved if my life is threatened and he wants to save me. Perhaps I'm not the piece that will be moved in for the kill. I don't know.

The phone rang.

'Margot, you've blown your cover. Kaput, you're off that job.'

If I had been still 'one of the boys' he would have said this over a few beers, given me more time, because everyone would have had to pay for a round. He rang off as cold and hard as a rock in the rain.

A bishop not a pawn in the game. There are two factions in the NSW police force and it's all coming to a head. I noticed in the car-park quite a few cars had exactly the same note under the windscreen wipers. Someone's joke. The Black Knights and the Cleanskins playing out their chess game?

V

PATRICIA PHILLIPS
A Madwoman's Diary

My psychiatrist has a cuckoo-clock on the mantelpiece.

I used to hang my stories around the house, flopped over dowel or pegged to fishing wire from Steve's box of junk in the shed. Documents hanging on the clothesline to dry. His shed. The boy must have his shed, he said. Hubby's cubby-house. Full of toys.

There are five minutes before each session when she keeps you waiting while she checks her notes or meditates or has a quick joint... the knock of the tock in the nick of the tick.

Bolts of white silk I bought and dyed. Or painted in metre squares. Sometimes sewed into shirts, skirts and pants. Or simply banners and scarves.

There is a sandpit in a box in her waiting room which can be freshly raked with a kiddy's plastic toy. Objects are lined along the cedarwood sides to decorate the sandcastles and waterways. A young public-hospital shrink, Doctor Anne Levin looks like the Eurythmics Annie Lennox, about ten years my junior, and she quotes poetry. *We die with the dying... we are born with the dead.*

The deafening drum of the rain won't stop. It is thrown in handfuls from the sky to splat on the ground like bodies splashing on top of one another, making deep evil-smelling ponds in the middle of the lawn. Growth cannot contain itself in midst of its own rot. Disgusting, like a fat man eating.

I take her on Gothic journeys through the rutted roads of stormy skies and Gormenghast tunnels of the imagination. *Words move, music moves/Only in time, but that which is only living/Can only die,* quoth she.

Still the clock, kill old Chronos dead. Tactfully, the Swiss antique is not wound up during sessions. I know my forty-five minutes is up through the bleep of a cheap chemist-shop digital. For three-quarters of an hour she takes seriously the contents of my brain and earnestly seeks its meaning: nothing is mere fantasy to her. We get along.

'The *bruja* of the waves carries me off into herself ...'

'The *bruja*?' she asks. Dr Levin sits down in her waiting-room, watching me play in the sand.

'Spanish for "witch". Her name is Leni di Torres.' I pluck Leni's underpants from the line and I am she, pounding through the spray, scaling the waves, with warm buttocks cushioned from the splinters of the crude wooden seat, for my knickers are kitten down, soft solid as nature's raincoat: mink to me, carrion to you.

We carry on. She takes me so seriously.

'My life,' I stop my sand-play, 'has become more real since my death.'

'Yes?'

She gets up and opens the door to the other room. I pass into it, in front of her as she speaks, telling her, 'I began as a crippled wanderer and then I learnt that if one is to travel one must carry a burden. The traveller is the carrier, I learnt. What one carried in one's pack seemed to be the chief concern and topic of conversation among all wayfarers at all manner of rest stations. When people worried, this is what they worried about. When people were proud, they were proud of what they carried on their back. Some were proud of weight, others of utility, others of design without care for the contents. I saw as a very young wanderer that quite a few walked along with other adult people on their backs or in pushcarts, and these seemed to fight with each other over the muddiest parts of the track. At times preachers would stop us and divert the god-fearing across ankle-twisting rocks and broken glass up the hill, and all that could be seen at the end of their pointing fingers were clouds behind the high summits. For sport, I noticed, the truly holy take on others' burdens, sometimes by force, and begin to crawl on bare hands and knees up these pathless treks, crying with bliss at the pain and torture they endured for faith. Others glared in their direction with incomprehension, envy or guilt.'

No psychiatrist's couch in this consulting room; the floor is strewn with bean-bags and cushions.

'Yes?' she says.

'It was a strange world I was born into. I was a cripple and people said I should be thankful for it. For a while there I carried along a bag with rocks in it and I went along the goat track on bare feet and showered only in cold water. In a way these were happy days, as others looked up at me with faces twisted in disapproval and I thought I was taking responsibility for my own life and suffering admirably. Living itself exhausted me and I hunted for jagged ice to sleep on.'

I remove a sprig of daphne from the vase and smell it. Her body is relaxed and her eyes are sharp as tacks.

I ramble on. 'Did I fall off that path or was there a general landslide? Everyone who could fit was down in the valley of daisies and golden daffodils for a brief shining moment, stripping off our burdens and dancing naked with each other. If we walked, we walked around in circles making rude gestures of love to the travellers up on the road. Refugees, we called the poor pathetic followers of roads on the way to or from some war, a human river. Yet we were indistinguishable from one another in our freedom, as our small parcels held the same small precious things.'

'Flower children?' She is with me in my allegorical landscape. It is so clear, before my eyes.

'Whereas in the crowd,' I continued, 'each wayfarer was

assured of a unique identity by the contents of his pack. I rejoined the sufferers.'

'How? How did you rejoin the sufferers? Was it a conscious decision?' She writes something on her pad.

I shake my head, I don't know. Sharp as a rat biting my amnesia, she wants this bit but I won't tell her. Trauma is fillet steak to the shrink.

'Once,' I shrug, continuing, 'I returned by that way again and no one was in the valley of daisies and daffodils. No one at all, not even those who pretended to be there. I could see them, sitting on packs, camouflaging suitcases behind tea-tree and scrub, quietly exchanging gossip about their burden and their journey, the distance travelled, the distance to go. They may have been planning to broaden the road, dam the creek and irrigate, or make it all into a drain beneath a concrete plaza. All I know is they weren't really there. Not as others had been there once, children of Pan with freesias in their hair and songs of criticism of the goings on up along the road.'

'Freesias.' Her turn to sniff the daphne.

'Now I am dead and that was long ago, through mists now, ages. The travelling of roads as grey husks of beings was a way of life.'

The seeds are dead as old wattles before their time, babes with faces of old men, decayed through and through. Take my shoes off to squash fat worms, squelching my way away from her rooms. But the blue bird comes to flap and sing in the branches of the beech. Autumn should be different from this. Where are the mellow days when the jacarandas lose their leaves to reveal their fine lines, the bones of the purple flesh which arises like Persephone Spring after Spring. My mother said she didn't have to see another Spring. And died.

I'm screaming at the rain, pushing pins into my skin in the mornings, but I don't tell my doctor. The flame trees with their love of blood brood over the choking grasses, sucking up the rich mulch of their sodden state, biding their time like assassins with brains. They won't let the Spring appear without their festive tents advertising anger and passion beside the passive jacaranda, pink and white oleander, overblown brief azalea, bougainvillea, and all the bushes at the fair. My mother said she didn't have to see another Spring. That little string snapped with me holding the other end.

Annie asked about the travellers on the road again and it was easy to remember.

'The happiest,' I said, 'were those with blinkers—people blinkers, like race horses have horse blinkers. They are rigged around their eyes like a pair of falsies with holes in the top where the nipples would be. The people with these contraptions are the happiest ...'

'Is that how you consider life, as a strange traveller in a strange land?' She caught my sarcastic tone.

'They say certain experiences make you feel alive. Do you feel alive, Anne?'

'I am not in the midst of an intense experience, but I'm interested. Go on.'

'Maybe I was alive last night, for today I am tired. Let's look at the grey water and the grey skies where the leviathans break through with wings and deafening jet-streams ...'

'You said you strangled down the birth canal with a rope around your neck ... You struggled, you felt the umbilical cord was strangling you ...' So she had a job to do, after all, and my fantasies were part of it.

'When one has a rope around one's neck, one is likely to hang or accidentally choke as it gets caught on something, or your sister ties you up in the ancient almond tree. It has been done.'

'Your sister strung you up to the almond tree?' Facts, girl, facts.

'I want to get back to the crowded road, the stream of human refugees, the husks of beings walking, walking. It's like a book I haven't finished ...'

'The birth canal?'

'The tunnel oozes moisture which clings to its soft-warm-strong-sucking-expanding sides. I am a stick figure no bigger than my own little finger. And when you draw me, I always have this rope under my head like a scarf, like Isadora Duncan's scarf, or the scarf of Amelia Earhart, flying out behind me. So I am tiny in this organic tunnel but my head is huge; it's a helium balloon. I'm looking for a hat-pin to prick it. I see a rope ladder. So I climb. I poke my nose into the world like a bunny, or a snake, or a badger—a mole.'

'It sounds like dreaming.' She frowns and hugs her raw-wool cardigan around her skinny shoulders.

'There they are streaming along the road as usual, the blinkered ones, plastered with the grins of self-achievement. They are no less violent in their jostling for position. The crowd masses tighter and tighter; the closer they are to each other the more selfish they become. It is completely illogical. They are fighting each other to be closer together. Soon, of course, some are killed in the crush. They are smothered. The air is squeezed out of them, and then they are used as springboards and stairs for those continuing to get a better position, which is forward, forward, forward—toward what is never made clear to me. Whatever it is must be starting soon, or must have started suddenly, as they are running, the fittest are running. And they are not running for their lives; they're running because they're alive, and crushing others under-foot. Those tripped regain their footing as soon as possible and take up running again. And so on.'

'Where are we?' She taps her chest-bone and indicates me with her eye-head nod.

'You are running. I am watching,' I state emphatically.

'Ha, I've tricked you out of this personality. You are making up a story.'

Harsh today, Anne? Even so, it is clear to me and as I see it I say it. 'You are a husk and you are running and your falsies on your head have little holes cut out of the cups, and it's all so amateurish and ill-done it's a wonder you're not cross-eyed. I am running alongside the road, a slight stick figure, with incredible speed, and I come to the head of the panicked procession and there in front is a huge forest. The trees are three hundred years old and they are graceful and gorgeous and impenetrable. But I am wrong. The front-runners plough through them. Their husks become grader blades of cast iron, tractors with chains pulling logs. They are not only clearing a path—which would have made sense in their terms, as they need the road to go on so they can continue running along it—they are clearing acreages. It's awful but everybody is very busy. It is then that I see another group, stick figures, gathered on a hill-top. Some have scarves drawn about their necks like me, others have tears painted on their full-moon cheeks. I am there in a flash and we are looking out to sea. Our cousins are being slaughtered, they say, and they point their stick fingers out to the horizon and there in nets the air-breathing dolphins are being drowned. At this point I go mad.' I open my palms.

'You're in here to escape. What, I wonder. The consequences of your actions, perhaps? The death of a friend? The death of a sister thirty years ago?'

'Get me my drugs, doctor,' I demand, and clench my fist to punch a cushion. I don't want to cry.

She is tough, now. The digital has bleeped. None of the sweet violet about her now. I wonder what happens when you make her angry? I was going to say mad.

'Frigging fuck off. You don't understand anything.' I punch the bean-bag.

'Calm down, I'm not going to hurt you.' She is writing on her pad.

'No? The bunch of stick figures, fools on the hill, turn and there where the acreage was cleared is a dam of dirty water. Not only is the water grimy and thick with silt, there are oily rainbows on the surface. Someone mentions cyanide and we all pull back and gasp. Cyanide-leaching, timber-cleaning, wood-chipping, water-polluting, gold-smelting, fossil-burning. We turn to the beach. There on the sand is the waste of all the people who have been throwing their packaging over their shoulders as they ran along the road, and there on the beach is human faeces, feeding only the blue-backed blow-fly. If we had anything in our stick torsos we would throw up. And you ask me, am I making this up? Am I mad? A great gust of wind, or let's say a universal and communal fart from the scampering multitude, comes and blows us little stick figures away and we all float off dangling from our balloon heads up into the sky with our little neck-ropes snaking like kite-tails.

'Keep writing,' said Annie Lennox as she gave me a quick hug at the door of her office.

I wandered down to the soccer oval where some old loony has four or five golden retrievers. I watched a young dog play with an older bitch. I watched like a cat, with aloofness and scorn. The young male had boundless enthusiasm and seemingly no independence. They have a game of chasey when the female wants to be chased. While we live in a greenhouse which is making it rain as if the atmosphere is sweating. It'll all leak out the ozone fence and we're done. We'll all lie doun an' dee, Annie Laurie, won't we?

Peter came down from the mountains. To Sydney. If I had known he was here, an inch away, a line taking off, off the page, out of my pattern, what would have changed? If I could have seen him, I would not have seen that look of hate in Steven's eyes. A look of hate destroyed my existence, shattered the glass globe of my world, and left the pieces like the tacks in Frida Kahlo's picture of herself, piercing the skin, and still she lives and still do I, just to feel the pain. No more.

The soldier sat in his car, waiting. Looking through the windscreen in the rain at the repeating arcs beneath the rail, viaducts, rain-softened misty colours. It would take patience topaint it: the jewelled saturated greens, then roofs, the muted hard-edged terracotta, the shape of hill and perspective. The driver of the car on the hill waits, frightened of the ever within. No plans. Always a watercress growing between paving stones. Rock-hard resistances. Who cares for those who dare?

Here, in waiting, searching, half-heartedly perhaps, for the risk, the brisk risk. Reaching to each other across the fresco. Still, apart. The thread-thin commitment should be non-threatening; yet, at the brink of the abyss, lacking the lust to jump.

He is not tame any more. He lives unseen in the Barrington Tops, unable to conform. His brutality is contained in his aloneness in the wilderness, invented and perpetuated by himself. He defines existence through his ability to survive, as if he were the first man, a cave man. Only there, at the mouth of the cave, does human life make any sense at all. He dreams the dreams of an ape-man, rolling his knuckles across the ground, growling to an imaginary ape-woman. He grabs the sword-grass with his toughened palms and yanks the hair of his mate whom he then drags into the cave to fuck ... uck uck. He has made a leather pouch to come in. He pulls the string tight about his erect member as it moves of its own accord and his hard hands encase the chamois, squeezing with infinite tenderness. But only sometimes can he get the fantasy right, only sometimes does the sun set on primitive treetops with golden beams, only sometimes does he convince himself. I am caged in another age.

'A savage man I am,' I hear him sing. Living in fatigues, beautiful bush-melting colours making him invisible to the holiday-makers; to the trekking greenies with their walkie-talkies and safety flares, walking and talking; to the rangers who know he is there but never find him; to the Narcs in their choppers — fopfopfopfop chopping — coming to get him as he attends his crop. 'Making me feel right where I belong, a savage man am I.'

The addiction to war made his nights cold. He accused himself. Twenty years ago, he was twenty. He was there, where the blood flowed, where he discovered horror in his veins alongside adrenalin, a coursing physical courage, mind-fucking power. Now his nights, cold. Even when it rained in Saigon it was never cold. He frightened himself sometimes, the fury backed by training. He was afraid of what he would do, what he could do if provoked. He couldn't sit by and watch. His anger. His ability to kill. He fought for a way of life —and that wasn't getting attacked on the train because you're a woman, because you're alone. He wouldn't witness anyone getting bashed and do nothing, not him.

'They don't deserve that,' he said when he came out of the woodwork one day.

'Alone I roar as I try to come and all that happens is the strength goes out of my penis.' Sometimes he is just bouncing along beside me, talking. 'I know it's worse for other blokes, ones with the wives who have miscarriages and kids suffering lung problems and hyperactivity. They don't deserve that. But when I came home you were into peace and long hair and dope-dreaming and hating us for being there. I was as grown up as a man can become, having gone to war aged twenty-two. A war no one but us could understand. The only blokes I can ever trust are the others who were there.'

Each time he makes love he rapes again the ten-year-old he raped there. He says it wasn't rape; he paid money for it. Yet he hears again her groans of pain. He feels again the tiny hole resisting entry as the little Asian face nods acquiescence and blinks away tears at the corner of her slant-eyes. Doing what her father said she had to. How he came in that tiny space, he can never imagine, but he did. He must have, because he slid out of her a shrunken thing, not wet with thick lubrication but with thin stuff like tears. He emptied himself inside her. His entire self seemed to go from inside him to inside her, that mere slip of a thing, sprog of the enemy. He cannot trust himself. Only with the other men who served.

The 1987 Welcome-Home Parade for those who fought in Vietnam—it changed his life a bit. He was not going to go to the parade, but here was something, the only thing since he fought there that was ever done for him, so he might as well. He served with 'The Team', the elite unit, a nasho with the cream. He cared, he fought along with other blokes to 'stem the tide of communism'. And he returned to Australia at night so that the demonstrators wouldn't be there. He knew I was among them. So the Welcome-Home Parade was graced with his attendance. After it, he had to see me, confess everything.

'Soldiers are the only real men who cry. They have something to cry for. When I returned, my emotions were fierce. No one home understood. I needed to be intense. It was like a drug. I couldn't tell my old friends what, say, sex was for me now. That didn't alter the fact that I loved you. My Felicity. I fought for you. If blokes who hadn't gone couldn't understand, how could I expect a girl to? I didn't want to try, I loved you too much. Felicity upon a pedestal. Married. I don't break up families. I found out from other student radicals. He was an any-bandwagon man, splashing his face over the newspapers, the type who would abuse returning soldiers with his educated voice if someone was watching, so he was safe. That made me puke. For years I roamed the outdoors, abalone fishing, camping out anywhere, kangaroo-shooting, bumming around, drinking too much, like an old-time drover. I married once—any woman. I wept in her lap and dissolved in her womb, the real home hearth. But the little Vietnamese girl haunted me. I walk along bush trails with the tread of a cat looking for sword grass and spear grass.'

He wanted to punish me with his confessions, I knew. He undid his fly and pissed carefully to wet the spines. He pricked his penis, he teased his penis, he forced this natural growth to hurt him, and hurt him more until it was agony and the adrenalin flowed up his backbone and with the help of his imagination he could come with immense pain. There were other things he did with his anus and bits of wood from the bush to try to experience her degradation, when he was desperate.

'Were you jealous of Steven, Peter?' I asked quietly. He ignored the question.

'After the Welcome Home, something changed, something simple,' he went on. 'I wasn't so afraid of you any more. Time is a slow old healer, and things are better. And with this all the old peaceniks were snivelling in their handkerchiefs for what we'd been through. The respect was there, finally. The respect we deserved made it into the culture. Now they're building us memorials in Canberra and other places. I started putting things down so that one day you could read them. I'm still afraid of what I might do. My temper is short.'

Felicity and Trish, two different women to two different men: who am I?

Those Irish nuns must answer for some evil. Their own poverty and mendacity meant every kid was screwed for all the extra pennies the families could afford, relentlessly. Those nuns warned, dutifully, against sins of sex and such, but never gambling. In fact, gambling was what they taught, for how else was God to display his penchant for miracles except by landing a pile of loot in someone's lap? The Holy Grail and the pot of gold at the end of the rainbow and bloody leprechauns teaching superstitions about Fridays and left-handed girls, sinister phobias ... He swore he'd have the gold or the grail by the time he was forty, but with neither money nor an ideal to carry him through, he is shy, outside the house of the beautiful Felicity.

But Peter was not brought up Catholic—I remember that now. Some other religion accounted for his pious father. It is Steve who is the gambler, the screwed-up Catholic. I have them confused. An everyman, an anyman, is my man, and I am the only individual. Peter appears, talks, disappears when my back is turned.

He said 'It happened dozens of times. The watching, then the going and getting drunk, and spending the money earned from dope grown in the bush, protected by booby traps and anyway well hidden. Then the returning to the wilderness and the remorse.'

He hides. He is watching. He, in his jungle greens, can disappear into trees and never be heard. He watches his Felicity. She turns out to be me, a bourgeois wife playing games. Cleopatra with Charmian and the other maids. He saw my fabric party.

Felicity seems to be in a state. She is crazed. She upturns her huge basket of fragments and the larger lengths of material and sits among the textures and colours in the front room. She doesn't notice him. She is staring into herself. Frenzied activity. She makes the house into a cave by draping fabrics everywhere over everything. She rounds the square corners of the room and hallway. All solids become anonymous substance. It looks like Arabian nights, carpets and chiffons and silks billow. A delicate, textured world in shrouded colours, for all the lamps wear scarves. She makes herself naked and then slings lamé around her hips and puts as much jewellery around her neck as she can find. She takes from the hall-stand a big man's gabardine coat and goes out, leaving the door open. He stays until she has gone into the corner shop. Then he sneaks through the place, smelling and feeling with stealth, and he is outside again. She glides barefoot, bejewelled, along the street at dusk.

He was struck by the pathos of it. This corny fantasising seemed to disguise a hearty hysteria. Still, healthier than his. The house was a den of chaos. He slipped along the side path, the shrill din of cicadas and the bickering of birds in the banana palm drowning the sound of the gate opening, the door slamming. The bright white light of the refrigerator showed him my face, my chin. Inside: camembert, stuffed and Spanish olives, fetta cheese, gherkins, strawberries, houmos, other cheeses. Corn-chips and biscuits are on the bench.

He knew Steve was away. He saw him load camping gear into

his car and drive off. He recognised a rifle. Steve had been gone several hours. A party in his absence? I threw a lace cloth over the already draped table and proceeded to decorate it with food. He left.

I knew I was performing for invisible eyes. The twilight was full of immaterial beings, elementals.

But after getting something to eat and trying to stay away, he returns and again lets himself in the side gate. A motor-bike is parked at the kerb. Through the first window there is a bilious green hue, and at the next he sees, reflected in a mirror, candles, champagne bottles and remnants of food. A cat hisses at his ankles and an unfamiliar kind of fear makes him shiver. He moves his position. Then he sees three naked women, drinking, laughing. One is big and tanned and jovial, another quite thin, more serious, and the third, his Felicity, the oldest yet the most beautiful of the three. Women being women, just as men imagine them, in covens, in caves, in trios. In paintings. His habitual fear of women and of himself near them and his guilt about the young Vietnamese girl made him turn away and go.

Did he also snoop through the window when I watched video after video, every damn movie that came out about war and Vietnam? When he saw that, did he guess that I was searching for him through all the dialogue, making my fair boyish lover into a man?

That heroism was bloody suicide. Kam Diem whatsitsname.
Charlie's on our arse.
You dumb horny bastard. Death then sex. Sex could be death
for you.
Da Nang, number one on his shit parade.
What a zombie act, you pussy-brained arsehole.
Who's suicide is it, anyway?
Medivac medivac medivac!

To the sweet sweet hospital ship.

There are no safe places, there are some really shitty ones,
where there are no white-nurse fannies, arsehole.
Don't fuck her around when she's so scared.

I'm angry, the fucking army wouldn't give a navy doctor a box
of bandaids.
A desert landscape, the bloody moon.
They pound shit out of us five times a day.
A spooky chopper pilot is the pits.
Suicide on the battlefield, oh yeah.
A bouncing betty blew his balls off. I got the other in the
windgate, and his face looked younger than my kid brother's.
The mother-fucker!
I'm dancing, making boogie, pity my guitar's a machine gun,
it's still slung low around my hips, let's boogie in the shower.
Call that a shower, arsehole, you stink.
Wouldn't you? Inserted it in the base of his skull and scrambled
his brains.
I can't write he was a suicide, I'll say he was a hero.
What's the difference, he's dead.

Rain pounding outside, cosy among the bean-bags and
cushions, I ask my shrink, 'Is it healthy to go into imaginary
landscapes?'

'Only if it helps you break through to your shadow,' she
responds.

Only if it unleashes the degraded other me and meets me in
mortal combat! I wish to research my times past, play Proustian
games like all the dreamy poetic ones, I say, and give her my
sister's letters.

'Okay.' She shrugs. Speed-reads in her time-is-money way.

Julie blamed me for the cheap burial—well, cremation— I
organised. My mother was a great fan of Gracie Fields and I

asked them to play 'Ave Maria' as the coffin slowly took itself
behind the curtain to incinerate, while we felt her passing from
this plane to the next. Instead they got the sides of the record
mixed up and 'Wish Me Luck As You Wave Me Goodbye' came
lustily through the speakers. I wasn't surprised because I wasn't
concentrating. It was an accident that I was prepared to live
with. I started singing along with it.

I thought Julie would be pleased it hadn't cost too much. But
then I wasn't thinking for myself. I let Steve do it. His thinking
prevailed. Julie wailed. I, in my embarrassment, laughed.

Anne tried to make me grieve for my mother, but I couldn't—
it was off the point.

I spent an hour knocking my head against the wall and going
to the mirror to check that a bruise was rising. I don't know the
difference between courage and cowardice. But I must find out.
Through action. I've thought myself into a corner. There is no
way out except to damage something.

I've had the awful feeling all my life that I was right.

The cool waters of Lethe can't protect me.

I have to know the truth.

My shrink really bored me today. What do I want from my
relationships, she asked, as if I were responsible. I can never
ask for my sister's help in remembering: she would remember
only her view. Her role, the tell-tale. Mummy, Mummy, Patty
pushed Kerry Anne under the train. I don't know what she said.
Three sisters standing on the station, me hating my youngest
sister so much and I can't remember why. Arguing. My mother's
broken heart. Soon afterwards she was a drunk. She couldn't put
a sentence together without the words tavern, pub or hotel in it.
She couldn't tell a story that did not end around a table
somewhere with other drinkers. She loved the garden, never went
there without a glass of wine in her hand. Going to the shops
meant patronising the establishment which hadn't yet banned
her, where she didn't owe an unpayable tab. All taxi-drivers

knew her, she said, but the bus which stopped outside her house she never set foot on.

Mum was musical and every now and then she sang an air, sitting, swaying, at the piano in need of a tune.

Cath wrote me a letter. Since it came the pain has been like mosquito buzzing, persistently, one then another and another. The buzzing never stops. The rest of my life has twisted and become tense, in a posture of sacrifice which has no surrender. No rest. No peace.

The boy in my brain is yelling 'Take care of our own fucking people!' amidst his imagined satchel charges, his combat fantasies.

Cath said, 'His penile arrogance has been inserted into my bones, like steel pins in an orthopaedic operation. The "he" inside of me is like an unnatural child, an incubus. I feel I was raped through the head by something made of gas and my being was infused with alien matter. It made me chunder, morning after morning.'

'He' is my Steve. For a while I would not believe such obnoxious impregnation could occur. My mind circled happily on trivia. But it has happened before, in pagan myth, in the Bible story of the Virgin Mary, Zeus making himself into a swan to rape Leda, and Cath felt it all. Then the unbelievable metal shaft starting growing in me, stiffening my joints, sinews, and feeling like sharp edges pressing outwards on my skin too.

I wrote back to Cath, 'We are all chosen, one way or another to perform in the Marquis' magnificat.' But I never sent the postcard. De Sade haunted me. In one movie the boy and I watched, a Nazi sadist tenderly tends a maiden-hair fern and weeps over the death of his cat, while viciously ordering mass slaughter in the gas chambers. The film is spiced with a little rape motif. The trouble is my boring, ordinary, vaguely handsome Steve can be as evil as this man painted to be the exceptional psychopath.

Steve has paralysed me, trapped, curtailed the real me inside myself. My imago couldn't emerge. Just a vessel, like the Virgin Mary.

For what?

It is, it is, a bright blue bird in the tree. It is quite big. Every day it is there for me. The misty air recalls the soldier off to war whose grime is streaked by the tears of the women on the pier. They shuffled them back from Vietnam in the middle of the night, debriefed them in secret and asked them to keep their war experiences to themselves. That would be wiser. Why didn't he come back to me? Because I was snivelling beneath the peace banners, shouting 'What do we want', singing 'We shall overcome some day'.

Sweet nectar of medicine, spin me out. The fog over the water obliterates view of anything, like the woolly fabric of lies that I have been living. The fog invites me into its folds. The fog is so quiet. No planes fly, no cicadas cry and the birds spend the day dreaming, snoozing. It is comforting because the sun is just a whiter ball in the sky. Distance has been destroyed. When it rains it is warmer. I am wearing silk; even so, I rip it to welcome the fog with a shiver. I'm standing chilled to the core. If I walked into the water with rocks in my pockets and in a knapsack strapped to my back, I could not feel colder. I can't stay with such a beautiful idea. The chemicals I am fed make me daydream. Nerveless. Nerves that go beyond the flesh, the sodden heavy flesh of the drowned body, waterlogged clothing. They connect invisibly into invisibility.

Leni, the loner, travelling in the leather boat, plucks me out of the ocean and we merge into one and continue.

I know leather boats existed because I remember my mother reading about St Brendan in a medieval craft, ice-island hopping from Ireland, to Greenland, to Iceland, to Canada, and quietly living there, praying to the god of mysteries with the natives. She would read and I would dream of being so holy and so free. I don't believe this flesh is necessarily real. I am quite cold now. I have learnt nothing. I understand nothing in the whiter and more ominous shades of pale. It's the witching lure of the little people. Why not piss off into the supernatural? What keeps me here? Pain and the dulling of pain.

The decade of the daydream has gone. That, I suppose, was what it was. For the first five years I was open-eyed, excited, beautiful, in my twenties, a woman whose love could heal the world. A beloved. An artist. Beguiled, dewy-eyed. Madwomen were selfish. They were unbalanced. *Unnatural.* What I see in the mirror is not what the others see when they look at me. I beguiled myself, and loved it.

If there were a million, pinpricks could kill you, even if they, like leeches, anaesthetised as they pricked. For ten years I felt no grief. Small hurts were discounted, ignored, de-sensitising and adding up. *Unos cuantos piquetitos.* 'A Few Small Nips', painted in 1935 by Frida Kahlo, depicts a naked woman on a bed bloody from her wounds. She has one stocking and one shoe on, and a fully dressed man, with a hat on and one hand in his pocket and the other holding a sharp knife, stands at her bedside. '*Unos cuantos piquetitos*' is written on a banner held up at one end by a white dove and at the other by a black crow. 'The Broken Column', painted in 1944, is her with back-brace, half naked, and all over her body are tacks nailed in, and white tears flow down her face. And later, in 1946, she painted 'The Little Deer', herself as hind with horns and pierced by many arrows. So things don't get any better. Leni di Torres is the incarnation of Frida's anger ... and a million pinpricks can make you kill. If the million humiliations go ignored they gather like grains of gunpowder until one day the slightest spark ignites the girl and she explodes.

I didn't need Cath. She came though, a dog-maiden, a sweet Artemis without arrows, an athlete without games. 'I hate the taste of tears,' she wrote. 'Tears and unburped air turn my stomach juices into poison. Somehow I am poisoning myself. I want to throw up and throw up and throw up until I am nothing inside, empty.' Go see your Aunty, dear, there's nothing I can do. You have youth and family. When the prissy side of me comes out, I know I really am mad.

When I convulsed with guilt at using a refrigerator which was making smelly awful holes in the ozone layer, I committed myself to an institution. But that wasn't the reason. Mad-am.

Now that I know love is grief and grief is love, and the decade of the daydream has gone, and now that I am mad, these paintings of Frida Kahlo make me double up with emotional agony. I had seen the 'exquisite corpses', I had seen many of her paintings and looked on them with curiosity. How was I so safe?

Like a rubber band, I snapped. I snapped when I saw the look of hatred on Steve's face. Hatred of me. For a moment he couldn't disguise it. All that I had known him to be for fifteen years was a persona hiding this naked hatred. Despite our intimacy and his stated dependency on me, he hated me and looked at me as if I were something to fear, a stampede of elephants coming to smash his house, garden, cranium and balls, to rubble possibly. But he could hold back this herd with enough hatred. Well, seeing he was giving me this power, I wasn't going to let it go. It was incredible; I kept shaking my head. I was not an individual but a flood of the loathed and reviled. I went into a frenzy. Then my fan belt broke—machine out of action. I babbled about the chlorofluorocarbons, fossil fuels and the greenhouse effect. I didn't see him go, but he was gone. I babbled about pricks and pricking. I became a blithering idiot dragging around the house looking for my copy of the Bard, mumbling to myself that if anyone could explain men to me, it's got to be Shakespeare. Then I got a couple of silk gowns, a cardigan and a bath robe and came through the gate of Rozelle Hospital, near the ambulances, and went through a door to find men in uniform playing Euchre and drinking coffee.

The first thing I said to doctor dear was: 'I strangled down the birth canal with a rope around my neck, as if before I even began I'd been tried and hanged for murder.' I remember because I repeated it like Caspar Hauser's only sentence, as if I were on stage all the way here. You see, I didn't know whether or not they would believe me. They might have asked for a referral or my name and address before I could enter. But fortunately, suddenly I was armless, drugged and sitting in a chair, and birds were singing in the air.

Did they burn out my memory with ECT? I forget Steve. But I don't care, I am remembering the sweetheart who went to war, whose boy I murdered in my womb, and they can do what they like to me. The boy has the face of my sister, Kerry Anne. I swore he was real. Then I had to escape and search for him, along the inner-west streets, or perhaps in the city near the Haymarket. I could see his face so clearly—I had but to find him.

Drugged to the eyeballs, I walked out and kept walking until I stopped. I stared at two people: a man at least fifty, a woman tucking a baby into a scrap-heap pram. 'You've stolen that baby,' I yelled at them. 'It's obvious, it's not an Etruscan vase.' Then I lost it. They looked so damned awkward with their treasure, but who cares? The lady's for burning.

I swore I saw a soldier on a hill howl like a wild cat in the rain.

Yearning blurred, blotted by drugged hysteria. *Las drogas, ma querida.* Don't tell me of your Aunt Jane, and her sister, your mother, Cath. Don't say a word.

My mother is dead and buried, and gleaming clean is her coffin in the ground.

'I wish it *were* a good clean rot in the ground, not a puff of smoke and an urn of ashes, as Gracie blathers inanely on with a male chorus behind her doing the high-step,' I said, as if to the Aboriginal woman who passed by me drunk as a skunk. 'She was a gardener after all.' My eyes sprouted tears like trees of water because she is so sad, sadder than me. Except for skin colour, she is my mother. 'The stories are all of the strong one, the one who got a university degree, the one who saw the sorry state and separated herself, but that's not you, is it?' I said, as I sat on the bench at the bus-stop. 'You just live,' I shouted at her swaying back, 'and life is a shitheap.'

We're both scared and we're both impeded by chemicals that we need. I got up and waltzed along the street and met up with Mission Beat in their neat little van. Self-respecting, pain-in-the-bum do-gooder men asked me, Would I like a ride home? They don't ask What's the matter, Why are you crying? They want to know where they can take you, what they can do. They want you to make them feel better. Better than all the saints.

I got taken back to hospital. So sick, so sad.

I started reading a book on Jung. It tells me my husband is my *bête noire*, my shadow, a projection of my animus. He is not himself, he is my *animus*. I am taking responsibility for myself. This book gives me no option. My animus is a depraved man, the worst of the worst, a liar cheat rapist traitor. I feel I'm an artist. I'm a nymphomaniac, if you listen and count. Jungians have me taped and labelled, a 'feeling-sensation' type, while he must be a 'thinking-sensation' type and Cath is probably a 'feeling-intuitive' type. It is all my pre-menopausal identity sexually, but no dice. The men's realisations of their destinies is the length of the tales ... Logic is generally avoided.

'There is a wall in me. I hit it with my head sometimes and punch as if imprisoned, grasping at bars ...' I mumble, trying to stick pieces of jigsaw together which can't possibly fit, trying to make another picture. 'The wall is in my mind. I want to tear it down and become free but there is only the constant scraping away of pebbles, the only escape is always digging a tunnel.'

Nurse and I go for a walk. We often go for a walk. I feel safe with her. There is the sea and I will drown; that's my premonition. I am drowning or choking to death.

'Perhaps they are satisfied with their wars and their death-dealing and death itself, their reasons for dying in honour ...'

She really tries, does Margot.

'But the woman's story isn't told. The hero comes through it to some fictional satisfaction; the tears and the gnashing of teeth, the grinding and damning and swearing at fate itself, as if they hadn't told the story in the first place, planned it all, then lived it.'

'I am addicted to men. But I'm sick of the wham-bam thank-ma'ams you always get, especially from the hunks,' Margot says.

This girl just doesn't understand what I'm saying.

Cath and I once made a dance in our minds, in correspondence with each other. But by that time I couldn't get it together to find a stamp. Can't quite grasp what love is right now. Crisis. I know I am not admitting five hundred thousand things and people don't care whether I do or don't, provided I fit well enough into their projections. 'Self-realisation' — the be-all and end-all. Me-me-me-me-me-me. I don't realise who I am. Doctor? Doctor, love me, fuck me? Doctor, doctor, do me up: I've unzipped myself. Do you understand, Doctor Shrink? I'm stoned out of my mind on these drugs you prescribe — don't worry I love it. *He* has made the sun's rays, which was the sun that I worshipped, sick with lethal cancers; *he* raped the earth of fossil fuels then converted them to poison to make the sun a killer. *He* is the sneak — the multi-national-corporation executive, the small-time hard-talking salesman, the slimy school teacher with an eye for teenage fannies, which are the immature, unsophisticated projections of his undeveloped, under-rated feminine side, called *anima*.

Steven couldn't rape *me* because he had had me a thousand times. There is only power if there's resistance. Perhaps each time we had made love he had fantasised rape. If the world were fair, rape would fail. Men's individuality means nothing to nature, their fiefdoms of personality and power are puny compared to the huge yet delicate balance of the earth. But they don't give in. They keep going on and on, raping. Pricking, stabbing, piercing with arrows. With 'dangerous unsentimentality'?

Cath gave me the Andrea Dworkin book with passages underlined: *Death ended her desire, put her back in her place ... his wife, in wanting another [man] had her own quest for love, her own heart and will and desire, and so he killed her, because he could not stand it.*

I have no worth. They have won. All newspaper cuttings in my scrapbook end the date I entered the nuthouse. I have left the world of the supposedly sane. They can have it. Death itself is just another pinprick.

Roo rode her motorbike down the road and parked it right outside the ward. Strode in and gave me my Frida Kahlo book. No, she didn't. She left it in a plastic bag by the bay on a day when the sun came out for a moment. Frida painted herself vomiting all manner of gunk upwards from her bed to hang over her on a frame. It is called 'Without Hope 1945'.

The nurse who never leaves me doesn't know anything. She doesn't know about Peter coming, and she didn't see Roo. But she watches me all the time. She reads over my shoulder. She is watching me now.

So I write: 'My eyes are awash with the men's games, the prickling salt of tears scratching at my lashes and the heavy snot of laden nasal passages ...' I can imagine Roo or Cath saying this: 'We are the victims of their pain'.

Duty calls and they must leave, love, stand up and suffer for honour, and the women, variously, support and desert them in madness or betrayal or submission, constantly picking up the pieces, being cannon fodder for the film, the book, the pamphlet ...

I am getting into this. I know Margot, the nurse, will nod with approval. I spin her marvellous tales. The woman's death, in a war movie, is sad, so sad, but mainly we are concerned (and we cry) for the two men.

The father and son are comrades in arms, peers in the sport.

I play with the jigsaw a while, tossing pieces in the air and catching them like jacks on the back of my hand. Nurse appraises my long-fingered, lovely hand, and I glance at her. The guard marches
the band is martial
the ship's funnel sounds the departure
the boys are off to war.

I am always making Margot little poems. I think she keeps them.

'The lover escapes, he is despised. The deserter even I can't respect, but where are my values coming from?'

'The man's world is on a larger scale than the woman's. That's just personal. Women's books leave me cold, especially if they're so well-meaning, they're nauseous.'

Margot on literature. Take note, world.

I'm terrified of watching films about the forests or the seas. I'm afraid of the cruelty to all-too-intelligent life ... the magic of plant growing from seed. The wholesale ugliness of poison, hundred-mile dragnets in the ocean ...

There was something else I was afraid of this morning. But I've forgotten.

Little girl looking at picture, but everything in it is moving.

Kerry Anne is on a rock digging into my psyche. There may be bones but they are no bigger than chicken bones. There are

sisters and sisters. And in that triangle of relationship
...Remember the sea. The hole and murder are love of mystery
and unreality. The reality is actuality being factual discovered
through the meaning of life and faith and the relationship of
sisters to each other and other members of the human race. I
want to go laughing to the scaffold for I was innocent as I am
now and will be more so, for martyrdom awaits surrounded by
the perfume of musk and other exotics from Araby. Alas, dream
after dream abates. And to be holy must mean to make yourself
into a hole. Opposite of whole. If I continue thinking and
knowing the labels they glue on my hide I might speak
mischievously with perfidy, for I stripped the skin off my rib-
cage with trust, I thought. Although the words they used were
accurate, they lied.

The boy is another murderer in his imagination. Boyo.
A skinny thug on suburban rail, devil with a spray can.

HE WANTS TO BE FIT ENOUGH TO KILL. TO BE MAN ENOUGH TO KILL.
STRONG, SKILLED WITH THE USAGE OF KNIVES, SAMURAI SWORDS,
HAND GUNS, THE GPMG M60 7.62 CARTRIDGE. THE HEAVIER THE GEAR
THE BETTER. (I wonder if that is big enough for my faithful nurse
to see.)

My cunt was so wide all the world's hungry and under-privileged
could dive in for succour ... Supper in womb? The
hallucinations and illusions often exceed a logic as plain as the
nose of your face.

The boy? It took some courage to talk about the boy, but when
I started to tell Dr Levin this morning, I didn't want to stop.
She was dressed in high heels, long black skirt and a blazer

with enormous shoulder-pads — a professional.

He is the Ba'al I never had. The boy, the son. His spirit, after my abortion, flew out over Sydney looking for a fuck in progress. He found a familial rape in Wentworthville or somewhere near there. It was short and brutal, as was the fight to be born among the bickering spirits hovering above the 'two-backed monster'.

She is so fat she moves only as jelly moves, flat on her back with her knees up. He lies on her flopped-over tits and flabby belly. He thrusts two or three times then he comes. And my son jumps in at that moment.

He wasn't winning the quarrel to be born: the other imps pushed him from the back and he fell into the world. His bad luck.

His mother, a slattern, tied him to the door-handle while she went down to the Club to ease her woes. His brother, in filthy nappy, was tied to the sink. He had not spoken for the five years of his life. There was a fire in the downstairs flat. That was how the boys were discovered. They were taken by the police to a Children's Home and given a bath by a brisk nurse. Then they were fed and shown their beds. The brother gurgled. The boy used his voice. He said, She couldn't help it. Of course she could, he was told. I can't help it she said, he insisted.

If he were American, they would call him a nerd. Except he doesn't have any glasses. His younger brother was the reason he stayed at the Home for the length of time he did. The social worker from the Department maintained that, after all they had been through in their lives so far, they should not be separated. The brother, blessed with the sunny personality of the terminally sick child, died when he, the boy, was thirteen. The one with the morbid nature and the other beloved by the gods, linked beyond language, spent silent hours together watching television and videos in the privileged privacy of an infirmary room.

At school the boy was quiet. In his brother's room he tinkered with electrical things. He made them work. The younger charmed the other kids and the assistants to bring whatever they could find of broken transistors, gramophones, televisions—anything electronic—to feed his sibling's obsession. When he had fixed them, they were traded for videos, hired and returned by what the boy called 'my brother's messengers'. They were a team, two boys on a raft in the ocean.

At school, the boy was considered by some of his teachers retarded, by others a strange genius. He believed in aliens, in vampires, in wizards and warlocks, in his brother's ability to fly. The house mother never heard them talking, but they did, secretly, in a language and of things which soared above the horrors of their early childhood and the dreary boredom of the orphanage, appropriating to themselves the happenings on the small screen and embellishing them further. Until quite suddenly the younger confided to his brother that he had had an encounter and that he was going soon. The boy imagined his brother taking off like the boy in *E.T.*, through the clouds on a bike into another dimension. He would speed so high, so fast, that in no time the Earth would be nothing but a speck in the distance. And he nodded; shrugged: Why not?

The boy came back from school on a Tuesday and they told him his brother was dead. Oh yeah, he snorted, that's what you think. That weekend was his last at the Home.

My imagined boy and I watch the videos together.

The knifing and the explosives and other training bits in the film—*Uncommon Valour*, starring Gene Hackman—show the decoy method. You hang something down to the right of the enemy's path; you are hidden to the left. Something is on the ground, you are in the trees. Something is in the trees, right in front of them a booby trap.

Scout's knife attack from *Uncommon Valour*: 'Come in low, under his line of sight from behind. Kick the back of the knees and leap in one movement. Take his head with your left hand, squeezing his nose, then twist his face away from your knife, then go in at the base of the skull to the right of the spine, into what the Chinese call the windgate, insert upwards and scramble the brains.'

Explosives: 'tomatoes' and the 'bouncing betty which blows their balls off', set in a zigzag so the next one catches them leaping away.

The boy watches his videos in the small room he has in a rooming house in Newtown. He fiddles with electrical things in a junk shop down the road. The owner lets him fiddle and sees him fix things—old black-and-white television sets, radios. Pays him. Gives him scrap. The boy's room is an electrical Aladdin's cave. He has a way with wires. He watches this father-loves-son movie over and over again.

Steve is all thumbs when it comes to electricals. He fears being electrocuted. He fears the invisible. But the boy is a genius.

From Timezone to Timezone on the Harbourlink he travels, because riding the monorail is really like being in *Blade Runner*, suspended between buildings at first- or second-floor level and coming suddenly across a change of scene: water, boats, sailing boats and square cruise-booze boats, buildings of the eighties half-finished and old buildings, bridges and that, and gravelly patches, spaces for bits of litter to hang about, ladders and staircases going nowhere and rusting machinery, full of mood. Then the Chinese garden, like something a graphics bloke thought up, just coming at you, and then you're faced with enormous holes in the ground with perpendicular clay faces, like the beautiful walls in a video computer game that close in on you as you speed through on a motor-bike or helicopter. The graphics are wonderful. He tries to see the world in their image and sometimes succeeds. The dragons, warlocks and wizards in the latest are as good as Disney animations. That's how they've always been described and probably do look, for who knows whether they're not somewhere? People don't make things up completely; they just change bits here and there.

Being on a motorbike in Timezone isn't like being on the real, boring road; it's a thousand times better and three or four times as fast. The seat heaves and weaves, leans into bends that disappear underneath your feet, and tall cities like stacks of gold bars come at you and are gone, if you don't dissolve first into a clang-er-er of flame. You duck, you weave, you are in control and you can keep going at higher and higher tension if you're good. And your score rattles over: the tally can hardly keep up with you.

The boy feels at home in Timezone, feels alive there, warmer than anywhere else emotionally. He's safe as houses there because he can be inside his own dreams.

He is a Ninja avenger, a robot, a swordsman, a boxer, a wrestler, jungle-fighter, mercenary, street cop, superman with a deadly punch. There's just him against them, Glytron-zombies because they're the computer. He's the human, his little man just happens to look a bit like them.

Some of the dollar machines you can climb in and you are in control of spaceship or chopper. Sound effects. Moves up and down and left and right, at least eight directions and all the time your head's cool and your fingers flash. He is good, the boy. One of the best. His initials are on the top scorers' lists on at least three machines in all the places around George and Pitt Streets most of the time. Dens of deception and delight. De-de-de-der ha-ha-ha-har, strafing, chattering in bullet-talk to himself. He can alter the state of play, in fact he is the reason for it. He is both Ross and Hardy, Rambo-esque characters cluttered with gun belts, grenades and fire power. In *Operation Thunderbolt*, if they don't kill all the terrorists, the hostages will die. Depending on how good you are, hostages and terrorists multiply at ever-increasing rates in countrysides and junglescapes and desert roadsides. You gasp with the excitement of it all. If you accidentally waste a hostage you lose five points.

The boy's timing on the joystick and button is perfect. His

pinkie lifts in delicate pause, then he fires, like manic like crazy man. At this he has few equals, his paws are pianists'. The few who are better, who are always ahead of him on the scorers' table, are Asians—flat-heads, gooks. And girls only play old-fashioned Space Invaders or Galaga—baby-stuff. There's hardly any of them anyway: they have no sense of adventure, no guts to try anything new, because they never do. Whereas the boy's pride is tied up in it. If he isn't on the latest from Namco or Taito, et cetera, and master of it in a week, he doesn't like himself, he gets mean. He never reads, he doesn't need to. His mind can roam to exotic places. He can be taken there for forty cents or a dollar, imagining he is getting paid for wasting the enemy. The enemy only has to be pointed out to him. Hey, there, over there, the ones that look like so. They come up on his screen and he fires.

He gets on the monorail and the world is all pretence. He shops at Kings Disposals because they have the Confederate gear that he loves. He knows the tall cypress forests of Virginee. He has been there. In Timezone in Pitt Street, Namco has a huge screen of this forest and a rifle on a chain and wired, so you can shoot. Circles of light come flying out of the trees and you aim and despatch them like clay pigeons. Beside that is a pistol-shooting game with a regular television screen and normal Glytron enemies.

If there were a computer-games Olympics for Kids, he'd do all right. He wished, after seeing *The Colour of Money*, that there were some way you could hustle this talent. If people collected around and watched and clapped he wouldn't mind—even if it were a real fight, he wouldn't mind. He'd just like to take these gooks on. Fair and square with umpires and stuff. The boy is a romantic with dreams of heroism. When he walks out in his long grey greatcoat, he takes them with him, the stories, the achievements. But they're his secret, no one cares about him and how good he is. His secret is like gremlins in the cellar: he keeps feeding them, wondering when they're going to grow and multiply and destroy. The fear is ace. There are a couple of stories Namco and Taito haven't thought up yet. What about Nazis for instance? And big-game hunters? In Africa, against mammoth animals and lions and things? And what about real sex war? Get the skirts. Or striped uniforms pop up — and pow! Beautiful polished grey and black boots, hats, greatcoats. He has his dreams, the boy. He is hero in his own movie. He's a moody loner with a taste for clothes.

I went down there once, looking for a lad with Kerry Anne's face and my colouring and the blue eyes of Norway.

'One day,' I said to my shrink, 'I got out of the shower, dried my body, threw a towel over my hair and dressed. When I went into the bedroom where the hair-drier is I found my hair was still sudsy with shampoo ...'

Anne wasn't into my discovery of my madness. She wanted to place my guilt. Confronting the 'shadow' in some people, she assured me, brings out powerful feelings of having wasted one's life, guilt at having lived a life of self-deception. I snorted with mirth. She's serious, is my Annie Lennox, so she told me a story of one of Jung's patients. Apparently this patient hiccoughed on a couple of words in word association, wherewith Jung found she was responsible for her baby boy's death. When he called her a murderess, he saved her from punishment by insanity by putting an enormous burden on her conscience. She wanted me to talk about Kerry Anne or say something about the boy or my mother, but I wasn't playing. I said, in the manner of Dame Peggy Ashcroft, 'Three guilts are like pebbles in the air and the juggler's hands are tied behind her back, but the pebbles go boing boing and crack down on her nut in a maddening rhythm. Time goes nowhere, it's a metronome. It's no more no less than a tick, sis.'

The blue bird with blue wings stays on the same branch of the same tree waiting for me. It's a kingfisher, I think. It's up there as I write, moving its feathers just a little.

Thunder rumbling like the great burps and farts of the gods—
bullish clouds head-butting—enters my head and I am part of
their angry play. One stubborn notion knocking out another, my
head a boxing ring. But I'm in no mood to beg for phenazocine
hydrobromide; sweet morphine is another trip. If I kick up a
rumpus, perhaps they'll quieten me down with something nice.
But really I don't want it. I want my headache.

Let go, have it out, I say. Kill one another. Nurse and her
jigsaw ... suddenly I'm panicked. Fear is my brace. Leni let
hers float away among the ice floes on the sea.

They are hiding themselves in the corner of imagination, the
bits I need. They're on the floor, I've lost them.

'That frigging sheila over there has been nicking pieces of my
jigsaw puzzle. Nurse. Nurse. Forget it.'

But I tell you, they're not here.

'Clean up the bodies, girls. Dead or alive, clean them. Dig
the ditches, say the prayers, keep the album safely somewhere,
remember all the names, use the sandstone in your mind like a
plinth for the forgotten soldiers. Let me tell you there are no
forgotten soldiers: the papyrus inscribed with their recall is
skin, the skin of their lady-folk ...'

They treat me like a schizophrenic and let me ramble on. So I
shout: 'Will someone tell that jerk to do up his fly! If he doesn't
I'm going to kill him ... Well, give him some clothes. He doesn't
have to walk around in pyjamas all day ... I don't frigging care if
he runs away.' Comforting having people around you all the
time, someone right by your elbow ready to pop you a pill. Jolly.
Nurse Margot never thinks of giving me anything out of the drug
cabinet, curse her.

Here I am. Help me. I'm going to have to yell ... El Alamein
ward's across the way. Everyone's shouting, notes Margot, no one

need take any notice of you ... I'm nothing special. Nobody listens to what the mad lady has to say.

'No frigging forgotten soldiers, unless of course it's the gels, the little nursies in the line of fire. There's a body six feet under quite near here and my mother might be a forgotten soldier.'

I'm going to sit out there on the rocks soaked to the skin, shivering and watching the yachtsmen and speedboat-riders, wishing I was already drowned so that I will not have to go through with it. They catch me, escaping into the storm, drag me up to Annie's office and lock me in her waiting room. It's cosy, but it's not home. My head throbs.

No spinning wheel, no weaving loom, no wet clay on newspaper, no old combustion kiln behind the barbeque in the backyard, no records with genuine Peruvians playing the pan-pipes between The Boss and The Brandenburgs, no pure white silk to paint on with meditated brushes, no fabric at all. I've lost all that. I could disappear into those activities, a sane artist. My crutches were of delicate tortoise shell and gnarled old Mallee root, oiled willow wood and straight steel. Now I have no crutches.

I did have a super Pfaff with computerised adjustments and sleek lines. I believe my sewing machine could even do smocking and embroidery. I had a huge basket—it was cane—overflowing with material fragments, a bucket of buckles, buttons and clips, another of sequins, ribbons hung from wire coat-hangers hanging from the picture rail, and when the wind blew through the house it was Fall in the Rockies. I had an enormous pin-cushion in the shape of a lady's torso and a little plastic skeleton someone gave me. A doctor gave me the skeleton from his desk. Men I could handle. You only have to fuck them, and when they're sorry you grab their head and hold it close under your tits and for them the world's all right. With men you make the world all right for them. Simple.

Dr Anne Levin seemed to have forgotten who I was. Does she

only know you by the time of day you're due on? Her attitude threw me off my fearsome mood.

'Perhaps I should talk about my relationships?' I suggested weakly.

'Should?' responded Annie, on automatic. Impatient, an extra professional duty. They get paid for it.

'I don't know if I can say I loved Cath. She merged with me somehow in a totally warm and sexual way and now when she writes it's as if she writes out of my head with different words. The only member of her family that I ever met was her Aunt Jane, a nun, now retired from teaching, amateur sleuth, and member of some radical organisation called Clergy for Freedom and Justice in Mozambique, or something like that. Maybe it's Catholic Clergy for the wiping out of Renamo, which is that mob of South African-backed thugs which goes around maiming children and burning crops and destabilising the economy and generally creating vicious mischief with the financial help of fundamentalist Christians in Australia and America. Or that is what she carried on about. I couldn't get over the feeling that these passionate clergy for freedom and justice in the third world were quite prepared to "condone" (her word) violence in pursuance of their aims. We had lunch. Cath assured me that her mother was quite different. Quiet and private ...'

'What's this got to do with anything?' she interrupted sharply, just when I was feeling easy-going and chatty.

'Lesbians in the house was the beginning of the end, I suppose. The way I had been was unquestionably right, balanced, classic, a man and a woman, and my man was handsome and had stayed through our mutual infidelities; a brave of the real world, who took the heat off me when I needed him to. You are nulliparous, he said, as free as a man. Likes long words, does Steve. His freedom was taken for granted. He could fuck anybody he wanted, and the worst he'd get from me was a tease. The Roos of this world inhabit the margins, ratbags on the fringe, no real threat to anybody. I listened as I rocked my head, or shook out the garment I was preparing for my stall at the market, to her wild political fancies.'

I heard my shrink sigh, glanced at her and saw her look at her watch, shrug and relax. I smiled and continued. 'Roo's arms were very tanned and a handmade armlet squeezed her bicep and lots of thin bracelets adorned the right wrist. One huge earring hung in her left earlobe. She would grab me up in a huge bear-hug. An easy, hollow hug, like a nook in the tree where the chipmunks are, so different from Cath's trembling, insistent affection, which can send shy electricity right into my veins. Roo expects her rudeness to be excused on the grounds of her lovableness. Why didn't she stay with Cath that night? Troubles with her own lover. That great big muscle-bound bikie-lass is jelly inside ... why am I blaming someone else when I have already blamed myself? The blame has been apportioned among the women, all should be well.

'When she has her severe depressions she doesn't move out of her own place, she becomes agoraphobic and paranoid, stares at television and doesn't leave her bed until it passes. To counter these depths, when she goes out she is an extrovert, an energetic liver of life. A show-off.'

'I don't think we're getting anywhere this afternoon, Pat. And I have an appointment elsewhere in about five minutes ...' My Annie Lennox started collecting her bags and putting files away, and I began to cry.

'Off with his head, off with his head.

But for red queens all dames are dead,'
I chanted all the way back to ward, just to keep myself together. When I got there I began a fight with another patient. I hate her. She says I'm lying. She listens to the mad ladies babbling. But she's not mad herself; she's in here for the drugs.

'I'm not lying.' I scratch her cheek.

'Yes you are. It's obvious. Like declaring you have nothing when the jewels are hanging off your ears, nose, neck, forehead.'

'Piss off, know-all.' I kick her. 'Get back to the world where you belong.'

'Your pretentiousness sits up there like a tiara.'

What an image. I laugh a laugh bordering on hysteria.

'I don't know how I look and seem, Fuck-face. Leave me alone, I'm writing down my thoughts like Doctor told me.'

'You started it.'

Wimp. I poke my tongue out at her. 'You know all about lying don't you? What lollies did you wheedle out of them today?'

I am a cat. I concentrate and switch to indifference. In desperation we could laugh! Or was it repressed hysteria? The careful joke shared among siblings. Reality a ghastly joke. A bloody lie. Now the urn is shattered, and we get a look at the ash in me. Trash I've hidden for more than thirty years.

A pall fell when Kerry fell, I suppose. Who marked out this tragic fate — my mother? In your eighth decade finally I asked you what was beneath and you revealed a sump of despair so deep and full it was black. Julie was dismayed, her tears seeped out of her face like a mountain spring. The question was mine.

All quests are futile. Knightly steeds are hobbled and nobbled at the outset by too much irony. I press my palms to the temples as if that could make it all stop. It makes me vomit to swallow the irony and take things seriously; it's too bitter, too sad. It makes me retch. It's only half the story. When you, my mother, finally faced death, you became beautiful. You were never more beautiful. The dreadful contradiction was over like a long and gruelling Eugene O'Neill play.

That water out there reminds me of Ezra Pound, canto tumbling upon canto like waves from the hungry ocean, a way, a rhythm, a wave ... dredged from the depths, perhaps. The incomprehensible babble of tongues or the static they call the music of the spheres or Milton's blind sight of devils in rhyme, all time swirls and now is then. Wasn't it Pound who said 'We're all writing the same poem'?

Well, Ezra, the boys are, that's for sure.

The idyll began to crack. I was taking everything in my
stride. I've always been elastic. When did I begin to get
stretched enough to snap?

Cath's letter. After that I couldn't look her in the eye. The
guilt was all mine, so in anger I did plenty to be nicely guilty,
luxuriously guilty.

At the proper time, Annie was charming and professional:
'What will we talk about today?' she asked, cheerily.

'The rape of course.' I pulled out of my pocket Cath's letter,
dated the day of my mother's funeral. I frowned at my shrink
while she read. Eyes alone moving. She reads like someone who
has years of solid academic study behind her.

'darling—
you were the most beautiful woman i had ever seen—my whole
being vibrated to the keenest chord of love. the ground dropped
away and i floated. the world changed colour. my character
collapsed into a million fascinating parts, to be recreated,
reinvented, rediscovered over and over.

i spent days in the pink clouds, pacing the flat like a tigress
trapped and restless. i was in a state of total distraction.

how did i get that invite to dinner?

you told Roo to tell me to come and i went and i came. what
else could i do but trust you? you were divine. and i trusted your
husband though i hardly even saw him, let alone assessed him
for myself. you were a goddess. the fabric party was like
something timeless, a ritual that happens forever in the centre of
the earth. i can return there whenever i want, though it is hard
to sit still and concentrate at the moment.

i think he came into Leichhardt looking for me. there were
three of us in the coffee shop. i noticed him sit down and
nodded. or was it just that he was there, that he happened on me
accidentally? do they do these things with malice aforethought?

he stared stubbornly back, hurt about something? i frowned a
question. he didn't bless me with a response.

i stood in front of him on my way out, to do the small-talk chat
bit that's done when you know someone's name. he mumbled
something like, 'what birds like you need is a good fuck'.
i really didn't believe my ears. i raise an eyebrow and walk
towards the door. say goodbye to the others.

'hey! wait. i'll drive you home,' he says, sounding
reasonable.

in the car i squeeze my hands between my thighs. nervous.
he ignores my directions. they seem to aggravate his already
aggressive mood. he goes out through Drummoyne.

on the Gladesville Bridge, he says, 'it's a nice night for a
drive'. there's a sinister tone men can put on. do they think
women are fools that they can't hear: it doesn't matter what i say,
you're lucky i'm saying anything?

almost dutifully i look at the moon and lights reflected in the
ripples on the water, the yachts and launches swaying at anchor.
he takes the Hunter's Hill exit. here the bays are inky dark,
rocky.

'i only want to talk.' it sounded false.

'about what?' i'm worried now about you and me, the worst
that can happen. i'll never be able to see you again. i shiver.

'you're young, aren't you?'

'why talk out here?'

'it's romantic.'

i have always been afraid of men. i'm careful to avoid contact
with them—this is me, who i am, i admit it. the expensive
houses in their tree-lined streets are beginning to intimidate
me. it'd be hopeless to scream here, if scream i could. nobody
would care.

i hold onto the thought: you love me.

his driving is loose, too fast on the corners. is he drunk? i'm
still giving him the benefit of the doubt. all these trees and the
houses of the rich absorb sound. there's no one else around. i
should never have got into the car. i'm trying to reassess things,

stack the odds on either side. he has the physical advantage. but
we're not fighting. as a little girl, once i nearly got into a strange
man's car. he flashed himself. i backed off and ran for five miles
on the adrenalin of that fear. i taste that same taste.

he starts swearing at me, monstering me. i couldn't believe it.
'you're a slut, dyke. is my wife moist enough? slimy enough?'

'you bastard.'

'no i'm not. i'm a nice guy. i don't mind my wife enjoying
herself, she always has, but why should i be a monk?'

he pulls up near a boat ramp. the water is dark. the small
movement of ducks in the reeds asleep is all. what is he going to
say to you tomorrow? it all adds up to rape. he rapes me. i feel
dirty, i want to dive into the muddy stream, i consider it ... his
awful, fixed expression, a violence of concentration, his cock is
enormous. he tears my singlet and pants. i see my white flesh.
my vagina is closed tight, a tiny button-hole. he forces, forces,
uses the strength of his arms and braces his legs. all my muscles
are rigid. then agony, i shout in pain. he keeps saying, 'relax
relax.' he's getting tired and he hasn't come. i am spitting and
pushing and kicking. his erection fizzles like a damp fire-
cracker. i sneer. but i'm angry. and shattered.

he puts on a little-boy look. it's incredible, do they think
women are so stupid? no words from me, no reprimand, no
comfort, no derision, no forgiveness, i can't speak. he drives me
back to Leichhardt.

the mental agony now is more than the physical pain, and it is
poison, pollution. it has entered my feelings for you. you have to
know. this is what all the other letters were really about. now
you know.

he's got to answer to you, darling.

Cath.

Anne kept shaking her head when she had finished reading it,
affected by more emotion than she usually is.

I told her, 'I said to him, it was wrong. This woman is out of bounds.'

'What do you mean "out of bounds"?'

'The girl had chosen to have nothing to do with men, and Steve thought if I could have her, he could too. He didn't think it was rape. He thought it was his right. A part of our agreement, but he did not respect her boundaries. Her choices. I don't think Steve would go and rape any girl walking along the street. It was because of me.'

'What did you do when this letter came?' she asked.

She is cool, is my Annie Lennox, whose hair is spiky and bleached, who looks as if she has never bought a box of eye-shadow ever, who has the clear irises of the New Age. What did I do? I said it was wrong. The wrong woman. We bickered. He said, By the way where are my socks? and disappeared. But in answer to my shrink I just let out a flood of tears and she let me pull tissues out the box and throw them on the floor.

I had been spending half the time at my mother's with Julie railing at me, I had to be calm. My nerves were stretched. Arrange the live-in nurse, live in myself, then arrange the funeral, and my grief was a mountain inside me. I could do it even with Julie haranguing me, Cath sending me agonised poems. I was leaning on Steve, taking him for granted. I hardly listened to him. It was his arms, his shoulder I wanted. I realise now that each moment of physical warmth ended in bed, making it. After Cath's letter came, I felt such a whore. I confronted him and heard begging, snivelling, crawling. I preferred it when anger erupted and I punched him and he took swipes at me. I could square my shoulders and take the blame and the punishment. Delayed shock after my mother's death, remembering my other sister's death, doing too much and none of it nurturing me, I snapped.

That truth should be silent I had almost forgot. Thunder's stopped and sunlight streaks through the dust lighting up the smokers' smoke. I have become uncomfortable as if the anger expelled from my body hangs in the air like the lethal atmosphere of an old asbestos site. I sit and itch. The sister comes around with the drug tray.

Staring at my frowning image in the dark windows I am a mixture of Frida and Cleopatra, both tragic heroines destined for the dirt. The flame inside me got as solid as a red marble column. There would be no shitting it, no puking it, no drugs can make it into powder. It is here to stay, I dare say.

Only as Leni do I have clandestine-piercing sight. Leni di Torres has an *ojo avisor*. Annie asks me to translate my pidgin Spanish. Like all bright young things she is quick to express ignorance, so as to get it out of the way. *'Sharp eye'*, I whisper it for effect. Then I shout at her cuckoo-clock, 'Leni cuts the crap.' She is out in the ocean with the mermaids and dolphins, away from spies.

Will the police report describe our place like this: Terrace house in Lilyfield, renovated at rear. Kitchen, dining, sun-room, polished wood floor made into one big space, brown tiles, white appliances. Open shelves of jars of rice, flours, dried peas, lentils, beans, semolina, pine-nuts, bread-crumbs, bran, wheatgerm, millet, pearl barley, rolled oats, raisins, sultanas, mixed fruits, herbs hanging to dry like dope-plants, garlic cloves in baskets suspended from the ceiling with the pots and pans and cooking utensils and an indoor plant called Chain of Hearts. Will they ask about Cath?

Doctor Anne is rapidly taking notes this session. Because she is my therapist, I have a feeling like love for her, which doesn't go beyond the walls of her rooms. Trust, anyway. I want her to know me. She is intelligent and she cares. She takes the piece of paper I'm fiddling with. It's one of Cath's raves:

'there is no other way. the battle lines are drawn. he sees me as
his enemy. the real enemy, a witch, a lesbian, an anarchist. i
am a piece of filth with obscenities sprouting out of my mouth,
out of all the orifices of my body, snakes extend from my
fingertips, my dreadlocks are asps. i am Medusa, i suppose.
this is how i am seen. as i am not even symbolically his mother,
my femaleness does not make me maternal, nor nominally
heterosexual so that his world may see me as one of them. i am
not his virgin sister, as i am a sexually potent being with no
allegiance to any of his systems. i am the enemy. though there
are hordes behind me, it is i alone who will have to stand up to
him. in short, i have to dispense with him, and disappear into
the marching, screaming, scratching hordes in any
demonstration. and i can do it, i must. for here the battle lines
are personal, domestic, one to one, cuckold and scorned. i
cannot trust his next move. it will be violent, as that is all he has
left. he may attack you, he may attack me, he may attack an
innocent woman walking along the street. with male sexuality
out of control what can you expect but the worst?'

That arrived before the letter of the rape, when I was still
putting my head on Steve's shoulder for a bit of comfort. Weary
was I about Mum and Julie and the sadness I couldn't dispel
about Kerry Anne. With my mother's death I wanted to rid
myself of my own life and start again.

'I didn't understand what it meant, Anne. Do you?' My doctor
is wearing soft cream trousers today. She reaches out and holds
my hand, grins and says, 'Is this little butch as violent as she
sounds?'

I laugh. 'Of course not. She's as gentle as a lamb.'

Oh Cath, you dream of freedom and power, but you're a poor
little masochist like the rest of us.

Quite without my realising it, the lovely Annie Lennox has
me describing the first night with Cath.

It was about June or July last year. Both she and Steve were watching me while summing each other up. He was deliberately getting her name wrong and enchanting her at the same time. We all ate, then he measured the port into liqueur glasses and I pressed the plunger on my coffee-maker. A comet passed overhead—you know it has come and gone. A moment of providence.

She shifts in her seat. He bears down on her, sordidly playing court, leaving ample room for innuendo. I smile, one on my left, one on my right. I hand over the coffee.

'She looks like Roo, doesn't she, Trish?' The attractive things about Steve are his tall handsomeness and his voice. But he is being cruel. There is nothing similar about the two lesbians.

'No,' I grunt, thinking she's going to trust him because of his thinness and his reassuring tones.

'We have different hair.' She shrugs as she watches his long, manicured hands pour more port.

'You all dress alike. Some kind of uniform?' He stretches back. 'You know what I'd love to do. You're a poet aren't you?'

Cath shrugs and blushes. 'No, what would you love to do, Steve?'

'Well, to put it bluntly, perpetrate a great hoax, one of the greatest. Use imagination. Like fake some secret documents. Give them to the media. With some political importance, of course, not just rhymes that no one reads.'

Cath laughs. 'I'm just a compulsive writer. Don't know what it's got to do with imagination.'

It moves me to giggle even as I write this. She thought he was joking and laughed.

'The Western world,' he continued, 'is so riddled with corruption, out for gain, with a memory no longer than six months. I'd like to rub their capitalist noses in something smelly. Have 'em shitting themselves because all of them have something to hide and know it. Even I have secrets—and Trish. One's secrets are part of one's identity—part of being human.'

'But—' she spluttered, still seduced by his voice, thinking

he likes her—'but you would catch innocent people in your net.'

'No one is innocent. We are all part of a corrupt system. Collaborators. That's the practice anyway. Theory can be idealistic.'

'What political party do you vote for?'

'That's my business. Anyway, they're all the same.'

She didn't mind having an argument with him, discussing and laughing about serious matters. They got onto poverty in Australia and went hammer and tongs until I interrupted. I said, 'Anyway, sweetheart, you've never been there, you don't really know.' To her I explained, 'He grew up in a roomy house on a decent block of land, the lawn of which Dad mowed every second weekend, and Mum grew flowers in beds which she tended in the early mornings so as to avoid the breakfast table. Breakfast she had already laid out on the table-cloth: bowls, spoons, toast, juice, mince or baked beans for Dad and the older boys. Milo.'

'I can take myself into the yard of a fibro house with a lonely swing and a rusting car, wandering jew and mangy cats slinking along the fences ...'

Romantic left-wing crap he comes out with.

'The cats in those places are always pretty healthy. It's the dogs which get a bit mangy.' She was still laughing, but it wasn't on her face any more. Under the table, she had grabbed my hand. Steve's eyes flickered and he made moves to get up.

With a wonderfully theatrical gesture, he declared, 'If it weren't a sin against the Holy Spirit I'd give in to Despair.'

'You a Catholic?' Serious question.

'Once a Catholic always a Catholic, they say. Excuse me, ladies, I must go and play with my new toy.'

'What's that?'

'A computer.' He was so charming and so slyly knowing. With that, he sauntered off down the hall to the room he calls his office.

'Fabric', 'fabrication' and 'Fab' —Cath makes a game of sounds and meanings. What does 'fabric' say about 'fabrication'?

That lies are a texture: recognise the texture, recognise the lie. And 'fabulous' meaning 'marvellous', which comes from 'fable', an unreality, the truthful? I make up my mind then and there to give her a fabric party, to have a girl-night in my home. It is all in the cut and fall, she says. Well you can't get the fall of crepe in a length of tweed, I say, going the whole hog. Silence in the tower of babel, monuments of knowledge weighed by wells of mystery, babble and jargon ... an exciting conversation. Ideas were erotic.

'I wish,' she suddenly said, 'that I could wake up in the mornings next to you, slip out to the kitchen, squeeze oranges and bring the juice with warm croissants back on a silver tray— I have one, it's one of my better trophies—and listen to you tell your whole life story. Indulge you.' Her sharp dark eyes, her tanned cheeks, little Artemis, lithe huntress. I wanted her. A flip in the heart, recognition of desire and wish to fulfil it. I smiled.

I led her out the back door, the back gate, down the cobbled lane to the gardens. We made love on the dead leaves and twigs near a Moreton Bay fig.

I didn't show Anne the rest of her letter, but it is here, in my scrapbook.

'i cannot stop thinking about it. if i don't decide on a positive, strong action and go about doing it, i will go mad. at any moment they may institutionalise me, and if i, single murderess, am arrested, what is the difference? i am institutionalised both ways.'

I had no idea what she was talking about. Steve and she had got on so well, dinner after dinner. Although he suspected we were close, I didn't think it mattered.

'dear goddess, i feel courageous. i fear the solid brick walls, as i am married to the wide open spaces. freedom, absolute liberty, is the cause for which i would die. martyr or moron, who cares? i care. i and my ilk, we care. our existence, our right to be what we are, Amazons, is denied. they have denied women the right to be violent while they glorify the male warrior. the political woman who passionately cares about the world is, through all ages, feared, attacked, slandered. there is nothing in the man that helps him shoot straighter than Annie Oakley.'

I told my shrink that Cath and I swallowed each other's identity for a while. There was nothing worth hiding from one another.

I wander on the edge. Never leave the grounds. I need a thousand hours to think. (Meet the soldier on the hill.) Time to think. In the shifting pools of my reflection, projection, or injection.

(He suddenly takes off and plays football with kids on the oval. What a dad!)

The nurse who follows me everywhere is centreless. She is a parasite, sucking out something. My madness? My shrink is different: for her everyone is sane. She is like a young parent who doesn't speak down to her children.

There is no earthly reason why this healthy hunk of a net-ball nursing-aide should so distress sick wraith-like me. But here she is chasing after me, rippling with sturdy muscle. No escape possible with her as my guard.

I have no need of another's masturbation ... find someone else. Especially in this Gunter Grassy asylum of the insane, where imagination is the preserve of the schizies with our oranges and milk ...

I need hours to think. (I see him running, my footballer.) I grow sick from thinking. Yet my writing is a long adjective with no noun. No nous.

The woman in the spotlight, me. Everyone is staring. Where's my sash? Where's my crown? Giggle giggle, what a giggle, girls! The white butterflies, the colourful moths and the fat caterpillars. These are in the garden. Along with the blooms.

> Thus I am proven by buzzes
> Bees to my flower, I am pretty.
> Gorgeous, brilliant.
> A genius, I hope.
> I'll bring the sandwiches; you ...
> Both Echo and Narcissus ...

Invisible green-grocers ringing to the traffic thundering along Victoria Road.

There she goes out into the world on her bike, carrying that big black hole of sexual frustration in the middle, to fill up on sensual experience. Even pain. She goes home to a little box made of ticky-tacky somewhere in the suburbs where they all look the same.

The crickets have quietened.

The kids we were, the three of us, would gurgle in the bath with thoroughly natural schizophrenia: that boat belongs to the aliens and they're coming to get me. Goody, I can scream. Both Julie and I pinch Kerry Anne, and now we cannot forget that we were torturers, childhood fascists.

When I confronted Steve about the rape, he said the only way he could relate to women was for them to mother him. I had no idea I had mothered him so much, giving him everything because I wanted to be polygamous, yet uninvolved in conflict, I suppose. But a man scorned is such a petty puny pusillanimous person ... How dare he? I couldn't cope with his violation. My mind could not surround.

Somewhere in my sluggard garden, I am neither mirror nor woman, and both. Vague reflections on others ghost my progress; my sun-thrown shadow is a far stronger being.

Myself itself actually
more elastic and fluid than the body I have.
Mistaken, ignored, paranoid and multiplying
with the lights of the nights,
dressed with hats and elongated by the slant of suns,
squashed fat in middays,
a different, darker me attached at the siamese twins,
sole and soul.

Leni is strong, strong as they come and solo.

King tides disintegrated the shores of his sleep. He tossed,
turned, then battered down the seawall and woke. He gave
himself a head-masterly tongue-lashing, deliciously exaggerated
his faults, indulged in mental flagellation. He was a sinner of
heroic proportions. Guilt was the storm in his subconscious. He
had grown used to the warm bed of having me there to comfort
him. He'd often have nightmares when he would wake up in a
cold sweat of fear, usually after his camping trips. He took my
comforting for granted. I would ask him to tell me his dream.
Queen of the inner world I am and it never occurred to me to ask
why he was tormented. I assumed it was his inner self getting its
own back as, for Steve, like all Australian men, the external
world reigns supreme and internal things are relegated to the
unreal.

Annie Lennox is leaving me. The cuckoo-clock is packed in a
cardboard box lying on its back. Inexplicably, it is ticking. Time
is running out. In the nick of the tick, in the knock of the tock
... I must tell her. She has taken away the sand-box, and the
comforting books on Carl Gustav Jung which filled the shelves
with his large avuncular presence have transformed themselves

into carryable brown cubes secured with masking tape and addressed, stacked. The grey bookcase is bare. The cupboard door lolls open, showing a few empty vases and a box of matches. The cushions have gone; two lonely bean-bags remain for my final session.

If I had been home maybe it wouldn't have happened. I had left a note but the wind blew it away.

Notwithstanding the lack of all her props about her, Annie gives me her complete attention. A concerned frown plays on her brow. I tell her about the conversation I had with Steve.

' "Where were you? Simply off for a few days. At the Hilton, champagning it, maybe, with some handsome devil." He was niggling and I was tired.

' "I thought I was free. Where was I? At my mother's sick bed, Steve. Julie came. She couldn't stay with her alone, she said. Anyway, I did leave you a note."

' "*And Sophie howled with an agony that passed for madness*," he read from my bedside book.

'I yawned; once he had adored me.

' "*Depravity, debauchery, dissoluteness, all connote exploitation of women, who remain inferior because of it, for pleasure,*" he read again, from *Intercourse*, a paperback with a black-and-white cover, by Andrea Dworkin, the chapter where "The Kreutzer Sonata" by Tolstoy is discussed. He glared at me in the darkness beyond his circle of light. "You never read this stuff. *My* love would never read this stuff. Someone planted it here."

'I felt him shudder.

' "*Men need inequality in order to fuck*. Why are radical feminists so foul-mouthed? Men need. They don't choose to need; they can't help it. *The dominance of men by women is experienced as real — emotionally real, sexually real, psychologically real; it emerges as the reason for the wrath of the misogynist.*"

'I went to sleep thinking about my mother. He read the chapter and it made him sexually excited. I felt myself being taken while semi-conscious.

'He loves to be punished. This schoolmistress, Miss Dworkin, this boarding-school matron, telling him off, suited him. He is a naughty boy, but boys are like that. Here goes. I am there, I cannot be raped. Though that, I suppose—no, I know—was the very night he tried to rape Cath. She was an object to him. Her personality fell away as he tried to penetrate where no hole seemed to exist. She was closed, locked. He had to break in. He wanted to burst into an inner sanctum occupied by me and this woman, and possibly hundreds of women. He wanted to delve in there and emerge armoured, triumphant, mounted on a horse like a knight. It did not happen as he wanted it. Though she "howled in an agony that passed for madness", she hadn't given in. She had swamped him.

'I felt his cool perspiration of fear return as he flicked off the light. Was he worried that she would go to the law? Now he realised that it was rape, and that rape was a crime. She could not be expected to act with his interests at heart—as his wife, his mother, his sisters were always expected to do and seemed to love to do. She was an unknown quantity. He was afraid the police would come knocking on his door any moment. He has never trusted the police.

'I'm inspired,' I say to my shrink, 'by urgency and clarity. This was the night he did it, and I seem to, suddenly, know everything. When then I knew nothing. Nothing.

'As I slept, he realised he had done the one thing I might not forgive. He had always been able to bare his soul to me, climb into my lap. Now? The girl would tell me. His thoughts grow sinister. If the girl doesn't tell me, I need never know. Something could be done about the girl. He had confessed to me all manner of weird sexual behaviour and fantasies and I had forgiven him. He had confessed practically every weakness he had, including pornographic fantasies of such amazing originality he thought they would make him wealthy through the blue book trade if he wrote them down. He confessed to me with religious regularity. I had had to swallow a lot of depravity. I was able to do it, to absorb the sewage like the ocean.'

Do all Jungian psychiatrists take copious notes, like my Anne?

Introverts can become pathologically under-involved in the world.

'I could bury my head in dreams, in art, in novels, in sweet femininity. Now the shit might wash back onto the beach. His early upbringing and his teenage years with the Jesuits had given him, in the confessional, a kind of flush-toilet for guilt. It was right to confess all these things, even exaggerate them. He could come out purified of the burden of sin.'

I could not see the chemist digital with its muted bleeping alarm anywhere in the room. Being our last time, perhaps she has forgotten time. Except that the cuckoo might yoohoo from its supine position any moment. I looked distressed and glanced at my watchless wrist.

'It's okay,' she said. 'Carry on.'

'There is always religion for a man like that. Piety, remorse, penance. He could be truly and would be truly sorry.' I ended flatly. The tissue of existence enclosed me like a cobweb hidden on a bush path, and I began to flail my fists.

Another thunder-storm was on its way. It was still, heavy, dark, for the middle of the day. The sky was about to fall in. Anne came over to me and began to play with my long hair with her fingers, smiling. As careful as a sensible mother saying goodbye to the child on his first day of school, she coaxed me to be brave, to leave her harbour stronger, having come to terms with certain things about myself. She really was going and, although she had hardly mentioned her before, she said. 'You really loved Cath, didn't you?' I nodded. By now it was raining and I was crying. She thought she planted a resurrecting idea: to see Cath, to write to her, to give her the exercise book that Annie had told me to use to get my thoughts in order.

I clung to it, hugged it to my breasts as I ran through the

storm to the ward. Lightning played like a faulty neon across the solid wall of cloud and wind whipped the rain in all directions. As I gained cover, it was all over. Just drizzle.

My mother was taken to hospital in the middle of the night.

'I have to go, again. My mother is dying, Steve, dying.'

He couldn't offer any help. I'd woken him from a dream. He thought my mother was a useless drunk. She was, but she only became that way after Kerry Anne died.

'I was stabbing him and I was making love to him at the same time,' he said, and I listened to his dream as I waited for the taxi to take me to the hospital.

'Films that make dreams represent what really happened are wrong. It's just art. Dreams don't recall logically; they exaggerate and juxtapose, even if they do make you remember. The place is and is not where you've been. If you saw what you dream on the screen you'd be scared, but you're braver in sleep somehow. Where was it?'

He smiled. 'The place was probably Vietnam, and he was a pretty youth. He looked twelve or thirteen, but they look younger than us. I knew in the dream he was the enemy. That didn't matter; he was beautiful and I had to kill him. It was like an olden-day sacrifice. And as I knifed him, I came. It was a wet dream. But on film — you're right — it'd look more like a nightmare. Then I was back here and someone was calling my name, saying Don't. It was only my mother and I didn't take any notice. There was something so clean about it in all the mud and blood and slush, something so open, so known, clear-cut, complete. Nobody's going to call me a queen.'

'You hate poofters because they give away your male secrets,' I laughed. 'They betray the silent language. You reckon men's eye contact can convey meaning beyond what the women around them understand, but we know it's all about sex. Poofters flaunt this and that is not on. It is not the beautiful moving experience of comrades in arms. Anyway what were you doing in Vietnam?

You're not the soldier.'

He shrugged. 'Anyway, do you have any homosexual friends? I mean men.'

'Afraid of AIDS?' I laughed at him.

'I'm giving up my homosexual friends. I'm simply not going to eat or drink with them again. But I won't tell them.' He was afraid of their germs on glasses and toilet seats. He was afraid of filth. Yet a friend of Roo's who hugged a friend dying of AIDS said he smelt like a baby.

It seemed we had no Summer this year; those days and nights are merged together until finally it was over. Julie and I came home, bleary-eyed, in need of sleep. I smoked my sister's cigarettes as we argued over the funeral arrangements. Julie left. There was no room for Steve in my time and he threw tantrums like a spoilt child. I ignored him and read books on feminism and conservation.

'By the way where are my socks?' He asked a few weeks later in a tone of voice I had grown to hate. It was the night Cath's letter had come. I got so angry. I bellowed and bit his finger. He looked at me with pure hatred and said, 'You bitch.' I saw red.

And then it's blank, Anne, I could tell you no more. When I recovered my senses Steve was gone. Perhaps he left me.

Puff. Dandelion in the wind. Dandy lion gone gone. Puff.

VI

JULIE SCHEMPRI
Letters

10/11/88

Dear Patricia,

       I'm just back from Japan, so haven't had a chance
to answer either of your letters. Horrid news about the old girl
but what can you expect? Thank you! For telling me. The tone of
the second makes me really angry.

But why does the very way you phrase yourself make the
hackles rise on my back? I 'owe it' to you! You really bring out
the worst in me.

She is your mother, too. You don't have any work
commitments. I see you count the cost of your labours. It is your
assumption. Not mine. I'm no good at it. What's wrong with
you? In the face of our differing on the meaning of
daughterhood, next time I see you I'll have it out. I could have
made a scene that took you unawares; I could perhaps convince
you, but more likely I'd get your back up. Or I could store it,
stow it, and wait for improvement in your attitude as evidenced
by deeds which you count as free, gratis, see something wherein
you are not a greedy little operator. But you're not, are you?
You're the sweet one. The one with the Mona Lisa smile and
come-hither eyes. Mum's been addled for years. It's not our
responsibility. Well I suppose it is, but...

It might be blessed release if she dies, actually. You know

how unhappy she is. I just have to go to Tonga next week. A very
short trip. There's simply no putting it off. You've successfully
avoided being anything but wife, so I don't expect you to
understand.

But you know I'm always here.

Because you do a bit of nursing it doesn't mean you are
automatically better nor am I worse. I see you as jealous of me—
my career, my independence, working mother, all that
(Samantha is getting on very well by the way. They love her, and
she loves it)—therefore prepared any moment to punish me for
it. Enough it is you think I owe you. The tone of your letter
really made me mad! But I don't owe you anything. Mum maybe,
but all my life I've been trying to get as far away from her life as
possible.

Even at the time you were asking—no assuming,
demanding—payment.

15/11/88

Later.

Thought this letter was important enough to leave
and come back to. How are things?

Those feasting in Tonga eat little of the meat; they send off the
pork and the chickens to relatives who were not fortunate enough
to attend the feast for the king in their village. The only time
they get to eat meat is when their relatives are feasting for the
king and they are sent some. This noble economy of sharing the
morsel is probably enforced by gossip. It relies on trust. But
really, in relation to what I was saying, one does things one
wants to and you always have the right to refuse. It is up to you
to enjoy doing it. So how come I owe you?

When I said I would be most grateful—I hardly concede that
I made this semantic slip—but had I said I would be most
grateful, it was not a euphemism for rewards in the future.
When my character and my motives are mistaken, I get
most upset.

I've had an enormously successful year. I've been so busy.
I'm my own woman, not going to be blackmailed with guilt.
You always were selfish. Self-indulgent. Well it's my turn now.
I'm making money. I'm busy with the company. Now's the
moment for me. I'm exhausted, far too much travel.

Well, I suppose our mother's deteriorating health will bring
me to Sydney soon enough, but I can't stay there by myself.
Impossible, no! I can't, I'm sorry.

Affectionately, Julie.

P.S. Samantha sends her love and asks you to paint some 'rad'
'rap' or 'rat' (???) T-shirts for some fair she is involved in.
She'll write. I can't remember the word. JS.

2/12/88

Dear Patricia,

What's all this rubbish about Steve? You know I
save and collect everything, especially letters. I'll have to put
on another room for the filing cabinet and the fax and I'll be well
set up. It only makes more work.

Right now I'd like to quote a description of this man written
by your very own hand a long time ago. Seventies? You never
date beyond what day of the week it is. Perhaps this will re-
awaken a little of that love you felt for him, then, and help you
out of the dark you're in now.

I've probably got it wrong, you're probably having an affair
with someone, and hence are seeing faults in the man you've got,
the bird in the hand...

I know I sound like a hypocrite but 'though it didn't work out
for me and Jim, I still believe in good marriages.

This is what you said then. 'The truth is he'd like to be
Greek. He loves his black hair. Groov-ee. Long and glossy. Far
out. Idle girls at parties have asked if he is Greek or Sicilian
and he has lied in the affirmative because he is handsome in a
lanky intellectual yet Mediterranean sort of way. His skin is
brown and he uses the mobile line of his eyebrows to emphasise

his smouldering, passionate look. His eyes are little slits of humour. He has a gift of being unbearably intense then he lets you off with his laugh. He is Hellenic, he's my Jason. Believes in free love. So do I! He is sexually attractive, exuding the calm confidence of a man with a good big penis.'

Now, Mum. The news is not good I take it. Well I will come. As soon as possible. Perhaps the both of us could stay with her a couple of days? Coming up to the 'final curtain' she should have close family around. I'll ring.

Your sister, affectionately,
Julie.

10/2/89

My Sister,

Oh my god, the painful decorum in the crematorium chapel. Her old neighbours and friends (each one proud of his/her own survival) in clutches of professional condolence and commiseration!! 'Commiserate'—I've never heard that word so often. I think it alone was making me howl.

So much easy-flowing sympathy. Death frightens me, and oh god, no Mum to worry about, to come and visit even though it was a duty. The truth is my mother was the only one who really knew me, who understood, whose care I trusted even though she was half-sozzled. I am shattered. I'm going to enrol in some calming classes. I've done enough self-assertion. I'm motivated in my work.

Nowadays there is desolation where there should be chanting and stamping, keening. Wasn't it horrible, the mistake they made with the music as the coffin disappeared into the fire? I thought you had deliberately chosen it until you started that hysterical laughing.

Afterwards, in her friend's flat, you were on the balcony staring at clothes billowing in the wind, like a zombie, and you said, 'Someone's wet wardrobe on the line against a background of sky and brick veneer is so beautiful I want to paint it!'

See these blotches, they're tears. You seemed almost bored. But of course, other things were going on. Must fly. Forgive me about the sibling rivalry bizzo in that letter a month or so back. I had to get it off my chest… You were marvellous, really. Thanks for organising the funeral, even though it was a cheap crematorium job and we had to put up with slack sound effects. I'm sorry I couldn't do it for you.

What has happened to Steve? He was most peculiar.

With love, affectionately,
Julie.

15/3/89

Dearest Patty,

Hope I've got the right address.

I'm sorry. Hold onto yourself. Just have a rest, let someone else look after you for a few weeks. I'm tearing out my hair, my calendar is chockablock until at least June.

Cultures are funny. You know all this corruption hitting the fan in Japan. It's just that they operate differently from us. 'Insider trading' doesn't exist for them, or rather it has for so long that it's acceptable and honourable. A bit like, say, 'usury' in Europe: that's become honourable in the West now. Anyway, before the war, all the traders acted that way: they spent heaps on meals, parties, geishas for a client, wholly, solely and openly to get the account. No wonder they made such a killing on the stock markets in the West. So different from poor little Tonga, where to expect return for your gift is not on. But the Japanese are the ones pulling the fish out of their sea …

Events in China are hotting up too, a pro-democracy movement is under way, and that, baby, will mean opportunities for me if I keep my head down and nose to the wheel.

Love to you. And relax, Sis. Okay?

Samantha sends hers.

Affectionately, Julie.

24/5/89

Sis,

   Just a note to say, sure, you can stay here any time, as long as you like. I've got business elsewhere, in this country as it happens! But Samantha is keen to see you. You sound really mad to me when you talk about ending your life. You have just had a nervous breakdown. I don't believe your mad ravings: you didn't push Kerry, and you can't have done the other thing.

   This year is shaping up a shocker for our crowd. Losing money. And China where I was hoping to expand looks decidedly tricky.

   Steve's just disappeared on one of his phony expeditions.

   Please don't do anything stupid.

   We're family. We care.

Love, Julie.

VII

MARGOT GORMAN
Private Notebooks

10 JUNE

Back from holidays. Another fortnight to go.

Apparently I was losing my grip because I'd blown it in front of that damn charge sister, whom I should have known ... Ding-a-ling. His phone-call as I was pumping up my tyres.

'Margot, you've blown your cover. Kaput, you're off that job.'

Shocked, I said shakily, 'Do you want me to come in with my report? I'm about to leave.'

'Good idea. See you in twenty minutes.' Those words ring clear even after two weeks in the fresh air.

'Ten. How much says I won't?'

He had laughed. We both laughed. I don't know why I laughed. Nerves probably.

I was in his office within quarter of an hour with my bike hooked over my shoulder. Feeling pushy. Looking distraught.

'Detective Senior Constable ...'

'Don't Detective Senior Constable me in that tone of voice. Not drinking is not a suspendable offence. Sir ...' I had decided to be ropable. But was pretty incoherent, I guess.

'Calm down, Margot.' I was taken aback because he had that beaut smile. He felt into a drawer of his desk and brought out a holiday package, fully paid for: bush-walking in Tasmania.

Stunning photo of Cradle Mountain.

'Well, you have been spying on me. I picked up a brochure on that a few weeks ago.' He regarded me with an attitude of fatherly kindness which brought me down.

'I had a look through your work sheets, mate; have you been working! It is—I suppose I don't have to inform you—over twelve months since you took a break. And that break appeared to coincide with your separation from Barry. With your very best interests at heart, my dear, I'm ordering you: No work for a month, Tassie for two weeks. Then,' he shrugged, 'ride your bike into the blue distance, refresh yourself. Enjoy.'

If there is something I cannot stand it is that American expression, 'Enjoy'. It sounds so condescendingly lazy, like when they put in unnecessary words like 'off of a case'. He wasn't dismissing me with his usual command. He was waiting for something from me. I held up my work and said, 'Don't you want a look at these?' I expected him to say no, but he took them. Scanned the diary and report, glanced into the notebook and read bits, and began frowning.

'What's all this crap?' He whacked the pages with a kind of affectionate slap.

'Records of conversations with her, mainly. My own thoughts ...'

'Well, Margot, your notebook is your business. I want you fresh as a daisy to work on a completely different case Monday.' He checked through his diary. 'Last Monday in June, twenty-fourth. How's some time in Adelaide affect you? Casino? City of churches?'

He was getting rid of me now and I took my notebook off his desk. He had wanted to see it, even though he only skimmed through it. I lingered. There was something fishy, but my mind was in such a whirl I couldn't think straight.

'Plane leaves tomorrow,' he tapped the ticket.

I grinned, yes, great, can't wait, I'll be ready, off. Fresh air, fitness essential, my sort of trip, but I frowned, remembered. 'There was something I wanted to ask about the case, Swan.

She's all right?'

'She's fine, Margot. On the whole you did an excellent job.'

'Thanks. I still have her scrapbook at home, and in it are all those newspaper cuttings about the body in Wiley Park, remember? Now I'm off the case, what did all that add up to?' She had given me her scrapbook, I shouldn't have mentioned it. They might want to take it.

'Oh, yes. Can't say anything about the Wiley Park cadaver. Why do you want to know?'

'Curious, that's all.' I opened my palms and realised I had grease all over them.

He continued anyway. 'A certain body had bite-marks on its fingers, which was considered curious. A vicious murder yet bite-marks on the fingers? A girly thing to do, bite—don't you think? Anyway. That's all with the Homicide Detectives, not our business.' He raised his heavy eyebrows enquiringly.

'Bite-marks?' Where was I? This was zeroing in on too fine a detail for my state of mind. 'Along with the slit throat? I take it they weren't, say, an earlier injury?'

He nodded. 'Probably. That body's nothing to do with us.'

The magnetic fields of the earth were screwed up and this dog had lost her scent.

I plumped down the stairs spitting invective. I hate being kept ignorant or idle or, I'll admit it this once, lonely. So after swearing, I started crying. I sat on the concrete in the smoke-stinking stairwell, sniffing tears. I really did need a holiday.

As I rode home, I concentrated my thoughts on letting go of Patricia Phillips and getting enthused about trekking in the bush.

Still, I was mad at myself—or Swan.

Even so, I was at the airport well in time for my plane, recognised an old friend from Wollongong and he happened to be in the same group. We flew away from the rain of Sydney and into the drought of northern Tasmania. The air was, as expected, crisp and clear. The hills were steep, the walk was hard, the sleeping bag was warm and songs around the campfire were great. I came back refreshed with a half-read detective novel in my pack and another two weeks of holiday to go.

A cat I called Owl had acquired me a couple of months ago. My neighbour had fed her while I was away. She looks like an owl, a tawny tabby with huge eyes, little ears and a wise brow carrying a startled frown. I didn't realise I'd missed her until I was home. She doesn't demand much: company in the evenings and tinned catfood on a plate. She doesn't mind living in a first-floor flat with only a tiny concrete balcony. When I'm off to work she is locked outside and has to seek a place to sleep or adventures on her own. No matter what time I return, there she is slinking along the letter-boxes saying, 'Hello, have a nice day?, hello,' again and again. She appreciates her independence, wouldn't have it any other way. But with cats, you feel they could take your human friendship or leave it. That's why I like them.

So here she is on my lap as I finish a P. D. James thriller. *What, after all, was the sexual act but a voluntarily endured assault, a momentary death?* I don't know why I find her a surprisingly cold crime writer. A friend of my dad's, the nicest chap you could meet, was a butcher at the abattoirs and his only hobbies were fishing and duck-shooting. A confirmed bachelor. Owl says I remind her of him, the way I read detective novels in my spare time. I usually devour them and forget them; so do lots of cops. But this line about sex suddenly struck me. Normally I would have passed over it, not troubling to think whether or not I particularly agree with the statement, because my standard response is: the world is full of all types and everyone's entitled to an opinion whether or not I agree with it.

But after watching Patricia so closely and without a clear brief this line in a best-seller snagged me. While I find sex for the most part a 'voluntarily endured assault', the momentary death bit seems just the man's experience.

Surprised Owl but I threw her off and went to fetch the scrapbook. Surprised myself too.

Patricia Gaye Phillips née Vickery, born Geelong, 1946, sister of Julie Susan Schempri née Vickery and Kerry Anne Vickery deceased. Her husband is Steven Sligo Phillips. He had been most mysterious, indeed like the last big hole to fill in a jigsaw. Her emotion for him seemed blanked out. Just blotted, blown, blobbed. It reminds me of shock. She simply couldn't bear to think of him. Anyway, not for me to reason why.

I let P.D. tie her loose ends up and Owl purr on my lap, curled tight as a football, wondering how I was to stop myself getting mad and bad through idleness.

I went to the phone-table and saw that I had started, in the beginning of my days with Pat, to sift through all the 'Phillips'. After phoning on and off, enjoying thinking up different guises and voices, I had narrowed it down to three. Two were in suburbs too far to ride this afternoon, so I took the third, Sans Souci. Bingo.

The place had a big yard that overlooked the Georges River estuary. An early twentieth-century building with plenty of bedrooms and open fire-places I surmised. Rang the door chimes, which sang welcome. A woman answered the door, smoking a cigarette and carrying a form guide. She asked me in. The amber glass-disc doors opened into a living-room with photos all over the walls. Sons and grand-children, or daughters, daddy holding up a fish and so on. It was a great display of successful motherhood. She had earned her place in the world and was comfortable with it. I saw Patricia in her wedding outfit and the handsome lean long-haired Steve.

I explained my business, showed her my identification card and asked where her son, Steven, was.

'We haven't seen him for ages,' she said. She didn't seem surprised that a plain-clothes cop on a bicycle was looking for him; rather, perversely, proud of having a black sheep in the family. I gestured at their wedding photo. 'Do you ever see Patricia?'

'Oh no,' she said, 'Patricia and I never did get along—too interested in her own pleasure for the normal woman, you know?'

I agreed. She isn't normal.

I could hear there were other people in the house, grown-ups. Steven's brothers? I asked her, would anyone in house happen to be in contact with him?

She yelled, 'Brian, you seen Steven lately? The cops want to know.'

Brian yelled back in the negative. The boys could do anything in this household I saw, including bring their girlfriends home to stay, even though they must be well into their thirties.

As I was leaving she said, 'Patricia never loved Steven, you know. Not the way I loved his father.' I stopped to hear more. 'I don't know why she stayed with him so long. I think it was because her true love was killed in Vietnam. I always thought that accounted for the way she was with men. Too easy. And never satisfied.'

I got on the bike but didn't push too hard along Rocky Point Road because I was thinking slowly. Here was a woman who had it all, including the prodigal son, but what did she do? Play the horses and cook, clean, provide for the sons and grandsons. Some women love it. There had been a cheap romantic fiction under the form guide on the tiled coffee table.

Pat's lesbian friends think differently. I wonder if they read romantic novels. Suddenly I was curious about them. Were they like Pat, relentlessly questioning the tide of human affairs? If so, were they all mad? One day during my holidays I'll ride over to the hospital and pay Pat a visit.

There are hundreds of women in Sydney who could be Roo. Early thirties, dyke. There are lesbians everywhere, so the public toilets from Mt Druitt to Watson's Bay tell me. Roo is the one on the motorbike with the dog.

Before I went to sleep I read the poem which was stuck with sticky tape on the back cover of the scrapbook. Unsigned, it reads:

'We must come by a way of destruction
to bring our opera to the park.
We come with banners and matches
and molotov cocktails to throw
at the status quo, to blast
the comfortable collaboration.
The cause
for destruction is hard to swallow
and the door to renunciation stands ajar—
but I cannot turn back
nor want
to feel as desperate as Emily Dickinson
or Emily Bronte who preferred, after
visiting Heaven, to be tossed lonely
into the elements on the moors.
First,
the weapons must be carefully handled
for some targets are in the self
and the enemy citadel deep in foreign land
and along
the road the spies and battalions:
in daily life the battering usage of women
is the acceptable way of being here.
I cannot know myself until I destroy a part of me.
I am
the subject of investigation and the object,
my own rape victim in many ways
—and that is too hard to admit.
There are no court procedures to clear me,
no confessional to clean my soul
to a state of grace if I am to remain alive.
A kicking,
living woman and not one of the undead,

who looks alive and female, but has man's blood
in her veins — man's thoughts in her brain —
who dies by day in endless service of another,
who collaborates with the Count,
Eurydice in another form, Mary mother of Christ,
Leda deceived by Zeus as Swan, Io the cow,
sea-woman battered and dragged by her hair
to be fucked by an ape in a cave,
making a queer species.
Both
investigator and investigated, trapped
in an unfair present and unable to see the future
through the threat of a mushroom cloud
and no perceptible cracks in masculine edifices,
built on deceit and conceit.
It's impossible to create a philosophy from here,
yet not one of these thoughts is mine alone.
We must come by a way of destruction
to bring our opera to the park.'

11 JUNE

No work is hell. Days off I've usually planned outings, a ride, a barbeque, a film, to do something I've wanted to months ago, that sort of gratification. But I can't not work for weeks. The sun came through the clouds. Owl stayed home on the balcony. Stupidly, I waited for the mail, but it doesn't come until two or three in the afternoon. Resisted the urge to get on the bike and ride to the hospital to see Pat. I made some thick pea soup to smell that smell of Mum's the time my Dad was retrenched from the coalface. All we could afford was soup from dried peas. Mum even made bread in the oven, telling us that she had saved forty cents or something. The memory of the bread and soup and unemployment made me think of life behind the Iron Curtain and of deprivation, as in romanticised stories of the Depression when there was nought but family love.

Actually, we experienced it and I remember it clearly. But it has nothing on doing a good job, feeling you are somebody worth something and drawing a pay cheque. My brother and sisters feel the same way. We're all earning well above average and I reckon that's got a fair bit to do with the way my father handled that period of retrenchment, and the age we were then. Dear old Dad.

He'd say, 'My mates'd be going down the pub, now, in my position. They're empty because a good day's work gives a man a pride he can't have otherwise. They'd be getting full on beer and then it's anyone's guess how they'll be getting on with their kids in the future. You see what I mean? So if I can't work on the coal, then I'm gunna work as a dad, be a dad to youse kids.'

The mine-riddled Escarpment dominates Wollongong. Everyone knows someone who died in the mine. Dad suffered a nervous breakdown after a big cave-in at Corrimal. He wasn't exactly retrenched.

First he'd ask us what we wanted out of life and what we reckoned we could do, and he listened. Then he'd ask us what we thought he should do and we would all ponder the problem of his future. Dad didn't know anything else to talk about, so we all put our teenage heads together night after night until eventually the five of us—that is Dad, my two sisters, me and my brother, all agreed he ought to invest in terrific, reliable, expensive lawn-mowers, hedge-clippers, later whipper-snippers, and exchange the station-wagon for a ute and go round mowing lawns, cleaning up yards. It took a while to convince him—he thinks like a miner, a worker—and then to save the deposit and get the loan from the bank. Meanwhile, I do think it made us—each of us—responsible. In fact, my brother and my sister still work the family business, tree-lopping, landscape gardening, grass-cutting. They're raking it in and Dad and Mum enjoy their holidays and reckon they deserve them. My other sister married a doctor and works as a radiologist part-time.

I started at university doing Law, but I dropped out and joined the police force. There might be bent cops, but at least police believe in right and wrong: lawyers don't. They can't. They play by another set of rules which has precious little to do with justice and guilt, with the innocent going free and the bad going down. They know when their wealthy client is a hood but they'll do anything to keep him out of the nick. I struck that in my first Criminal Law exam: List three ways to get this filthy scumbag off on a technicality. I couldn't hack the mental hoops and moral gymnastics you had to go through just to get the degree, let alone to practise in the big bad world. The trouble with police work is that we have to spend so much time in court, dealing with the people you've already arrested; everything has to be juggled around court days and trials. It's all right fighting to nail the guilty, putting your nose on the trail and ending up with the quarry, but then you've got tortuous court proceedings, often a bad judgment, and overcrowded jails, and politicians making decisions that spread the misery farther and wider.

After brunch and daydreaming about my past and family and smiling at the workers' songs we sang round the camp-fire in Tasmania, I looked through Pat's scrapbook again. The thing had some kind of magnetic hold over me, damn it.

'...that, along with the amazing phenomenon that my generation of women all over the world are literate, educated, hard-working, independent-thinking, and have published, as well as established themselves in the institutions of state and marched on the streets ... my personality would have accepted hook line and sinker the full catastrophe and tried to be "normal", even saintly ... like you my lovely, like you? ... but, ignorance is not permitted me ...'

I skipped the letters and ended up on the pages with the newspaper articles pasted in: Marijuana Discovered in Wiley Park; Strange Dope Find; Religious Sister Helps Police; Missing Legs Eleven; Exclusive Interview With Nun Discoverer; Body In Banana Leaves.

Everything was unrelated: what had Pat to do with this body

or why had she collected these clippings? What had Pat to do with any specific investigation by the NCA? Had or has her husband any espionage links, and do these involve international crime syndicates?

Why am I more interested in her than I should be? Why can't I just dismiss her ravings and her friends' ravings as other people's business and get on with my holiday, or go out and find a boy-friend? Why don't I go to a boring foreign film with Angela or something?

Owl stared at me with those big unblinking eyes and, as if she had suddenly remembered a very important matter, checked for dirt between her toes, then resumed staring intently at me. There was no mistaking what she was saying. I opened the front door and she continued gazing at me. I picked up my money-pouch belt and buckled it around the top of my tracksuit pants which I rolled to the knee. When I swung the bike around, Owl sprang into action, slithering down the stairs with unseemly haste. Myself behind her with the crossbar of the cycle over my shoulder. I had no idea where I was going. I had been ordered out of the house by the cat. It's dangerous to establish a routine you are not prepared to stick to.

Thinking of the cat, who so quickly had become part of my life, I pushed off down the street. Paperbarks on one side and flowering bottlebrush on the other, it is a fairly wide road and not a busy one. There is a thirties block of flats which looks as if it were designed for Nazi Germany, several modern unit buildings with strata titles, individually owned like mine, well secured and kept, old houses which in their day must have been mansions, and several single-fronted terraces rendered to look European with tiles, white paint and arches. I know the area; I didn't need to take myself on a tour of Dulwich Hill, Canterbury, Hurlstone Park, Earlwood, even as far as Roselands, but that was where I was when I realised where I was going.

Wiley Park. I didn't really want to go there. There would be nothing of interest for me. Homicide would have let this little murder enquiry shuffle itself to the bottom of the pile by this time. To ask the local detectives about it, or maybe get a look at the running sheets, would require more preparation. I couldn't just swing off the bike, enter their shop and ask on this one. Why? I could on others. This one wasn't mine.

Unaccountably shy, anyway. Memories of Dad, no employment, no pride. My confidence was shot. Patricia-talk had nibbled into my corners like rust. I lowered my chin to the handlebars and started pumping. I kept in the wind shelter of the lorries travelling at fifty-sixty ks, poisoning myself along Canterbury Road into Milperra, and approaching Liverpool, puffed. I turned off at a slower pace into Henry Lawson Drive and ended up staring at the waters of Lime Kiln Bay, thinking about a woman who let me see the colours of her mind. As I watched the ducks scrape around the wormy wet earth, I made a decision: to find out who was wrapped in banana leaves and interred six feet under, and maybe who did it. A purpose, a holiday job—I felt better.

I needed a piss. Soon I found a public toilet off Roberts Avenue in Oately Heights Park. There, stuck on the daubed anti-graffiti paintwork was a 'rape crisis' sticker. It seemed ominously helpful, the timing. I memorised the number and thought that as I rode home I would stop at a telephone box. I would say I was a lesbian who had had an affair with a married woman whose husband brutally raped me, and would there be anybody who had had a similar experience that I could talk to? It would be a long shot, but maybe they'd put me onto someone called Cath?

It had troubled me all along why this Sister Mary Ignatia had assumed that because the freshly dug earth was disguised by dope it followed that a body could be hidden underneath. What sort of man would draw attention to his crime? If it was a man.

The convent, set in among the red-brick houses on suburban blocks, had a Spanish look with that half terracotta piping along the fence and enhancing the portico. The facade was cement-rendered, painted cream and adorned simply with a cruciform window of stained glass. A circular drive surrounded a lawn spotted with beds of petunias. The Little Sisters of Jesus did not seem an order of great pretension or wealth.

A murderer would find it cheaper and probably easier to steal or buy, say, petunias, and petunias, like the ones here in careful beds on the convent's lawn, would be less likely to attract attention. If the gardeners discovered them, even if they hadn't planted them, would they be as likely to pull petunias up or kick up a fuss about them? And if the murderer chose, as this nun argued, to cover the greater crime with the lesser, how could he or she be sure that they would be discovered by a law-abiding citizen? I doubt whether 'law-abiding' in this instance would apply to ten per cent of the park-walking population. I wouldn't nick a Lebanese matron or Pakistani begum for smoking hashish: it's part of their culture. Even I—if I weren't a cop— would think twice about the three or four grand these plants would fetch. I'd probably keep it to smoke or even give it away. In fact, the likelihood of a nun, of all people, discovering his plantation is very slim indeed if you take it from the murderer's point of view. Then that nun jumping to a strange and horrific conclusion, and that conclusion being right, all sounds pretty suss to me.

This reasoning is why I found myself in front of St Benedict's on the way home.

The schoolyard behind the convent began to rattle and squeal with children scattering from classrooms. Perhaps the rare sunshine made them exuberant. I'd hate to be taken for someone with a suspicious interest in kids, so I rode up to the main door and rang a bell, which seemed to echo far away, in a kitchen? The door was answered by an athletic-looking woman in her late sixties. She was wearing a white sweatshirt with the motif of a couple of koalas gaily wearing shades driving a comic convertible, and a cotton skirt likewise bought from Best-and-Less or Target. As a pendant, her cross hung from a chain around her neck. A good fifteen centimetres taller than I, she wore flat Chinese happy shoes on her stockingless feet, no make-up. Her grey hair, once curly, was now like steel wool and her neck a marvellous maze of deep wrinkles. Expecting to see one of those chubby nuns with several chins and high-coloured cheeks, I was somewhat surprised as I asked for Sister Mary Ignatia. She looked down my rolled-up tracksuit pants to my smooth bronzed calf muscles and slowly lifted her eyes to my face in a way that made me thank my Protestant stars I never went to a Catholic school.

'I am she,' she replied.

'You are not as I expected. I'm sorry, Sister. I'm Detective Senior Constable Margot Gorman of the National Crime Authority.' I automatically pulled out my ID. 'But I don't know why I'm saying this, because I am not working at the moment. I'm in the middle of a ride on my bike and I was passing.' I understood how they got the truth out of those poor little beggars. Her steady gaze didn't waver. I cleared my throat to continue. 'Er. It has to do with the body you discovered in Wiley Park a couple of months ago. As I said, I'm not officially on duty: you don't have to answer any questions. It's just that I want to understand; I would like to know why you rang Homicide at the same time as notifying the local detectives. And of course the Narcotics Squad. Why did you bother?'

She ushered me into a hallway with a gleaming wood floor and prints of famous religious paintings on the wall. A plaster statue of the Virgin was painted blue and white and gold. All I could think of was leaving my thousand-dollar bike outside unchained and not being game to mention the fact.

'You think I saw something?' She sat down on an upholstered chair with the spindliest of legs and gestured that I do the same on its partner the other side of the hall table. 'You think I saw someone. You think that a nun is the last person who would guess murder most foul. You think that curiosity in the world doesn't account for that unlikely but accurate guess about homicide. Most of all, you wonder why the marijuana was not uprooted by someone in need of it, or simply by anyone else.'

Notwithstanding the cheap, comfortable clothing, this woman

exuded the authority of an abbess and I felt I must ask questions, ape the eager student.

'Why, Sister, did the murderer choose marijuana in the first place? Why not anything that may be grown in a public park? Seedlings? Annuals?'

She put the tips of her fingers together under her nose and responded, 'Why, indeed?'

The interview was not going brilliantly. My concentration was undoubtedly bruised by worry about the safety of my machine and somehow I had anticipated more sympathy, more generosity of spirit than was forthcoming.

'You call the Bingo numbers up at the church hall on Saturdays, Sister?'

'And Wednesdays. My nickname about this place is Legs Eleven. A couple of the nuns are fond of *The Golden Girls* on telly and tend to call me after that Beatrice Arthur character, as well. Yes, well the proceeds go to the Catholic Church. I'm retired, why not?'

We never trusted Catholics in our household. Deep Irish hate of Papists. They'd do the sign of the cross with one hand and stab you in the back with the other, my uncle maintained.

'I read something about you in the local paper. That's why I want to know what you think. Why marijuana?' I got up as I said this as I could see another nun scurrying down the corridor and wanted to avoid having to refuse a cup of tea. I reached up to the door-handle. She stopped my hand.

'Never let yourself out of a house until you have known the occupant seven years.' She used two hands on the deadlock. Superstitious, my uncle said, as well.

'The trouble with both police and a majority of crime-writers is that they are far too logical. You would be surprised how often this week the number one came up. Who said the world was logical? Not God Himself. Let the marijuana implausibility work for you, not against you.'

I was so relieved to see my bicycle still where I propped it, I said my goodbye quickly without seeking further explanation.

Remarking on the firmness of her grip when she had stopped me letting myself out, I wondered why she distrusted me. Her attitude was odd, but then my seeking her out was odd.

'Let the marijuana implausibility work for you.' She said that as if she knew I was embarking on an investigation alone and unassisted by my colleagues. Then there was the look in her eye.

There are no petunias in Wiley Park. Mainly natives. I rode down into the ex-velodrome, converted in the bicentennial year to an outdoor theatre. Work was still being done, as hills of bare clay to the side indicated. Then, starting at the little waterfall, I followed the path which crosses and recrosses the creek down to a water-lily pond. A nice little park, I thought as I circled it. While King Georges Road and Canterbury Road on the western and southern sides are always very busy, the north and east edges are quiet suburban streets. There is a car-park with toilets, tables, council barbeques. Few people around, but then everything was wet today.

It was 'H. P.' of the *Courier* who had written the 'exclusive interview' story. I knew her! I decided to drop into their office.

Hattie Porter is one of those wonderful part-Aboriginal women who work with enthusiasm on all—and I mean all—street campaigns. Veteran of a hundred demonstrations, she was there, delivering posters reeking of fresh ink advertising a public meeting in bold letters—*Stop The Second Frame Up Of Tim Anderson*—to someone in the *Courier*'s office. I know her from my days as a constable, when she helped me not make too many mistakes around Redfern. I had one of the toughest and most educational probations a lady detective can have.

Hattie married a GI on R & R leave, back in the Vietnam war. I have seen photos of their wedding. They are wearing tee-shirts saying 'make love not war' and flowers in their hair and me smiles on their black faces of pure happiness. It was a match made in heaven, she always said, showing her son as proof. The GI was killed later in the war on one of those American missions where the grunts were sent up the Mekong to be ambushed.

It sounds like *Apocalypse Now* the way Hattie tells it. She is an authority on war. Sycophantic journalism I did not expect of her.

'Margot? Gidday. Long time no see.'

'Hi, darling.' I gave her a big hug, almost lifting her off the ground even though she is not small. Skinny arms and legs but rather rotund in the trunk, she invites affection somehow ...one of the few women I can be demonstrative with, without suggesting anything more. 'I thought the doers weren't the writers. What's this suburban journalism wicket?'

'Bread.' She trilled her high-pitched laugh. 'You know me. I'll do anything I'm asked. Anyway I don't do much 'ere. What's your bug, Margot?'

'The nun.'

Hattie's shrewd eyes waited for me to explain. I didn't. She shrugged. 'Oh? Legs Eleven? That was a whole lot of luck, because I was one of 'er pupils way back. Only little black face in the room, back then in the fifties. Long before I discovered who my folks were, I mean my real mob. She struck the fear of bloody God into everybody. It was all right in those days for the nuns to whack, you know, and whack they did. They didn't feel they had paid Him his due every day until someone got six. But 'er, she was a bit different. Intelligent with it, in places. And strong. Shit, she didn't have to hit: she'd lift you up in the air and have you dangling in front of the class.' Again the trilling giggle. 'Dangling 'em. One in each hand choking on their collar and tie.'

'What about this more recent business?' I gestured around the small newspaper office.

'Well, Mike over there knew I knew 'er, and everyone knew she found the stuff and they thought it'd be a cute angle if I went over and interviewed 'er. So I did. Was gunna do some more. But the whole thing went real cold real quick.'

When Hattie gives talks at universities she can sound as educated as the next person, other times she is definitely downwardly mobile in her language.

'What kind of a hold has she got, this nun? Is she just nosey, or what?' The Sister Ignatia I had met didn't seem the type to waste her time.

'Curious old bugger.' Hattie shrugged again. 'Tough as they come, and will be when she's a hundred. I tell you, Margot, she could have dug that grave herself, all six foot deep and six foot long and three foot wide of it.' She burst into a peal of laughter.

'But she didn't?' Mike looked up from his desk and smiled.

'Nup. She was hard on us kids but she was fair—if you take a pretty narrow political analysis. More worried about Biafra as I recall than the Aboriginal Protection Board.'

The words 'political analysis' always manage to get into Hattie Porter's conversation, no matter what the topic.

Thunder and lightning and a sudden darkening of the day sped my purpose. I wrote down Hattie's address, asked her permission to get back to her, and took off.

When I did get home, soaking wet, there was mail, my copy of *Freewheeling*. The funny thing with magazines is you start flipping through them straight away. *Good winter clothing is hard to come by in this country but not so in North America. This stunning women's outfit from Cannondale consists of a windbreaker jacket with large flap protection over the zipper and multipanelled winter nicks.* I read this still wet and wanted one. It'd suit me fine. My unit has one of those stupid half-baths under the shower. Didn't matter, a bath was what I wanted. *A well-run Ironman triathlon is a wild, lavish, excessive party* ... —only a fanatic would write that. I love it—*a day-long mobile celebration of human endurance, discipline, determination, courage, co-operation and sacrifice.* To the bath to read and forget about ... and dream about ...

Woken by the phone.

'We found her cardigan washed up at Five Dock, near the drain, few pebbles in the pocket. And on the Hospital side of Iron Cove a back-pack with rocks in it.' Swan sounded drunk.

'What? Patricia Phillips? Dead?' I practically screamed.

'She walked into Iron Cove Bay under the cover of fog early

yesterday morning with rocks in her pockets.' There was something odd about his voice—and I could hear other male voices in the background.

'Like she said she was going to do? "Remember Margot," she said, "I could drown." I told you.'

'Well I don't think so,' he said, mollifying me, 'but she has left the hospital.' I fell over backwards, stunned. Literally.

'She could have been murdered. I was supposed to protect her from something, wasn't I?' I argued.

'We weren't officially involved with one mad woman from the suburbs, you realise. Anyway, she was a voluntary patient, allowed to go and come as she pleased. I don't think she's dead. Just gone.' How could he be so casual about that brilliant woman's life?

'One last thing,' I said. 'Have you considered suicide?' It was quiet behind him now.

'And *we* haven't considered murder, either. Because it is not *our* case, Margot.'

My Chief, Detective Inspector Samuel Lake, doesn't have to tell me more than he wants to and he was using his full prerogative. But the phone-call almost sounded like the blokes making a practical joke. Of which I was the butt?

He sounded almost apologetic when he said, 'Just thought I better tell you, in case you decided to go and visit her, seeing you're on holidays. You did take a bit of a shine to her.' Could I hear male laughter?

I went as red as a lobster, ground my teeth and replied, 'You know I'm not like that, boss.'

'Night, Margot.'

12 JUNE

Dreams made my sleep a stormy journey through the night. The waves were watery mountains which I skiied barefoot and alone. Perhaps there was thunder and I woke. Anyway, rest is the last thing I got.

Magazines littered my laminated breakfast bench. I shuffled them aside to put my porridge down. *Police Gazette, Freewheeling, Push On.* Flipped through them. Rolled oats is comfort food; as well as warming the blood in winter it reminds me of Mum. My sister was afraid of getting fat on porridge but Mum would say she wanted to give us a strong foundation, and that the fat would fall off soon enough. All fat was puppy-fat to my Mum. Overweight adults are emotionally undeveloped, according to her.

'Anybody who can finish a 3.8-km swim, then follow immediately with a 180.3-km bike-ride and a 42.2-km run, is a champion,' I read. *'Whether they do it in nine hours or fifteen, they have beaten pain, boredom, despair and the doubters who said they never could.'* The trouble for me would be the swim. I'm not afraid of water but I do tend to plough up and down in one spot, no speed. I don't have a swimmer's physique. Not like Patricia Phillips who was afraid of drowning. What I couldn't have done with a body like hers!

'Louise Bonman (9:53:48) became the first Australian woman to beat ten hours and she had not even specifically trained for the Ironman, as she was preparing for a hectic race schedule.' Dividing it up, you've got to say it's a bike race with a bit of a swim and a run either side. A run? A bloody marathon.

There's a road race at Pitt Town advertised in the *Gazette.* I'll probably be the only woman, but why not go? I'm trained for it. Get to see some fellow coppers. It's too hard being alone. Other people—well fifty per cent of them—automatically hate you. You're a symbol: the executive arm of Law and Government. I'm just a cop. Tears stopped me reading. I shouldn't be crying over a practical joke. But I felt she was dead. Call it intuition. I try to pull my thoughts together.

Even if I were right about Pat, if the very worst had happened to her, I'd still have to cut off. Nature of the job. I fed the cat and rode up to Leura and back, hoping pain and effort would rid my mind of Pat and her troubles. When I got back I was buggered.

The weather had turned into that nasty constant drizzle, but I was warm from my ride, back to reading my mag. Owl was confused, suspecting something out of the ordinary was happening but not sure how she should capitalise on it. I started working out a training schedule for the next few days and reading about these hardy solicitors and diabetic nurses who beat the fifteen-hour mark when the phone rang. It was getting dark.

It was Barry. A friend in need. I wouldn't say Barry was bent when he left the police force, just weak. Now the fuckwit is using. I don't understand, it's stupid. But I suppose the latest pop psychology would call me an addict too: what's the difference between being addicted to challenges of mental and physical strength and being hooked on chemicals. They're both ways of distracting your nerves. Anyway, he said he had hit his girl-friend. She was screaming she would get the thugs in and would only keep quiet if he promised to ring me. I've graduated from ex-wife to big sister. I could hear her in the background. Empty threats, possibly, as he has more friends on the force than she. It's strange that either of them would ring me — over a domestic. It made me curious.

He used to get frustrated when we were married, and lash out at me too, but I'm trained, strong, fast, and it never came to anything. I divorced him quite amicably. He lives near Petersham Station. Miserable part of the world. The name Terminus Street adequately conveys the end-of-the-line feel around there, although I bet the house prices are nice enough. I thought about Barry as I drove there.

First major promotion, Drug Squad, then what does he do but slip in with the easy riders and start skimming? It's a tragic flaw in his character, balancing his compassion and sensitivity, this propensity to get drunk or get stoned. A Starsky-and-Hutch cop. Yet that's the reason why I'll always have a soft spot for him. His mate, Bill Locus, caught the lead from a sawn-off shot-gun in a bank robbery they were both called to. There was no back-up psych for Barry. He put on a brave face and got promoted, but after a few years and when the opportunity presented itself, he let go. He started sampling. Free heroin. Cocaine. I'm not quite sure how corrupt he has become. He does security work these days.

Drab weather and time of night. I pulled my Ford Laser into Fishers Reserve.

Barry opened the door then started thumping his head into the wall. I kicked him in the back of the knees and growled, 'Get hold of yourself or I'll squash your balls.' Susan was crying. She was bruised in both eyes. She cringed on the well-used couch. Theirs is the one terrace house in Sydney that has undergone no renovation whatsoever. Gloomy workers' cottage it still is, except for the television that dominated the small sitting-room.

'What did you say, Sue? What's this about?'

'Dope,' she croaked. 'But he can get it. He's got the contacts.'

I turned on him with a sneer. 'Are you that badly off, Barry? Have you slipped a few notches since I last saw you?'

He didn't answer me. Why bring me into their drug row; they know I'm straight as well as a fitness fanatic.

Their kitchen was through a narrow doorway. I went in and opened the fridge. When Mum was making do for the lot of us on next to nothing, the four kids would come home starving after school and hockey or rugby practice and go straight to the fridge. There'd be jam and pikelets ... something. Pikelets are not only flour and milk, they're care and time. I can measure poverty of spirit by what's in a fridge.

There was poverty of spirit in this one. (a) It was iced up. (b) No one's digestive juices would get going on what the shelves offered: a plate of cold crumbed lamb cutlets, several with a semi-circle bitten out of them, hard-looking cheese, cream with use-by date long gone, ancient taramasalata, some tinned dolmades lying in greenish slime.

'This fridge doesn't know the Ice Age is over,' I yelled. 'You both need something hot to eat.'

Barry laughed at my joke. Susan is a couple of years younger than I am but she looks and dresses about sixteen, like the pop star, Madonna. Such clothing is not cheap, not where she buys it anyway. All the same, my Barry is far more suited to such a creature than to me. She exudes a femininity that somehow asks for it. I don't know what. The situation was beyond my district-nurse hands. To feel sensible I had to do something.

'I'll go down and buy some bacon and eggs, or whatever I can find at the local deli. Look after each other until I get back. Because first I think you both need to eat. Then secondly, perhaps, talk.' Both watched me go into the hallway.

There are several shop-fronts which suggest that once a small shopping centre thrived: a jeweller, several delicatessens, a gift shop, fish and chips maybe, across the road a butcher is still there. As I proceeded to the corner store, I noticed Women's Liberation House now inhabits one of the old shops.

There was some kind of meeting happening behind the curtains. A handwritten sign stuck to the window gave the date and time: 'Rape Action Group'. I couldn't linger without arousing suspicion so I carried on. What is rape action about?

I was aghast at the price of tinned steak and veg. My concern was to get some home-cooked food into them so that they might warm to each other again. There was always hope for Barry, he's such a big-hearted guy. I got half a dozen fresh rolls, frankfurts, tomato soup, bananas and milk. Just my doing this for them, being around, would make them look to themselves, pull up their socks for a while. Barry doesn't ring me often. Why now? What's unusual?

I was frowning, distracted, when I stopped on the footpath outside Women's Liberation House. Behind the synthetic curtains, women were in a huddle over a coffee table. A large person had just left the room and her absence had instigated this hurried heads-together. I peered through the lacy curtains; they were too engrossed to notice me. I watched until a very young woman with an angry expression lifted her eyes and glared straight into mine. I turned and walked away just as the other came back.

I let myself into Sue's and Barry's. Both were silently watching television, rigid and glum. I went to the kitchen and did what I call 'a mum'. Mum's kitchen was her cave and refuge and in it she performed wizardry. She was an eternal creature, like Mother Courage following the wars, she provided food through disaster and bitter argument.

'First get some food into yourselves, then you can talk about it while I do the washing up.' Doing 'a mum' makes me feel the big tidal wave could come and I'd cope. Nowadays, with all her holidaying, Mum says, 'It's nice to have someone cook for you for a change.' I loved Barry. In different times I'd have stayed his wife, I suppose. He would have been the cop and I the housewife keeping him on the straight path. But I'm glad I don't have to be a housewife. I love being a cop, earning my own money, managing my own affairs and pursuing my own interests.

Barry devoured the soup, rolls and frankfurts, and Susan ate with an appetite I didn't know she had. I was hungry but as I don't eat white bread or meat, I just picked while they argued it through.

Their argument drained me. But it kept me busy—that is, not thinking about Pat Phillips. I stayed until about eleven. It is hard to remain robust when the last decent meal you've had was a falafel sandwich from a take-away shop in the hills, hours earlier.

Before I put the key in the car-door lock, they hit. Three of them, young girls with inexpert karate kicks and punches. The sort that are taught in ten-week self-defence classes, to be used for defence not attack. Dojo exercises. I could have injured all three easily. But there was a fourth I hadn't immediately noticed. I react. I'm a cop. I react to violence with violence.

I gave better than I got. They were so young, so angry, and girls. Girls hitting a woman who had, as far as I knew, done them no wrong. I had the feeling it was a practice attack. I threw a punch at the one in the background. A mistake. Lightning fast she slammed my head into the footpath. It seemed as if she hadn't moved. The scarf around her neck fluttered a little. Then another and I was unconscious.

Barry was there when I came to.

13 JUNE

'We'll get an arrest for this one, Margot.' The Petersham cops brought me home in a squad car and drove my own back. Service that only members of the club can expect, I suppose. I told the sergeant I had concussion and couldn't remember who came at me. 'I mean, they came at me from the back.' I really did not want a wholesale purge of women's libber places all over Sydney by trigger-happy cops. A lot of the libbers do a really good job, in their refuges from domestic violence, drugs and alcohol, and in their health centres. I've seen them succeed where social workers and cops, and even the Salvos haven't, with some really hard-bitten cases. In any case, I wasn't a hundred per cent sure it *was* the women libbers.

Tender as I was, nothing vital was damaged. I plastered calendula ointment liberally over any swelling I could see or feel. The back of my skull was augmented by a large lump. My hands and face were fine. I'd been roughed up worse in my time. But they—whoever they were—meant to hurt me. This knowledge was more of a headache. Why? Had they used the word 'raggings', or had I dreamt it? Jumping to conclusions is not a habit of a good detective, not the way lawyers are these days anyway. That meeting of theirs had struck me as pretty harmless and I recognised none of my attackers as the women I'd seen through that window.

I mixed up some bean sprouts, cottage cheese, grated carrot, walnuts, yoghurt, tahini and whatever else I could rustle up and laid it thick over a rye bread slice and a cold lentil rissole and chomped.

Why me?

I toss and turn, doing no good for my aches. Weary consciousness. As a tough young plain-clothes constable on duty at a small station, I once had to look after a rape victim, a woman, who kept saying 'why me?' Fate singles out some people and gives them a hard time. She was walking along the street just like anybody else and she turned a corner just like anybody else when suddenly she was attacked, in daylight. Her husband blamed her. He tried not to but he couldn't help it. He brought her to the station and there was accusation in his tone, as if he had blamed her for everything that went bad for him. 'Why me?' she wailed.

We caught the rapist fairly quickly, a recidivist out on parole: skinny little bloke who would know exactly what he was inflicting, having—I dare say—had it inflicted on himself inside. My anger was directed more at the husband who had pecked and scratched at her self-esteem over however many years so that she had become a featherless chook. Her wail was just a plea to the capricious gods.

I got up, made a milk drink and flipped through Pat's scrapbook. It was like taking a dip in a psychic pool.

Maybe she did just walk away.

R A G, Rape Action Group, rag, raggers, ragging. I wonder how far these girls are prepared to go in getting revenge on rapists. Have the radical feminists decided they will take justice into their own hands and deal out punishment in the anarchistic way? Revenge, they say, works. It rids the heart of the obsession. Something is achieved. He gets his just desserts, eye for an eye. So, maybe raggers are avengers of rape. If they are a successful underground movement, why leave a note on a window? And why slap me around? I don't care if they threaten to snip off dicks. I'm a national crime investigator not a domestic one, except in my own time.

Now there was, I remember, a big woman there, at the meeting. Large women I know include, so far, Roo, the most likely to be there, Hattie, who could be anywhere, and Sister

Legs Eleven who is the biggest of the lot.

In the morning, at quarter to six, I received a phone call. 'Are you all right, Margot?'

Why was Hattie asking? 'No, I'm bruised all over, with a rotten great headache. Who did it? What do you know?'

'What are you talking about?' My bullshit detector, at least, had been recharged. She sounded genuine. 'I have some information for you, but I'm going down the south coast in about forty minutes. They're bombing our sacred sites near Jervis Bay. If I'm not arrested there I might lend my considerable weight to the side of the trees near Bega.' If she did know, she'd be worried about police retaliation.

'What information, Hattie? And why did you ask if I was all right?' Somehow first daylight is colder than the darkest hour. I shivered.

'You sounded husky, subdued ... not your usual self. How come you're bruised anyway?'

Then again, you don't know with her. I cleared my throat and toughened my tone. 'Do you know anything about R A G, Rape Action Group, by any chance?'

'Now that'd be talkin'.' What she doesn't know she'd like to know. She'll find out.

'Okay. What's the information?' The cat appeared, yawning, stiff-legged, yet tail arrogantly aloft.

'Legs Eleven was out on the night in question. She attends some kind of secret gathering. I have no evidence that it is not a bridge circle, but ...'

I interrupted her, 'Do the other nuns know?'

'The one who told me does. She does it once a month and gets home late. Fridays.'

Informants handle information like poker-machine players handle money—you've got to risk some to get some. 'Interesting. Does she walk alone at night? Not a black belt in karate by any chance?' No drop from me, Hattie.

'Tai chi, maybe. She's got a driver's licence, moron. Hey? Do you think it's going to keep raining? I've got to pack mildewy filthy clothes and my japara's got holes in it and my sleeping bag's not waterproof ...' Her old self, a friend. She wasn't very insistent about 'how'd yer get dem bruises anyway missy?' Why should she be?

I looked at myself in the mirror. I was pale. There was nothing I had to do today, really. I could read, cosset myself, play with the cat, worry alone. Catch up on some sleep. It is aggravating being singled out haphazardly and thumped.

What was that nun's group: Catholic Clergy for Peace and Justice in the Third World?

It must have been very difficult to keep the press so totally ignorant about that mystery corpse in Wiley Park. Except, when you look at it, there aren't that many police-rounds reporters, and they do have to have mates in the force or they get zilch. But that body was in the morgue; where is Pat's?

Let me go over what I've got again. First, the local uniformed cops would have checked the corpse and called detectives, cordoned off the area, and sent for the Forensic police. Both detectives and Forensic would have attended, then called for the District Medical Officer who has to check the body at the scene. Forensic would have taken photos prior to moving the body. Then they examine the site around the body for physical evidence, and any that is found is photographed before being moved for analysis. When the examination of the body is completed the government contractors take the ex-person to the morgue. Body and clothing are booked in by police and all recorded. A detective is present throughout the post-mortem.

Now which coppers would have been there? How many? Say we have two of each, plus Ballistics if a gun was used, so ten or more people in the NSW Department could have been on the scene. There are running-sheets and photographs somewhere. Who in CIB is or was handling it, I wonder? Narcotics would have been around too. Barry would know someone bent enough to give me under-the-counter info. Are drugs involved? His mates will clam up on me. Sue could have threatened him with drug-heavies; she's been around, that girl. They're afraid I'm a

whistle-blower because I hate corruption and I'm not afraid.
Barry, unfortunately, is not the snooping type but he could ask
a few questions on my behalf, seeing he owes me one, at least.

It seemed easier to work on a straight homicide investigation—
as a puzzle—than Pat's disappearance. I did ring Rozelle
Hospital. They confirmed she'd gone, but said nothing of
backpacks with rocks in them.

I want to figure out how to get into the Phillips' house in
Lilyfield. I have been kept well out of the know by my own crowd
here, and that's got to be deliberate. In fact, I'm on enforced
vacation. I'll have to break in. I wonder how much surveillance
there'd be.

Start making lists, Margot. Psychopaths. Boy with an unholy
hatred of women, specially mother. Weirdos with the glory of war
in their blood and the frustrations of peace coursing to an
alcohol-befuddled brain.

The ex-soldier? Is he the classic weirdo?

Cath, the lesbian. Yes, well.

What about Steven Phillips himself?

Then there's Julie Schempri, business woman, from Victoria.
A couple of phone calls should find her. But if I go to see her,
because it is much easier to glean intelligence face to face, I'll
have to have a good cover.

Start with the son? I asked my friend Angela to interview
some lads around the Haymarket. I didn't tell her why, chiefly
because I couldn't. But there may be some way of finding the
son. A rich girl with nothing much to do, she loves my little
assignments.

My work is cut out for me, if this is what I want to do with my
holidays. I wish I didn't have suspicions about a big woman who
knows me and maybe, just maybe, ordered up a few bruises on
my hide.

Julie Schempri had her answer-phone connected and very
helpfully it informed me that she was in Sydney until the 17th.
Urgent enquiries, ring this number. I rang it and found that
Mrs Schempri was in Sydney.

A motel at Bondi Junction. How fit do I feel for this expedition? I have a long-sleeved, calf-length, hip-hugging number which I don't look too bad in, with my straight blonde hair, brown skin, flat stomach. It should hide the black-and-blues. I don't mind adding to my height with heels; it's the walking I hate. She could see me between seven and eight-thirty. Tenderness around certain areas made me walk a little gingerly.

As I was driving through Redfern I thought I saw Hattie Porter sitting at a bus stop. But it must have been a woman who looked and dressed like her because she went down the south coast this morning.

It wasn't a particularly classy motel in Bondi Junction though none around here is exactly cheap. I told the clerk at the desk that I was expected. He pointed in the direction of the lift and told me the number.

'Come in,' she called in reply to my knock. The door was ajar. It opened to a narrow corridor between wardrobe and port rack, miniscule bathroom, into a bedroom box, a double bed with a print of condors in a South American landscape over it, a couple of Danish Deluxe chairs, a bench with television, motel stationery, kettle and tea bags. Awful orange curtains I hoped did not hide the multi-million-buck views that can be bought round here. It smelt of air-conditioning and smoke. Handbag, cigarette pack and bottle of sherry were the only things on the bench that made the place at all individual.

She was smaller than her sister, wearing designer jeans and jumper with padded shoulders, little make-up, hair untidy, thin, wispy. She was lying on the bed shoeless. Hardly looking up, she gasped in indignation at the ABC News. The old men of China had brought out the troops against the students. Dragging on her fag she exclaimed, 'Momentous events occur when I'm in motel rooms. It always happens.' She was obviously someone who felt comfortable in the anonymous environment. 'Sit down. Margot?'

'Thank you. Margot Gorman. I don't suppose Pat would have

ever talked about me to you?'

For all her deflecting attention, her eyes, lidded like a snake's, didn't miss much. 'Yes, I've heard the name.'

I didn't expect that.

'In a letter, I think. Do you want anything to drink? Look in the fridge. Brandy, whisky, gin, beer ... ?'

I took out a soda water and poured some into the Duralux glass, sat down on a chair and crossed my legs.

'Where are they? Do you know?' My miner's-daughter-at-cocktail-party voice.

'Who, Steve and Patricia? Wherever they are, they would not be together, I can assure you. Men have it so much easier, don't you think? They don't have periods, menstrual cramps. I'm really in pain today.' She rolled into foetal position, groaning. She knew and she wasn't going to tell me.

I glanced at the sports news. 'Could Pat swim? As a child, I mean—really swim, do the crawl, the breast stroke and so on; did she get her *Herald* certificate?' I let the strand of hair I usually hook behind my ear flop over my face.

'Of course, everybody round our way could swim. She could swim as well as anyone else. Why do you ask?'

'She said she was afraid of water, and that she could drown. I'm worried about her.' I wanted to convey a neighbourly, gossipy relationship.

She leapt off the bed and dug in her bag and eventually lit a Marlboro. 'Are you for real?'

She knew I wasn't. 'What do you mean?' I responded weakly.

'She walked out of the hospital, signed herself out.'

My instinct told me this woman was lying. She started talking about Steven. 'He's a misogynist of the first order that man, and no one would guess it.'

I shook my head and ruffled my hair and asked, 'Where is Pat now?'

'So far as I know, they are holidaying for a while. Apart.' She began collecting her cigarettes, matches, glasses, and pushing them into an overcrowded handbag.

'Where do you think your sister would go at a time like this? Any haunts? Any old lovers? Why didn't she go to you? Wouldn't she need some t.l.c.?' My bag felt heavy with the Smith and Wesson as I got up.

'I don't know. I'd lay down my life for her, of course, but we're not close. There was one old lover … Peter. But. Thorns had grown, ships floated away from one another, hands reaching out not touching sort of thing. Very romantic. In one of her letters I found a piece of torn paper that wasn't meant to be there. "P.O.W." was printed on it. That's all. Very mysterious.' Pat had written to Julie from the hospital. She had never asked me to handle any of her mail. Someone else must have.

'Peter? Could it have been Peter's initials, for instance? Prisoner of War? Pow! as in Batman? Peter Owen White?' I said, trying to bluff more information out of her.

'Not his surname. Something German, Polish, maybe Dutch. It's a long time ago and I only met him once.'

The heels made me tall. The dress slowed my usual pace.

'I haven't met Steve yet. What's he look like?'

'He looked Italian—tall, dark and handsome. My husband was Italian. Passionate, paunchy and sexist. At one point along the way I wanted them fused into one to make the perfect man for me. Steve's still tall, narrow about the eyes and mouth.'

I went to the bathroom to wash out my glass.

'I had an affair with Steve,' she called.

'Did he hurt you?' I yelled, looking at myself.

'He just used me.' She came to the doorway behind me. 'He's cold. Oh it meant something to him all right. He meant to well and truly hurt us both. But he didn't hurt Patricia as much as he wanted. She knew, she tolerated. She is sort of lazy, laissez-faire, vague—and free, she felt, to have an affair of her own. When he realised that bonking her sister wasn't going to get to her, he dropped me like the proverbial. I'd meant nothing to him and I wasn't as beautiful, he said. He had to make it cruel.'

'Total creep.' I leaned into the mirror and applied lipstick.

She dragged a brush through her wispy hair, gauging me.

Then she lit another cigarette, picked up her handbag and aimed me at the door.

'But he's a charmer. Both snake and charmer.'

We were waiting at the lift doors when I managed to phrase a question about Cath. Julie didn't know her.

As I was going, she surprised me with the question, 'Do you play tennis?'

I nodded. There are only a couple of sports not in my repertoire.

'Want a game?' She threw her cigarette butt into an ashtray in the lobby of the motel.

'Okay. I haven't played for a while but I've got a racquet, shoes ...' She cut me off.

'In a couple of days. I'll hire a court. Ring me.'

'Right-oh. Bye.' I minced away in the high heels, knowing I hadn't fooled Julie Schempri one bit.

Fortunately I keep a canvas bag in the back of the car with tracksuit, sweat gear and towel at the ready. I went to City Gym in Oxford Street, paid the money and got on the equipment to perspire and tire before wilting in the sauna. There my mind crawled around this puzzle like an ant in a ball of cotton wool.

14 JUNE

Soon after dawn, I got on my bike and rode out past the airport to La Perouse and then back down Anzac Parade to Maroubra Beach. A girl from Wollongong can never forsake the waves for too long, surfer that she is. The sea clears my pores. An onshore breeze was blowing quite stiffly. There was a decent swell. I wouldn't have minded having my wet-suit and board with me.

I gazed for an hour, trying to figure out things. Maybe she had just walked out, as Julie said. Julie was one of a type, a chatterer who swamps deliberate misinformation with a flood of words.

Why was Julie lying to me? Was there any real evil in their sibling rivalry? My feeling was still that something terrible had happened to Pat.

I was being treated shoddily. Shut out. I wondered whether I should blast back into Swan's office, demand an explanation and risk being called an hysterical female making a mountain out of a molehill. My poor little head wanted answers and my body wanted to plane waves.

Detecting crime and solving it was precisely why I joined the force, but something deeper was bothering me. I have never wanted to be mistaken for a dyke, though it has happened because, as they say, I'm a tough sheila. So why has her disappearance got emotional undertones for me?

I walked along the beach. I saw a figure that looked familiar. It was Big Frank, Swan's friend, the poofter, flying a kite. He was making it dance on the sea breeze. It had always seemed incongruous: Frank Farouk, heavy-weight wrestler, and his hobby, making delicate, pretty kites. He is one of the best gossips in Sydney because he has lived with Morrie Bishipp for years. What Morrie doesn't know would fit on the back of a postage stamp. Frank still play-acts at the odd bout in the clubs with his cronies. They enjoy it and so, it seems, do the patrons. I watched the kite fly, glide and dive, sometimes skimming the grass. This kite was electric-blue, lavender and green, in black borders like a stained-glass window.

He had been to Vietnam, I knew. I walked up to him. Maybe he'd know Patricia's Peter. Talking about Vietnam is okay these days; the vets seem to like it. I told Frank the little I knew about Peter.

Frank said, 'I knew a lot of Peters.'

He turned away. I got a hunch that he knew exactly what I was about. He's usually such a chatty man. He wasn't giving. I had to convince him. I ended up telling him about Pat and my job at the hospital, and saying I didn't know whether I loved her or not. That brought a smile and he talked.

'Sounds like it might be Larsen. But Larsen had the mark of

a hero, you know. Not a big fellow, not a loud fellow, but a
beautiful man, you know. Handsome in a sandy kind of way.
His skin tanned reddish, his eyebrows bleached. They seemed
to beetle more and more over his clear blue eyes, as he got
deeper into the war. A beautiful man, really, far too sensitive for
that war. I say "that war", because it was no war. It was
officially something else, an "engagement"? Nobody declared
war.' The contrast between Frank's physique and the light,
affected voice made me smile, as it always does. It would be an
amazing coincidence if this Larsen bloke was Pat's teenage
lover, but stranger things have happened.

'Therefore,' he continued, manipulating the kite's strings
with both hands, pulling delicately against the wind, 'I guess we
were just murdering people, and being murdered. It didn't take
Larsen long to figure that, or any Australian, corporal or officer
or private, for that matter. We all knew. We wanted to fight a
proper war, like Dad did, sort of thing.'

A gust came over the back of the kite. It stalled. I watched.
I was sure it would splinter all its balsa wood bones on the
ground. It didn't. He manoeuvred it so the wind came
underneath. It climbed into the sky. 'We'd drive out and pull
the dead Yanks from their jeeps. Week after week.' Frank gave
me a sharp look and asked, 'If this is professional ...?'

I shook my head madly. 'No, it's personal, only personal. Tell
me about him, please.' The look, the size of Frank is enough to
make you not want to argue.

Larsen. Frank, hiding his real nature until well after the war,
was obviously madly in love with him. I was listening to him
describe the beautiful man, the warrior poet, the hero.
'Anyway' — the big man could talk when he wanted to — 'the real
hero is one who goes to his limit, not in a self-destructive way,
not in a stupid way, but in a thinking way. They're always the
ones who do the most work, by the way. You'd understand that,
Gorman? Larsen was a bloke like that. He didn't shirk anything,
and he didn't like anything. But the war screwed him up
somehow. His little picture of Felicity couldn't always hold up

against it all, and he'd go to Saigon ...' Again he choked up, but as he turned his face into the wind, he cleared the sadness.

'Yes,' I prompted.

He sighed. 'There was a hairdresser there, a barber. You'd go for a shave he'd get you a girl—young ones, kids. Larsen went one time and came back different. Saying he could never see his Felicity again after what he had done. He'd talk to me. Not that he talked a lot but I saw the quality in him. A thing I remember he did say was that her name wasn't really Felicity; it was just that she was cat-like and spread happiness about her. I got a cat called Felix, for Larsen's Felicity.'

'He wouldn't be a P. O. W. —prisoner of war? He wouldn't have gone back and turned up missing-in-action or anything, would he?'

'Lars? Nup, get that idea out of your head, girl. He's mad, but he's not stupid. He was a great soldier but he's not Rambo.'

This Larsen bloke had a fairy-tale quality about him. I wanted him real. This was a man I wanted to see, whether or not he was Patricia's warrior. 'Have you seen him?'

He took his time. If it weren't Frank, I'd have sworn he was lying—something about the way he shifted his shoulders inside his jacket. 'Yep, saw him at the Welcome-Home parade. We cried in each other's arms. Him and the little bloke who is now in a wheelchair, Paul—and Swan was there too. We were together in Nam and we were together again. Doesn't your boss talk about it?'

I shook my head. 'Do you still keep in touch?'

Frank hesitated. 'Not much. Morrie hates old soldiers. So ...' Everybody in Sydney knows about Morrie Bishipp and his bodyguard.

Frank started to reel in his exotic bird. 'The little bloke is in hospital. Prince of Wales. Broke his wrist. Big thing when you're in a wheelchair.'

P. O. W? I got Paul's full name and was off on the bike, around the coast road to North Coogee and over to the Prince of Wales Hospital.

The little bloke turned out to have none of Frank's explicit and Peter's reputed qualities; Paul Murphy was shifty. I took an instant dislike to him. He was still trying to avoid the bullet. I could tell by his eyes. I suspected he knew where Peter Larsen was. And he, for his part, immediately knew I was a cop. Sharp as a tack, or maybe it's obvious, I don't know. I wasn't trying to cover it.

I threw him a few questions, interrogation-style. The odour coming off his woollen cardigan was a give-away, for a start. 'So where do you get your dope from, Smurf?'

Flicker of the eyelids. 'Don't smoke that stuff.'

'No?' I felt down into the pocket of the wheelchair, pulled out a packet of ready-rubbed tobacco and smelt in it. 'Don't give me that. I'm not going to bust a poor little cripple. I'm not interested in you.' Felt in his shirt pocket, pulled out a twist of plastic lunch-wrapping, 'Pretty obvious.' I held it to his nose. 'Peter grow good stuff?' I asked.

'I'm not saying anything. That's final. Leave me alone.' I angled my head to read the signatures on his plaster.

'So Larsen supplies, does he? Seen him recently, since you did your wrist?' I stared at his face very closely and saw in his fear the affirmative, even though he shook negative. It's funny, that type gives more away than truth-tellers. They think they've got something to lose when they've got precious little to start with.

For the first time I had a link-up. The soldier supplies marijuana and his name is Peter Larsen and he is a beautiful man.

Sister Mary Legs implies the real solution to the problem of Mystery Body is tackling the most difficult part. If the marijuana on the grave is hardest to reckon with, then the marijuana holds the answer. Being an illegal drug, it draws attention. Kind-hearted Peter Larsen grows and or supplies marijuana to the poor vets who need it to ease the pain, at prices the rest of Sydney would crawl for. To them, he is a hero. To me, he is a supplier, a criminal. He could also be a double murderer.

When I got home I discovered my cat, Owl, killing a mouse on the lawn in a routine feline fashion. She kicked it, made it run so she could pounce, then threw it, ignored it, fooled it and pounced again. When she saw me, she simply picked it up in her mouth and crunched. She protested when mousie bit her tongue, but she is stronger, bigger-brained, and might is right. You're dead, Gerry. She followed me in after discarding the warm corpse, boasting that she does that sort of thing every day. She's a comic character. I pick her up and tickle my face with her whiskers.

I stare into her Egyptian wise-plus eyes and get an idea. That drunken crime-writer, ex-*Sun* reporter, he'll know something about the mystery corpse beneath the marijuana. A hearse-chaser, that one: what was his name? Max. I went to the Journos' Club and found him asleep on a pool-table upstairs, having pulled the cover over him like a blanket. Everyone around laughed. I left wondering what would be the best time to find him sober. Max lives in a room above one of those Broadway hotels and probably starts on the piss as soon as he wakes up.

15 JUNE

'Caucasian, male.'

Thanks Max. Bite-marks on the fingers, knife through the jugular. I traded. Fair's fair. I held back on the attack method and its Vietnam suggestions.

'Looking for a set of molars, Margot?'

'Oh, yeah, last count Sydney had — what — four, five million residents?'

'Divide by two. Men don't bite.'

So a white man was buried swathed in banana palm leaves in a public park. Getting a sober Max was easier than I'd expected. A simple telephone call early in the morning. He didn't know much more. I could tell, because he wanted to.

Incurable snoops, journos. Curiosity flows in their blood like alcohol. And nobody apparently knows much. Unanswered questions keep a man like Max awake at night, needing the company of other shallow theorisers. Everyone to his own poison.

Today looked as miserable as all the rest had been lately. Blustering, wintry, any sunshine lacking warmth.

Today I would break in. If Patricia had walked out, or even gone for a holiday, wouldn't she go home first?

It turned out to be an easy matter of squeezing through the bathroom window which wasn't locked. The bathroom was one of those new cramped corner boxes tucked into terrace houses, when an outdoor one had done quite nicely for fifty years.
A small bookcase faced the lavatory: cartoons, poetry, Marx and Freud. Glancing into Marx or Freud each day for a few minutes indicates a taste for the quotable quote. A couple of coloured catalogues, Japanese dyed cottons, Aboriginal bark paintings — more her style — were also there. Soap in the miniature sink and in the shower alcove. Big fluffy towels still hanging behind the door. I flicked through the Freud and found a couple of sentences underlined: *A mother is only brought unlimited satisfaction by her relation to a son; this is altogether the most perfect, the most free from ambivalence of all human relationships.*

It made me think of something in Cath's letter describing the rape: 'he puts on a little-boy look. it's incredible. do they think we are so stupid?'. Women had to cater for men's needs in the same unlimited way they catered to the needs of children. No other way, my mum would say, no other way. Without these great men telling us how things are, how do we know?

Pat certainly had not been home. The kitchen-dining room was as she described, tiled shiny brown (broken glass territory). Some mould was showing on the sauce bottles. The couple of unwashed coffee cups looked as if they had been there for ages.

I thought to rinse them and then realised that I shouldn't really move a thing. This living area felt a bit like the Marie Celeste: all occupants spirited away in the midst of eating, talking, being; beams creaking, doors flapping.

A narrow passage fed three further rooms. In the first, a king-sized double-bed dominated; it was covered with a patchwork quilt of the most beautiful colours — warm blues and pinky tans. Two bedside tables with reading lamps and a built-in wardrobe completed the simplicity of this room. Irving Wallace's *The Seven Minutes*, which *brings the reader directly into the vortex of today's storm over pornography, sexual freedom, perversion, nudity and human rights* lay open with its spine broken on one side, and *Intercourse* by Andrea Dworkin was neatly closed on the other. Flipping through these books, there seemed to be more lecturing in the Irving Wallace. The best-selling entertainment must come from the juicy bits in between. I wanted to take the Andrea Dworkin and reconsidered my earlier resolution to leave everything as is.

A movement in the tree outside caught my eye. The one window of this room faced the back fence along a narrow pathway beside the kitchen-dining room. The back yard, though narrow, was long. There was a bricked area with a barbeque, beyond which were quite a few trees. There was someone in the garden, I could feel it. I watched for some time, but nothing. I must have been mistaken.

The middle room had no window but a sky-light, and was fairly dark today. Obviously it was her room. A large white L-shaped working bench had a silk-screen frame lying on it. A sewing machine. A huge basket full of remnants and folded cloth. A length of white cheese-cloth hanging from a line, long since dried. The scene on it was of the bush, an abstract in greens and tans and blues. A small fire-place in the corner contained the partly burnt silvery remains of a cigarette packet and some butts. A ghetto-blaster sat on the mantelpiece. Easy to imagine her quiet industry here. Unframed paintings stuck on the wall with Blu-tak. I could have sat and kept her company in this room with no effort. All they had said was wrong: she couldn't have walked—or swum—out of that hospital of her own volition, because she hadn't been home to collect anything. Why not?

At the front was his study. Miniature bay windows gave out onto a tiled verandah with wrought-iron fence and a crowded plantation of Aussie natives: an acacia, a tea-tree, a gum, a bottle-brush, a couple of straggly kangaroo paws.

Again I had the sensation of being watched. This time from the street itself, the footpath. I turned back into the room and there, facing me, was the face of the handsome Steve Phillips. A large colour-photo portrait in a standard frame showed a man with a head of thick black hair, a high forehead, neat close ears, a straight nose, moustache and mouth covered by a fanning hand of long fingers holding a cigarette. The eyes are looking directly into the lens with a half-amused, crinkled glow. I stared at it for minutes and minutes. The eyes had smile lines about the corners and seemed to express much interest in the camera or the beholder.

The desk was covered with the paraphernalia of teaching: a little Apple IIe computer, a few floppy disks spread about, books and papers everywhere. Not as though someone had searched and tossed—although they well could have—but rather as if this were its usual state, the mess denoting work half-done rather than neat completed travail. I came back to the man's face. That look in the eyes. A look designed to seduce women. I pulled it out of the frame to see the photographer's name, F. R. Pollack. If F. R. is not a woman then he is in love with himself. An ambiguous look. I peered around for something to convince me that Steve had gone for a holiday. But no, there was an interrupted feel here. Whoever left here only went to get some more cigarettes or something. Nobody leaves floppy disks out of their sleeves unless they'll only be gone a minute.

I got the fright of my life when a face suddenly appeared at the french windows. It was there and then it was gone. The front door was double-deadlocked and I couldn't get out. I tried the windows. He stared at me for a few seconds. Greying sandy hair, eyes narrowed under bushy eyebrows as if used to bright sunlight, the red-tan skin of an outdoors man, torn work-shirt over muscular arms.

He looked just long enough to size me up and then he was gone. I didn't recognise him. But then, I don't know everyone in the Authority. Just possibly, he was Internal Security. I recalled Swan's warning about Harry 'the Heat' Clarke. If my boss calls me, I'll have both answers and questions ready, remembering that I had broken in here. If this was one of our chaps, he was a maverick. You get to know the look of the loner. I was glued to his squinting eyes for less than thirty seconds. They were blue.

An armchair in front of full bookcases emphasised the masculine feel of this study. I picked up the portrait and sank into the armchair. Glared into those unsmiling, terribly-terribly honest eyes, asking myself: what was it about them? Their invulnerability? Would this face murder? Wondering about the face at the window distracted me. When I looked at the photo again, it struck me: these are the eyes of a liar, a deep and successful liar. A confidence trickster, perhaps. Steve Phillips. Sligo guy, Galway boy.

I considered stealing a couple of the floppies. I considered giving myself a hands-on lesson on a p.c. I had never used. But it wasn't my home. One thing was certain. Pat had not been here since her spell in the asylum. I couldn't get the idea of her suiciding out of my mind, since I'd been so convinced of it on the job.

Tonight I got the phone call I anticipated. A muffled voice said, 'We're pawns, Margot. Get it? Pawns, not players.'

Nosing into the Phillips house was apparently encroaching on someone's territory. I checked through my list of enemies — people who had a grudge against me — quite a few. Barry's there because a couple of his friends are there — bent coppers who know at any time I could sing. But what they might have to do with the Phillipses beat me.

I'd done enough to get the heat if I was a 'pawn' in the NSW police factions game. Everyone had the feeling something was going to blow and, when desperate people are pushed, the innocent sheep become scapegoats and Cleanskins get tarnished.

16 JUNE

While I was in the shower, I thought I heard movement on the balcony. When I dried and dressed, a bit shaky, I went out there. Owl meowed from her position on the pot-plant table and I saw a saucer had broken on the concrete. I looked into the street. There was a figure running—a youth, or a fit woman? I had to get out of the place. I rode north, to sweat the worry out through my skin, across the Bridge, down Pittwater Road and back up along the Wakehurst Parkway and down into Manly. I sat in the Corso exhausted. The figures strolling past me seemed distant, alien. Patricia was dead, for sure. Forget she ever was. After eating and resting, I put the bike on the ferry and chugged home from Circular Quay.

The place had been burgled. The window on the first-floor verandah had been forced. My video, my television, my hi-fi, my camera and my jewellery were all still there. Owl was as indignant as I was about the intrusion. The remainder of the day was a write-off.

17 JUNE

Tennis with Julie. Styles: I drive from the base line; she runs to the net and clips some fine volleys. We have two close sets, which I win. She comes off the court puffed; I could play another hour. The sky is overcast but it is not raining. Saturday morning in Prince Alfred Park: a large group of black people congregate under a tree; a couple of joggers with headbands and red faces; a few people strolling, others walking through towards the city.

Julie and I make our way towards Chalmers Street and a coffee shop there. She, smoking and swinging her big canvas shoulder-bag, with racquet grip protruding.

'You know, it looks so natural for them—to be outside. Whities would be having a committee meeting in a board-room.' She laughs. 'Shelter is the Caucasian nightmare. Have you looked at the real-estate prices lately?'

We were in the café ordering, when she looked directly at me for the first time. Though surrounded by a mild hysteria, her core seemed hard and fixed. Her look sliced the water and was away again like a silver bream in the sea. I mentioned Steve.

'His eyes,' she said. I nodded. I too had stared at them.

'His eyes try so hard to make you trust him. Great effort, like a hypnotist, seeing he had so little to work with.' She laughed, meanly. 'Maybe he made her mad. When they were both into the mind-bending drugs, mushrooms and LSD, you could never tell whether or not he was pretending, even to be high, spaced out, hallucinating. He would kill rather than be a victim. He wanted to be looked after as though he was a victim, but that was part of the ruse to make anybody—everybody—his victim. Isn't it funny that a woman can see right through a man and it doesn't make the slightest bit of difference?'

'Strange.' I spoke distractedly as I was trying to work out whether to blow my cover with Julie: would she be more willing to help me if she knew what exactly I was about?

'I'll give you an example if you've got the time?' She laughed.

'Yes, I have the time.' I sipped my mineral water through a straw and she ordered another cappuccino.

'You know he goes off on these hunting expeditions, all over the place. Duck-shooting, boars, kangaroos, and so on. He'd pack his rifle and take off for a weekend, a week ... It was a regular thing, all the time they were together. Well, he once told me a story about some duck-shooters. They sat in their flat-bottomed boat—a sturdy one with no leaks. There was no wind. The lake was calm. One of the men said, "We're going to fall in." He clasped the side of the boat so hard his knuckles went white. "We're going to fall in." The sky was blue overhead. It was quiet in the early morning, except for the occasional flutter of ducks taking flight, or other blokes shooting on the shore. They were further out. There were weeping willows to one side and reeds on the other side of the lake, a few dead ring-barked trees sticking up. "We're going to fall in," he repeated. His mate in the bow asked, "What's got into you, ya mug?" The one with the oars started to row. The man in the bow scowled, swore and said, "Shut up." His blunt forefinger tapped the weapon on his knees.'

'You really get into a story when you tell it, don't you?' I interrupted, being friendly, smiling.

'It's the way Steve told me. I've never forgotten it. The three men have guns; they have a wooden duck and a honker which they blow. They are all set up, except that the chap now says, "We're going to drown." It starts up a tension in the boat. "Christ it's deep here," says the one with the oars. He watches his blades dipping into the water, not where he's going. The angry one in the front looks down into the water and sees snags and buried trees and other muck and he shivers. "We're going to fall in," thunders the prophet of doom. He shouts it so loud and with such conviction, the one in the front stands up, cursing, and overbalances into the water, making the boat rock dangerously. This is not helped by the oarsman who leans over, trying to help the one in the drink. He won't let go of his rifle and his heavy duck-shooting clobber is dragging him down. In the confusion, something sharp pierced the floor of the boat and it started to sink. The three men drowned.'

'This is supposed to be true?' I grinned disbelievingly, because I felt it was expected of me.

'Oh,' she said, 'I don't doubt it's truth. But the way Steve told it to me I knew he had never been duck-shooting in his life.'

Fortunately I had brought my car. The bike was screwed onto the rack at the back because I intended to train later. She would be able to help. I told her I was investigating Phillips. She knew

Steve pretty well. She may have a key to their front door, and she may even know how to operate the computer.

'So you believe that he never went on hunting expeditions at all? What kind of a man is he, Julie? Is he neat and tidy? Would he, for instance, go out or go away hunting leaving the floppy disks for his p.c. all over his desk, out of their sleeves?'

'Heavens no. No way. He's the type that would keep them under lock and key, all of them ... What are you, Margot, a private eye?'

I grunted. My investigations were certainly private and I had eyes in my head. I flashed her my NCA card.

'I want to show you something. Come on.' I paid for the refreshments. She didn't even offer. That's how they make a quid, they say. In the car, she continued raving on about Steven Phillips. If the blokes were watching the house, Division or Authority, it wouldn't seem so strange—me being there with Patricia's sister, even if I do have to break in again.

I pulled off Victoria Road into a narrow side-street.

'You are in Sydney, and you haven't tried to contact Pat, or Steve. You're not close?'

I insulted her with that remark. I said it sharply. She chatters on so generously, she plays a reasonable game of tennis, she avoids meeting your eyes and she doesn't let you know anything about how she is feeling, until suddenly she is offended. 'I told you: they're on holiday.'

Why is she lying?

I stopped, boldly, outside their house. She looked at me before opening the car door, and asked, 'What do you want to show me?'

'I want you to have a look in here and tell me whether you think they left deliberately, went on holiday, as you said.' I got out and asked, did she have a key.

She shook her head, but shrugged in a she'll right way. I followed her into the tiny, crowded front garden and she hunted around under a couple of sandstone rocks and found a key in a plastic bank-book cover. 'Voila!' She smiled. We opened the front door and went straight into Steve's study.

Julie gasped. She was quite pale, trembling about the lips. Gone was the confident little money-grubbing business woman, back was the character Pat described who cried buckets at the funeral of a mother she loathed. She ran her finger through the dust on the disks and blew it off the magnetic surfaces. She picked up his portrait and croaked, 'So, it's true.'

Something struck her suddenly and she ran down the hallway to the kitchen dining area and searched around. She found a dish rag and held it up to me. There were rusty stains on it.

'He was just a bullshit artist.' She collapsed into tears.

'What is true, Julie?' She had gone silent. 'What is that on the dishrag, Julie?' No answer.

I convinced her to run the computer so that we could read the floppy disks that were scattered on his desk. Expressing contempt for his cheap computer, Julie got a print-out of the disk labelled 'Personal'.

Later, after I had driven her back to her motel and parked the car at head-quarters, I was riding towards Newtown through Redfern when I was passed by a motor-bike, the rego of which I remembered. Astride it was a big woman, with a dog on the petrol tank, sure-footed and panting with a toothy grin. I was sure it must be Roo. I clicked up a few gears and put my head down. I had never pursued a motor-bike on a push-bike before, but I was not short on technique even if I lacked power and acceleration. I had more than I thought, threading my way through the traffic on the inside, using the footpath and running red lights. I kept her in sight until she stopped. I came up beside her, breathing fast, and yelled: 'Hey, Roo! Have you seen Cath, lately?'

'Cath?' She smiled and frowned in one, clearly wondering who I was.

I smiled broadly. 'How are you, anyway? I've been on the lookout for her since I came to Sydney.' I bargained on the scanty understanding I had of Roo's character from Pat's scrapbook that she would know hundreds of women, and I could have been one she hadn't taken too much notice of wherever it was we met. 'Cath wrote to me, told me about this wonderful woman she was with—Pat?—and when I saw you sail past I thought might as well ask Roo, she knows everything.'

'She didn't give you a return address?' Roo had turned away from me and was on the footpath, checking her panniers on that side. Her bitch was leaping about, sniffing trees and returning in a neurotic but cheerful manner. I looked up at the house. In the window a small sign read: 'S O W: Beware'. 'Hey, what does "S O W" stand for?'

She stood up, her arms full of copy paper, and regarded me narrowly. 'I don't remember you,' and shook her head. 'Didn't Cath tell you about S O W? "Selfish Outrageous Women"—it's a little magazine we put out. A kind of network, noticeboard sort of thing. Anything you like: the love life of lesbian kookaburras, sexuality and law reform: you name it. The patriarchal press never takes up our concerns so we've got to get off our bums and do it ourselves. I think Cath sent us a poem for it. Hope I can find it.'

It shouldn't be hard to infiltrate this little scene. I locked up my bike and followed her inside. It was a small dark room with bright posters on the wall and paper everywhere, on three desks, each with a lamp. A ladder in the centre of the room indicated that there was some trouble with the overhead lighting. I glanced up and recognised the skinny woman on top of the ladder: a veteran of many arrests. The last time I remember seeing her was Anzac Day a few years ago when this particular sheila went kicking and scratching into the paddy wagon. I pulled my peak-cap down. Roo made loud friendly sounds and was greeted cheerily.

'I have to fly. If you've got Cath's address, I'll be away.' She was taking her time.

'Here's a copy of the poem. Envelope's gone, I'm afraid.'

'Before I go, I wouldn't be able to use the loo, would I?' I pleaded with an ingenuous grin. She told me it was out the back. I disappeared over the fence. When I went around the front for my bike, I had the padlock key ready. I knew the one on the ladder would recognise me soon, if she hadn't already.

Maybe infiltration would not be so easy. In these lesbian organisations, for every one who trusts you without question there are another three who suspect anybody they haven't known for ten years or who haven't otherwise proved their colours in the Movement.

I was just mounting when Skinny leaned out the window and yelled, 'Why don't you coppers get onto the real crooks? I had my tyres slashed last night by right-wing thugs. Why don't police take any notice of *our* complaints?' She had recognised me, but she couldn't have overheard my business with Roo.

I grinned again. 'I'm on holidays. But if you want I'll drop in on my way home and get them to take notice of your complaint. When did you file it?'

'This morning.' The accusation was loud, clear and terminally impatient.

'Okay, I'll do that. No worries.' I waved and went. I rode down through Stanmore to a dead-end near the railway line. I got the poem out of my pocket. I read it quickly and made a mental note to put a copy in Pat's scrapbook with the rest.

I rode up to Petersham Police Station, flashed the NCA badge and asked if I could check the Occurrence Pad for the day. The complaint and the address were there. I asked if it was happening a lot, that sort of National Action thuggery, like the slashing of land-rights activists' tyres. The constable replied that there was no evidence, no culprit and precious little they could do. I listened to him suggest that it was harmless fun, and the dykes deserved it. I'm an exception in the job, I'm not racist, but I'm afraid most of my colleagues are.

I leaned over the counter and whispered that I was working on a pretty delicate matter and that I needed to cultivate a gig in the dykes' household and could he please drop around there sometime and make it look like he was taking their complaint a little more seriously.

'Yes Detective Senior Constable Gorman,' he said.

The Station Sergeant came out of his office. I was pleased to see he was an old friend of mine. George and I had worked together at Redfern when I was on probation, the first woman to stay longer than six weeks at such a tough division. I was all of nineteen then.

'Margot.' He gave me a peck on the cheek. 'What brings you here?'

'How's me old mate? Your constable here will explain, won't you, son? But while I'm here, George, do you mind if I punch a name into CIIS on your computer here?'

'Be my guest. How about a drink in a while? Across the road.' He roared with laughter at his own joke: the Oxford Tavern is not exactly the kind of place you take a lady for a drink.

'Why not?'

It has taken me some effort to convince people that I am still kosher. I used to sock it away with the best of them, especially after an exciting operation. We'd play cards and drink all night. If you don't unwind, you're a basket case.

I brought up 'Larsen, Peter,' on the screen. The name was listed on the Criminal Intelligence Information files. I noted down the details.

The desk constable was telling George about the tyre-slashing report. George came over to me. 'Would it help if we drove over to this place together? I'm sure your cycle will be safe in a police station. Just run it into the kitchen.'

'Yes, yeah. Just let me photostat this.' I ran Cath's poem through the machine.

It was important for me to repair my reputation with these radical lesbians of S O W magazine. So turning up forty minutes later in a cop car and apologising for accidentally going off with the Cath poem might help. We went through all the details of the tyre-slashing again. It had happened several times in the last few months and always to cars owned by women with stickers on the windows: Aboriginal land rights, along with anti-logging, anti-nuke and 'give the girl a spanner' transfers. Though they were pleased to see the police bothering with their case, I could feel they were seeing through me, my charade, asking themselves why I claimed to be a friend of Roo's.

Retrieved the car, returned to the unit. Looked for Pat's book to put in the poem, and to browse a bit more. No scrapbook, not there, not here. Not anywhere. There must have been a thief here. Yet that is all that was taken. Why? I hadn't read everything in it, but what I remembered reading did not seem worth stealing.

The image of the face at the window at Pat's and the idea of Larsen hit me together. Were the snoop's eyes blue? They were.

18 JUNE

The quick notes I jotted down in the cop-shop about Larsen showed him to have married and been reported for domestics in Newcastle and Hurstville. Once for 'possession' of marijuana.

None of the charges had stuck. Perhaps he had been remorseful and, maybe the mitigating circumstances of the after-effects of war held in his favour. Mates in the force? The wife was noted as sixteen stone with one child and capable, probably, of giving as good as she got. Nothing about his 'supplying' grass. Earliest date in the intelligence file: May 1975; each entry ends with charges dropped. Means of support regularly noted as invalid pension. *Was* he the face at the Phillips' windows?

Julie Schempri was plainly upset at her sister's house. But not about Pat particularly nor about the ugliness of Steven's mind as revealed by his files, especially the dull, pornographic record of intimidation labelled 'C', the product of a warped mind in my opinion. Julie was more interested in a few data-bank files, which seemed to be a gambling ledger.

'So that's what he was always lying about,' she breathed out as if relieved. 'Probably that's where he went on his phony hunting trips — to casinos?'

I suggested that he was a double-agent and his 'hunting trips' could relate to that.

She laughed with scorn. 'Steve was a wimp, basically a coreless, greedy man, Margot. He wouldn't have had the guts, I'd bet on it.' She said 'was' quite definitely this time.

Whatever was deeply worrying her — and I felt certain something was — she wasn't confiding it to me.

A sleepless night before a cycle meet in the bush with other cops is not the best thing. I tossed in the bed; Owl, curled up in the crook of my knees, was continually disturbed.

The only woman competitor in this particular road-riding session, I came in seventh. I used to feel more comfortable in the company of men than women. Now, I think I was naive. Men were playing me along, or could be, like Swan ringing me at two in the morning to upset me. To find a chink in the respect I've earned. No use pretending to be feeble when you're not. Yet one of the chaps at the barbeque sneered at me. He was in that bunch I reported when I was young and green. Normally it wouldn't have troubled me; today I couldn't get it out of mind. It hurt.

Wandered around the sausage sizzle, wheeling the bike. I laughed loudly at jokes I didn't find funny: What do you call a lot of our indigenous people falling over a cliff? An abolanch. Ha ha ha.

Introduced myself to three blokes, looking handsome in skin-tight lurex shorts and luminous tops.

'Detective Senior Constable Margot Gorman, NCA.' I grinned girlishly. 'Who are you?'

'Highway Patrol. Constables. Bob, Macka, Bill.'

We talked. Bill is one of those fit young men whose face is clear and healthy, whose eyes dance with the joy of being alive. He rides his bike to work each day: from Coalcliff to Sutherland.

Like me, he doesn't eat sausages or drink beer. There was a chemistry between us. And what do you know? —we're off riding down the road together, and doing it in the bush.

Drove home, wondering whether we'd see each other regularly. We both had a box of condoms in our cars. But I'm sure he's got a girl-friend; sex is just a part of his general healthiness. He'd do it anytime anywhere with a condom and a smile. I humiliated myself on my back on the twigs with a young buck. Well, it has been ages.

Undercover detectives are dogs. That's not disparaging. Dogs don't ask questions, they serve the master. Like Samurai of the Shogun, honourable in obedience. Yet, so far as my job of guarding Patricia Phillips was concerned, I had really been left dangling. I want to go somewhere and lick my wounds, like a dog which scratches and scratches until he makes a sore and then licks and licks. Self-sorrow gets me absolutely nowhere. I always held that if you can't bear life you might as well go and help in a leper colony as commit suicide.

I sat down at the phone-table and rang around.

Sister Mary Ignatia's monthly midnight peregrinations? Clergy for Peace and the End of Oppression of Indigenous Peoples Around the World or something was the name of one of the groups. My informant told me that 'clergy' includes nuns and deaconesses and ministers of the church and priests, several rabbis and even a renegade imam. It is an extreme left-wing group dedicated to the service of those suffering under violent oppression in places like the Philippines, Mozambique, Burma, South America, everywhere. Although all members are seriously religious, the group is not pacifist. They believe that in some cases violence is justified.

Why did Sister Legs Eleven deduce the existence of a body underneath the marijuana plantation? Was she afraid no one would find it? Is it possible that this murder was so political that the identity of the body must be kept secret? Only high authority could manage that. Did manage that?

Angela Credence-Blackhouse lives in Bellevue Hill, shops in Double Bay, sounds like the Queen herself and has been my friend since my one semester at university. As my Nanna would say, 'like Madam O'Grady and the Colonel's lady we're sisters under the skin'. I rang her, found myself crying and confessing my confusion. If a man can do it like that, why can't I? Why do I feel guilty?

'Darling, you were frustrated. It happens to the healthiest of women, believe you me. You needed it.'

I heard her and imagined her face. She looks like a raven, with blue-black hair, hawk-like nose and wide gap in her front teeth. Her mind is full of fantasies. Life is one tragic romance after another.

'In fact, you're so healthy, I'm surprised you're not after it more often.' Sexual exploits are her specialty.

'I have typed them up as if they are speaking themselves,' she said.

'What are you talking about?' I had forgotten I asked her.

'The records of conversations with young lads about the Haymarket, Darling Harbour, George Street. Loved it.'

'Right.' Pat's son. 'Was any called Brendan?'

'Can't remember. Meet me at Centennial Park. Usual place at half eleven. Tomorrow. Au revoir.'

Sometimes I think she only likes me because I am some contact with a side of life which she sees from her safe distance as terribly exciting. She, I might add, never looks for or at the probable which is likely to be staring her in the eye. Far too boring, darling.

19 JUNE

Yesterday's love-making beneath the gum trees put me off riding my bicycle, as was our custom: she in jodhpurs and helmet on her horse, me as perfectly dressed for cycling. Chatting as if by accident, we meet casually where so many like us are doing their exercises. She loved pursuing this charade with a real undercover cop; it was always a game for her.

So much so that she has turned up with huge sunglasses and a white chiffon scarf tied under her chin Princess-Anne style, trying to appear as neurotic as Audrey Hepburn in some sixties thriller. While I was glad that I was not completely alone in the world with my worries, puffy eyes and headache, I didn't want to assist in yet another of her frivolous movies. But.

I encountered her on the bridle path.

'Is that,' she leaned down over the wither of her steed and whispered, 'the pond where they fished out poor Sally Ann?'

I shrugged. 'I don't know, Angela.'

'Where's your bike?' she demanded imperiously and began to trot off.

'I don't have it,' I yelled. She turned and began practising some moves with the animal. It looked like a live rocking-horse, especially its colour which is deep dappled grey. I watched her bring it back at a canter slower than its walk; it must be pretty hard to make a horse do such an unnatural action. She finally pulled up beside me, out of breath, patting the sweat on its neck.

'Very nice,' I commented, playing a movie role. 'The goods?'

'Nothing much really, darling.' Her tone of intrigue impressed me. 'In England one woman charged a group of women with assault.'

'What?' I vaguely remembered asking her, when I was guarding Pat, what she thought about lesbians and violence. I didn't mean for her to do an assignment on it.

'But that was after she had tied one of their friends up and whipped her. They were paying her back.'

I patted the nag's soft nose.

'I didn't ask you to do it, Angela.' I must have sounded sharp or weary, not my usual patient self, a cynic with a heart of gold.

'I know, darling.' She gathered up the reins and threw me a manila envelope. 'A woman charged another with assault in Balmain recently, but the police didn't follow it through.

But, to the job in hand. Wait till you listen to my boys. The twenty-first century is here, complete with the moron-glytrons.' She tapped her temple and squeezed her heels into her horse's belly.

'Bye.'

'Bye.' Off she rode towards the showgrounds, where her horse is stabled. What a life!

Old women walking in track-suits with jogging shoes, poofters with Afghan hounds, teenagers on hired yellow push-bikes, and families in pedal-cars, lanky polo-horses thrusting their necks out with long-legged men pulling their bits, retriever dogs swimming good-humouredly after ducks, the soil still soggy and the grasses too sodden to be mowed, young Kiwi nannies with precocious upper-class toddlers, serious cyclists and determined picnickers were all there, though not as many as on the weekend. The Park seemed open and empty. I wandered about, thinking about the patrolman and sex.

One of the blokes I once worked with said, all women must be masochistic, otherwise he couldn't understand why the world was the way it was. It was after we'd attended a domestic and the woman, recently punched about the midriff, obvious from the way she stood, made us go away. The complaint had come from the kid, or one of the kids. She spent three-quarters of an hour at her door shivering in the draught, telling us that her husband was asleep and she couldn't understand how we had got there, suggesting that it must be the house next door. All sorts of crap. Another chap would have let it go. But this bloke wouldn't; we cruised around all the phone boxes in the area looking for the kid who'd rung, up and down laneways, checking in clothing bins to see if he was hiding from his father there. Then we got drunk after work, discussing the way of the world, and unwinding.

Now my way of unwinding was sweat, and more sweat. I turned into Wilson Street from Erskineville Road, heading for the Police Academy in Redfern. I wanted to punch the bag so hard my knuckles would bleed. I wanted to tear the muscles in my legs and arms with weights too heavy for me. I wanted to wipe myself out. Maybe I am masochistic.

When I got there I was too weary. Brain work makes me physically tired. I just went down to the armoury and asked Jock if I could shoot along with the lesson he was giving. Shooting is steadying. Like playing chess.

When I got home I decided to ring my boss. Too many things had happened; he would have to know. I would have to tell him that I'm not one of the boys, his joke did not amuse me. That if Patricia Phillips was alive and well, I would have to see her face to face, otherwise I would continue my private investigations.

All I said was, 'Can we meet, Swan? Please?'

He said, 'Lunch tomorrow, Margot, at the Friendliest Club in Town.'

His quick acquiescence surprised me.

20 JUNE

Swan is fatherly to me, stern and just; a captain, who can be counted on when the going's tough to play a captain's innings. He is a master and I am an apprentice. I convince myself that the man must have compassion. I have to put myself at his mercy and throw my cards on the table. I have no alternative.

My real father rang. They are back from their trip. They loved it. Hoping to see me in Wollongong soon. Yes, Dad, if I can get the time off.

'You're on holidays, aren't you?'

Well, I hadn't mentioned it to any of my family. I haven't had contact for a month. They've been away. Dad is going deaf. Selective about what he hears, he did not answer me when I asked how he knew. Just said, 'Your mother and I are looking forward to seeing you, sweetheart. In a few days then? You can be bored by our slides.'

'Yes, Dad, 'bye Dad.'

Now, to make some notes:

Dead body in park. Bite-marks on fingers, sliced throat. Deep grave, improvised shroud. My guess: the body is Steve Phillips. I guess Patricia bit him. Bites do not a murder make. A scar on my own little finger tells me: angry women bite, and it hurts. But biters aren't murderers. Nor are they always women.

However, if Pat did kill him, how did she get him to Wiley Park, dig a proper grave, wrap him up and get home again and never mention it in her mad ravings? (Or was there some clue in the stolen scrapbook that I missed?) Was her madness a cover-up and she a clever member of an international drug ring? This would account for why I was put on the case in the first place.

Maybe the body is not Steve.

Whoever did it, why did they draw such blatant attention to it?

The nun says, 'Let the marijuana work for you not against you, Margot.' What does she know?

She is not a pacifist nun. She is a passionate idealist. She condones political murder. However, neither she nor any of her organisation would have cause to kill Steven Phillips; unless his espionage exploits led him to support right-wing terrorists somewhere else in the world.

Maybe the body is not Steve, but its identity is so politically important that it's not released.

Yes, Sister, the marijuana works for me. It points its serrated finger at Peter Larsen. Perfect soldier, kills quickly, quietly, thrusts a blade through the wind-pipe into the brain and turns it. His motive is jealousy.

Okay: why did he draw attention to his crime? And, if he was so jealous, why wait so long? Why didn't he do it in the late seventies?

Steven Phillips, alleged deceased, tried to rape a radical lesbian. Are women as capable of violence? I was bashed up by a group of girls. R A G may be into vigilante martial arts to pay back unreported rapists. Man-haters: why bash me? Dangerous assaulting a cop. Did they know I was a cop? Why, anyway?

Did Barry and Susan have anything to do with my being bashed?

Were the women in the pay of some international or political network that had something against me because of my work with the NCA: this job, or last job?

Or was the attack personal, on me, Margot Gorman? Who are my female enemies? (Forget it, kid.)

Pat? I, who know nothing, do I know too much?

Dead Caucasian male may be a dirty Yankee agent who was also into international drugs while posing as a draft-dodger; seen as responsible for the loss of lives of a couple of Australian soldiers. A wild Viet vet who lives in the bush cultivating marijuana behind booby traps finally uncovers his identity and offs him. Avenges the death of mates. Very much on the cards if the dead person is a traitor and the vet a crazy.

Young son may also have a reason to kill, even if it is psychopathic. Life-long hate of step-father? (Fat chance, Margot.)

I'm assuming that the body in the park was as Max described, male and white. Is Max a reliable informant? Maybe he passed on rumour. Rumour could be deliberate misinformation. Body could be female. (Not likely ... ?)

Steven Phillips, 'the Phantom'. Maybe the ghost walks. Jealous of his wife, he makes her disappear from the hospital, and he attracts no attention whatsoever.

Is she alive? Is she dead?

There does not seem to have been much domestic violence in the marriage of Patricia and Steven Phillips.

Questions:

— who in truth is the mystery body in the park?

— why was there a hush-up concerning all details in relation to it? Furthermore, how?

— why did Sister Mary Ignatia call Homicide?

—where is Patricia Gaye Phillips née Vickery?—
was she suicidal? was she mad?

—who took her scrapbook from my place?

—what is Julie Schempri née Vickery hiding?—
where is Cath, the lesbian lover?

—is there a creepy boy out there?

—is there a boy who would kill a man in the manner of a
Vietnam scout which he had seen in a video movie?

—who rang with threats to my person and called me a pawn?

—was the man I saw through the window Peter Larsen, a bent
cop, a drug mate of Barry and Susan or of Steven Phillips, an
operative of the NCA or a dog from CIB?

—did the marijuana plants have anything to do with the
body? (Maybe the nun was wrong.)

—why did Detective Inspector Lake give me the job of
putting on a nursing-aide's uniform to watch a madwoman?

—and, finally, why did he warn me about Detective Inspector
Harold 'the Heat' Clarke?

Detective Inspector Lake, you can't put a good dog on a scent
and not expect results. And if all this has something to do with
the corruption in either or both the New South Wales Police
Force and or the National Crime Authority, both boys' clubs
which think they are above the law, then I reckon I might start
up in private practice: Margot Gorman, Gumshoe.

SAME DAY

The luncheon hours at the Catholic Club, 'the friendliest club in
town', as proclaimed by its coasters, remind me of the old Coles
cafeteria—minus the children. The grandmothers are there
gobbling up the cottage pies made from yesterday's roasts, or
hoeing into today's roast of the day. There is always a gambling
priest or a priest with an Irish accent accepting drinks from
somebody's parishioners with alacrity and easy blessings.

Catholics come in all shapes and sizes and walks of life and there's something mildly dowdy about all of them. A businessman playing the poker machines has a group of followers around him trying to catch morsels of stock-exchange gossip. He is as jolly as the priest. It is only the sycophants around him who betray his power, and with that power, his ruthlessness. Of course, there's some of our people, plain-clothes men making deals over the tables behind the ten-cent machines on the other side of the bar. The inevitable poofy barman, living up to the Club's claim, is as friendly as ever, as are the ladies who pay out jackpots and guard the door as if they were manning stalls at the annual church fête. There is a homely atmosphere at the Catholic Club.

On my way, after dropping by my bank, I backed so quickly, so furiously, so nervously (for me) out of a parking spot I nearly staked a lad on my mack-rack. He was wearing a long grey greatcoat with insignia of pop groups AC/DC and Kiss, so like Nazi SS badges and iron crosses. I've been a bit hysterical this morning, half laughing, half crying over my notes.

The walls of the Club are decorated with square canvas banners all depicting the same circular mess as if a tin of blue paint were spilt on a spinning surface then red drips fell on it. As I stare at them I discern that although they are not all the same way up they are all exactly the same mess.

I had noticed as I walked past the Timezone in Pitt Street gangs of boys there who seemed so bored, so latently aggressive. Pointless thrill-killing could happen as easily here as it did in New York a few months ago, when a bunch of boys raped and killed a girl in Central Park for no reason other than fun.

My boss had not said a time, it's true, but I did not expect him to keep me waiting so long. I have my big accommodating bag with me, as I always do when I drive. As well as the novel I'm never without, it contains my official-duties diary, my pistol, my notebook. I am writing in this like a student in the refectory catching up on an essay. Cup of tea in front of me. Strung out, waiting, I decide to break my pledge and have a bloody mary. Once I start I'll keep going. No one else will mind.

At the bar I see another long grey coat. This is soft, worn gabardine, a man's coat on a young woman. She is buying money for the poker machines. She has dark hair, brown eyes, fine features. She smiles at the barman but the droopy grey coat seems to express depression. She is wearing it like some people carry chips on their shoulders; childhood patterns of behaviour trying to fit into the adult world. I guess quite out of the blue that this is Cath. I laugh at the irrationality of my knowing. Hunch.

I could heavy her if she goes to the toilet, or whip her handbag away. It is a black leather shoulder-bag which she leaves at the machine when she goes to the bar. She knows after a while I am watching her. She stares back at me with an enquiring frown as if she could know me, giving me the benefit of the doubt.

'Hi Cath,' I say, casually, holding my pen as if to continue writing any second.

'Hi,' she says. My heart is pumping at such a rate I wonder what my problem is. Maybe she knows who I am. Her face was asking: How do you know my name? I feel followed. I look over my shoulder and back again. She is already engrossed in losing money.

A tall thin man with thick black hair enters. Could it be Steve Phillips? He's with another, a shorter man, a bit older, jolly, Italian possibly. Surely it couldn't be him Cath is going over to meet? Something intense is happening between them. Of course it's not Phillips—my mind is swimming. I had no more than two hours sleep last night.

I notice a group of old ladies around a single ten-cent machine. I think it's the legs I recognise—no stockings, brown, in cheap vinyl men's shoes, the sort with tiny zippers instead of laces. Legs Eleven. Sister Mary Ignatia, with, I suppose, other sisters, who have come to the Catholic Club for lunch after business in the city and are now having a little flutter before they leave. One of them knows nothing about it and exclaims with wonder each time they get a two-coin drop. The one in the middle is determined to win. She has the look of a person to whom money means just about everything. On the far side, Sister Mary herself calmly presses three-coin multiple play, to get her go over quickly perhaps. She sees me. Her look is shrewd. She neither smiles nor waves.

There is a commotion at the door. I can't believe my eyes. A man in a wheelchair being manoeuvred by another: it's that slime, Paul Murphy, wheeled by the man of the face at the window. So this is Peter Larsen? Both are merry. I am further surprised when I turn around and see that the little Italian chap and the girl in the long grey coat are sitting together organising some deal. My eyes must be playing tricks on me, but now I see the tall man behind a few people with some woman who resembles bloody Julie Schempri. Same type, same height, same style of yak yak yak about her, but back view, and it really couldn't be. Could it?

Finally Swan comes. I see him at the door. He doesn't see me right away. He has friends all over the place and he is accosted by one. He nods in the direction of the plain-clothes men I noticed earlier. They glance towards the girl in the grey coat, who is saying awkward goodbyes to the older man. Then Swan greets Larsen in the manner of combat mates, big hug, lasting that little longer for the memories to come back, even a kiss.

Swan is an extremely nice fellow. He listens, he nods, he slaps the little bloke's arm and moves towards me.

I wonder if I'll tell Swan all the things that are going through my mind.

'I'll be with you in a minute, Margot. What are you drinking?'

'Hello to you too. Bloody mary, thanks.' He is served straight away at the bar, and my vodka and tomato juice this time has a slice of lemon on its rim and gaudy straw. My boss gestures with the worcestershire sauce bottle. I might as well, I nod.

When he eventually sits down opposite me, he has one eye on his watch and I am about to burst into tears. I never would, of course. One of the pre-requisites of the job: don't burst into tears. His shoulder I want, to lean into and tell him all my troubles. But I am official and shy, my not being at all sure how he will take my enquiries.

'By the way, the husband of the madwoman—remember?—is doing his darndest to be a first-class shit, but we've got him running scared. He's scared all right, and running short of cash.'

'Whereabouts?' I don't believe Swan, and show it on my face.

'Cairns. He keeps hiring cars in false names. Another?' He holds up his glass.

What does he think I am, a moron?

'Swan. What's the NCA got to do with a bloke suspected of espionage? And ...' He cut me off with words I had heard before. I keep telling myself I am being spun a line. Even more bothersome is my eyesight; it is becoming decidedly foggy. I could still see Larsen, getting drunk near the bar, making jokes, and the nuns ... it struck me as bizarre indeed that all of them were here, like some curtain-call. But what about her—Pat? All had something to do with the track I was on, and Detective Inspector Lake was not telling me the truth. I sighed loudly.

'Okay Margot, okay. He *is* the mysteriously wrapped and buried corpse in Wiley Park.' He wrapped thick, ugly fingers around the schooner glass and gulped. 'Another b.m.?'

'Yes, I will.'

I waited for him, feeling sick and stoned, the lunchtime scene of the Catholic Club swimming before me. But I concentrated enough vision to watch two detectives walk up to Swan at the bar.

He returned with my drink, smiling. 'We've made an arrest, Margot.'

'Who did him in?' I lisped groggily, flopping my elbows onto the table. 'And, tell me, where is Pat?'

'For your bashing, Detective Constable, we have someone in custody ...'

I put my head on the table.

'We're opposing bail, naturally ...'

The next thing I recall is waking up in the Church of Scientology at about five in the afternoon. I staggered out of that building to see that the vacant lot between the Catholic Club and Church had a building at the back which in effect joined the two at first-floor level. I know I was not dragged out through the front entrance of the Catholic Club in Park Street, so I must have been passed in a drugged state from window to window. When I came out onto Elizabeth Street, my sister, the radiologist, turned up in the traffic, plucked me off the footpath and took me home to be doctored by her husband. The neighbour would look after Owl while I spent a couple of days down with the folks. It was all organised by my family. That's why Dad was so sure of seeing me.

VIII

CATHERINE BELGRANO
Monologue of a Victim

the walls are awful and i'm glad i've got my coat. here i am in
the lockup. Caterina Belgrano was my name: a recently
beheaded chook. waiting to be eaten. eucharist. drink my blood.
eat my flesh. i'm yours, boys. Christ, i'm cold.

perhaps i'll write poetry all night. i don't feel sleepy and the
light is always on. they let me keep my black leather bag, but
took my nail-clippers and swiss army knife and money out of it,
all for my own protection. they charged me with assault and told
me not to say anything until i got a solicitor. okay.

i recognised my alleged victim at the Catholic Club because
she was the cop who was spying on our rape meeting. some were
talking that night about rapes that happened many years before.
rapes that had been buried in their minds for so long yet
somehow surfacing in the consciousness, the memory. there's
nothing good about rape for any woman: no woman can ever ask
for it. ever get over it. some of the older women had blanked
incest rape out of their memory for forty-odd years, and one day,
they woke up and remembered. even after all that time, it felt
better to talk about it. forgetting's just wall-papering over the
cracks.

i did not feel alone in that company and i didn't talk much.
i watched and listened and sympathised. agonised vicariously
too, disturbed by those who were raped by their fathers.
i frowned and would have cried. must have looked sooky

because a big black woman came along and hugged and comforted me. she enclosed my face in her big tits and rocked me. it was kind of professional of her, but i liked it.

i was at the Catholic Club because my father rang me. i couldn't believe it. but there you are. i went early so that i could gamble and drink a few beers and get myself into a relaxed frame of mind for whatever onslaught was about to happen. i felt good. there was a Viet vet there who looked like Lloyd Bridges, who was plying his crippled mate with grog and good cheer and making the bar-men laugh. a clown with the edge of real sadness in his humour, as if he had been to the bedrock which says, well, you've got to laugh. standing at the poker machines i was smirking at his gags. everything for this man seemed fodder for jokes. and everyone—glad he doesn't know me: he's the sort who'd put a carpet-snake in your bed.

i'm a gambler like my dad.

Belgrano, Spanish-Italian. my father's family has been in Australia since the gold rushes of the eighteen sixties. my mother, Irish-English-Scottish, prefers cleanliness to fashion. spic and span in pointy collars passing the test of time, she is sharp. my eyes are dark and my hair is brown; my wrists are thin and my fingers long. my skin is sallow because the sun has gone away, probably for good.

it has been raining for months, possibly years, in Sydney and i feel the coat, the clouds and i are one colour. grey. i feel the coat, my favourite, so soft, smooth with age, roomy. my shoulders are a coat-hanger.

i am terribly sorry for myself.

they said i looked like Evonne on the court six years ago. i was a champion tennis-player in the junior ranks. i started on the circuit at fifteen years old, my father pushing and pulling and there all the time. then i fell in love with a woman, an older player, who did seduce me. i adored her. she was magnificent and for a few months we were an item, hiding from my father.

then as quickly as she picked me she dropped me. she found another lover, or went back to a previous one. she is very fickle. she still wins her matches so she only thinks about herself. it's what you have to do, i found out. be highly motivated. i wasn't. i thought about her and about my dad, who was egging me on to success, and i couldn't watch the ball.

then the humiliation. i was out on the court, playing in a tournament and my form had been bad for three weeks or so, ever since she cut me dead. but Dad said i had the character to forget that and concentrate on my game. the more i tried to force myself the worse i played. every forehand went high, every volley into the net, my serves were wild and i threw myself so furiously about the court i fell over a lot. it was humiliating to my father and all my mates on the circuit said, you don't have it, kid. you're not a killer.

my father left my mother soon after i started losing. i wear my failure like a coat, i wrap it round the real me; you'd think it is who i am. i feel like the bod from the New Testament who couldn't multiply the talents while others could. i betrayed a god-given gift; well, that's how my father finally put it. he considered himself a religious man and he reckoned God wouldn't be too pleased about his generosity being scorned. i can't argue with that; i don't play tennis any more.

shrouded by coat and weather i go out to gamble. i am terrified of the phone ringing or going to the letter-box for my mail. he will turn up on the phone or in the letter-box. i am awaiting the blow. metaphorically. i don't have the strength not to know what is in an envelope. truthfully, i can say i never left a phone unanswered, an envelope unopened. my soul is the soul of a no-hoper. i think it's getting dark outside. i don't even have my watch. the snow-droppers will be out tonight and there won't even be any washing left on my line ...

time is punctuated by food. they brought me a hamburger in a take-away container. i'm alone in the cell and there is no window,

but i can feel the darkness outside. the night ahead of me seems
eternal and the coffee is wishy-washy and sweet. assault and
battery on a cop does not exactly get you sympathy in the clink.
i saw the lady cop in the club before they picked me up. she
frowned at me and said, 'hi Cath?'. she was afraid of me and her
voice asked a question. what is frightening about me? i am
totally powerless.

    i don't feel tired.

    he had no idea of the creativity in the giggling of girls
    arranging the posy with laughter
    and hardiness and sprigs of maiden hair
    we made a flower arrangement for Nemesis
    matching the other i was raped
    through the sympathetic nervous system
    my mind must know as much as my body
    for me to be his equal was his abnegation
    and that is not on
    he had to prove his power and defile me
    the pornographic and doctrinal minds
    are both based on the duality:
    women, nature, filth;
    men, god, immortality, cleanliness;
    causing a repression of a part of males
    of which they're then afraid
    so they must control or lose control
    rampage, rape, make war
    i know it is not churning in his guts
    there is no blade growing in no womb
    no knife turning in the stomach
    i retch bile-flavoured air in mornings
    cloudy and silent except for bird-sounds

    i wear my old grey coat with love. i read my rape poem at the
RAG meeting and they nearly all agreed that it was the mental

anguish that was worst, even those who were physically hurt badly.

it follows. i'm in gaol, he is free.

in meditation you are told to listen to the outside sounds, one by one, and only gradually come to hearing the breath in your own nostrils. that's what i try to do, hear nothing but the breath in my nostrils. but i hear the sound of my grinding teeth, i hear a drunk woman swearing, i hear the traffic in Oxford Street.

my mother gave me an obsession and i thank her for it. i am obsessive about housework. sweeping, dusting, making windows glisten to nothingness are joys. i favour the straw broom over the vacuum cleaner because of noise. machines are like torturers, they want your mind. brooms are lovely, like sporting equipment. i know my shower recess has no grime, no 'grout-plaque'. i am not alone, though, in my obsession about cleanness, enjoying the therapeutic and satisfyingly physical effects of housework. others have the same thing—some said it happened after their rape. they became guilty about specks of dirt.

people will get guilty over anything. at really radical places and meetings among women you are not allowed to say 'people'; it assumes we are men. the words 'person', 'human being', 'mankind' etc. disguise the inequalities within the species. silence is the ideological tongue for women if you want to be logical, i guess.

i just read a couple of Borges' poems. this night is going to be long.

in the morning, perhaps, i will ring Aunt Jane. my mother's sister is a nun. she's the one to ring.

there was a church with a very high ceiling in Lakemba. i used to be taken to it as a small child. way up high hung Christ on his cross. this Christ was grossly hairy on his shoulders, on the bridge of his nose, on the folds of his loose loin-cloth, on his knee-caps, on the top of his feet and over the protruding nails.

i was frightened of this monster. i thought he was a werewolf someone had tried to pin down while he was in the process of changing. i had a total freak-out at midnight mass. there was a fairly bright moon. i stacked on a turn, and it was supposed to be a special outing for me, symbolic of my getting to be a big girl. i screamed in absolute panic. Aunt Jane proved to me that what i thought was hair was only dust and nobody could get up there and clean him. so God was not only made of plaster but filthy. Aunt Jane appreciated my logic. and has liked me ever since, even though i don't believe.

love is a shithouse thing. look at Syd and Nancy. the other members of the Sex Pistols didn't end up like that; Syd did because he and Nancy were an item. Yoko is blamed for ruining the Beatles. no one doubts that love is good. for a while i tried to convince myself that the heavens in their infinite mercy and mysterious ways contrived to have me fail on the tennis court to strengthen my character. i apologised to my mother often for making Dad go away by my failure, but every time she'd shake her head and say, 'don't be silly, it wasn't your fault. i'm glad he has gone.' she probably liked the fact that we were away so much. a tennis-circuit widow. i lived with my mum for three years and then left.

i had known what it was to love and make love to a woman and i wanted, in fact, needed, that more than anything. so i left. Mum was probably glad i was gone too. i confessed my lesbianism to her one night with tears rolling down my face. she was not surprised. 'there's always a bed here, you know that,' she said.

the complete opposite to her husband, she expects nothing. she left me to myself and my world, and i will never find out what she thinks. perhaps she is just a selfish woman. better selfish than suffering. she has the second half of her life to do what she wants with and i don't expect anything from her either. her careful indifference is unchanged but it is not carelessness. she fulfils her obligations as a mother and lives her life. she's cool, i'm cool in respect to her. i reckon too much is put on mothers, anyway. she's just another person, and in a comfortable way i love her.

Kate Belgrano played in Paris, New York, London, all the exotic places. i became Cath after i gave up tennis. tennis stole my adolescence in a number of ways. but that's all boring.

as Kate i could have been a millionaire. now i want money won to comfort me. what little i have i throw down the machines. and i'll end up a wise old crone.

i miss my bed, my little weatherboard house, my neighbours. the boy in the boarding house a few doors up fixed my record player the other day. we were both in the street watching a rabbit hiding under a car. a brown and white household pet, the bunny came when it was called, quivering its nose and flopping its long ears. the boy fell in love with it. he asked me could i look after it until he built a cage and i nodded and told him where i lived and he could come and get it whenever. he came back in two hours. before he left he fixed my hi-fi. mysteriously to me, the radio in it just couldn't hold itself on a station. magic — his fingers fiddled and it was fixed. i hardly ever see him, but when we do see each other, we nod and act like neighbours, friendly but distant. we're both so moody; it depends on the day whether or not the other gets a smile.

Pat never answered my letters, poems and philosophisings. didn't matter, i sent them anyway. i couldn't see her. it would have been too much. i was too scared of him. it was a couple of months before i could even write the letter describing the rape. it took me days to compose that letter, and days more to send it. i could hardly move out of the house. even there i wasn't safe from the telephone and the mail-box. the only safe place was a club, a games parlour of slot-machines, where everyone is about the same business regardless of creed, class, colour, ethnicity or literacy. numeracy is universal.

they, a couple of ships, disappear over the back horizon of my life, assuming i'm facing a future. one is a dark horror vessel with the devil on board, the other golden with sirens singing, laughing and dancing on the taffrails as she recedes into the sunset. it's safer for me to be sorry for myself than to follow sirens or tussle with the devil and i am not alone at all, no no not at all, at all, i have my images, my imagery ... my washing hangs motionless in the night. i hope it dries while i'm inside. 'inside', they call it. i guess it'll rain again.

coming to terms with myself, not really trying to throw off the dismal coat of failure that's hung on my shoulders through this year of sogginess; all i manage to grapple with are images, imagery ... it happened to me. he tried to rape me. in the summer, such a long time ago. he did not succeed in coming, or properly getting inside me. i did not go to the police because i couldn't even tell Roo, at first.

my friends tried to say the right things and i'm glad they have a crisis group for me to attend, even though i hardly say anything.

i've been accused of beating up a lady cop. well i didn't do it, but i think i know who did. someone has to take the rap, might as well be hardy little martyr me. i can't believe this is happening to me, but then lately i've been so inured with thoughts of unfairness, it just very well could.

am i too fond of failure? the night is about to suck me into its black hole. my pencil is the staff, the stick, i have to ward off tormenting thoughts.

Pat called me Artemis, fawn of the forest, athlete without games, lithe huntress. she could call me beautiful things, and i was all those things.

in the midst of my love for her, she disgusted me, and that is exactly how he wanted it. the disgust was to do with my imagination being unable to cope with her sleeping with him all those years. her loving him, even. what he has done since the rape has been a clever torture, attacking our love, describing our love-making in the vilest way, giving me her supposed secrets, saying things men are interested in and i am not. yet i had to read, i had to listen to him. i think i was looking all the time for an apology, a recognition of the damage he had done. he would start so reasonably, stretching out the hand of friendship and in it slime. i showed my group his letters and they groaned. but i didn't feel they knew it was a psychic attack. i wanted to give him the benefit of the slightest doubt so that i could go back to Pat, talk it out with Pat. Patty darling, your lithe huntress has been cheated out of her speed, her grace. there's a dark cloud over the moon and all the world's in gloom. because he disgusted me, he determined, so shall she. he must be a part of everything that is or was hers.

i was in a cleft stick. no good going to lawyers. my only line was letters to Pat, explaining and trying to figure out what he said or wrote.

like: 'what silliness not to join the free-living, free-loving society, of the truly liberated! you believe in liberation, don't you? what do you suppose freedom is made of? like the rest of your generation you probably only think of yourself, having a good time and making pots on the stock market. your generation, who drive pink, chop-top v-dubs, want a return to the nineteen fifties, which my generation re-evaluated and found wanting. you have no comprehension of freedom, the give-and-take mechanics of freedom, the commerce of care!'

he had no comprehension of freedom, my freedom. it made me shake all over as i walked from the letter-box to the toilet. where i sat shitting. my arguments came full and strong, but i couldn't say them to anyone. what did he want?

then the throwing up started. every morning, anxiety stirred the juices in my soft organs and they churned and turned, leaving me wrung out like a smelly dish-rag. i showed two letters i had from him to Roo and friends at SOW and they laughed at how pathetic men are. said this one was a real jerk. seeing my distress, they put me onto RAG.

he rang. i exploded, unleashing a string of swearwords, chiefly meaning that he was a dickhead. he responded coolly saying, 'calling me names, ranting impassioned invective neither moves nor convinces me.' his coolness was — i don't know—stupid: so what?

they have invented God to pretend that there is a man with a higher mind beyond the stars who deals out life-everlasting rewards: *in my father's house there are many mansions* ...

i said this to my aunt one night when we argued about the existence of God.

'it's obvious that it's pretence,' i declared.

she was eager to discuss theology. the First Person of the Blessed Trinity, the Father, receives her prayers of adoration, for His world is complex, brilliant and beautiful. prayers to the Father, she says with a twinkle in her eye, consist of lists of the wonderful things about the place, followed by gratitude that she has the wherewithal to appreciate so much. He, so far as He is a harsh judge, and mean and nasty as to the locations of famines, droughts, plagues, earthquakes, cyclones and floods, is also very frightening. thus she must admonish herself for her dreadful pride in trying to understand the Almighty. the Son is the compassionate One. she demolished my theories about God being useful only to men. He is, apparently, useful to her. but i don't buy it.

when, a couple of months ago, Aunt Jane sat by the bedside of a young man dying of AIDS, she prayed to Jesus, for He loved men. the Son of God and of woman, Jesus is aware of human frailty. her prayers were also addressed to His mother, for intercession. the intercession she sought for the suffering sinner was peace of mind, courage as he approached the unknown, and finally trust, that the next world would be Heaven. she wished for him to have the intensity of experience she had when she knelt and worshipped. she says she pleaded fervently as she was trying to brush from her mind impertinent questioning of the Divine Will.

she discovered the marijuana in the park and figured it hid a mysterious body. when she heard it was shrouded and dug in deep, she said, 'perhaps it was a mercy killing.'

if my father couldn't explain something, his god could. here i was with a talent, therefore i must sublimate everything to pursue this gift. my personality had nothing to do with it. when you look at it, it was all for him. by being a money-spinning girl, i could almost fill the place where a boy should have been. being a failure, and a failure as a woman as well, in that i didn't want to be a girlfriend with a boyfriend, made me an excellent scapegoat.

if Dad had pretended when he left my mother that it was only her he was leaving, that even though i lacked the killer instinct, he still loved me, if he'd tried to show me that in some way, i don't reckon i'd be in quite the mess i am at the moment. but he didn't. he resented me, because i robbed him of a job too.

i am kept awake by how bloody miserable i am. what else to write? it must be near midnight.

two women live in a big house in Stanmore Road. they always welcome me because i framed a few pictures for them, at cost. my trade, a picture-framer, is all right if you don't work too hard, become clumsy or get RSI. these pictures were the weirdest drawings you can imagine, probably valuable erotica of the future, but i could see why they didn't want to take them to a shop-front. so i go there and get tea and sympathy, beer, dope, whatever. they're sweet to me and roughly twenty years older. i got them talking about the generation gap, how they felt about us, those in their twenties, and they, disturbingly, expressed opinions not unlike Steve's. the student revolts of 1968 were the beginning of everything that was good: idealism, dope and liberation.

Micki, the one whose mother owns the house and lives in the back, is a big diesel dyke in leathers most of the time; when she is not, she wears a brocade smoking jacket. Em, her girlfriend, has one of those pinched faces that ages really quickly; she is a secretary. a regular Gertrude and Alice outfit. the sleek black cat is called Nancy, and the dog with his butch studded collar is Syd. they greeted the story of the rape that i finally told them with a kind of muted sympathy. 'poor little kid,' said Em, and gave me a hug.

now in the cold police lock-up, i can't believe i'm still shivering here with my wits about me. light from the passage comes through the bars and i hear scraps of conversation from the night shift. even games of chance are ruled by probability. life seems improbable. games of skill are logical. life is not a game of skill, therefore.

i read i dozed i read again and having read must write:

in all the world one man has been born, one man has died./to insist otherwise is nothing more than statistics, an impossible extension.

to insist otherwise is nothing more than statistics:
a man dies
a man is born
there is nothing more,
he says. Borges says.
but i am here, blind prophet of the Andes,
here i am—a statistic,
who is never born, never dies
so importantly; woman
is in endless supply—a natural resource:
i speak of the unique, single man, he who is always alone.
my tears are for the uniqueness of the single woman
who is always accompanied,
having to provide and provide
so that *del uno, del unico,* might have his pride,
make his poesy or stand
astride the gaping hole—the mined mine—
the open cut into the body of the earth—
proud of his exploitation, his greed,
his violence, his violation.
one man alone has looked on the enormity of dawn.
if only a woman could stand on a rock
and say i alone have seen the dawn
without someone calling on her time,

seeing her naked beneath her clothes,
demanding to be her son—
an ugly cuckoo chick weighing down the nest
of the tiny hummingbird, devouring
and tasting nothing—she would be free
to meditate on the nature of her soul,
physics and metaphysics with a mind cleansed
of the violation, intimidation, misunderstanding.
she has digested the reality
that she is an impossible extension,
no more than a statistic,
so her mind cannot be alone,
a nest with eggs of her own kind,
shell-delicate, exquisite.
a fat, ugly cuckoo sits in there
pretending to be her son.

i bought myself a flick-knife at an army disposals store. there,
the boy from up the street was buying himself a pair of Doc
Martens lace-up work-boots. i sat down beside him and tried
some on myself. this seemed as close as i could get to any male:
a neighbour buying the same shoes on a wintery day exchanging
hints as to how to grease the new leather with dripping, both in
long grey coats, lonely and closed up in our individual selves.
bye, we said, and i walked off in the opposite direction.

i bought myself a flick-knife because, after all the letters and
phone calls, Steve might come around one day in the flesh, and
having failed in his rape attempt, try to hurt me physically. you
have to be brave just to handle a flick-knife; takes practice. i am
the huntress, the sportswoman, proficiency with this knife was
not hard for me. i could fight him off, now.

'killing is lovely,' said Aunt Jane. she came to the rape action
group meeting with me more out of curiosity than moral
support, 'who doesn't,' she asked, 'bend their back further and
work more furiously rooting out weeds than sowing seeds or

picking flowers?' the women went silent, thought about it. 'who doesn't love to squash snails with vicious delight when they see the holes in the vegetable leaves made by the soft, greedy things? of course we Christians allow ourselves this pleasure. the Buddhists don't.' always provocative and cheeky for an old woman, Sister Mary Ignatia, but i thought i'd prefer to be a Buddhist than a Christian, even an extraordinary Christian like my aunt.

no killer instinct. here in this hollow, echoing cell with lines of shade across the floor from the bars interfering with the corridor light, i am laughing hysterically. that was my big problem, no killer instinct on the tennis court.

how much further can you get towards the ends of your own earth than here? grey coat, grey blanket, grey walls, thrice grey, my surrounds, and here i huddle, hands in deep pockets, too bloody sensitive to throw my body in the path of the gunships heading for the citadel, not courageous, too frightened to shut my eyes even, for jails aren't safe places and i'm not capable, without a knife, of throwing an attacker on her face and knocking her skull on the bitumen of the pavement in the space of a second. which is what i'm supposed to have done.

sleep, sweet sleep; dreamt of still lakes and snowy mountains, hot fires and gluhwein. the first woman that i loved was there on the slopes in her tennis gear, serving tea to people on a table with a red gingham cloth.

dawn dawn grey dawn ...

i fell in love and she gave me crystal glasses, one of which broke recently and i slashed at my wrists with the shards. perhaps my privilege as a child makes me dramatic.

my father is all men to me. he loved me beyond the call of duty. he turned over his life to make mine great. as i write that, i see i could have said 'to make mine his'. but the inside-outside nature of our relationship was: he was totally committed to me and I was cocooned in a shell of fatherly protection. i was spoilt.

my life was a panorama of promise stretching out before me: money, fame, grace and stardom. i viewed this from beneath the canopy of my father's care. nothing could touch me. he would kill. he was invincible. i thought it could last forever.

that he could turn on me so completely hurt and continues to hurt so much, but i look at it and see that he only withdrew what was his. that others were without this beaming father-sun all their lives, and i must be lucky to have had so fiercely as much as i did, should make me grateful. i should be so lucky. lucky. my emotions didn't exclude him when i loved her. he thought i should be able to beat her because she was nearing the end of her illustrious career and i was at the beginning of mine and i had a natural, flowing style; the racquet was an extension of my arms. all i had to work on was my concentration, my commitment.

our matches for a while were brilliant, like love-making, combative, exciting. because of that touch of class, i merited a mention even though i was way down on the world rankings. my father was riding me like a jockey, thinking i'd finally got it— the deadly desire to win. but he was wrong. what i had was love and it enhanced my talent. especially on the high backhand volley, i could fly and flick.

she left me with the crystal glasses and disappeared into the American heartland, taking my tennis with her, more or less. the few weeks on tour after she left, on court in Cairo—the Egyptian Open—i played like a cripple. with a limp wrist, face-on to everything, i could not remember how to hit a ball. my father's world collapsed like a card castle. he was flabbergasted, and wrong about the reason for too short a while. he knew enough about the game and the circuit and he knew who it was before i told him. but i wanted him to comfort me, to fold me up in the tent of his care and let me repair myself. he felt excluded from my emotional life. he was only pushed to the side for a while; not, never, excluded. but he couldn't see that. what he saw was: two women, no men. what he saw was: when she cut me off, i couldn't play tennis. he said i couldn't have won the C grade championship at Shepparton with that class. what he also saw was the co-incidence of my real brilliance and the height of my romance, and it disgusted him. from that day, prostrate in a Middle-Eastern motel room, i knew i was an outcast for the rest of my life.

yesterday was bright with sunshine and icy wind; seems years ago. my father's phone-call out of the blue. he rang again to say come to his Elizabeth Bay apartment to meet his new wife. i was curious as to what he wanted after so many years. two phone calls in half an hour. we drank and we laughed a little desperately, a little boozily. it looked like my father had become some sort of entrepreneur, taking off around the world quite frequently, and his new missus was the type to enjoy it. she'd look good in any dining room. my mother hated travelling.

for all the easy conversation and bonhomie, it took him a while to come around to the proposition he had for me. when he did i roared with laughter, it was ludicrous. i was to be a horse, a fly on the wall for his bet; there'd be money in it for me too. he had staked a fortune on a boast he made at his golf club. he bet some joker that i, his daughter, not ever having played golf before, could drop my handicap from thirty-six to sixteen in a year. he still had faith in my sporting ability. i could, in the profanity of illegal betting, get some of that sunshine beaming on me again—daddy's attention. i said i'd become a gambler too.

later at the Catholic Club we made the deal with the other guy, who apart from his eyes which are big and wide open and as sincerely honest as a car salesman looked very like Steve Phillips. whose eyes are very small. i said i'd give it a go to please him. it slipped out, the bloody need to please.

well, he didn't stop my arrest. i don't know whether he could have, but he could have tried.

breakfast interruption. i eat with appetite. they offer me a phone call. i will ring my aunt. funny, i saw her yesterday and we hardly spoke. she's a distant sort of woman in a social environment, no time for small talk, except at Bingo when she calls: 'it's a garden gate with a doctor bevan, a garden vine and a legs eleven, a life-saver ...'

the keys rattle in the lock. i'm free.

ANNE LEVIN
Psychiatrist's Report

Name: Dr Anne Levin.
Date of birth: 2 April 1954.
Qualifications: BSc (Adel.) MD (Syd.) PhD (Berkley).
Practice: Visiting Psychiatrist, Rozelle Hospital, 4 Oct. '88 until 15
May '89.
Now Senior Lecturer, Mental Health, Bond University, Queensland.

Psychiatrist's Report prepared for Detective Inspector
Harold S. Clarke, CIB, NSW.

Subject: Mrs Patricia Phillips.
Date of birth: 27 June 1946.
Address: see file.
Marital status: married.
Occupation: housewife.
Medical history: no serious illnesses.

History given:
I saw the patient three times a week during May and June this
year, for one-hourly consultations, in my room at Rozelle Hospital. The sessions were informal, conversational and at the time of
my work with Mrs Phillips I was not aware that she was under
suspicion of murder. My examinations were terminated when I
resigned my position at Rozelle and took up my present post.

Opinion:

Much of Patricia Phillips' talk was delusional raving, which in itself was interesting on a symbolic level. However, there were pieces of repeated gibberish which could indicate a deeper guilt or sense of guilt. For instance:

'Off with his head, off with his head,
But for red queens all dames are dead.'

Her several personalities included Leni di Torres, a sort of wild woman of the seas, a boy whom she imagined should have been her own, or would have been her own, but for an abortion some seventeen or eighteen years ago, a traveller after death and several others.

The boy's biography was clearly mapped out in her mind. In her fantasies, he watched war movies. She herself watched them, becoming the boy in doing so, over a short intense period beginning sometime in 1988. Her memorising of scenes or quotations from these is astonishing; for example, this description of a scout attack: 'Come in low, under his line of sight from behind, kick the back of his knees and leap in one movement, and take his head with your left hand squeezing his nose, then twist his face away from your knife; then go in at the base of the skull to the right of the spine, into what the Chinese call the windgate, insert upwards and scramble the brains.'

In understanding her relationship to her husband, I think it is pertinent to make a few general comments on his possible state of mind. He was disturbed by her expression of lesbianism which in itself was, in her case, quite a natural and unthreatening thing, as it would have been in other cultures and other times. She alluded to a relationship as being like that of Cleopatra and her faithful servant—nothing the man need worry about.

But he did and I offer this explanation as to why. The lesbian is invisible in our culture, as werewolves, vampires, and witches are invisible, and to see the invisible is to fear it to the point of wanting to destroy it. In his seeing it and seeking to control it he sought to destroy it. Everything outside man's control is considered monstrous, its independence fearsome. So rightly, as in all vampire movies and monster stories, he could embark on a mission of destruction. If this culture is right, and it glorifies such actions, he was courageous.

The pertinent thing is Pat got mad. Her anger was triggered particularly by a small comment he made: 'By the way, where are my socks?' and this set a ball rolling in her psyche. She was confronting him about his sexual advances to her friend and lover, Cath Belgrano, who was 'out of bounds', and bit him on the finger. He said, 'you bitch', or something, and at that moment she saw a hate in his small eyes that astounded her. She saw it as universal: men's hate of women pin-pointed in her own husband's glare at her. It took that thinnest of stiletto looks to break her ... or make her.

I say 'make' advisedly — make whole. She had spent years with him, but only partially. She was in fact largely preoccupied with a parallel, but dominating, emotional life, showing itself in two ways.

The first, expressed in sibling rivalry with her sister, was the death of a third sister. The two of them had made a fairly constant practice of tormenting her — Kerry Anne, the youngest, their mother's favourite. It doesn't matter what actually happened because the guilt was real. Patricia felt that either she or Julie may have pushed Kerry Anne under a train. I doubt whether Julie ever thought there was anything homicidal or suicidal about her younger sister's death. She seemed to be the type of person who can express her emotions fairly quickly and openly. She saw her mother's grief, her increasingly hopeless alcoholism, as proving that Kerry Anne was the special one. Even Patricia was more favoured, so Julie divorced herself from her family and set out to make a life of her own. She made money and, in the process of setting up her business and being a working mother, separated from her husband. It was different for Pat. The burdens of her sister's death and her mother's pathetic state stayed on her conscience, even though it may not have been her fault.

The second thing that constituted her preoccupation, in her vague all-accepting life with Steven, her husband, was her love of a soldier. The national serviceman left her, when she was pregnant with his child, to serve his conscripted time in Vietnam. She, like many of her generation, became involved in student politics against the war. She was still young; most of her friends had also had abortions, and maybe knew boys off to war. Peer-group pressure is enormous. It would have been death to her independent, free-loving, free-living lifestyle to go back to the soldier after he had been to Vietnam. It was impossible. She endeavoured to forget him and the abortion. For five years or so, she probably succeeded. Without her recognising it, that love, especially as she idealised it, was constantly shaping up against her love for her husband.

This explains to some extent her fascination for war movies. Her addiction to them contributed to her coming to the hospital. Her involvement with several women friends and their politics had also created an unbearable friction between her feminine and her masculine self.

Since I've known of the possible murder, I can see that her knowledge of video Vietnam could have provided her with a means of killing her husband. I think she stormed off after biting his finger in anger and went into his office, where she read some of his computer files. I imagine Steve Phillips suffered from something like 'the Nixon syndrome': that is, the pathological desire to record all your sins. There she saw what his malicious teasing could have done to the sensitive little lesbian, her 'thin-faced, lithe huntress'. It is well to remember she had only recently received a letter from Cath describing Pat's husband's advances as 'rape', though the event had happened in December and the intimidation had been going on for months. Pat's pent-up scorn and disgust of her husband—of his attitude to women— turned to uncontrollable fury.

She had memorised the scout attack from the war videos. Also, in her fantasy emotional life, she had an extra persona (only a dream until this stage), the cat-killing loner, Leni di Torres, capable of extreme violence.

Patricia is tall for a woman. She is neither skinny nor weak. It would not be hard for her to galvanise her strength and become as ruthless as the wild woman of the seas or (her words) 'man enough to kill'. She could have pounced on him as he sat moodily at the dining-room table, inserted a knife into his windgate and scrambled his brains. I understand this is how Steven Phillips was murdered.

Psychologically, it is credible. I would have to examine the patient, Mrs Patricia Phillips, further if I were to give an opinion as to her mental well-being or sanity at the time of the murder. I declare that this statement only establishes the possibility that she may have committed the deed. It in no way suggests her actual guilt or supposes that she was responsible for the death of her husband.

SIGNED: Anne Levin. 30/9/89.
Department of Social Management, Bond University.

BOY BRENDAN
Record of Interview

(transcribed by Angela Credence-Blackhouse)

Who wants to know? Brendan. My name's Brendan. Is that a tape? Are you a reporter? I'm not a street kid. I've got a job. I don't care.

What do I believe? I've always believed in things. Because I'm gifted I could wire up Lady Luck and she'd come stepping down the escalator towards me with rainbows of money flowing from her hands, but that's not what I want. Dungeons and dragons, why not? Civil war, why not? I could kill my father, if I had to. If I saw him mounted on his horse with the blue colours of the Union around his neck, a fucking Yankee, I could line him up in my sights and shoot. Shoot clean, through the heart.

A spooky chopper pilot is the pits. I was thinking about Vietnam on the train. A bloody old drunk was opposite me, thinking I'm a railway ratbag, thinking I'm lurking on the station to pick up Asian girls to screw and kill. But I wouldn't do it with him there. He reckons he's a soldier. Drunk and maudlin as he is, he'd probably have my guts for garters. I'm a young hoodlum that he watches through his tears. He could have been my dad but.

I groan, and look away. This soldier has no webbing, no machine-gun slung over his shoulder, no flame throwers, no fire-power, no jungle greens, no bandana, no beads of sweat in the no tropical heat, no sneer of violence. He just keeps his eye on me. His eye is sharp as tacks, too. Not my idea of a hero, just an ordinary dead-beat with a skin full. But he talks anyway.

'I felt—I believed—I was fighting communism. The North were invading the South so we went there to stop them. Australian soldiers always go away to fight. They help people. Got a great reputation.' He starts crying again, and I try to look away, but he is the real thing. I frown at him. 'The professional soldier has to follow orders, otherwise the whole kit-and-caboodle falls down. If a good soldier doesn't follow orders there are dire consequences. Court martial. In some places, summary execution.'

If I could choose my dad, and I can, this would be him. Some one who was a hero, but heroism was too strong and he never came home. He just wandered the world thinking about the war and drinking with his mates, leaving me to look after my mother. She would be the most beautiful big woman. With big tits. No fat, just muscle.

Yeah. I was on the monorail and I got off at Darling Harbour and then I saw her. Because I had a clear picture in my mind of what she looked like. She got off a rowing boat. She was soaking wet. The breasts weren't really big but big enough and I could see all their shape and they would have been heavier than pears to hold, and soft. She was as mad as a cut snake but, if someone's come back to Earth for you, you don't expect them to be ordinary.

'I swam away from the loony bin,' she said. Yeah, that'd be right. I mumbled. I'm glad she had to swim to the boat because how she looked was making me drool. But mostly I only see her in my mind. I said, Stay there, and I went and ripped off a couple of tourist tee-shirts and gave them to her. Then we walked across the walkway to Chinatown and had a Chinese meal. All she had with her that she could use was an ANZ transaction card, so she got some money out of a hole in the wall, and bought a pair of jeans.

She never stopped talking all the time, and I listened to every word. But I can't remember all of them. She knew I had a hard-on because of what she looked like and she said Freud said that we could have a beautiful relationship and it would be ideal, be cause she could tell me everything and I would do her bidding. I'm glad she escaped the funny farm, even though she was as screwy as a two-bob watch and she made me think I was screwy too, but what do I care.

Next thing was to get her on a train to Melbourne where her sister had a place. I did the details and felt like a real gentleman. I put her on the train and waved goodbye like we were old mates.

Most things in my life could have happened, but I swear this did. I helped a woman with big bones and skin like expensive peaches, a mad way about her and old enough to be my mother, get out of Sydney. And I'll tell you why I did it. She just looked straight at me and expected me to. It felt like she trusted me. Well she did, I could have run off with her train money. But as I said, that's not what I want. I wanted someone to treat me like I was a gentleman and a son, and she did.

No bull.

SISTER MARY IGNATIA

An Address: 'Justice at Home'

(prepared for Clergy for Justice and Peace in the Third World,
4 August 1989)
Opening reading: Isaiah 55: 1-13

The Little Sisters of Jesus are followers of Charles de Foucauld, who took a contemplative approach to the problems of the world.

It was, however, activism during the Vietnam War that matured some of us towards a more radical social ministry. We, if you recall, were quite often in open conflict with our superiors in the Catholic Church over Christian moral issues, such as conscription, and its relation to the Vietnam War. A number of us were influenced by the writings of American Catholics like Dorothy Day and the Berrigans. While Pope Paul VI and U Thant, then Secretary of the United Nations, spoke up for a negotiated agreement to the Vietnam struggle in 1965 on the grounds that it threatened a nuclear confrontation, Melbourne Catholics like Santamaria and the NCC (National Civic Council) urged the West to take firmer military action because at the time China was suffering a famine and therefore was at its weakest. The Catholic peace group, Pax, was started at the end of 1966 to work against nuclear proliferation.

These times threw us back to examining our own consciences in the wake of Vatican II. The Church was divided. Archbishop Knox attacked the Moratorium and supported the war. I was in Dandenong at the time a young priest was preaching to a congregation of about 700 at Sunday Mass about solidarity with the Vietnamese people and the protestors (disagreeing with the Archbishop in his own see), when the senior parish priest strode out across the altar to the pulpit and physically pushed the young man away from the microphone and denounced all he was saying. Vietnam had become a showdown between Communism, the church's traditional enemy, and Democracy, the free world.

Things have not become easier. Freedom of conscience, freedom of thought, freedom to interpret for ourselves true Christianity has hardened divisions within the Catholic Church, and probably within other denominations. On the one hand Ecumenism is growing and on the other Fundamentalism is strong.

Theology has changed. We can no longer think the Pope is infallible when it is clear the latest encyclicals from the Holy See are right-wing, anti-women and give lip service to the desperate needs of the indigenous races throughout the world. Unfortunately, the reign of the present Pope seems to be tainted by the continued employment of proven corrupt financial officials. Scandals rock the Vatican as they did in the days of Martin Luther. Public excommunications are not the rage these days, or perhaps Liberation Theology would become another major religion.

We find we must take up arms against oppressive regimes. Their crimes are more horrific than those of the Inquisition. Compassionate Christians cannot stand aside, nod in abject humility and accept that it is the Will of God. It cannot be. It is logically impossible for it to be the Will of God for He is just and gave His only Son to suffer crucifixion to save us from our sins. The troops of the One True God have been severely routed by those of the Devil and false gods in recent times. Now is the hour for us to put all our efforts into preserving the temple of the Holy Spirit in its widest meaning—the Earth and her people. Especially, the downtrodden. This may mean revolutions, and my heart quakes at the cruel repercussions some may induce, particularly, for example, in South Africa. We can only work within our own parameters. The greater successes must be left to the Greater Intelligence. I realise that according to Council of Trent my remarks could be considered excommunicable. But my blood literally boils when I witness the scale of injustice being done.

Further from the reading in Isaiah 55 is a verse in 56—verse 3: *Neither let the son of the stranger, that hath joined himself to the Lord, speak, saying, the Lord hath utterly separated me from his people; neither let the eunuch say, Behold I am a dry tree.*

My talk is entitled 'Justice at Home'. And for 'eunuch' here I will take the meaning to be homosexuals and lesbians and quite clearly read that God will welcome them into His House if they embrace His covenant. And I take that covenant to be true Christian values: justice and peace.

While I thank Father Geoffrey Clarke for his reading of Isaiah 55, I'd like to interpret the meaning of Chapter 56, wherein, in verse 5, the Lord reveals, *Even unto them will I give in mine house and within my walls a place and a name better than of sons and daughters: I will give them an everlasting name, that shall not be cut off.* The Lord is saying in this chapter that the pure of heart, no matter what their sexuality, will be more treasured and rewarded than those who are deserving through heredity or privilege, who have not the virtues of Faith, Love and Hope uppermost in the manner in which they live their lives.

A particular story—the Wiley Park murder—has been on our minds as a group which meets monthly in the area. Aspersions were cast in my direction as I happened to be in the vicinity of the Park on the night of the fifth of May when it all started, coming home from one of these meetings. Accusations have been rumoured around that we had something to do with this unidentified corpse.

When I could not understand why marijuana plants suddenly appeared in the Park, I deduced there must be something hidden beneath them, something buried. I apologise to this group for bringing scandalous attention to our activities. I was curious. I happened to be near the place twice: on the night the interment took place, and on the following afternoon. My insistence on further investigation seemed out of line, for a passing nun.

I'd like to say that while the grand questions of peace and justice in the third world are important, so are the little queries, which if not asked do not uncover wrong-doing at home. Theresa of Lisieux spoke of the Little Way. The Lord, in Isaiah, invites all, including eunuchs, to partake in His covenant of peace and promises them a place within his walls and a name better than those of the sons and daughters who pollute the sabbath.

The Little Flower, St Theresa, is a saint wholly and solely be cause she refused to be raped. She was murdered. Her rapist and slayer consequently became remorseful. My niece has been raped. Her rapist is free and probably not in the slightest remorseful. It happens too much in this society for us not to take notice, and do something.

Look at the world today. How many times *does* it happen? My God, My God, why hast Thou forsaken us?

My niece is a lesbian. Where in the Commandments does it say, Thou shalt not love, Thou shalt not display affection? If one can not feel love, how is one to understand the Commandment to love thy neighbour? How is one to understand the meaning of '*no greater love hath a Father that he give His Only Son...*' Why not? I ask.

My God, please forgive me for my constant questioning.

Now, at the conclusion of my talk, I would like to offer my resignation from this group for two reasons. My interference in the Wiley Park murder mystery has brought unnecessary and uncomfortable attention to our activities. I feel I should resign on this score because I featured in the newspapers. The second reason is a personal one. While my heart bleeds for the sufferings of those in countries less fortunate than our own, I feel, in the light of recent events, I would like to work for justice at home. I would like to work among the victims of rape and incest.

In respect for the ecumenism of this group, all my readings from the Bible come from the King James version.

Thank you, ladies and gentlemen.

SAMUEL LAKE
Extract from Personal Papers

On 5 March 1989 Larsen rang me in the middle of the night. You don't ask why when a man like that asks for help. You rather wish he would ask more often. If there is the slightest thing I could do to make that man's life happier, I would. Any time.

Within twenty minutes I was at the destination he had told me, a place in Haberfield. Big Frank Farouk had been called also. We both waited under a tree in a dark part of the suburban street for a while. We knew it had to be special because there were only the two of us. Among a wide circle of mates, we were the two men Peter Larsen trusted. The address we had been given was derelict. You could not see the house for a jungle of overgrown banana palms. Frank and I wandered down the driveway. The house was unsecured but there seemed to be nobody about. We returned to the footpath. Within two or three minutes Larsen's ute pulled up. He had a tarpaulin over the contents on the tray.

Peter said he had some explaining to do. We followed him into the jungle of banana palms. He started slashing a few fronds and we helped. It was evidently difficult for him to get it out. So we worked silently for about fifteen minutes and put the leaves on top of the tarp in the ute. When we were doing that, Frank asked, 'What is under there?'

Peter replied, 'Get in.'

The front seat of Larsen's 1972 Valiant accommodated three big men closely. He started explaining. He had been watching in the window of his Felicity's house. He had been doing this for years. There was an argument. The woman bit the man on the hand. The husband was in pain but did not fight back. He apparently expected that she would return with first-aid and apologies. He was mistaken. The woman returned and knifed him in the throat. She saw him sitting at the table feeling sorry for himself and approached from behind, a stay-sharp carving knife in her right hand. She quietly put her left arm around his neck and suddenly grabbed his nose and yanked it around to the left and inserted the blade with her right hand, using full strength with determined power. Then she dropped the weapon and paced about the house in a distracted manner. Larsen heard her run a bath. When he was satisfied she was in it, he entered the house through the front door. He used a spare key that is kept under a stone in the front garden. Quickly and efficiently he removed the body and put it into his utility. Then he returned and cleaned up the blood and disturbance.

Peter has the tread of a wild cat, no one could hear him if he was choosing not to be heard. The bathroom, where the lady remained, is situated at the back of the kitchen. Larsen was working from the dining area to the front. It is unlikely that she heard him at all. He removed evidence of her crime. She could believe it had never happened, depending on how mad she was. He double-locked the front door and returned the key to its hiding place. His ute is always full of junk—tents, tarps, hurricane lamps, camp ovens, axes, spades and tool box. He hid the body among the junk and threw a tarp over the lot and drove to the closest pub.

In the pub he rang us and downed as many drinks as he could in the time he thought we would take to get out of bed.

After explaining himself he turned the key in the ignition. He should get his muffler fixed, not the best car for clandestine operations. We proceeded in a westerly direction. He trusted both of us. I could feel that the big queer was going to do anything he asked. A friend of Larden's was a gardener working this week in Wiley Park. That was where he headed.

Frank wrapped the body carefully in the banana palms with some binder twine. For a huge man with huge hands he has a delicate touch with small work. Carrying a load of banana palms across a park, even at night, would not be particularly remarked upon. Peter and I brought spades. They dug the hole. I cased a fifty-metre circle around their activity playing cockatoo, ready to waylay any passer-by.

When they had finished I returned to the site. It had the appearance of a fresh interment. Frank suggested removing flowers from nearby beds and planting them here. That would immediately attract suspicion, I said. Larsen snapped his fingers and laughed. He ran back to his car. He returned carrying two large hessian bags. 'Here goes a couple of thousand bucks,' he said. He displayed a number of young marijuana plants. He would tell his gardener friend some story about not being able to get back to the bush, and having to plant them somewhere. He would say they were a free gift to the populace. A practical joke, especially one based on generosity, would be believed by anyone who knows Peter Larsen. We decided I would say something similar to a mate in the division around here and Frank would get Morrie onto it. In fact I said it to Sergeant Millar who has had a drink or two with Peter Larsen that my mate had planted the dope in the park and that there was nothing suspicious about it. Just a crazy joke. Take no notice. No big deal. I spoke to him at seven a.m. when he arrived for duty. We all knew that someone would notice them sometime the next day and we wanted the rumour to circulate as quickly as possible. They'd be ripped up and the disturbed earth would be explained.

Back in the Valiant and proceeding along Canterbury Road towards the city, we discussed the victim, Steven Phillips. We never knew whether he was in fact the informer who masqueraded as a draft dodger or not. There was somebody at Sydney University in those days who was working Yankee dirty tricks on our ASIO chaps and the demonstrators. Maybe it wasn't Steven Phillips. Apart from that detail, he could have been a regular shit of a man. Most men who are murdered by wives after a few years of marriage are. The others are wealthy and the wives are money-grubbing poisoners.

Frank expressed both his and my loyalty to Peter Larsen in sweet terms. In words I would never use. The midnight mission was romantic, no one can deny that. There was only ever one woman in my life too and I would have gone to the gallows in her place if I had to. I understood that Larsen was busting a gut for this lady and would probably get no rewards, or no thanks from the woman herself. Although I did remind him that she had carried a photo of him in her purse. I still had it in my wallet. I showed it to him.

'You bastard,' he said.

Independent incorruptible women are proving to be the bane of my life: both Sister Mary Ignatia and Detective Senior Constable Gorman. The good nun was simply too nosey and too brainy. Perhaps if she had known Peter Larsen she would have lent the weight of her pristine conscience to his side. Why didn't she just go up to a park attendant and say, 'Hey fella, you've got marijuana growing over there' and let him deal with it? But no, she not only rings the locals, in the same phoning session she manages to involve Homicide and the Narcs. Far too many people for me to convince with the first story. I did manage, however, to keep the press pretty ignorant. I don't want Larsen to go to jail. I am an honest cop and I don't want to go down as a corrupt one. I let Homicide alone. I had someone in Special Branch intimate to them that there could be international espionage involved and it was better all round to stay ignorant for the time being.

Larsen dropped us off at our vehicles and drove back to the Phillips' house. He watched her being a total loony at home then take herself off to Rozelle Hospital a few days later. It was his chance to talk with her.

When the story did hit the media, he asked another favour; could I just manage to have the murderess protected until the basic Homicide investigation was over? So I put Margot Gorman in a nursing-aide's uniform and spun the line about the husband being our subject.

Margot is a dedicated policewoman and a comrade whom I would trust with my life. She tends to be a bit of a maverick, but that is all right because she understands the code of obedience and professional solidarity. She is one of the best dogs on my team. If the mission had been fair dinkum she would have been a great asset. Her nose is good but she is not a man.

When I flicked through her notebook I saw she was getting into too much detail. Homicide had taken the bait and were letting it shuffle to the bottom of the pile. Sister Mary Father Brown had not got enough info to keep nosing. Larsen had, finally, after fifteen or twenty years, spoken with his lady love and settled something in himself. So I pulled Margot out. I would have told her the real story, or more of it, if she'd relax with me over a drink now and then and share a joke. She is not a mate. This was proved to me when she decided to lie about the attack on her outside her ex's place. She started protecting someone. It'd be girls. Larsen got me the girl who had been having an affair with Mrs Phillips. Showing my good faith and care I sent Margot off to her family.

We'll have to see how she pans out. Keeping her service record excellent and a new and exciting job may make her forget. I bet she still wonders who doped her at the Club. All the same, a good tracking dog never forgets a scent and what's at the end of that trail is me.

AFTERWORD

Finola Moorhead

There is a parallel life we each live, an individual place where the
conditional tense reigns over the past, present, and future.
I suppose it is about time, or rather timelessness, but that is
another, more moot, matter. The producer of fiction creates a
door between individuals' private places, or, perhaps, a mirror-
window. What I mean is the author and reader communicate in
their parallel worlds in the same space with no personal
interaction. If the fiction reaches the depth of something I might
as well call timelessness then the fiction approaches classic status;
that is, it really doesn't matter when you read it. It survives the
fads of living history and contributes to documented history.
A good story can come from anywhere and be appreciated
everywhere. The more exact the precise time and intricate the
local detail the more exotic the tale for strangers; the good story is
universal if told well. My theory of the fiction aesthetic includes
rigorous accuracy of the mundane in its supposed date and place;
if you can't be trusted on the everyday little things, why should
your insights into the meaning of life be believed?

The expression for honesty is 'coming from the heart'. The
stuff matters as much to the writer as to the reader. I prefer to
use the word truth, although I know it's old-fashioned. I respect
the truth in each sentence. Beauty is Truth. If Keats wrote
nothing else about a Grecian urn, the lines at the end of the ode
' "Beauty is truth, truth beauty,"— that is all / Ye know on earth,

and all ye need to know', are worth the repute of his name. Using truth instead of 'from the heart' enables me to include the mental as well as the emotional effort, the legwork of research as well as the enlightenment of a political point of view, in the construction of a story that aspires to breaching the boundaries of our private worlds. A timelessness grasped in a temporal second, the moment of a page being turned, sets off bombs in the dreamlike landscapes of our minds luxuriating in the reading of good fiction.

As we can copyright not our ideas but the way we write them down, the style and format of a work is as important as the subject matter. The title *Still Murder* came from the words *still life* referring to a picture painted of apples and pears on a kitchen table or similar still life drawing, not as later conjectured by reviewers to mean something in the region of: here is what happened, is it still murder? My first published novel had dance as its formal blueprint, so it followed to me that the next be about stillness: how? A painting is still and a still picture moves when it is a jigsaw puzzle.

A stillness if it is art is generally framed.

Both formally and philosophically *Still Murder* is about frames and boundaries. The murder having happened is still, like a photograph, a captured moment: where are my socks? you've gone too far; slit his throat and scramble his brains. There is no mess either side of it; it is framed. The man, the husband had gone too far, trespassed. His transgression is attempted rape. A demand for sex is nothing much in the life of a handsome man with libertarian morals. His action is the pinpoint of light that comes from a greater source, the shaft of sunlight which outlines the subject of a portrait in the umber school of painting, perhaps. Rape is the point of *Still Murder*. From his domestic transgression the novel reaches out to the immense prevalence of rape, especially in wars. The sympathetic character, the opposite male, the Romeo to the central Juliet character, is a Viet vet who on his tour of duty happened to buy the sexual usage of a girl in Saigon from her father. Although he punishes himself his sexuality never heals.

More importantly, rape has psychological consequences for women: any man can do it; all men benefit from that possibility. The rapists have been called the storm troopers in the battle of the sexes; the citizens of the occupied territory, those in power have what they want. Most men are not prepared to relinquish it, or even begin to think how to. The warrior in my story is an outsider, a renegade; yet the warrior is a great figure in the history of Western civilisation, the epitome of manhood. *Still Murder* points out that the nicest possible bloke is a rapist. War is and was a horrible thing for many servicemen; being emotionally, psychologically, physically crippled for life is not an unusual story among veterans. In all wars women are raped, villages pillaged, infrastructure broken, bridges bombed, food supplies shortened; war gives men a terrible licence. Even the most libertarian woman, as I wished to paint Patricia, has a boundary which must not be crossed without consequences. Too frequently the consequences are assumed by women. In her case she turns to madness. Madness is a sane response to realising how widespread, stupid and violent are the powers that be.

She has a therapist. Another frame, another pun. A sharp-edged successful woman, with spiky hair, who gives her point of view in the book, a fog of Jungian psychiatry and bureaucratic jargon which misses Pat's malady completely. The world being what it was there is no way of treating madness officially, except taming. The madwoman prowls like a wild animal behind a fence, in asylum, in the zoo. She is trapped, free to speak her mind.

Speaking Patricia Phillip's mind was my main enjoyment in writing *Still Murder*. No one in her life understands her. This is an isolation many women feel in our culture; the dividing has conquered. We may relate sexually. We may enjoy each other's company. We may love our man. We may truly love other women. We may enjoy the idea of Woman, or everywoman. We may have discovered a politics which gives us a sense of belonging. We may have accepted the life-wasn't-meant-to-be-easy trite response to hardship and buried our minds in trivia. We may have surrendered. We may even have collaborated. But, secretly each woman is alone. I speak of a cultural aloneness. We lack ritual. We lack a coherent spirituality which would give sharing and joy to our insights. Patricia speaks to the inner woman reader; she passes through the door in the parallel world. She is allowed poetry by her author. She would not have been understood even in this context if I had not framed her with genre. I could not write a book like Charlotte Perkins Gilman's *The Yellow Wallpaper*; at least, not yet. Then. *Still Murder* was basically written in 1989, although drafts began in 1985 and ended sometime in 1990.

The madwoman is framed by several genre; the murder mystery and the grand romance being the main ones. Anthony and Cleopatra, Romeo and Juliet. In love on the campus at the same time I was at university (1965–1968), Peter and Patricia were happy and free. Peter drew the lottery, drafted under the conscription act in the middle of this period. He had a choice. An individual man has the choice not to rape or harass women and girls. As Buffy St Marie sang in those times, the universal soldier is to blame for what he does. However, Peter was a team player, a sporting bloke, ignorant of the dire consequences of obeying the state. He went, leaving his one true love pregnant and heartbroken; but she was young. I meant to leave it an open question whether the child lived or not. In Patricia's mind he did and he was called Brendan after the saint who sailed a leather boat to Canada by the northern route past Greenland long before Columbus claimed the Americas. One of her alternative personalities, Leni de Torres, also recalls that journey. For me this is a little play on the nature of history; truly amazing stories of heroism and humility are sadly forgotten in arrogant dictators' greed to be remembered; historians and popular general knowledge going along with them. Imagining a lost son is how a woman would quite logically cope with an abortion. So many of my friends in those days had to have an abortion. The peace movement swept us up: make love, not war. It is logical that Patricia would have understood and agreed with the antiwar movement; as logical as taking up another lover for husband.

If I had been male, I would have been called up. This little conditional case has often played its fragile melody in my parallel life as I changed. As I was a woman I did not have to choose, but if I had, would I have chosen the peace movement? I don't think so, not as I was then. However, I may have been a draft-dodger, merely out of independence of spirit, never one for the institutions, a truant at school and that sort of thing. But Peter was popular. An A-grade player. Patricia was gorgeous. A cliché filigree in the framing. Split apart by events, history, politics, they were on different sides and their lives turn tragic.

In 1987, there was much to-do about Vietnam because of the Welcome Home parade, but earlier in the 1980s we marched in black on the Sydney streets, mourning the fate of all women raped in wars. I'm afraid that would be dangerously unacceptable today. Even then, we were hustled into paddy wagons and charged with public nuisance. The Montague–Capulet divide of my present in history was alive and kicking. It wasn't much of an imaginative leap to set this into fiction. I researched quite deeply into the Australian experience of Vietnam, and strangely when I told the bloke at my local video store that I wanted to watch every war movie he had, he told me of his Vietnam experience. He, too, was a member of The Team, and called up. It was the best two years of his life, he said. I also spent a lot of time haunting RSL clubs, sitting at poker machines listening to men talk to each other. I let Patricia stay vaguely outside the feminist movement because she was already lost in her dreams, the torn fabric of her life just billowing along. So the book starts with Peter Larsen.

The other main genre frame is Margot Gorman, whom I found relatively boring to write, a detective senior constable and a good cop; yet, a woman who felt she was one of the boys. Again I was fortunate to know a female detective senior constable as she was studying to achieve that rank. Margot, however, bears no resemblance to that woman, she is a figment of my imagination. She grew more than a figment; I must have an ordinary fit working class girl hidden inside me; she was a breeze to write and to like; she is derivative of Sue Grafton, Sara Peretsky et al.; lone detective, honest as the day, energetic and independent. Nevertheless, I treated her quite badly in not allowing her to solve the crime. Leaving her in the haze of a Mickey Finn was my way of signalling this was not really a murder mystery. Funnily, ever since *Still Murder* was published, it has been treated as detective genre, which must irritate the aficionados no end. I read the book yesterday, twelve years after having worked on it thoroughly or looked at it at all; Margot as a rounded character , in my opinion, is okay. As I recall during the decade of ignoring or remembering it, I had the madwoman as a jewel in the centre of the crown, so to speak; it doesn't seem that way to me at all now. I mean it is not uneven. Margot has much more enduring strength than Patricia as a fictional character I have found in my writing since *Still Murder*. She singly carries half the structure and narrative of my epic novel of lesbian separatism, *Darkness More Visible*. While *Still Murder*'s open-endedness suggests sequels, and all the characters have possible futures, Margot Gorman, being a type of everywoman Australian, is, in *Darkness More Visible*, a bridge between the two worlds of mainstream ideology and revolutionary feminism.

Cath's voice is as strong as the others. Here is a minor edging in the frame: the lesbian novel. Because I am who I have become in the world of Australian letters and am anyway, I could not, and would not, leave out the lesbian point of view. Deliberately, Cath is not a particularly political lesbian, although the lesbian political environment is around her. While domestic violence, female poverty, rape, injustice in the court system, refuges, and other topics of concern outside the mainstream should enter novels, it is annoying to be hectored, being told how to feel, act, and what you should do with your money and time. Bad writing is always caught out by the mundane detail I referred to earlier. In case I fell into labouring my radical feminism, I gave Cath no consciousness of those issues, as such, only as she herself experiences them, i.e. the rape. The date rape, the attempted rape, the almost happened unwanted intercourse. Her sensitivity was incredibly important. She couldn't even spend much time with men without becoming a nervous wreck, as each incidental thing their egos let fly in her direction would be felt as an annihilating insult. The thousand pinpricks of Frida Kahlo's self portraits Patricia refers to are probably more about Cath than herself. She sees her as out of bounds of Steve's predatory philandering.

There is real love between Patricia and Cath; it is like the love of Cleopatra and Charmian, womanly. Cath would grow out of it. Patricia, having spent so much time with men, has a toughness I find fascinating in heterosexual women. We, lesbians, wouldn't dare announce aloud the sort of things these women say daily about their chaps; we would sound like raging ball-breakers. Instead we let our behaviour speak for itself. We do not give them our energy, or our time, without putting a valuable price on these resources. Similarly in novel writing, the politics must be in the action of the plot, spoken in the mouth of an appropriate character with consequences in the story line. Being as lovable as she is, in her acceptance of the ways of the world, Patricia is the type to think more of other people's hurt than her own, especially if she loves that other person. That is why, after putting up with him for so long, she suddenly turns on Steve. And she can with a guiltless vengeance. It is not her guilt at murdering her husband that has sent Pat mad, it is the freedom of finding herself, of freeing herself from her world of veils, of illusions and daydreams, the return of Romeo, the possibility of the boy, the son. To symbolise this, I have her seeing a blue plastic bag caught in the branches of a winter deciduous tree as a magical bluebird. She is obviously short-sighted, so am I, so I didn't think I'd make a big thing of it; it's a bit of imagery, but if you missed it, no matter. She is also emptied of her love for Cath, which is something I hadn't noticed until this recent reading. I guess I did think of that loose end when I was working on it, but after working in the timeless prophecy of fiction, you don't remember much. You don't have to; it is there on the page.

I have no doubt the reason *Still Murder* is more successful than my other novels is that it has men in it, and deals with male issues. Conscription was the catalyst for student mobilisation when I was twenty. National Service had been upgraded from three months to two years to provide manpower for the engagement against communism in the divided Vietnam. It was as controversial as it had been when Billy Hughes was Prime Minister in the First World War. The Holt and Gorton governments introduced amendments to the National Service Act which became more and more outrageous as far as we, the age group involved, were concerned. I am pretty sure my birth date was in the ballot, and certainly some of the blokes I knew had to go, or burn their papers and go on the run. In the 1960s, that particular issue included only men. If it were reintroduced today, women would be included. The whole Vietnam experience for Australians, Americans and New Zealanders changed the world; and opposition to it led to an explosion of creative work in the popular culture, especially among singer-songwriters. Protest was our word. It absorbed the energy of women, ordinary women; the Save Our Sons organisation was emotive and effective. Because it was war, it captured imagination in a way, say, the mobilisation against the spread of AIDS which also absorbed the energy of women, especially lesbians, in the 1980s, did not. It reeked of heroism, sentiment, atrocity and glamour.

Hopefully all students will protest against the injustices of their times as the breadth of knowledge and living history dawns upon them. Now, it is against international finance and banking practice. It is interesting that although the pornography industry has far outgrown the wildest nightmares of the Women's Liberation movement, no great protest is waged against it. This, I fear, is connected to the fact that feminist subject matter is not appreciated in literary books. I refer back to my point above about cultural aloneness. The popular culture, the air we breathe, is dominated by the male ethos; it follows that taste and standards of literature, and the jobs which arbitrate quality and worth, are equally dominated by that ethos. If I was to be successful in terms of reigning literary judgment, I had to care about what it was like to be a man. Understanding men is not hard for women, not because women are especially understanding and listening creatures, but because that is our education: to understand men. When the generic term men was questioned when it associated all humanity together, the light bulb flicked on in a lot of dark corners. As Freud said, for men, woman is the question. The controllers of thought have a vested interest in keeping women mysterious. We are relatively mysterious to ourselves. Being the mystery, being the muse, being the madonna on a pedestal, the sexy model, the porn star, is no help for a woman to know herself while she may have a thoroughly good understanding of men, their needs and weaknesses. They are an open book, the white noise, the lift muzak, wallpaper in a variety of patterns. It was not, and it is not, hard for me to create male characters.

The outer frame of *Still Murder* is the voice of Samuel Lake, the detective inspector who is Margot's boss at the NCA. He is the personification of power in the world of this novel. He is neither corrupt nor a whistle blower, he is the wise leader; the embodiment of the status quo. The point about Swan is he breaks the rules to help a mate; his greatest allegiance is to the contract between men which is sentimentalised into tearsome mateship. A greater cause doesn't bother him; he is a realist. Or rather his fantasies, or ideals, are those accepted and appreciated by the culture around him. It is easy for him to make a fool of Margot. The only one who feels that humilation is Margot. Parallel to Cath's rape and Pat's madness is Margot's indignity. All her best efforts become as the movements of a puppet on a string. Again it is the cultural isolation and the nature of power as we know it.

The inner frame of *Still Murder* is Steven Sligo Phillips. I was interviewed on radio in a closed ABC cell with a voice coming to me live from Darwin; the first thing she said was, (I can't remember the exact words): the dead guy's the most important character in the book, isn't he? I wasted valuable air time being speechless; cleaned bowled. I had to think in ten seconds of an angle I had never approached the work from before in all its changes. Our interaction followed a news item about filming *The Phantom* in Rum Jungle or somewhere up there. So I gasped and replied, Yes, he is a phantom. Relating my recently published seriously thought out novel to wispily remembered fiction entertainments of my childhood — *The Phantom* (I remembered his dog, his horse, his girlfriend) and Rum Jungle, a radio serial which followed the Argonauts at 5 p.m. in the 1950s — for the entire interview was the best I could do. What a contortion! Steve is the opposite of The Phantom, just as he is the opposite of Peter; he is a coward, possibly a sly spy. He spends his time with women not men. He is Dionysius to Peter's Apollo. He is a ghost in the midst of living characters. He represented something I was quite happy to kill: the peacenik of the 1970s who strode high on student politics, grabbing the megaphone, taking the podium to shout other people's words and ideas; a demagogue without responsibility, charming the ladies with bullshit, sending them mad with drugs and alternative pseudo-spirituality; eventually becoming apolitical doing an ordinary job like teaching, reflecting the epithet: those who do, teach. He is so lame, so jealous of everything, that the best he can hope for, having no children, is to perpetuate a hoax on the public he hates so much (as to want to do that). He is a case; although I know him well, I didn't want him to take up too much space in the fiction.

The boy, on the other hand, I love in some atavistic recall of a pre-Babylonian matriarchy where the women in Spring had the youth in sexual joy then sent them away to become men and live elsewhere; thus there would be children. But I do not expect readers to love or even like the boy. He is an essential part of the masculinity within the book if I kept to my word of dealing with men's issues and the male aesthetic: he allowed me to look at and be horrified by the implications of the turn popular culture was taking, specifically the interactive killing games of high tech computers and futuristic videos. This may be a little dated; it's the fifteen years since I wrote that stuff. The teenage boy comes unbidden into my fictions and I don't know whether it is me personally or because, as I said before, the air I breathe, the hegemony of the culture I inhabit is so infused with boy mythology I can't avoid it. The boy is also in *Darkness More Visible*, which novel makes no claim to representing the male point of view.

Legs Eleven, the nosey nun, was an idea for another novel I could have written, and did write some chapters of; parts of it are in *Still Murder* and bits in *Darkness More Visible*. I couldn't, however, maintain her through an entire work; she becomes here a colourful character. A free woman wandering around the place with passion and curiosity, making deductions, gathering facts, having opinions, entertaining herself; she is, I think, a fairly common phenomenon among the post menopausal female population.

Julie, the sister, is also a type; the probable sibling. Successful, neurotic, single (divorced), energetic, different from Pat, but giving Pat a normal family-life context. I think the number of male and female characters is about equal; the flavour of the novel tantalises with balance while pointing out that equality in the acreage of the imagination doesn't exist. The claim that our assessment of literary quality lacks gender bias is not true. In the cultural landscape women's material is not considered beautiful in and of itself, while it might seem startlingly so lit as a detail in an overwhelmingly male environment. Hopefully, for that is how I mean the insights of Patricia's madness to appear. Read *Still Murder* again; you'll see what I mean.

Finola Moorhead,
August 2002